Secrets of
THE PRESENT

Echoes from the Past

Book II

Sam Caffrey

ISBN Ebook -   978-1-969324-07-9
ISBN Paperback - 978-1-969324-08-6
ISBN Hardback - 978-1-969324-09-3

Published by **Parker Publishers**

"The Journey is the Fun of it.

The Act is just the Destination"

Table Of Contents

Chapter 1

Two weeks have passed since Paul asked me if I would like to work for him and manage the Manchester office. This period has been a complete whirlwind of emotions, comprising some of the most difficult choices I've had to make in my life.

I walk into the office and Joan greets me, as she always does, her smile a constant in the ever-changing office dynamics. And perhaps, one thing that I can rely on every morning, the rest of the day is a brawl against the frustrations building up in me. It's a brawl, I repeat, to suppress such a rage.

We go through our morning's itinerary, the familiar rhythm of our routine grounding me amidst the chaos. As on any Monday morning, I am heading for the planning meeting early, to review our ongoing projects and assignment work, the fluorescent lights of the boardroom flickering to life as I prepare for the day ahead.

During the meeting, I advised Jack that the London job with the sports shops had finished, and we were within a couple of days of finalizing the pharmacy due diligence. My desk, once cluttered with files and papers, now holds a certain emptiness. I have no other major projects on my desk. Or more accurately, all major projects were redirected away from me.

I listen to everybody else outline the status of their projects. Jack advised that there are two new jobs soon to be starting, and he is giving one to me and one to the other team. He slides the folders down the desk to us, the sound of sliding paper momentarily filling the quiet room and asks us to review them and come back later. Taking the folder and heading back to my office, I open it and review it. It is not a bad job; it is a company we are to restructure and get ready for sale, a challenge that would usually spark my interest. I know it will take a couple of months to do a full analysis and restructure the company. I take the folder and head down to Jack's office, the corridor's silence accompanying me as I rehearse my next steps. Walking in, I ask him if he has two minutes. He sees the folder in my hand and says, "I hope you're not complaining about this job; it was the better of the two."

"It looks fine and interesting; however, I will not be able to do it." Looking at me quizzically, he asks, "Why?" and I handed him back the folder and a letter. "I am handing in my notice I and I'm leaving the company." Jack looks on, his expression a mix of confusion and concern, pausing for a minute to compose himself, "What happened, and why?" His tone transitioned from brisk to empathetically concerned just like that.

Glaring back, I say, "You know why. I have been stagnant here for years. I work hard, bring in more fees than most, and do everything asked of me and more. Every time a promotion comes up, there is a reason I don't get it, and I see people I've trained, promoted above me. It is very clear to me that I have gone as far as I can go here. The walls of this office, once symbols of aspiration, now feel like barriers to growth. I should have done this two years ago."

Jack is still looking, in shock. He spends the next 10 minutes telling me how valuable I am to the company and that I am one of the best at my job, his words a stark contrast to the actions that have led to this moment. He asks me what he could do to change my mind, I tell him that I should have done this a long time ago. He takes another longer pause, as if articulating his response but before he can say anything, he dismisses the thought and finishes by telling me he will talk to me later in the morning. I head back to my office and get back to work, knowing my resignation will not be taken lightly and it will bring in all the bitterness of these past years. They won't let me go easily and I need to leave this place. I clicked away my keyboard, the only sound I could hear as I contemplated my future.

I haven't told Joan I am leaving. I want to see how the day unfolds. Lunchtime comes, and I get a call from Jack. "Can you meet us for lunch? We want to talk to you."

"We?" I ask, my tone tinged with wariness. "Yes, myself, Malcolm Adams, Greg, and other directors." I agree if for no other reason than politeness. We head out for lunch in an exclusive and private restaurant nearby, the scent of gourmet food mingling with the tense atmosphere. Upon arrival, it felt a bit intimidating, with the management team facing me, their expressions a mosaic of concern and strategic calculation. I know they all have conjured up a plan to convince me. But I was convinced, convinced about leaving them. Jack does most of the talking. "We would be extremely disappointed to lose you. What can we do to change your mind?" I listen, take a moment, and looking back stone-faced, say, "I don't know. You had your chance and passed me over, and then when I complained, I was given menial jobs and put in my place. I gave the company my all for years. But every time a promotion came up, you passed me over and said it was not my time. The empty promises echoing in my mind like a broken record. It showed me my value here." Malcolm interjects and says, "We will give you a pay rise in recognition of your work if you stay." I look at him, rather shocked at his offer.

"I don't need a pay rise. That is not what I am asking from you." I pause and finish by saying, "When are you announcing my promotion to partner?"

Staring back, he replies, "We are not due to appoint new partners until next year. You know that." His words hang in the air, heavy with implication and the weight of unfulfilled potential.

"Alright, give me a letter saying I shall be the designated next partner appointed within the next year."

He gets serious, his brows knitting together as he tries not to get annoyed. "You know I cannot do that. We will look extremely favorably on you then if you continue performing as you have."

"Thank you, but that is not enough. I have been getting that excuse all too often, and I know that no woman ever made a partner here. Maybe that's what holds you guys back from promoting me. So, sorry, I am not changing my mind."

He reminds me, "Just remember you can't work for any other practice or compete as per your contract. If you try, we will protect ourselves against any breach."

Staring back, I have thought about this, I knew they would bring this up. My voice steady, I say, "Oh, I know what is in my contract and the restrictions. I am not going to work for a competitor or a client, as per the contract. So, sue away if you want." I see the surprise in their faces, or is it anger? Not the reaction they expected.

"Who are you going to work for?" He asks.

"That is none of your business. Just know I will not be breaching the contract."

"It is a simple question, who are you moving to?" He starts to get annoyed.

"It is, and my answer is the same, none of your business. I am not breaching the contract, so I will do what I want. I will work on my months' notice. From today." I keep my resolve, somehow, I know it won't last that long.

Agitated, Jack cuts in, "Is that your final answer? You should reconsider your decision. Think about the respect and position you have here. All the people here know how hard-working and respectable you are. And honestly, you deserve all that. You have earned that all by yourself. Think about it. Will you leave all of what you have earned after years of work? It will be unjust to your hard work."

I stayed quiet, it is these kinds of words that broke my resolve. I want to scream at them for how they underappreciated my years of hard work. "Yes, as it appears management don't respect my hard work and position, that's my final answer. And I value my hard work, that's why I am leaving. I can't see my hard work go to waste anymore. You have offered me nothing meaningful or concrete and you knew how unhappy I was."

"Ok. Well, when you go back, clear out your personal belongings and from today, you are on garden leave. You will not be attending work and can't work anywhere else while the month runs down."

"No problem. I will pack up and say my goodbyes when I get back. I will leave my laptop on my desk and the phone is my own. Anything else?" I purse my lips, waiting for this conversation to end.

Jack interjects, "What about your work in progress?"

"What about it? If I am out, I am out. If you want me to work, I need to be here. Or maybe you need a few minutes to decide what you want. Excuse me for a minute; I will be back." I stand up, push the chair back as hard as I can, and walk away.

I head to the ladies and give a big sigh when I go in. The pressure is there. I was shaking, and I am usually not confrontational. Confrontations make me shaky; I am not the type of person who likes to hurt people, and confrontations does thar.

I lightly pat my hair with my wet hands, trying to get rid of the frizz and freshen up my lipstick. I can't look like I lost, or I am hurt by this. '*I am winning this confrontation,*' I tell myself. I walk back in, my steps resolute. Sitting down. "Well, what do you want?" Jack comes in. "Garden leave. So, clear your desk today."

I nodded in agreement and announced I will head back now. Gratefully, I thank them for lunch, though I ate little anyway. A very expensive meeting for them, as the near full plates are cleared. A sarcasm-filled comment bubble up. This felt more like a tribunal than a lunch. But I resist the urge to say it aloud, I don't want this to prolong any longer.

"I will be gone in an hour, and you can send on my salary and expenses due."

I stand and stride out. Heading into the office, I meet Joan, who is still on her lunch break.

"Joan, you should know first. I quit this morning. Lunch was a final effort to get me to stay. I won't. I've had enough of the crap and politics here." Joan is visibly shocked. "Why? When?"

"Joan. I'm clearing my desk now. They're paranoid I'll steal clients or information or something. So, I'm being put on garden leave. I'm 'honored'—it's usually reserved for senior people." I laugh, trying to make light of the situation. However, deep down, I want to sob right now. I expected it to be bitter, but so ungrateful – I didn't expect that. Like a silent ending to my career here. When I am gone, I am of no more use and to be forgotten.

"We'll catch up for lunch soon, and I'll spill all the details." "Where will you be working?"

"Don't worry about it. I'm sorted. Who knows, maybe there'll be an opportunity for you too."

Within minutes, rumors spread like wildfire. I packed up and left before I was bombarded with too many questions. Nothing much to take. I have moved my personal items over the last few days. So, by the time I was ready to go, only my briefcase remained. I refused to do the walk with a box in hand.

On the way out, I ran into Jack and the others coming back from lunch. "Bye, Jack. Hope you enjoyed your lunch. Call me for whatever you need over the next month. After that, I'll be starting my new job and will be quite busy."

I keep walking, so they don't have time to reply, and out the door, I go. I can almost feel the intensity of his angry gaze on my back. I enjoy their annoyance at my resignation. If they are ungrateful for all the work I did, I'll like them to be agitated at my resignation. They better be agitated.

I immediately texted Paul.

Maria: Well, that's done. They tried to keep me, even offered a pay rise. Are you sure you can afford me? 😉

Paul: Well, I'm stuck with you now. At least you've signed a contract, so no more negotiations!

Paul: And no, you can't make me submit, not even with a whip in your hand.

Maria: Might be fun trying 😊.

Maria: It's a relief to have it all out in the open, and it's exciting to be making a fresh start. It's a bit scary, too, but I'm looking forward to it. I'm on garden leave and can't work for a month, so I guess I won't even try to redecorate the office. They'll probably be watching my every move.

Maria: Catch you later to fill you in on the lunch and the rest of my day.

I ventured out into the afternoon, seeking the sanctuary of a quiet coffee shop for a chance to decompress and take a breath. Settling into a secluded corner, I pull out my phone, not to send another message but to look up some news and enjoy a moment of peace. After ordering a coffee, I decided to call Mark. Better to fill him in as well.

The conversation with Mark was as succinct as most of our other chats. He was curious about how the morning went and whether I had handed in my notice. Again, his main concern was whether I was certain of my decision. What would we do if the new job fell through? I relayed the events of the lunch and the subsequent meeting with the directors; it only solidified my resolve.

Mark had to run, his final words before hanging up were, "I'll be home late this evening, we can talk more about it then." And I know, that later never comes, even if it does, it will again be just as brief as possible. There will be no deliberation, a very outward consolation, maybe, but nothing more.

As my coffee arrives, I sit back, sipping it slowly, my mind wandering through the events of the past two weeks, replaying each moment, and silently preparing for the new chapter ahead.

Chapter 2

One Month Earlier

I sit down at the familiar, cozy kitchen table with Mark, the aroma of coffee in the air, and take a deep breath as I tell him about the last few days in London, at least from a work perspective anyway. As Mark got ready to interrupt, with that characteristic impatience of his, to start speaking, I just stopped him short. "Just let me speak for a minute so I can try and explain for a minute where my head is at." Mark, with a look of concern creasing his forehead, is taken aback but nods and decides it's best to say nothing.

I continue and dive deeper with Mark about everything that has been going on, and how I've come to appreciate the new job and the vibrant energy of work in London. The hustle of the city, the challenge of new tasks—it's been invigorating, yet telling him that I am nothing but unhappy in my current role and that I feel completely unappreciated is like admitting a difficult truth. I draw attention to the recent occurrence where I was passed over for a partnership. The sting of that rejection was still fresh, when challenging Jack has landed me with some less-than-stellar jobs, it just made me seriously think about my future.

"All I can think is that I'm so unhappy in my job and I don't think there is anything more for me here except the pay packet. It's like I'm stuck in a loop, waking up with the same grey feeling every morning. I know the salary is good and had nothing changed I would probably have endured it. But then, Paul surprised me completely unaware today, when he asked me, coming back from London, if we could make a slight detour. He asked if we could call into the Manchester shop to review some paperwork briefly. My curiosity piqued, I agreed, that explained why he asked we take the earlier train back."

"I thought nothing of this; he certainly gave no hint as to what he was thinking. As we walked through the quiet streets to the shop, suspense built up inside me. But then, after we went to the shop, he escorted me upstairs in the building. He showed me that the upstairs floors were empty and had previously been occupied by an IT company, so was already outfitted with a modern setup and he had freshly redecorated it. The potential of the space was immediately apparent to me. He then told me that he wanted to continue running the business but with a primary focus from here in Manchester and limiting the time in London to only 1 or 2 days a week when everything was running smoothly. I already knew that he had ideas to expand into Holland to create an export hub for online sales once that initiative kicked off. As he shared his vision, his eyes lit up with a passion that was infectious. I could see he was charged with optimism about the future of this and had arranged with his own employers to move to a part-time position."

"The last thing I expected was for him to offer me a job and invite me to come and run that section of the business as a chief financial officer. The offer hung in the air, weighty and significant. I never expected this offer to come, let alone see myself in this role. It felt like the turning point I hadn't dared to hope for."

Sitting back in the chair, I run my hands through my hair, "I have no idea what to do, I need to take some time to think about this. The idea of a new job, the CFO position, and new challenges to develop a company are alluring, however, there is obviously uncertainty as Paul is as new to this business as I am. He has told me that he will continue working in his legal practice and just wants to take an overarching ownership/supervisor's role in the management of the new company. He needs somebody who has the knowledge and experience to run matters for him, financially and commercially."

"So, ... what do you think?" I ask, seeking some kind of affirmation or advice. I hope he helps me clear things in my head – my chaotic thoughts are driving me crazy. And I need to think clearly. This is no ordinary decision; this is about my career and my family's financial health.

"Maria, where to start.... What about the salary, what will it pay? You really want to give up the security you have?" Mark quizzes me, his brows knitted together in concern. He obviously starts with the apparent question.

"Well... he is matching my existing package and a performance bonus at year-end. I need to see the details, but he assured me the basic matches what I am on at least. I have no reason to doubt that. As for the security of my job now, yes, it is secure, but I hate it." I confess, feeling the weight of each word. *I don't have to doubt anything, I can trust Paul. I trust Paul,* I affirm myself before Mark presents me with another query.

"What do you want? Do you want the job? Will there be much time away? You mentioned Holland as well as London." Mark continues, trying to piece together the puzzle of my future.

"The new offices are here in Manchester, so it would be based here, with or without me. London would run as is and I understand that I would be there maybe one or two days a week, no more than I am now. Holland, I don't know, a new base would be set up there, I would hope not too much time there, after setting up. Look, let's all sleep on this." I propose, hoping time would grant some clarity. Quite surprisingly, Mark and I talked about it for more than a couple of minutes. And I, perhaps, am not used to this. It was an actual conversation.

Also, I could not tell Mark that a significant factor here is that I have fallen for Paul, and this would be a chance for us to be together and get away. The dilemma is more personal than professional, a complex weave of heart and career. The difference now is this would no longer be a job to hold the status quo, I would need to make this company work, develop it, grow it, and structure a new company. I am so used to fixing what is broken and working with structures that just need streamlining. It's a daunting yet thrilling prospect. I must think, can I do the job?

Coming back to my coffee, I sip it. The warm, bitter taste grounds me as I relive the past few weeks in my mind. And somewhere in my recollection, I drifted to the good old days, when I first joined Jack and Co. The applause at every accomplishment, the celebrations we had together, and the complimentary introduction Jack used to give to every trainee. It disheartens me, the ungratefulness and bitterness – I never thought after all these years, all they'll have for me was a cold, cold farewell. Was all that trying to pay me compliments rather than real recognition? Stroking my ego to distract from what I was not being given.

Sleeping on it did not help much. Not that I got much sleep, the thoughts were relentless, swirling in my mind like a storm. I remember, first thing in the morning, Mark asks, "Well, are you coming to your senses and staying put? You know you barely exercise let alone know how to run an outdoor shop." His skepticism is clear, almost tangible, and somehow, I think it seems reasonable. This was the Mark I knew would come out. Who I expected last night.

Sitting in my kitchen, all I could feel was alone. The silence of the room amplifies my solitude. It was clear that Mark did not want me to make the move and for no other reason than he preferred the job security that I had. His perspective was limited to the practicalities, unaware of the emotional currents running beneath. Paul did not come into the equation.

Emotions surged within me like waves in a stormy sea—from the unhappiness I had in my job to the excitement of starting something new and taking on a new role. A new challenge and lastly, and probably most importantly, the feelings that I have for Paul. I can't suppress those feelings; how do you stifle a raging torrent? You can't, you are overwhelmed, thrashed, and defeated by it. I am defeated by the torrents of my emotions – conquered by his love.

What would this new job mean to us? There would be a meaningful change in the relationship. I would be working for

Paul full-time. What tangled webs we might weave in both love and work? What would happen if the relationship ended? Leaving any question of a contract to one side, how could I balance the personal and professional? Could I continue working for him and then where would this leave me?

I feel dizzy. I take a long sip of my coffee, hoping it will clear the answers for me. My mind is so distracted I can hardly taste what I am sipping.

It was Saturday morning, and the house buzzed with the imminent chaos of family life. Everything was going to be busy with the children and as soon as they began to surface, normality took over. Mark did not mention any more of this to me during the day, but my mind was constantly slipping back to it. I was craving a distraction from the dilemma I faced.

Suddenly, it felt like the axis of my world had shifted. All of a sudden, my entire future felt like it hinged on this moment. The choices before me were stark and life-altering. Do I stay in a job I hate, in the marriage that was just trundling along, or do I take a chance and take the new role with Paul and try and develop the company for him and with him? This chance may never come again. The potential for a rekindled joy in life beckoned—while at the same time beginning to live life again and explore some fun and pleasure, passion, and love which I felt was lost forever.

Any conversation I could have with Mark would inevitably circle back to job security and income. From the outside, it appeared that this was an excellent job, with a good salary and a good future. And seemingly our marriage was the same, it was intact from the outside, but unraveling from within. But what guarantee do I have with Paul?

The 'what ifs' started to crowd my thoughts. If I handed in my notice at work, what would they do? Could they sue me under my contract, because I am now working for what was a would-be client? How would that work and what could I lose?

By the end of the day, clarity emerged from the fog of my indecision. My mind was clear, and I had decided. I was going to make a list and arrange a business meeting with Paul to discuss the offer in full and explain to him my concerns. Determined, I decided I would send Paul a message. For now, I keep my love life aside, my professional life needs intensive care and attention.

When all was quiet in the house and I had some time to myself, the glow of the screen in front of me felt like a beacon in the dark. I sat down and began to compose my message to Paul.

"Hey, love…" I backspaced the message. I don't want this message to hint the slightest at any other intentions. It can't be too flirtatious.

"I hope your weekend is going well for you. The time we spent together in London was unforgettable. You threw my world into a complete spin with the offer you made me last night. You know how unhappy I have been at work and the changes that I dream of making, but never thought possible. Your proposition has sparked a fire within me but also terrified me in many ways. I would like the chance to sit down with you over the next couple of days and arrange a meeting. I know both of us are back at work on Monday and it would not be possible during the day. For a change, it would be possible for me to say to Mark that I am arranging an evening meeting with you to discuss the offer that you have made.

Until that meeting, I would like to just continue enjoying ourselves, as we would any other weekend with our messages and texts rather than spending all our time discussing this offer.

The agenda for the meeting, and my concerns, are as follows. The accountant is now coming out in me and the professional side of how this needs to be dealt with.

1. How long of a contract are you offering? Will there be room for renegotiation or extension depending on how the role evolves and the direction the company takes?

2. If this does not work out, either you decide to sell the company, or find that I am not working out, what are you proposing? Is there a contingency plan, and will

there be some sort of severance to ensure a smooth transition if it comes to that?

3.	Is there a probationary period involved? During this time, what benchmarks will we set to gauge the right fit for both the company's needs and my personal career goals?

4.	What happens if my current employers decide to sue me for breach of contract? Would the company be able to provide legal support, or how would we handle this potential challenge together?

5.	On a personal level, things will also have changed, suddenly I am no longer collaborating with you, but I am working for you. You will be my boss, whatever way we may dress it up. What happens if there is a personal falling out with us? Could we establish some ground rules for separating work conflicts from our personal relationships, ensuring one does not negatively impact the other?

You know how I feel about you and how I look forward to the amount of time we can spend together and the new life we have begun exploring. I do not want to lose that and whatever my decision is here, in relation to this job, impacts that significantly. The last thing I would want is for our professional dynamic to overshadow the personal connection that has brought us so much joy.

My thinking is that, if I take the job, we obviously have the ability to spend a lot more time together and get away to London as we have been for the last couple of months. Even the prospect of the occasional trip away for trade shows or exploring the Holland project. These opportunities are not just career highlights but also chances for us to make memories outside the confines of our routine lives.

If I don't take this job, obviously our ability to spend time together is hugely limited and we would be down to looking for the occasional meeting in a hotel or something similar. I have gotten so used to spending days, evenings, and nights with you, it would be hard to settle for much less. The thought of reverting to a more distant relationship, after having tasted the closeness, we currently enjoy, feels like stepping back into shadows after basking in the sun.

You can see my dilemma, if I take the job, it gives me a new chance from a work perspective and it gives our relationship a chance to develop and grow and an ability to explore. If I don't take the job, it would make any relationship a lot harder, simply the ability to make time.

The intersection of our personal and professional lives is delicate, and I find myself walking the tightrope, trying to balance the weight of my decisions on either side.

I'm sorry if this is rambling, but this is where my mind is going. Really, I want to have time with you soon, to sit down and talk about the work side of your offer and the personal side going forward. It's a conversation that's as much about us as it is about me, about the future we're both invested in.

Just so you know where my head is in relation to us. I know neither of us has said this, but this is what I'm thinking.

ILU Xxxxx"

I hit send, and my message is gone to Paul and no taking it back. What will he make of the ramblings in my message? *It's going to be okay. It makes sense,* I convinced myself after rereading my message.

A few hours passed and there was no reply, I know I have asked him just to arrange a meeting, but I'd hoped he would say something. *He will say something, he is a very sensible person. It's Paul. It's Paul.* My heart and mind are in a race, neither of them lets me rest and relax.

I hear my phone ping with a message, and my heart jumps and drops at the same time. I know he really cannot be saying anything bad, but my head is in such a spin I don't know what to expect. I make an excuse that I'm going to tidy up the kitchen, so I can sit down and read the message in peace. I need some peace. All the noise simply adds to the chaos going on in my mind. I really am not in a headspace to appreciate and enjoy the time with my kids. As guilty as I feel for this, I know I needed some time off to resume having time with my kids.

Paul: hey baby let me start by saying that I understand everything that is going on in your head. I know that I landed a bombshell on you last night and that you did not see it coming. This was not a rash decision on my part, I thought long and hard about this before I made the offer to you and many of your concerns I would have expected.

Let me jump to the end of your message first. If you don't already know my feelings towards you, they are the same, and they have only deepened with each day we've spent together. I've never felt I would feel like this about anybody again. The time we have given each other has created a new lease of life in me and an optimism for the future that was not there. I had settled into a mundane life of routine. Your energy has been like a beacon, reigniting passions I thought had dimmed forever. I feel the same way about you as you do about me, I just did not want to say it, for fear it would put too much pressure on you, knowing your family situation. I was having too much fun and enjoying life too much, to risk losing you by scaring you.

I do not want to do anything that will risk us, though I do know your decision on this job also has massive implications for us, both as regards being able to see and spend time with each other. It's a pivotal moment that could reshape our landscape, together or apart. I agree completely that we need a meeting next week and I would happily meet you any night or evening that you wish. A dinner sounds perfect; a chance to lay everything bare, not just our plans and worries but also our hopes and expectations.

What I will say to you on this before that meeting is as follows:

1. The contract I'm offering you is open-ended and is not for a fixed term. This flexibility is designed to accommodate both our professional and personal growth over time.

2.   There will be no probationary period as you have well and truly proved your abilities over the last few months. Your skills and commitment are clear, and I have every confidence in your capabilities.

3.   If anything happens between us personally, that makes it impossible for us to work together and you feel you have no choice but to leave, I will propose that we build in a no-quibble severance package that gives you at least one year's salary. Moreover, if you would like to build any other safeguards, please tell me. It's paramount that you feel secure in this new phase.

4.   In the event your existing employers decide to sue you, we will fight too. We stand on solid ground, and I'll stand with you through any storm that may come our way. I do not think they have a case. We have an email from your boss which says that the sports companies were not clients of your company. You are taking on a new role, which is different from that of the accountant, though you will be overseeing the accountancy of the company. In the event that your company does decide to sue you, we will build into your contract that all your costs of defending such a claim will be paid by your new employer and that you have no financial exposure. Your peace of mind is a priority for me, as is ensuring that your professional journey continues without undue burden. I hope from what you've seen of me over the last period of time, the natural way I deal with people who are working for me or under my direction is clear. When I was given control of the shops and the business in London my objective was to treat staff properly and fairly and build a good working environment for everybody. I believe in a leadership that nurtures and a partnership that respects boundaries. I will always try to be fair, but I understand that you need certain protection in the event that things go wrong.

The decisions we are about to make are like threads in the tapestry of our future, each one significant and each one contributing to the larger picture we hope to create.

If you have any questions in advance of our meeting next week, please let me know.

But for now, how are you baby? Have you done anything nice this weekend and let's talk about something other than work. Life is more than the sum of our decisions and the work we do; it's the laughter, the shared silence, and the small, mundane moments that truly define us.

Can't wait to see you.

ILU2 xxxxx"

I smile and send a quick reply: Maria: xxx I am exhausted… it is all your fault 😊 and not even any fun in it, what is the newfound power bringing out in you …. BOSS. Not easy to message here… but good we are on the same page, I presumed we were, but just good to hear it. It's like we are dancing to a song that only we can hear, perfectly coordinated even when the rhythm changes. I am going to bed soon…. Send me off with a nice mental picture if you get a chance.

Nite xx.

And I hit send.

I watched Paul typing just immediately after he received my message. It's this attention that I enjoy with him.

"Ok, baby. you get some sleep. If you want something to imagine, think of the London Apartment, the shower, and you and me …. and let your imagination go from there. Picture the steam rising, the water a gentle cascade, and the rest of the world fades into insignificance. Drop me a message at any stage, if you want, on any front. Remember, regardless of the hour, I'm here, a constant in your whirlwind of thoughts."

I close my eyes and put that picture together, every goosebump rises up as if on command. I head to bed, trying to keep the mental picture alive, and try to sleep. It doesn't help much, and my head keeps spinning. It's like my thoughts are a carousel, circling endlessly, each one a blend of anticipation and trepidation. I decided to text Paul.

Maria: How about dinner on Monday evening? Please lay out exactly what is on offer and not and what work expectations are there. Let's map out the territory we're stepping into, not just the contours of our roles, but the landscape of our joint future.

I hit send. Put the phone away. And lay with my eyes wide open. The ceiling above seemed like a blank canvas, on which my apprehensions twirled and curved. With every passing minute, my eyes become heavier, and I am determined not to rest.

Chapter 3

Monday morning rolls around and I head to work. I am hoping today will help my decision one way or the other.

Joan met me and asked me about my weekend. Telling me I look tired. I just pass her off that I am fine and just tired.

"You'll be fine," Joan says with her bright smile. I appreciate her attempt to cheer me up. I am a bit late, so just head off to the Monday meeting.

Walking into the meeting, only about half the staff are there. I end up next to Jack and he asks about my weekend and London. "Is it nearly over?" Again, asking who the beneficiary is "It is highly irregular that you are keeping information from your boss, who inherited." Looking back, I just say "Jack, my responsibilities were clear – maintain discretion until the process is complete. It's about respecting the privacy of all parties involved. I don't want to be in the middle, ask the solicitors and the executor, they gave the instructions. I don't think you knowing, or not, makes a difference to the work. If you ask the executors they may tell you, after all, they are the clients here."

Jack is looking annoyed, but the room is filling. He quells his quiz and proceeds to look through the documents in front of him. I feel the weight of his scornful gaze he grants me with after every minute, but I'm determined to keep a professional boundary. My thoughts drift to the potential consequences if I transition to Paul's company. It feels like I'm walking a tightrope between my future happiness and professional integrity.

I outline, "London is nearly done, and I am just winding down the job. Nothing much left for us there, a few more weeks for handover." If only he knew what was happening. In my mind, scenarios of conflict and confrontation play out, each one ending with the same question: What am I willing to risk for this new beginning? Thinking really, if I go over to Paul, there will be murder here. I will be accused of cultivating the job and can't exactly argue other reasons, that I am sleeping with the boss already. *Good God, the shame of it,* I let out a sigh, trying to regain my composure. I need to be here and not anyone here knows that I am apprehensive about this new job. They can't know.

A few small new jobs are passed to me to get ready to take over and I take them as usual. The meeting ends and I head back to my office. Heading back Joan brings me a coffee, "You look like you need this, been a hell of a weekend." I look quizzically at her and wonder how she knows about the weekend, and she comes in "I just figured, you've had a lot to contemplate, it must be draining." Her intuition sends a ripple of discomfort through me, but I'm grateful for the coffee and the unspoken understanding between us.

I work away for the day and leaving at 5 I head to meet Paul for an early dinner. Paul is at the restaurant ahead of me. Sitting down, I smile a tired smile.

"Hey, how are you, Maria? Was work ok today?"

"Paul, my head is all over the shop. Jack is asking who the beneficiary is again and getting annoyed that I am not saying. His persistence is like a thorn in my side, relentless and sharp. There will be real trouble if I go and take this job with you. My company will say I lined it up while with you and they should be managing the accounts and likely to fight me. The unfairness of it tightens my chest, the injustice of being punished for seeking happiness. Mark is all over the shop, on the one hand, he wants me to stay in my job and at the same time encourages me to take jobs that have me travelling. He doesn't want me to take the new job in-house. He is also worried my salary may drop. He is no real help to me. The only right decision for him is to continue doing what I am doing and stay put, he does not care that I am so unhappy there."

"And what do you want Maria? Forget the issues for a minute. Perfect world what is your wish list here?"

A glass of wine arrives, I need it, "I am driving, fuck."

"Don't worry I will drop you home after the meeting or get you a taxi. I think you need a drink for this." I agree, as I do need one badly, and take a large sip of it.

"Ok well, perfect world. I take the new job with you, have job security and a salary that Mark is happy with, and I know I am covered. I yearn for a clean break, a smooth transition, but life is rarely that accommodating. I know there will be no problems left behind in my old job and I am not worried about problems there. I want to close the door gently, not slam it shut. We can continue as we have at least. Just as well I am not demanding." I laugh. The laughter is a mask, hiding the fear of uncertainty and the deep desire for a fresh start.

"Ok, I am not going to make this easy to say no to. I will match your salary plus 5%, which should sort Mark, project bonus when integration of the shops finishes and based on overall project success. Annual bonus to be discussed. Usual travel and other expenses. You will be your own boss effectively and get to recruit your own team. You can come up with your own job description, CFO, director, Operations manager, etc. whatever works. The autonomy in crafting your position is a rare freedom, a canvas on which you can paint your future. I will pay legal costs if there is a dispute with DAF, but you will obviously still be in it. Honestly, they may react badly to you taking the job, but I don't think they can stop you. Particularly as you are not going in as an accountant. With this reassurance, the bridge to the new beginning seems sturdier, less swayed by the winds of consequence. If any help, knowing how our bosses get along, I don't think I will be very popular either and there may be fallout there, but I am lucky, I no longer need the job and assume all is going to plan when I tell the family in a year or more what happened, I may move into more of a company role. But that is my problem." His willingness to face his own battles makes the offer more gallant, and more genuine. "So now, where are you?"

"Oh, it is so tempting and scary, was so easy to moan about my job, knowing I always had it and no chance to move and be an accountant. Now I have an offer that is life-changing, professionally, and personally, as I know it gives a lot of chances to be together. The threshold between the known and the unknown is a precipice where fear and excitement mingle." I took another sip, this time with ease.

"Maria, I know it is not easy. But leave me and us aside for now. If I were any other company offering you this role and package, what would you do? We will work something out somewhere. If DAF is the big issue and you are staying there. I could look at DAF as company auditors on the condition you are managing the account. That would give some chance." He's offering a lifeline, a way to bridge the gap between past allegiance and future potential. "Just decide whether you want the new job or stay, we will work from there. Black or white, should be easy for an accountant. No grey area. Yet life, unlike ledgers, thrives in shades of grey. Now let's order some dinner."

I glance at the menu and order some dinner, not that I am hungry, I should eat something, as I have not eaten all day. We talked a bit more about family, vacations, our dates, and a bit about how the new offices look.

"Let's get you home at a normal hour also, as it is a business meeting and no more. Let's not give Mark any reason to ask where you were." The precaution is a balm to my unease, a nod to the complications of personal entanglements in professional spheres.

We finished at about 8, Paul was talking about some of his plans and again said if I take the job, I can pick the accounts and admin team for the new office and he said, if I don't take the job, he will still be setting up in Manchester. This affirmation of his commitment to both the project and to me, independent of my decision, is comforting – very comforting.

I take a taxi home and leave my car. I relax my head all the way home and take in the night sky and the city's rush in. Arriving in, Mark greets me. "A taxi? Is everything ok, where is your car?"

"Yes fine, I just had a glass of wine and was tired. I would not risk driving. Not worth it. Prudence is my shield tonight, my safeguard against the unpredictable currents of change."

"Ok, I will drop you in tomorrow to work. So, what happened?"

"It is hard Mark. He offered me my existing package plus 5% and a bonus structure based on annual performance and a bonus once we finished setting up shops and Holland hub and integration. So financially, it is better than what I am on, more responsibility. His question is a weight, adding gravity to the reality of the decision before me. He said a guaranteed contract for 2 years so no chance of taking me and letting me go if I am concerned about that. I get to set up my new office and staff, and more work, but I can pick my own team in consultation with him and integrate with the London team. We would be the group financial hub effectively and online sales depot. The lure of control over my domain is a powerful draw, like a siren's song beckoning me to uncharted waters.

I am wanted to help advise on the new shop and EU hub for sales. Meeting suppliers also for negotiating new credit terms and supply, etc. Effectively, I am being offered the role of financial controller/operations manager. This role could propel me into a realm of new challenges and responsibilities, a testament to my capabilities and potential. He has said he will give me a week or so to consider before advertising the roles, either way, this is happening with or without me. The clock is ticking, an ultimatum of sorts, but also a sign of his respect for my decision-making process."

"Wow, he wants you badly. What about the work, can you manage it and the extra? Will he pay more now? I don't know what to say, who would you employ? Money sounds good."

I just looked, and wished for this conversation to end, "I will think about it this week and I told him we will talk. We will be in London on Thursday anyway and can talk there. So, I need to have an idea. The big issue will be a fight with DAF to try and keep me or stop me going. The intrigue of corporate chess plays out in my mind, pieces moving in a silent war of wills and wants."

"Could they? How messy could this get?"

All the questions I can't answer, Mark somehow knows how to ask the most pricking questions.

"Well, Paul said that the new job is not covered by their contract, so I could take it, and if there is an issue he will pay for the defense of it. He is happy, as I am not going in as an accountant, there is nothing they can do. Also, the shops were not clients, the estate was. He has that in writing. He walked Jack into that one, obviously thinking ahead and he had this in mind. But either way, they will be pissed. His foresight is my safety net, the strategic moves plotted with precision. If I went, I would look at maybe recruiting some staff or former staff from there for the accounts section, who did not have restrictions in contracts. But that is down the line."

"Who, Joan? Someone else?"

"I don't know, I am not thinking that far ahead. That is a small question, as I must think do I want the job or not, first. The immediate question looms large, casting a shadow over the finer details of a future still in flux."

The following day, I get up and sort the children. Ursula arrives and I see her and Mark talking for a few minutes before we leave. I am going into town with him. Usually, I am gone before him.

Looking at him, I say, "What was that about?"

"Nothing, at all, just seeing can she work late Thursday as you are in London." I wonder about it, as that is a standing evening for her to work now, as I know Mark has a site meeting, so he is nearly always late. The routine is disrupted, a ripple in the still pond of our domestic life.

I say no more. Mark drops me at the office, and I head in. It is a quiet day, I work away, but my mind is straying all the time to the offer and Paul. We exchanged some texts. Over my coffee at lunch, I am thinking that I am missing Paul. The more carefree times when we were just working on the job and enjoying each other. Memories flit through my mind, and sweet nostalgia mingled with the bitter tang of reality. I hope this does not change everything. I am lost in my thoughts. And I stayed lost in thoughts, I didn't have much work to do.

I got home that night and Mark is again asking what I am doing. "Can you tell me what you think I should do, one way or the other?"

"I don't know, great offer, but I wonder about security. I don't know." Mark shrugs his shoulders. About as useful an elephant in a minefield.

"Ok. well, I am not talking about it anymore, it is exhausting, I will just make up my own mind as you are not going either way here. My declaration is a line in the sand, the weariness of indecision becoming a call to arms for my own resolve." Mark is a bit taken aback. But before he can say anything "I am getting dinner ready." I sort dinner for the children and try to be as normal with them as possible.

Heading to bed Mark asks, "Do you want to talk about it?"

"No Mark. If you want to express an opinion one way or the other, then I will. But not otherwise, I am tired thinking about it." I fixed my pillow, pulled up the comforter, and turned away from him. The offer, heavy with promise and peril, sits like a stone in my mind, one I'm not ready to roll just yet.

I am heading to bed and sending Paul a quick message, "Nite baby xx."

He replied instantly "xxx and I have booked something nice for dinner on Thursday, you need the distraction." The thought of the dinner is a beacon, a small light in the tumultuous seas of decision, a reminder that life, despite its complexities, also holds simple joys and little escapes from our overbearing realities.

Some days, I just wish to switch off myself and rest like a dead bee. *Wow, I want to be a dead bee, now. I need a break.* I pulled the blindfold on my eyes; the dark might help me subside the pricking thoughts.

Chapter 4

Thursday morning, as the sun peeks through the city buildings, I am never so happy to be getting on the train. No more Jack, office, and Mark. I feel tired and the weight of the week seems to hang on my shoulders. I look every bit of it, my weary eyes reflecting my state of mind. I pass Mr. 24a and he smiles. His usual cheery demeanor contrasts starkly with my mood. I don't have the energy to smile back. I sat down and no Paul. I glance around, feeling a bit anxious, but thankfully he is just arriving behind me. I feel like all I want to do is kiss him. Forget the decision.

He sits down and smiles. "Hope you are ok, don't worry. Not a heavy day. I have booked hair and the works for you at 4. Just thought you might like some relaxation."

"Thank you, that sounds nice. To be honest I'm too tired to work. But I want to see the office and hope that might help." I ran my hand through my hair, wondering if my hair looks that bad. Or perhaps it's just for relaxation, as he says.

"That is fair enough, I have also booked dinner at a burlesque club in Soho. It should be a light-hearted, entertaining evening. I booked for four and it is up to you if you would like to invite Nicole and Adam or not. Did not know if you would like just us or maybe a distraction. Think about it."

We order breakfast as always and follow the usual Thursday ritual. Our breakfast routine is comforting in its familiarity. We drop our bags to the apartment. Today is a little different. Everywhere I go and everything I do makes me think of the decision that I have to make. The walls of the apartment seem to echo with the weight of my impending decision. As we walk into the apartment, I look around and wonder if this will be one of the last times that I arrive on Thursday morning. The Lilly tapestry hanging from the hook where it all started.

We drop the bags quickly and head down to the office. Walking in, I look around and see a new pristine office, with modern furniture, happy staff, and an energetic buzz. The newness of everything symbolizes a fresh start, a new chapter. I inwardly hope everything stays this way, and the mundaneness, office politics, and biases don't swallow all of it. I don't think I could work in such an environment anymore.

I hit my office and reviewed the post from the week. The incoming figures from the various shops and the up-to-date statements from the banks. I sift through the paperwork, feeling the responsibility of my position. As I sit behind my desk and look around at an office that is mine, at the same time it is not mine. There is a sense of authority here that I have not felt in other jobs, here I am perceived as being a manager, in charge, I am respected for my role, and no longer feared. Is this what I really want, or is there something else out there for me? Is this the only right option for me? Or am I missing out on anything else?

I know Nicole is at work, but she called me back and said it would be lovely, it is a great club. Been years since they were there. I am happy, and would love an evening with Paul, but just want to forget work and my decision. The rest of the day passes as normal, I grab a Starbucks for lunch, and I head off at 4 PM. Paul is coming back from the private office and here.

Why do I look forward to seeing him? Like just a glimpse of him, and I have butterflies all over my body.' I need to keep it together in the office, can't afford to have people talking about us. As much as I believe and may claim that I don't care about people, I do – I do care if talking crap about me or not. I think we all care, to some extent. No one wants to have their reputation questioned.

Dinner is booked for 7:30 and when I get back to the apartment at 6, it is time to change, and freshen up and get sorted. Paul is on the phone and dealing with some issues back in Manchester, his day job as he calls it. It all feels more normal, and relaxed. I call home and speak with the kids and Ursula to make sure all is ok. It is and Mark is still at work. I wanted to call Mark, but I ran that conversation in my head and knew it would be the same conversation we had a thousand times before, so I dropped the idea.

Dinner is lovely, and the dark sultry feel of the club, the life of the music, and the buzz of the atmosphere. The club and performers show such confidence in what they are doing. It was so different, dinner, a show, and such an erotic undertone to it all. So provocative, so daring. Exciting. Not something I would even think of, let alone go to with Mark. Maybe before the kids, but now he would have no interest. I watch the lead dancer, wow her costume, the tattoos, the dancing, and the music. I wonder if there is anything like this in Manchester. Maybe there is, it's just that myself and Mark never explored much. All I can do is sigh, what have I been missing, or missed out on?

Nicole and Adam are just chatting away as friends would. From work to the shop and they tell us about the next event they are going to soon.

"Adam, I am curious, what are the people like that come into the shop? Don't get me wrong, I am not judging, simply curious. The closest I ever got to this was local lingerie shops."

"Mmmm, well I could answer you, but maybe if you want a real answer. Tomorrow is Friday, one of our busiest days. Why don't both of ye get a takeaway lunch and enjoy the home comforts that my office doesn't have to offer? Come in and watch the shop on camera from the office or wander out if you want. It may surprise you. But needless to say, we get a mix, from the long raincoat brigade that you probably imagine. But with where we are, most of our customers come from the offices, businesses, and companies in the area. We are one of the few that have a broad selection of Latex also, so some come just for that."

"Thanks, Adam, at least you suggested lunchtime, you know what the boss is like. God knows what he would do if I skived off again."

When the night ends Nicole and Adam head off home, Paul and I stroll back to the apartment. It is a nice night and a 20-minute walk, so we decide to walk it. Streets are busy and fairly safe. I ask for the walk, some air and again craving some alone time and normality with Paul. The feeling of being together and alone, while surrounded by people. Something we could never do at home.

When we turn the key in the door and walk in, I can see our bits and pieces in the apartment, coats on the chair, handbag on the desk. It all keeps dragging me back to my decision. Paul snaps me back, "Lovely night, but you look exhausted. Let's just go to bed."

We curled up, me in his t-shirt, and Paul in his shorts, we headed to sleep. I love the feeling of my head on his chest as I fall asleep, the security of it. When I woke up in the morning, Paul was gone. I look at the clock. Panic. It is nearly ten. I see a note, you need sleep, so relax, you are not late. I am in the office and telling the girls you have a bank meeting to centralise all shop banking and see what rates are on offer. So, take your time.

I curl up with his pillow, taking in his scent.

Rolling into work at 10:30 I meet Paul at the reception, "Good meeting, was it?" I can see the smirk behind the look.

"I got sorted" and head to my office. At this point, I wonder why I am even here. I have no real decision to make. Nicola and Helen have this place humming and I see the changes around here and now I am a spectator. Do I even make any difference here anymore?

12:30 Paul calls me. Come on, we have a job to do. Nicola and Helen watched us leave. At this stage, they are used to us coming and going, so they pay little attention. They were too busy themselves. Paul has actually piled work on them. They are taking it with a smile and enthusiasm. I actually don't think they realise it. They just seem so happy in their jobs.

We grab a takeaway coffee and sandwich and head to the shop via the back door, and into Adam's office. He has cleared the desk for us, it is usually cluttered. The few times I have been there, you never know what you see lying around. The pile of sex toys and lingerie is now stacked in the corner making way for our lunch. Where else could this be normal?

We sit back and watch the customers come and go. A real mix. Some walk in with confidence and say hello to Adam, recognizing him as regulars we presume. Others, looking a bit hesitant, carefully browse through the aisles, their eyes occasionally darting towards the door. More are skulking around and picking items up, looking around hoping not to be seen. More just browsing as if they were in M & S. Among them, a young couple, giggling and pointing at assorted items, adds a touch of lightness to the atmosphere. The one thing that grabbed me was that most were well dressed, either fresh from the office or smart casual, professional-looking people. Almost what you expect not to see but they are the customers.

After about an hour, Adam comes in, leaving the shop in the capable hands of the shop assistant. "Well, what do ye think? Learn anything?"

I smile back "Everyone seems so normal, professional."

He laughs "What were you expecting, everyone in long raincoats and looking like little freaks? We have a good professional base here. They know what they usually want. You have shops at all levels, there are cheaper, seedier-looking ones and tourist shops with cheap and cheerful toys. We don't do much by way of the cheap and cheerful, we go for quality and the club scene and for those who want to properly explore this and enjoy."

"Well Adam, it was an education," Paul says. "Good idea to observe."

Heading back to work I meet Helen. "Hope ye had a nice lunch, I am heading away now, I am on a half day. Remember I am away next week, booked a holiday months ago, and never knew we would be so busy, but said if I don't take it now, who knows when I will get another chance. It was lovely having you here this year, made the transition much easier. To be honest, nice having a woman in charge. Paul is lovely, we are looking forward to having him as a new boss. I know you are nearly finished here. If I don't see you, please don't be a stranger and call in if you are passing, we would love to see you. You've really made this transition easier for all of us, we were so nervous of the changes."

She said it so nicely and really meant it, I could see, but it was like a slap, a wake-up call. This really is the end. I knew it, I could see it. But avoided facing reality. "Thanks, Helen, have a great holiday. I am sure I will make it down again sometime. I may be here for a week after you are back. But if not, I will drop in next time I am in London. Take care of Paul, he looks like he will be a fair boss and good. But he is only learning the business."

"We will. He is picking it up fast. Said he may even go to the trade shows to see what is out there and explore what we sell and could sell. We got lucky with him; I think. But I think you know that too," she says with a little smirk, like she knows all we have got up to, but how could she? "He's got big shoes to fill, but we're all here to support him." We smile and she heads off. Watching her leave with a spring in her step and a purpose to her job. I am sure not casting me a second thought, now I am gone.

I sit in the office for a few hours, make a few calls and check in with Joan. Killing time as much as working. Joan fills me in on the office activities and headline office gossip she thinks I need to know. All is fine at work. Nothing exciting. We talk for a few minutes. "So, you are nearly finished in London. Will you miss it? You seemed to enjoy this job more than most." Now, I know she is searching for gossip with a volley of questions. I go for a simple reply, "Yes, it was a nice job and a change of scene." She is fishing, but that is Joan anyway, and knows when to stop pushing.

We grab our bags and head for the cab to the train. Paul leaves with his usual casual goodbye, "See ye next week."

Finally taking our seats, moving his attention to me, Paul chats away about anything but the elephant in the room. his kids and their plans and ask me about mine. He is talking about anything but work. I know he is avoiding it intentionally. *I avoid it intentionally, too.*

As the train pulls into Manchester and the bustle of passengers around us move to grab bags, as if getting up that extra 30 seconds before the train stops will get them off sooner, we wait and let them move before we pack up. Dragging out the farewell we both hate. We walk down the platform, like all the other suits. Paul smiles his goodbye, as we part company, "Have a great weekend, get some rest." I look back, "I better, I am starting a new job soon and the boss I am sure will have me tied every way he can and work me to the bone."

Looking back in shock. I smile, "My turn to shock you this week. Draw up that contract, I am yours."

I turn with a smirk on my face and a sense of excitement in my stomach and head off. "You won't regret it, Paul," I call over my shoulder, my heart racing with the thrill of the unexpected decision. Thinking, I had not planned to say anything, but in a moment of clarity there, I knew if I did not take the job, I would regret it. Whatever happens, I am tired of playing safe and being unhappy. My days in London showed me an excellent group of people to work with and a sense of escape. There is a huge challenge ahead and working as part of a good team. Not to mention being given a chance to be close to the top of the food chain there. The icing on the cake is Paul, of course.

I laugh to myself. I bet he got some shock, getting an answer in the same way that he popped the question. I see the glances from passers-by as I laugh to myself and grin like a Cheshire cat.

The train arrives and departs around me as everyone's lives move on. I think and wonder how many other lives are changing on this platform and does anyone ever know what is happening?

Chapter 5

Arriving home after a long day, I walk in with a weary, yet tired smile. "Hey guys, how was your week? Anything new from school?" Mark looks at me as if I have two heads, a hint of surprise in his eyes. The kids all turn their heads as if to say, 'What's up with mom?' The question on their faces shows me the weight that was on my shoulders and how it was for all to see. I drop my bag and head to the kitchen, feeling the weight of the day lift slightly. I couldn't face my kids, not yet outside of hello.

Mark follows me in. "Are you ok?"

"Yes, I am, for a change. I took the new job. It feels like a load off finally." I turned and left the room and went upstairs to change, feeling a mix of relief and apprehension. I hear Mark follow me up, his footsteps echoing my own and telling me the conversation is not over and the next part is he is not going to support me.

"Seriously, don't you think we should have spoken about this properly?" I can hear the annoyance in his voice and see the frustration on his face, I just snap back, "Mark, I asked and asked. I asked you what you wanted me to do. I could not get an answer and all you seemed worried about was the money. Paul is offering me more than what I am on, so that solved that. After 2 days with nice happy staff in London, a new challenge, and a way out of the job I am no longer happy in, I said I would go for it. If you really want to know what I am thinking, I wonder why you were not more concerned about me being unhappy at work and only caring about the money. It is not like we would go short on one wage for a while, we would have managed." My frustration has never been this obvious. But he continues on his own agenda.

"Why didn't you call and tell me when you decided?" Mark remains concerned about himself.

"I wasn't sure until I got back this evening, and I told Paul then at the station, I would take the job and could he send me the contract. He was surprised." I just continued to change my clothes as the conversation went on, stripping down, I realise I was still wearing some nice lingerie, nicer than usual. But it goes unnoticed, as usual.

Having changed into jeans and a comfortable top and back in mommy mode, I headed back to the children. I have no real interest in talking about this, my mind is made up. I need to sort my own head on this and see how I will tell Jack. I go back down to the children and play mom, immersing myself in their world to find some normality. Mark, I can see is annoyed and probably does not know how to manage me. He is not used to the pushback he is getting from me. He wants his opinion heard and obeyed. I have no more interest in it.

After dinner I sit down, taking a moment for myself with a glass of wine, and check my phone. A text and a Snapchat from Paul. Why both, I wonder. I opened the text, "Maria, thank you for your answer this evening. I will email the contract to you this evening or in the morning." Very formal, I think.

Paul: mmmm hey baby, kept me waiting and then landed it on me. I am so happy on many levels. You are the woman to help me bring these shops forward and also means more time for us. There will be an executive summary of the contract, show that to Mark if you want, so he sees the package and travel and other expectations. Might give you some idea of what I have in store. I had the contract ready, in case you agreed.

What has he in mind, my mind races from work to everything else. Typical, thinking ahead. I know the contract is all work, but my mind runs to any expectations and ideas he may have,

Maria: Was I that much of a sure thing? The paperwork was ready. What have you in store for me? Can't wait to hear your plans. I gather from Helen that you have more plans than I have been made aware of. Than any of us are aware of.

Paul: Lol maybe a few diary dates for you when you get the contracts. Very transparent for Mark.

Maria: Can't wait. Send it to me.

Paul: …. for landing the surprise on me, I will make you wait until tomorrow.

Maria: Spoilsport. Good, now that I have told you I am so excited.

Maria: Horny as hell for you now, as well as the idea of the future.

Maria: The decision had me tormented until I made it.

Heading to bed, I feel my heart pumping in my chest. There's a mix of excitement and fear about what lies ahead. Almost scared about the reaction in the office, but who cares? My mind is made up and I am with my decision.

Mark turns to me, clearly his mood has not improved, "Well, are we going to talk about this now?"

"Ok, Mark. What do you want to say?"

"Are you sure? What about the kids? Will DAF let you go without trying to stop you?"

"Mark, yes, I am sure and since I made the decision earlier, never so sure. The kids, I won't be away that much, not much more than I am. You wanted me to take the other job. Almost sounded like you preferred me away for a night or two in the week. Ursula seems to be coping fine, after all, you seem to be missing most Thursday evenings also. I gather she spends the odd Thursday night here, so she is here in the morning. So that covers that. You could always pitch in. They are your kids too. As for DAF, they had their chance to keep me. They keep passing me over and punish me for other's mistakes. I will get the contract in the next day or two. If it is not what was promised, we can look. I will give you the contract if you want. See what is involved. Now I am going to sleep, thank you for all the support."

I can hear him taking a breath as if to react, I head him off at the pass, "If you want to do more than talk in bed, great otherwise go to sleep." As I turn my back to him. I wait for a hand to touch me anywhere. It doesn't, not that I expected it, not that I really wanted him to.

The following morning, I woke up, feeling refreshed after I eventually got to sleep. The best sleep I have had in I don't know how long. The wake-up was unexpected – it was Mark, offering a peace offering of coffee and breakfast.

"I am sorry Maria; I did not know you were that unhappy. Look, whatever you want, we will make it work. Just such a big move. I will talk to Ursula and hopefully, she will fill in. She has up to now. His voice is tinged with a mix of concern and nerves. Are you telling the kids today about the new job.?"

"No, I want to see the contract and sign it before I give my notice and make sure the package is all that was promised. I am sure it is, but I don't want to move too fast and regret it later. A few days will not kill anyone." His response catches me off guard, and I ponder his sudden change of attitude. I certainly did not expect that. Is he on board? As he stands there, the kids' storm in and save me from the rest of this conversation.

I spent the day with the kids, enjoying their energy and the simple pleasure of living their lives. Heading to town shopping. The part of my life that won't change, can't change, being mum, I tell them, "Come on, I am taking everyone to lunch today." Their faces light up with excitement at the unexpected treat. The food court, a cure for all childhood ailments. Fast food and fizzy drinks. A fun day out was had, the children talking at knots an hour, and at times I felt like I needed a universal translator to understand them. *God, do I not know my kids?* Mommy's guilt settles in.

I checked my phone and saw the contract was in. Paul obviously drafted it himself. I feel a buzz of excitement at the thought of reading it, and for a moment I forget I am outside with kids. I can't wait to get home. My turn to be excited. I have not been so relaxed in a while. The kids are all asking why I am in such a good mood. I can see the change must be obvious, and I wonder how bad I was that they were enjoying the change so much. Wondering why they notice, "I just am." Not sure if it means I am in a great mood. Or have been off lately?

We get home at about four and I quickly head into the study and print the contract. Watching it come page by page it is like a script for my future I can't wait to read. I head to the executive summary first:

Contract Executive Summary

1. Job Description - Chief Financial Officer.
2. Place of work location – Manchester, England. With travel required to London and shop location and trade shows where required.
3. Contract Type – Permanent.
4. Salary - £85,000 plus bonus.
5. Holiday entitlements – 30 days per year.
6. Expenses – paid to cover travel, hotels, accommodation, standard mileage, and subsistence.
7. Company car to be discussed.
8. Clothing allowance to be discussed.
9. General Job Description – Chief financial officer for group and associated companies to include any foreign based retail outlets or internet based companies.

I print a second copy of the executive summary and give it to Mark who walks in behind me, curious as to the content of the pages. Taking a breath reeling off the headlines, like an excited child, "Well Mark, here is the package and offer. All that was promised. Even extra holidays, not that I ever take what I am due anyway. The heavy workload for the first year, I suspect when trying to set everything up. But exciting, like a start-up. Look at it and see what you think. I see there is a trade show in Holland he wants me to go to in November, most of those are weekends I think, and the set-up of the Holland shop. At least a short flight if I need to do day trips."

Mark reads it and his expression is hard to read as he digests the information. I watch his reaction, his eyes moving over and back the page and raising an eyebrow, at what I am unsure. I am happy with what I have read. But I would be happy with almost whatever it said. "What are the bonuses?" he asks.

"I don't know, but I am already 10% up not 5%. So, any bonus is a bonus and I suspect he will be fair from what I have seen. He said all performances were related to the group. What property is there?"

"Well, he owns all the shops, and warehouses and some of the shops have either offices or apartments overhead. London has a few ground-floor units also. They tend to run themselves to the greater part. Really rent. Paul will be involved also. So, I suspect we are overlapping a lot."

"Maria, are you sure? Looks like way more work."

"I have never been surer. Now I am heading for a walk, I have had the kids all day." I can see the change in his mood again, back to questioning my decision. I don't need this.

I need some time to myself, to think and breathe in the fresh air. Clear my head. It is a nice evening as I grab a jacket and head out. Ringing Paul. "Hey baby, can you talk?"

"Sure, have you got the contract?"

"Yes, I have read the summary, I trust you on the rest. Sounds like an amount of travel, will I be away much? Anyway, I have signed it and will drop to you tomorrow."

"What about Mark?"

"Honestly, he was very off when I told him first. Then he did a 180 and seemed to agree with the idea. I am not sure what happened. Now turning back again, I think. Maybe my strop made him think, he did not have much of a choice."

"Good, on the travel, don't worry, you won't be alone. November is Wasteland, said I would call it a trade show. Booked to go early and if we can, just enjoy Amsterdam or go to Wasteland, worry about that when the weekend comes. The other weekends, really, just an excuse for you and me to get away. Maybe sunshine for Sunny sports gear trade shows etc. I have told Helen and Nicola to continue buying as is and make a list of trade shows well ahead, and make sure the usual buyer goes there. We may attend the early ones, to learn about the market. Ralph never really did any buying; trade shows were an excuse for a dirty weekend away." He laughs. His laughter is infectious, and I find myself smiling as I walk. "Better follow in his steps and keep up the tradition. Anyway, we can deal with that in the coming weeks and see what is needed. Don't worry, I will work you hard, your expertise is vital to making this a success. We will also have fun times and relax."

"Thank you, so now how to approach work? When do you want me to start?."

"Honestly, we are driving on, so the sooner the better. I would like to have as much admin and set up ready, and centralisation sorted to start the new year fresh and organized for the year ahead. So as soon as possible. But I know you have notice to give and need a plan. Let me know."

"Now tell me about your weekend. Memory serves madame was a little horny last night."

I laugh. "Was I what, really like a weight lifted and a major shot of adrenaline? Not like you did anything to release my frustrations, the idea of time and the future is so exciting. Ok babe I need to head here. I will call you tomorrow. I need to plan for work. When to tell them etc." I end the call feeling a mix of anticipation and nervous excitement about the future. I headed home, relaxed, for the first time in a long, long time. Or perhaps, the first time since I met Paul.

Chapter 6

Monday morning arrives, and I head into work as normal. Joan comes in with a coffee in hand, ready to plan for the week. She looks at me with a smile, "Any news from the weekend or London?"

Guarded as I have become, almost paranoid, looking for double meaning everywhere I respond, "No, this is my last week there. Then finished. Not much left to do, really."

But Joan persists, and I can't help but feel suspicious. "So, anything interesting on the horizon now that it's finished?"

What's she getting at? Am I just being paranoid? I move the conversation onto the tasks at hand and just ignore the question.

Later at 10 AM, the Monday meeting starts. I enter the conference room almost last, hoping to avoid any interaction with Jack. When it's my turn to speak, I tell the team that this week marks the end of my involvement with Michael's estate. I explain that it's just a matter of tying up a few loose ends and handing over anything I have been doing in London this week.

I confirm that all billing has been submitted, including this week's work, to ensure that the invoice can be issued now.

The usual workload is distributed, but then Jack drops a bombshell. "Oh, and by the way, there's a new acquisition coming up for one of our prominent clients in about a month. They specifically asked you, Maria, to handle it. I told them you were available, but I need to make sure you can manage the workload to allow for that coming down the track."

I respond casually, "Fine." But inside, I feel a blush of discomfort wash over me. I won't be here in a month.

I spend the next few days working diligently as usual, but I don't talk to anyone about my thoughts or decisions. Each day, as I leave the office, I make sure to take a few of my personal belongings in my handbag. I hope that Joan doesn't notice the office desk missing items, and the picture disappears from the shelf; she's the only one in the office who I'm afraid may notice the gradual disappearance of my things. I ensure that some things always stay in the office, and it doesn't look strangely sparse. Deep down, I want to be carefree about it, I am leaving anyway.

I made a firm decision to wait until after London to tell anyone about my resignation. I decided to inform Jack after next Monday's meeting. God knows how many times I have rehearsed the conversation with him. He will be disappointed, dejected, and maybe even bitter about it. *Will he be able to convince me to stay a little longer? No, no, no, I am gone. I have spent and wasted time and years here. I resume my firm stance. I can't back off now, I've promised Paul.*

I talk to Paul most days, at least once. I confide in him about my plan to give notice next Monday, which means I'll start a month later if they don't waive my notice period. Likely, they'll be too upset to do so.

We talked about telling Helen and Nicola. Paul asks, "When's the right time to tell them?"

"Let's wait until I give notice at work. I don't want it to get out there before then. But I do want to tell Nicole. I need to tell someone," I respond.

"Ok, that makes sense. There's not much work this week, so why don't you work on Thursday and see if Nicole is free on Friday for shopping or lunch, or whatever you two like? You can use your new credit card from the business to shop for the apartment if there's anything else we need."

I chuckled. "Might be dangerous. I didn't see a clothing allowance in my package."

"Well, I was tempted to put in a lingerie allowance but thought it might raise questions. Just shop till you drop, babe! The credit card bill will come to your desk at work, so no one else will see anything, just you."

As I hung up the phone, I decided to call Nicole and tell her that I'm free on Friday and ask if she'd like to meet up for lunch or some shopping. She's working in the morning, so I offered to meet her there at a convenient time. We agreed to meet up for lunch. She likes Mexican food, so I booked a table at one of the Mexican restaurants that I know of, and I braved through my spicy food. Nicole promised me a dessert, sympathizing with my red face due to spice. Once the food and dessert were done, we headed for shopping. I bought a few decorations for the apartment, and a couple of jumpsuits and sneaked into a lingerie store to buy something interesting. We wrapped up our shopping trip and I returned to my kids waiting eagerly for me.

Mark seems quieter this week and checks in on me to see if I've had a change of heart. He tells me that he has spoken to Ursula and she's happy to cover for me while I'm away. She's willing to do overnight stays as well if needed, and she could use the extra money.

I can't help but wonder how cozy they sound, but I say nothing. There is tension in the air between us. Almost like what I have done is driving a wedge even further between us. Mark almost sounds like he has checked out and is going through the motions. And I simply distance myself, like Mark and I are together only because of kids. We live like two strangers under one roof – only concerned if the other person is alive and well – there is no love, no intimacy, and no tenderness.

My married life is in shambles,' it has been this way for years, then I met Paul. These shambles don't bother me too much now.

Heading down Thursday morning, I assume my usual seat, savoring the familiarity of the routine. Paul arrives soon after, the ritual of acknowledging 24A and storing bags for the journey and we order breakfast with a side of coffee. The sound of the train moving off and of the departing station and the stale air of the carriage almost provide the comfort of 2 days ahead.

Today is so relaxed and peaceful, it doesn't feel like work. Instead, it feels like a much-needed break from the hustle and bustle of everyday life.

Paul drops his hand onto my thigh, gently rubbing it as we talk, like a habit - unintentionally, consciously, gently touching me. I missed his touch as I felt his fingers through the soft material of my black suit pants and after a few moments of conversation, I could feel myself craving his touch more and more.

I know if someone looked closely, they may have seen what we were doing. But I don't care today; I'm so content at this moment.

Suddenly, 24A passes by, heading for the restroom. He looks down at us and stares for a second. We both look up, and Paul just shrugs at him. He moves on, and Paul says. "Well, my lucky seat."

We arrive in the vibrant city of London and seamlessly slip into our usual routine. Nicola, always warm and welcoming, greets us at the door. A customary gesture, she calls me over, making it almost a ritual now.

As we exchange pleasantries, Paul, the ever-busy figure, continues on his way. It's during this moment that Nicola, with a gleam in her eye, presents an unexpected proposal.

"We were thinking, I know this is your last week here. The girls and I are wondering, would you join us tonight for a farewell celebration? A delightful dinner accompanied by a few drinks at a charming restaurant we've already booked. We've genuinely enjoyed having you here and simply want to bid you goodbye in a meaningful way."

Intrigued, I responded, "Okay, I say. Who is coming?"

She chuckles, "Pretty much everyone working here. Helen is practically going mad, regretting that she'll miss it, but she sends her best wishes. We decided not to invite Paul, being unsure of his availability. Since he's the new boss, we thought people might feel more at ease if he's not there. I'm certain he's arranging something special to acknowledge your last week."

With a mix of surprise and anticipation, I conclude, "I look forward to it. Just let me know where and what time."

I head to my office, the imposing desk and executive chairs dominating the room, the new smell still hits me, the pile of posts sitting on my desk and already open and organized by Nicola. I follow my routine, checking the incoming and any notes left with them when Paul arrives.

"What was that about?" He inquires.

"They have arranged a going-away dinner and drinks for me. Really nice of them." I laugh. "The boss is not invited."

He sighs, "And so it begins. Being treated differently. But so be it. Looks like a McDonald's Happy Meal for me tonight." He laughs. "You go and enjoy; it will be good and a good sign. They like you, obviously."

We work away for the day, and dinner has been booked at a local bistro for 7:00. I get back to the apartment with Paul at 5:30.

I wink, "Heading for a shower and freshen up before heading out. You get your Happy Meal yet?" I laugh.

I pick out my dress for the night, lingerie, shoes—determined to dress to kill, even if Paul isn't accompanying me. Lovely lacy black lingerie; only the best for the occasion. Laying everything out on the bed. a nod of approval mixed with apprehension of one-upping everyone else, I undo my hair bun and rub my scalp.

Undressing, I step out of my clothes and head for the shower. Stepping into the steaming shower, I relish the feel of the water over me. I tend to lose myself under a hot shower and today is no different. The room is steaming up. Running my fingers through my hair, washing it, I am lost in the feeling and sound of the water. Relaxed and happy., the day being washed away for a fresh start after.

Woken from my daydream, I get a shock, feeling a hand on my waist. I jump. and turn a little to see Paul resting his chin on my shoulder. Even though I should have known it could only be Paul, I still get frightened. Then I feel him move in behind me—his hands and then his naked body and arousal against me. Oh, this feels nice. Tilting my head so my cheek rests against his skin.

Turning to face him, my hands move from my hair to around his neck. Kissing him hard and deeply, looking up at him.

"Mmmm, this is nice," he whispers. Kissing me as he presses me back to the wall, I just hold on harder. I love his touch in the shower, naked, aroused, and just a desire to be touched. His touch. The water comes straight down on us, we just kiss, our hands exploring each other.

Feeling him so hard, pressed against me, he pushes me up and guides himself into me. As he pushes up and deep inside me, I hold on, and he whispers, "I love you, baby." His hand finds my ass, lifting me up, I feel him going in and out as he starts slow and works up. Water everywhere has us stuck to each other. The pace and desire mounts and I can feel the buildup and his ultimate release and that every familiar way. his fingers dug deep into my skin, holding me tight savoring the moment.

We enjoy this shower for the next few minutes.

"Now where were you?" smiling as he takes some shampoo and starts to wash my hair. I didn't have the heart to tell him that was done, and I loved the idea of him washing and caring for me.

We take a few more minutes in the shower, washing ourselves and each other off. Finishing, we both dry off and wrap in fresh towels and head out to the bedroom.

Looking at Paul, "That was a nice surprise… "

"You have no idea how often I think back to that first shower in Fort William. I always love the feel of a shower and now imagining you in it, such fun."

"Paul, you do this to me, and now I have to go out, all hot and bothered."

I stand back and decide to have some fun. As he watches and listens to me, I very slowly put on my panties and roll on my hold-up stockings, making sure my fingers trail up as Paul watches. Then the bra—I see Paul hardening through his towel in front of me.

"Now who is teasing?" he jokes, glancing at his aroused manhood.

I just laugh aloud, "You deserve it."

I finish dressing and get ready to go out. I put on the dress and shoes that I bought on the first Saturday in London.

"Maria, I love that dress and shoes, and here was me thinking you would save them for me."

"I feel a bit guilty about this; I know I am not leaving, and they are giving me a going-away night."

"Don't worry about it. We'll think about it later. For now, go, enjoy, it will be a good night and have fun. This is a chance for you to connect socially with them and enjoy the experience. This will stand to you later when you are working with them."

I head off out, feeling the early evening bite in the air, and the sound of the city around me and head down to the bistro. It is a lovely spot, the hustle and bustle of a busy restaurant, and the sound of cutlery on the plates. I see some familiar faces heading to the back area. They have a room booked in the back. Weaving through the tight tables I pass into the rear area and hear everyone in a great mood. I suspect some have had a few drinks and been out for a while. Nicola meets me and welcomes me, asking what Paul is up to and if he minds not being invited.

"He is fine; I think he's meeting a friend for a drink. Don't worry; he said he understands. The boss could cramp your style on a night out." I wink at Nicola, and she winks back - that lazy wink is a surefire sign that she too has had a couple of drinks.

About halfway through dinner, the waiter arrives in with several bottles of wine. When we say thank you but explain it's the wrong party, he says, "A guy named Paul called in. He ordered this wine and paid for it. Said to bring it back. He said to tell Nicola to tell everyone, an hour late tomorrow is fine." He leaves, and Nicola's phone pings. It's from Paul. "Enjoy the night out, have a drink on me, and tell everyone to come in for

10, not 9 tomorrow." She reads it to everyone, and there is a cheer. I give him this; he knows his staff relations. They are singing his praises.

Nicola turns to me as she sits, "I feel guilty now, I did not invite him." Smiling back "Don't worry; he understands, I am sure, and if he was put out, you would not be drinking his wine."

I really enjoyed the night. Everyone was chatty, way more so than usual. Maybe they do not mind, assuming I am gone. They all came across as a happy bunch and content with the new management. So far, anyway. The laughing and joking got louder as the drinks were flowing and the volume went up. I saw a side of many that I had not seen before. I now see how guarded they were around me or at work. As the restaurant encourages us to leave, because of the time and the noise, I headed back to Paul.

I get back to the apartment around midnight. Paul is already in bed, having turned in early. I am a bit drunk, making a bit more noise than intended as I stumble through the door. Climbing into bed next to him, I wrap myself around him. Falling asleep quickly, the alcohol-induced drowsiness takes over. Too much wine can go either way. Make me horny as hell or knock me out. Tonight, the latter prevailed.

Waking up around 9am, oh god the headache is like the sound of roadworks in the head, a jackhammer followed by a siren. How much did I drink? Looking around, Paul is already gone to work, leaving a cup of hot coffee next to my bed. His side is a crumpled mess, and the tea is still hot, indicating he is not long gone.

Head pounding a struggle for paracetamol and then a hot shower, and finally forcing myself to work for 10am. I inform everyone I'll be there until 12:00, expressing gratitude for the previous night's festivities. There is a distinct lack of energy today, with many sporting sore heads, a testament to the lively celebration. Throughout the day, no one spoke too much or bothered anyone too much, we had a mutual understanding of hangovers. 12:00 ticks in and I gulped my last cup of coffee before leaving.

At 12:00, I head off to meet Nicole. Arriving at 12:45 at the medical practice she works in, I wait in the reception area. She emerges, wearing sensible shoes, dark pants, and a white blouse, holding a Biro and file. She looks every bit the professional. If only her patients knew, that this unassuming woman, dressing like any other similar professional, has a very interesting dark side, a fun side.

She gives me a smile "5 minutes." I watch her interact with her receptionist before disappearing back into the office, reappearing shortly after in a coat with a handbag over her shoulder. She gives me a nod, and off we go. Heading down the road, we decided to grab lunch at a local pub. "This place makes a good lunch. Might be a good place to start," she suggests. The pub is filling, there is hustle and bustle around the bar and dining areas that contrast with the quiet suburban streets outside. The staff obviously knew Nicole, I saw one gesture on seeing her and leading her down to a table marked reserved. It has a small pub feel, timber tables, and padded stools and chairs. Sitting down, I order a diet Coke before the waiter leaves us to the menus.

Looking at me I see a half-concerned look on Nicole's face, "You, okay? You seem a bit worse for wear today."

Smiling, "Tired. It was a late-night last night. It was my last night in the office, and the staff took me out for a meal and drinks and more drinks. A bit hungover, to be honest. You know how it goes."

She just laughs, "That does happen. It is a shame your work is done here. Was lovely seeing ye both, and we had a lot of fun with ye. Will you get down to London much? Must get ye both out for a night or two if ye can manage."

"That is why I wanted to see you, not sure why, maybe because you are the only one that knows about us. But Paul offered me a CFO job; he is centralizing operations in Manchester, a new online shop, a huge revamp of the company. It would keep me coming down here. I took the job; the staff here don't know, and neither do my employers. I am telling them on Monday, and a month's notice is needed. I Wanted or needed to tell someone. Paul and I really want to keep exploring. Ye really are the only friends we have that know us as a couple. Just felt like meeting you and sharing. Sorry, that just all came out as one."

"I am happy for ye; well, life will be interesting. Ye have not only a double life but a triple life. Anyway, love to keep exploring with ye. Do you mind if I ask, what will Paul do with Adam's shop? He is a bit concerned." That was a conversation direction change, but for the better, I think.

"Don't worry, nothing happening there, Paul is not going to wind up or close anything. If anything, if Adam had any ideas, I bet Paul would be open to them. Paul likes the shop. On a similar note, he booked me for a trade show in Holland in November, for the shops. Really it is the same weekend as Wasteland. Not sure if we will go, but going to Amsterdam anyway. Are ye going to it?"

Nicole just laughed. "Wasteland! Ye two don't hang around do ye. Running before walking. We toyed with it, who knows, I will say it to Adam."

We enjoy a leisurely lunch, engaging in the usual chat about life, work, and kids, allowing the conversation to flow naturally. Afterward, we decided to explore a few shops, taking a leisurely stroll. I really can't get my head around shopping; my head has calmed but still suffering from a lack of motivation. Eventually, it's time for me to head back to the city center and catch the train back to Manchester.

Paul meets me at the station, as we walk, I share all the details, including Adam's concerns. Paul listens attentively and decides to address it immediately.

While pushing through the Friday afternoon crowds at the station, Paul gets his phone and just hits a speed dial option.

"Hi Adam, have you a minute? Maria is here with me; she just had lunch with Nicole. I hear you are wondering what I am going to do with the shop. Don't worry, you know Ralph's direction about no changes. But that aside, why would I do anything to the shop? It looks like a great business, and you are doing an excellent job. If you think the shop would benefit from anything, let me know. Trust me, the shop is at no risk other than developing."

I watch as they exchange conversation until some small talk, and Paul hangs up. "That sorts that anyway."

Looking at him, I say, "Told Nicole that we will be in Amsterdam for Wasteland. I asked if they were going. I hope you don't mind."

"Not at all, to be honest. I hope they are; it would be a major event to go solo. Babysitters would be good and more fun. The company would be fun."

We enjoy a relaxed trip back to Manchester, talking about last night and the trip to Holland and Paul asks, "How are you feeling about the new job, leaving the old? It is not too late if you change your mind. Honestly, we will work it out."

Taking a moment. "Paul, after the last few weeks and months, I am ready to leave. You have made it possible. I am nervous to see what happens when I tell Jack next Monday, but otherwise, fresh start and a new beginning."

"Well, enjoy your weekend, and I look forward to a new beginning."

As I stir my coffee, memories of a relaxed weekend flood back. Mark was quiet, just asking if, I was sure. And here I am now, Monday afternoon, and the day unfolds. There's no going back now.

Chapter 7

Heading home, I can only feel relief, excitement, and drained. The journey out almost felt longer than usual, watching the houses and traffic and for the first time in years, I did not have work to do, deadlines to meet and a boss to deal with. The weight off me was immense as I walk in. Mark is there to meet me. "Well, are you gone?"

"Yes, it was a rough morning. Jack and Malcolm are raging. Everyone seemed stunned. They did not see it coming." After I told him it was like a swarm of angry wasps out for my blood.

"Did you tell anyone first? What about Joan, did you give her a heads-up? Ye have been together a long time."

"No, I told her after. It will be different without her. She worked well with me. She was colder than I was." Laughing, "I was afraid of her at times, me, and everyone else in the office. She certainly got the job done. But a fresh start and a different job and new beginnings with new people."

"All change. Well, I am sure you know what you are doing. Now, what would you like to do for the evening?"

"How about we just take the kids out? I want to celebrate a little." We call around and find a nice Italian and book dinner. The kids are all happy when we tell them. They do like to go out to eat, especially surprised for a Monday night.

Walking in we are shown to a table, I have dressed up a little, want to make this an occasion for me, after all, it is. Why shouldn't I feel good? I tell myself.

It turns out to be a lovely evening; I tell the children that I have a new job and will be starting in a month. We are celebrating now. It is an excellent job, and I will be away a bit, but no more than I am now. They are all happy, asking a little, and in many ways, it went over their heads. They lost interest soon after I told them.

"Have you always been working in this field? This seems so boring." My eldest one remarked and couldn't help but chuckle a little.

"Adults do boring jobs," I explain myself.

"When I grow up, I'll just ride unicorns and ponies." My youngest one has the most imaginative mind.

"Good for you, love."

I enjoy a bottle of wine and feel it going to my head. I am giddy, and I'm sure the kids put it down to the wine. Mark says nothing, though I can see judgment on his face. That and, he can't drink as he has to drive. I think he does not know what to do with me these days, probably thinks an early midlife crisis.

As bedtime for the children approaches, we ventured out. The evening air hits me with a rush of oxygen to mix with alcohol in my blood. We wandered our way home, and the children head off to bed. I go straight to crack open another bottle of wine. "Take it easy, Maria; we have work tomorrow." "You may... I am on garden leave and taking advantage. Anyway, I want to celebrate."

I know Mark must have shaken his head in disapproval and thought '*Whatever the heck is wrong with her.*' But I don't care, I really don't.

I finish half of the bottle before heading to bed. I passed tipsy some time back; now I know I am drunk. Heading into bed, I am giddy, and playful, and start teasing Mark as he gets into bed. Jumping on top of him, stretching him out on the bed, I take my clothes off, down to my lingerie, grab his tie, and start to tie his hands. As he is stretched bare-chested on the bed, I straddle him.

"You're so sexy, look at you." I mess up his hair and give him a long kiss on his lips.

"What are you doing? He wipes his lips from the back of his hand, my wine must have left a taste in his mouth. "You are drunk."

I laugh back, "Come on, let's have some fun." Mark stops me and rolls me off him, "You are drunk, I have no idea what has gotten into you. Go to sleep." He gets up and heads for a t-shirt and puts it on as if to hide from me.

I sulk a little as I want to play, but Mark does not want to do anything. I am playful, horny, and full of fun. He does not want to do anything with me, all I wanted was to be taken. How much I wanted to feel aroused and feel a little better about our relationship. Disappointed, I fall off to sleep or pass out. Not sure which, but here I am.

Morning comes around, and I wake up. The sun pierces through the open curtain and then my eyes, like lasers cutting into me. Mark calls me, "Get up, we need to move." My head is pumping, "Let me sleep, I have no reason to get up; you and Ursula can sort the children. Not like I have work today." Mark grunts and heads off, not too happy. Rolling over, pulling the quilt over my head to block out the sunshine and I head back to sleep.

10 AM comes around, and I wake again. Feeling rough, I struggle out of bed and head down for a coffee. After a long shower, I freshen up and feel a little normal. The light flashes on my phone, sitting on the bedside locker, and picking it up to check, I see a message on my phone.

Paul: Call me when you get this.

The morning feels heavy with the weight of change, and as I glance out the window, the uncertainty of the future looms. The weight of my decision comes back to me. Snapping back. That is an unusually direct message from him. So, I called.

"Hi Paul, what's up."

"Get your ass in here for a meeting with me at 11:30. I see Jack and Malcolm have a meeting with Leonard at 3 today. If this is about you, I want to make sure you instruct us first in relation to employment issues. This may get messy, so let's get ahead of them."

Paul's voice on the other end of the line is urgent, and there's an undeniable tension in the air as he instructs me to join him for a meeting at 11:30. The impending clash with Jack and Malcolm adds a layer of complexity to the situation. Paul's strategic mind is already at work, wanting to ensure they are well-prepared for any potential employment issues that may arise. The weight of uncertainty looms over the conversation. Paul is in work mode; his day job was a different personality to the usual. He is more relaxed in London. I like Paul in London.

I breathe a big sigh, and after hanging up, my phone rings again. I see it is Joan. Somehow, I am certain that she wants to report on a similar matter. So, I pick up, wanting another person's views on the matter.

"Hi Maria, you certainly gave everyone a shock here yesterday. Not least me. Anyway, Jack is like a lunatic, Malcolm is storming around like I don't know what. They are going through your files and panicking. The files are perfect, but they need to pick up the pieces. I heard from Jack's secretary that there is a large job next month for which you were specifically asked for by the clients. The clients have said they will go elsewhere if you can't do it. It is you they wanted. Jack is now worried about what other clients may walk. They are desperate to find out where you are going and for whom you are working. Everyone is asking me when you decided and where are you going."

Joan's voice at the other end holds a mix of surprise and concern. She reflects on the shock that has rippled through the office in the wake of my unexpected departure. The chaos within the office is palpable—Jack's frenzy, Malcolm's storming around. Joan shares insights into the aftermath, revealing a frantic search through my files, perhaps in a desperate attempt to salvage what's left. The clients' reliance on me for an upcoming project puts unnecessary pressure. The air is thick with uncertainty as colleagues scramble to understand my decisions. They must all think I am a lunatic to throw away such a position. Little did they know how exhausted I felt about my position.

Joan's words resonate with a sense of chaos and apprehension within the office walls. The implications of my departure ripple through the team. The weight of responsibility on my shoulders becomes clearer as I learn about the client's specific request for my involvement. The uncertainty about my future destination is a crucial point of discussion among colleagues, creating an air of suspense.

"What are you saying, Joan?"

My response carries a mix of confusion and concern, mirroring the tumultuous atmosphere that has unfolded since my departure. Joan's inability to provide concrete answers further intensifies the sense of mystery and speculation surrounding my sudden career move. The dialogues reveal the intricate web of relationships and expectations that now hang in the balance.

"What can I say, I heard the same time as everyone else, and I don't know where you are going. I don't think anyone believes me. Anyway, watch out, just so you know I expect they will either try and get you back or go after you."

Joan's words, tinged with uncertainty, convey the brewing storm within the office. The fear of repercussions is evident as Joan hints at potential attempts to reel me back into the fold or, more ominously, to pursue me aggressively. The air is thick with anticipation, and the shadow of the unknown looms large. I need to be in the right headspace. I can't take my frazzled mind in the office today.

I get sorted, put on my trouser suit, get my makeup and hair done, and head for town. I want myself to appear confident, I can't let my uncertainty, confusion, worry, or anything of the sort be reflected by my appearance. I arrive at Paul's office at 11:25. I am escorted to a small meeting room, and soon Paul joins me.

As I physically move towards the meeting with Paul, the atmosphere is charged with a sense of urgency. The time constraints add pressure, and the small meeting room becomes a stage for the unfolding drama.

Paul pours two coffees. "You look tired; retirement not suiting you?" "Oh Paul, I hit the wine last night big time, I don't even want to think about it."

The casual remark about retirement and my tired appearance creates a moment of levity, as both enjoy the joke, breaking the intensity of the situation. The mention of hitting the wine adds to it, in the midst of the unfolding professional drama.

"Anyway … I have opened a new file for you personally this morning, marked employment matter. I have already had a long attendance done on you leaving and going to a new job, etc., and what I know. Just so there is no dispute about your file being opened first if DAF is looking to hire us against you. We have never done much for DAF in the past, so safe enough to argue no conflict. I suspect I will come under pressure here about you leaving also. My suggestion is we take this head on; I will tell Leonard in passing at lunchtime that you have left DAF, and I am employing you as operations manager here in Manchester to centralize everything for me and set up online shops, etc. You wanted to leave, as you were unhappy, and so I offered you a job. I will say there is no secret, but I don't know if you have told DAF where you are going."

Paul's words in the meeting room unveil a strategic plan, shedding light on the meticulous steps taken to anticipate potential challenges. The opening of a new file marked "employment matter" underscores the gravity of the situation. Paul's proposed narrative, positioning me as an operations manager in Manchester, becomes a pivotal element in shaping the unfolding narrative. The complexity of navigating relationships and potential conflicts is palpable in every word.

"Paul, you think that is wise?"

My inquiry into the wisdom of Paul's plan adds a layer of skepticism to the conversation. The tension in the air is thick as they grapple with the potential consequences of their chosen course of action. All that can be done is to ponder the risks and rewards inherent in Paul's approach, creating a sense of anticipation for the repercussions that may follow.

"Well, I don't know what is to be gained by not saying it. At best they may go away, and at worst, we find out if they are coming after you to stop you working. Let's see how it all plays out. For now, let's call you operations manager, keep anything financial out of your title."

Paul's response is a calculated stance on the unfolding drama. The air is charged with uncertainty, and the decision to refer to me as operations manager while excluding financial implications reveals the intricate dance of strategy and diplomacy. All that can be done is see how the plan unfolds and whether it will be carnage or will actually work favourably.

"Paul, I am feeling rough; I don't know how much I am up to today."

Feeling rough only shows my vulnerability in the soap opera that is now my career in the balance, contrasting with the professional life I am constructing. The intersection of personal and professional challenges is palpable, adding a layer of complexity.' The juxtaposition of physical discomfort with the impending professional showdown heightens the emotional stakes.

Paul laughs aloud, "Just as well you are not on my books yet; what would your employer say.'

Paul's laughter serves as a momentary release of tension, offering a brief reprieve from the gravity of the situation. The banter shows the relationship behind the situation.

I blush, "Feck off, no sympathy from you. I will go home and sleep it off. Let me know what happens.'"

At 12:00 we head off, and as we do, we meet Leonard in the hallway. He stares us both down.

"I'll take my leave," I try being as formal as I can in front of Leonard. As I leave, I see Paul follow Leonard to his office.

Paul calls me at one, "Just to let you know, I told Leonard, and he is not too happy with me. Said I poached you. I assured him I did not. You made it clear you were leaving and looking for a new job before I offered anything."

"From what you have told me, they just kept passing you over and treating you badly when you complained."

He did not mention the appointment with Jack later and I did not let him know that I knew.

"Let's see how the day goes."

I sit down and close my eyes at home for an hour, drinking mid-week is not a great idea.

The rest of the day passes uneventfully. I sit and think, do I want the uneventful, the certainty of routine, the predictability or a new happening in my life, and the adrenaline of uncertainty? I wondered if I truly wanted my life to be this mundane as it was. Nothing goes wrong and just the usual disappointments of life. Every day comes with predictability and certainty. Children arrive from school. I pull myself together and start making dinner. And that's how uneventful my life has been recently, until now.

One text from Paul at 4:30

Paul: Jack and Malcolm left a while ago. I have heard nothing. Assume now they know where you are working. I suspect Leonard may have said, even if now he can't act for them.

I have put an ad in tomorrow's papers seeking an in-house accountant and support staff for a start-up business for RM holdings.

If you know anyone, I suggest they look at it. You might as well tell people where you are going.

Maria: Thanks Paul

I give Joan a quick call. "Hi Joan, how is Armageddon going?" I laugh.

"It is not funny, Maria. It has been hell here all day. I am being quizzed on your work and where everything is and 2 minutes ago Jack asked did, I know you were going to work for the sports company. Are you?"

I rolled my eyes before, "Yes Joan, I am, I was ringing to tell you now. They are setting up here in Manchester. A new online shop and centralising stock and controls for existing shops and expansion. I was offered an operations position, and I took it. They are advertising for support and admin staff tomorrow under RM holdings, just so you know."

"What are you saying?"

"Nothing Joan, I am just passing information, I can't go near the place or work for a month. I can't have anything to do with them until then."

"Maria, you are a dark horse, not telling me you were thinking of leaving let alone where you were going."

"Joan, I did not want to put you in an awkward position, ignorance is bliss. You know how unhappy I was, and you are welcome to make that clear."

"Well, I can't argue that. Let's meet for lunch."

We end the call and agree to meet at my favourite spot for lunch later in the week.

The rest of the day and evening pass off. Heading to bed. Mark jokes, "How is the head, do I need to lock up my ties tonight."

At least his humour is light. I blush a little. "Hey, I tried at least."

"You are watching too much 50 shades, Maria, we are beyond that now, maybe in the good old days."

"You may be getting old, speak for yourself. I am still young." And we let it at that. I don't have the energy tonight even if he wanted to.

Am I young, still? Or maybe just overwhelmed? Or this lack of love, the love I feel with him makes me feel young? Am I not myself anymore? What has been?

My sleep is often prefixed with a long questionnaire where I lose myself in the labyrinth of self-exploration – and I only get lost there.

The following morning, I am surprisingly feeling more human, I get up with the children, shower, change, and face the world. Kids off to school and at 9:30 my phone rings. It is the office; I presume Joan again.

I answer and hear, "Maria, Jack. We want you to attend a meeting in the office at 2 PM today."

About to protest, "Yes Jack, what is the agenda? Do I need someone with me?"

"No, you are fine alone, it is to discuss your leaving."

"Ok," and I hang up. I text Paul.

Maria: Jack has called me into a meeting. I am going and will let you know what is happening.

Paul: Good luck.

I spend the morning preparing for 2 PM. I mentally rehearse every possible scenario in my head. I compose all the lines I need to say to them, no matter if they further harm my relations with the company. Well, my relations with that company really are finished, I am attending the meeting because I care enough to clarify, and they are still paying my wages.

2 PM comes, and I walk into the office. I walk with confidence and my head held high, even if I am a bag of nerves inside. The ice maiden returns. All I get are looks as I walk in, and silence.

I head straight to Jack's office. Knocking at the door, I am called in.

Jack asks me to sit and tells me Malcolm will be along shortly. He makes small talk and asks how I am, "You gave us all a shock, we never saw your leaving coming down the track. It has left us with problems."

I try and be polite, but confident in my tone. I can't show any weakness to him, any sign of questioning my decision. Holding eye contact, "Well, we all must do what is right for ourselves and I have not been happy for a long time, you know that. I am sure ye will be fine without me." It is all I can do, not to say they have Justin. I cannot sound bitter; I have to stay as professional as possible even though I want to remind them of all the mistreatments and unjust passing overs.

Malcolm walks in and sits down. He looks stone-faced at me. I can feel my resolve weakening, he could always intimidate me. "Maria, your leaving was a revelation to us all. Have you had a chance to think about this?"

"Of course, I have thought about this for a long time. But my treatment here in the last few months showed me how little I was thought of. So really, I should be of little loss to ye." I know I am a loss, but act as impassively as I can.

"Can I ask where you are going?"

"Yes, there is no secret, I am taking a different, non-accountancy role, Operations Manager with a chain of shops, primarily focused on setting up an online retail outlet and an EU base of operations, while setting up an office to centralise administration."

"Who with?"

"The new owner of the sports shops asked me if I would like the role. They had got to know me and see me overtime. I looked at the role and took advice on my contract and was advised that the restraint did not cover this.

"Maria, the restraint does cover this. They are clients here. So, we can stop you. We are losing their work because of this."

The tone of the conversation immediately turns adversarial.

"Sorry, they are not. The Michael estate were the clients, not the shops as such. Though we helped, there with some support. The client was the estate and its executor. Ask Jack, that was clarified way back. We never did their accounts, and they have seven auditors and accounts offices one for each shop. So, we never had them to lose."

Malcolm looks directly at Jack, the look being a question, before returning his attention to me.

"Maria, what will it take to get you back?"

"Nothing, it took a lot for me to make the decision. If a partnership was offered yesterday maybe I would have wavered, but the reality is, that a new challenge sounds good. I have been offered a good package and they know I can't do anything for a month, and they are happy to wait. From what I see, the restriction is working for a competitor, in an accountancy practice, or for a client. I am not doing any of the above. This is a new venture linked to the shops. I am not an accountant there. They are hiring in-house accountants; I understand to centralise accountancy for all the businesses. Rather than using external accountants. Much cheaper to have central accounts and employ full-time staff than pay so many offices and no co-ordination."

"Maria, we would argue the shops were clients. If I said I was going to file an injunction, what would you do?"

I take a moment and compose my answer. This was a threat I should have anticipated and didn't before coming.

"Simple, I will fight it and if it cost me my job, I would claim for the loss of earnings and into the future. But in the end, I will still be gone and could not come back. There is no version of this where I could return."

"You know we are losing some large client work because you are not available."

I start to get annoyed being blamed for that. "Well, good to see my clients at least saw my worth."

The grimace on Malcolm's face. "We know your value. Always did and .." I interrupt. "Look, Malcolm. I knew my worth also. I billed more than anyone and gave my all. Yet he kept passing me over. So maybe you knew. But never showed where it mattered. If you stop me from working, and I lose this job, what do you think I will do. ….. I will sit out the year and in 12 months take a job with a competitor and target my old clients here. That would do damage to you as I would have an axe to grind with ye. Or if I am left go to this job, you won't find me targeting any clients, and I am not competing, all going well at any time. So honestly. You are in a loss, loss really. If you stop me, I will chase clients through a competitor in 12 months' time, if you sue and lose, you are paying me damages. I will suffer loss of earnings for a year, or my new employers may employ me in the London office. They said if ye try and sue they will cover the costs as they are happy, that they will win. They took advice on it."

I pause, no one speaks and before silence settles, I resume.

"Look if nothing else, it is best I will go. Let me know what ye are doing. If ye want to take the higher ground, ye could release me from my contract now and cancel garden leave and stop paying me and let me start the new job. Who knows we may cross paths down the line?"

I get up and leave, not waiting for an answer. I walk out with a confident expression on my face. I am not even sure where I came up with some of that, but it did sound good. I stood up for myself, I value myself enough to not let anyone threaten or bully me. *You're a strong lady, Maria,* I tell myself. After exiting the office, I smile and wave farewell to everyone staring at me. Not all, but most returned the gesture.

I call Paul and fill him in. "Maria, remind me not to mess with you. Good for you. That will put them in an awkward position."

"If they fight me and stop me, what will we do?"

"Don't worry, you can work from London, we will give you a role there as you suggested. We can arrange hybrid work from home. I will deal with the claim against you. They have way more to lose if they think of it. The risk that you may end up with a competitor in 12 months and target them is a serious consideration. Working for me, you are not going to do any damage. Either way, we will work it out."

"Thank you."

I head home and wait for the phone to ring. That is almost all I am doing, waiting for the next call and what it will bring. Answering each with a sense of uncertainty.

The day passes and I hear nothing. My anxiety simply rises, and I want someone to hear me out and tell me everything will be okay. Mark arrives home.

I let him know all that happened, hoping to find the consolation I needed.

"What if they stop you working?"

"It is fine, Paul has said I can take a role via the London office if needs be and just work on the EU project, we will work it out. The only reason they would try and stop me now is spite. I told them there is no way back now."

The kids arrive in the kitchen, mid-sentence about their day, and leaving me fill in the gaps and guess the part I missed. The upside is it stops the conversation, thankfully. There was no consolation there, anyway.

The week passes off quietly. Nothing is heard.

I meet Joan for lunch on Friday. I have relaxed into my decision and now looking forward to the story of what is unfolding from the outside.

We have a nice lunch, and she tells me everything.

They are passing my work out to whoever has the capacity.

"Jack and Malcolm are meeting a lot, but I can't find out what is happening. I am being frozen out; I think they are afraid I am reporting to you. There are a few clients that may leave if you are not here, and Jack is going mad as they are large clients. He is scrambling to appease them".

"What about you Joan, how are you coping?"

"Tough going, I don't have a new boss yet. I feel the freeze out, and some are nearly even afraid to be seen talking to me. It will be hard to get used to someone new. We have been working together for a long time."

"How is Mark, how is he in all this? Is he ok with you moving jobs?"

"He is fine, he will cope."

"Good, you are lucky to have his support." I am not sure where this is going. I look at her and she changes the subject.

"What were you saying about those jobs, is there a position there?"

"This is a start-up; all positions are available. From accountants to office managers. The only job filled is the boss. Me." I laugh.

Little more is said, and we finish lunch and Joan heads back to work.

I sit back and relax; I'm imagining my usual Friday in London. A new city and new people. It has been a while since I met new people and worked with them. I somehow am certain that this change will be a good one in my life.

I have relaxed as the week goes on. Time heals everything, it really is true.

Sipping my coffee, I pick up my phone. *I am craving Paul.*

Maria: Hey baby, how is your day?

I have a problem. Another one.

10 minutes passes.

Paul: What happened now? Are you ok?

Maria: No

Paul: Why…. What can I do?

Maria: … Typical how can you fix it?

Paul: Well

Maria: I want you. I am feeling playful and need my Paul fix. Come on, book a room somewhere, let's have some fun. I need some.

Paul: LOL … you are playful. How about Monday? You, me, a morning in a hotel.

Maria: Look forward to it. I need some fun and games.

Paul: Maria, if you are at a loose end. Why don't you take your kids to London for a few days or next weekend? Use the top floor apartment. Take a break away and enjoy it. All go if ye want.

Maria: Thanks Paul, I might just do that.

Paul: I will tell Adam ye might be around and your family in toe, so remember our situation. He will be discreet, but easier if he is forewarned as the shop is so close.

Paul: Chat over the weekend.

I have not been so relaxed in so long. For the first time, my head seems clearer. Stress reduced and a sense of excitement for the future. Moving jobs seems to have taken a weight off me.

And maybe because I have Paul now.

I have Paul, do I really have him? My mundane days really make me question everything. Every question ring in the emptiness of my mind. What do I have if anything real, I wonder.

Chapter 8

Monday morning, I can't wait to see Paul.

He has a room booked in the Hilton in the company's name and told me to just check in using the company card. He will get there about 10.

What to wear? I have plenty of options, but I want to go a little extra today. Mark is gone to work. I made sure not to change before he left.

I want today to be fun, Sexy, playful, and have some plans in my head.

I go for the lingerie I bought last Saturday. Sexy lace stocking. Suspender belt. Bra and panties. A simple elegant black lace. I put them on slowly. Enjoying the feel of them against me.

I put on dressy black pants and a crisp white blouse that opens down enough to show a little cleavage and loose enough that if I lean over you can see into it. Black high heels with red soles. Just as I put them all on, I imagined how they might be coming off, soon. All of it, soon enough, won't be on me.

The excitement builds in me. Even more so than when we are away. A daytime hotel, now this feels daring, exciting almost dangerous.

I grab a briefcase and head off. I look every bit the professional heading to a meeting. If only they knew what was in my briefcase.

I head into town. Giddy to see Paul, though we have spoken daily, it has been nearly all work and weeks since we had some sexy time together. I wanted to play. I felt like sex on a stick, and he wasn't going to be safe unless I was satisfied.

But which way to play it? I still wasn't sure.

I arrived at the hotel at 9:15 and checked in. I order coffee and scones for 2 at 9:50. I take my key, thank the receptionist, and head up. I share a glance from the receptionist as she hands me a key. I wonder does she suspect what the room is for.

I text Paul.

Maria: Room 812. I hope you are well-rested from the weekend. You are in trouble today :)

Paul: Will be there at 10, boss. Whatever madam desires.

Maria: Thanks baby. In that case, just so you know. Be prepared to obey.

I put the phone down and take in the spacious room. It won't be silent here, soon. A plan formulates in my mind. The seduction, I think to myself. I open my briefcase. I take out a playful little vibrator I picked up in town. Simple really, let's see how he likes a little stimulation. I hide it under the pillows, must keep it a surprise.

I take out a blindfold and some oil. I place them on the nightstand.

Mm, this will be fun. I imagine myself, blindfolding him and taking him. Commanding him, to make up for the lack of recent attention. Satisfy me.

9:50 and the coffee arrives. I have the tray set down and signed for it.

10:00, a knock on the door. It's Paul. I can't wait to see him.

I let him in and offered the coffee I ordered. "Let's enjoy a cup and take a beat."

We sit for about 15 minutes, chatting and catching up with recent events, outside of the drama. Paul said he took a day's holiday, as he had loads to take, so no rush.

I turn to him.

"Take your shirt off." He pauses, questioning my sudden instruction. But then decides to obey.

He stands up. Takes his tie and then shirt off. I just sit and watch him. My legs crossed.

"Now stretch out back on the bed." He obeys. Sitting back on the bottom of the bed.

"I said stretch out." In a commanding tone, as I stand up and walk towards him. Feeling so tall on my heels.

I watch him stretch out on the bed and then I crawl up next to him and straddle his hips.

Mm, I can feel his arousal already.

I grab his two wrists, leaning over him, pinning them. I see him looking down at my blouse.

"You like what you see?" I smile down at him. I am enjoying the control here.

I release one wrist, grab the blindfold, and put it on him. He was not expecting that.

I sit up on him and he can feel me grind against his erection. He feels good. I can sense his throbbing erection.

I lean back down and see him inhale my perfume. His other senses heightening now that sight is gone.

I grab the vibrator and holding it next to him he hears it spring to life. I notice the look on his face. I have never used one on him. I smile as the look of anticipation on him.

I kiss his cheek. "Your ass is mine now." I laugh.

Oh, this control. I needed this. I have spent a week being pushed around and fighting back. Nice to have fun and take charge. Not waiting for what is coming next.

I stretch out next to him, "Hold your hands over your head, don't move them." I watch as I rub my hand over his pants. He begins to move his arms. "Stop moving, or maybe I make you suffer a little."

I watch his reaction as I touch him, he bites his lip as I squeeze him. He feels the vibrator against his skin, moving down to his waistline. I can sense his entire body tense up, his teeth going deeper into his lips, and his fist clenched tighter.

I open his belt and then pants and zipper, slow teasing him, torturing him.

Sliding my hand in, I wrap my hands around his manhood.

I missed him. As I slowly and gently massage him as I kiss him. My other hand runs the vibrator over him.

I move down off the bed. I start by pulling his shoes and socks off.

Then pull his pants down. Leaving his shorts on.

Leaning back in I kiss him over his shorts and then slowly pull them down and release him. Mm, he stands straight up.

I wrap my lips around him and slowly take him in. I hear him moan.

My eyes fixed on his facial expressions, as I watched him react, his head tilting back. Oh, I have been waiting to taste him. Aroused, I watch him get closer, fighting the desire to lower his hands at the same time.

I then release him and pull those shorts down and off.

I continue to rub the vibrator, now teasing his erection with it. Oh, I watch as he clinches his fists trying not to lower them. I know he did not expect this.

Kissing back up his body I take my time and enjoy his naked body. Massaging him, relaxing every muscle of his body. How ironic. I tense him up, and I massage him. That's the control I have been hoping for.

"You've been so good, baby," I whisper to him.

Thinking of what to do next. I decide to tease him more.

I am enjoying the power. He is obeying, even though he could move, he just obeys my order.

I lift his blindfold so he can see.

Standing back, I slowly open my blouse. One button at a time. Never breaking eye contact.

I watch him react.

I can see his erection twitch as I slide the blouse off. He looks me up and down. Seeing my lacy bra his eyes stop at my suspender belt.

I open the top of my pants. Slowly I slide the zip down while holding the pants.

I then let go and watched him watch it fall to the floor. I step out still in my heels.

I can see myself in the full-length mirror in the wardrobe. I see what Paul sees.

Is that really me? Wow, I look amazing, I think. *Like someone else*. Also seeing Paul stretched out. Like a picture of some erotic scene framed.

I walk around to the bottom of the bed so he can see all of me.

Watching the anticipation on his face, his body reacts. I know he is close to release. Depending on what I do next. Will I just tease him and make him suffer? I feel my inner smile.

I slide my panties down over my suspenders and off. I can feel how wet they are. I leave everything else on.

I then move onto the bed. Grabbing him in my hand, I move over him and slide myself down onto him. The playful glint in my eyes as I hold his gaze.

I take him all the way in. Then sitting astride, I begin to slowly ride him. My hips move slowly first as I sit upright. I watch Paul and see him turn his head.

I see the pleasure, his light moans synced with my movements, his head tilts back again, his knuckles grow whiter, and his breathing stays in the frenzy.

He is mine and his eyes just soak me in.

He realises if he looks in the mirror, he can see everything.

I begin to move faster and then lean down over him. My hands run up his arms, I move over him, and his face is buried in my chest.

I move faster and then hear him moan, his eyes close and face tightens, and he releases into me before relaxing. I don't stop, until I finish and then move to kiss him.

I kiss him hard, deep, and passionately.

He is sweating, panting as we kiss.

I can see he is spent. I lean in to kiss him. I stay on top of him, and he lets me be there.

"Oh, baby. I needed that. That was fun. "

Smiling back at me. "Who are you kidding? That was amazing. Sorry, I did not last long."

I head to the bathroom and when I come back Paul is under the sheet.

"Come to bed. Just curl up with me. I see a bottle of oil. Let's relax a while and then maybe I can give you a massage."

I take off all the lingerie and climb in naked, next to Paul.

I love to rest my head on his chest and curl into him. My leg up over his thigh.

This feels so nice. No pressure on time. His fingers gently caress my lower back. Just gliding over my skin.

I could fall asleep here now. The most peaceful sleep I will ever have.

After a long, relaxed time, just close, I am so blissed out.

Paul moves and slides out from under me. So, I roll onto my front. He says, "Relax."

My arms under my head as he straddles my ass. I hear the top of the bottle of oil. He pours the oil on my skin, and it twitches against the sensation.

He starts on my shoulders and massages in the lavender oil.

Slowly massaging down my arms, my back, and taking his time with every touch.

This is so relaxing. I watch him in the mirror. In between closing my eyes and savouring the moment, I feel my body giving in to his touch.

He massages every inch of my body from head to toe.

Then sliding a pillow under my hips. He leans in and slides slowly into me. Our two bodies rubbing smoothly against each other with the oil.

Paul slowly makes love to me. I am lost in time.

Before we know it Paul whispers. "Hate to say. It is lunchtime. Can you spare time for lunch?

Oh. "I have to be home at 3 for the kids."

"Come on. Let's have a quick shower and get some lunch in the bar."

We sort ourselves and head down. Briefcase in hand.

As we get off the lift in reception. Paul says.

"Hope nobody spots the blouse is inside out." I gasp and look around, panicked.

He laughs. "Just kidding. Come on."

The shock. I could have hit him.

"I will get you back for that one."

We enjoy lunch and Paul says, "You head off and I will sort the hotel."

Driving home, I still smell of lavender. What the hell? Call it a new perfume if asked.

I get in just before the kids return from the school. Ursula is collecting them. I washed my face, in case there was any makeup left, and a quick change of clothes as I put my jeans and jumper on.

I shed and hide the suspenders and stockings. But unwilling to let the day end I leave the bra and panties on. I want to feel them against me.

I check my phone.

Paul: Thanks for a gorgeous day. I can still smell you on me. Oil and all. So, did my son. He came into the kitchen and smirked. Love the new aftershave. Wherever you picked that one up.

He left grinning.

Maria: At least I can call it perfume. What did you say?

Paul: honestly, I think I went red and could not come up with a reply.

You have a good night there and talk tomorrow.

Tuesday, 9 AM:

The house is empty. Ursula is going shopping.

Sitting relaxing with a coffee my phone pings

Joan: Heads up, Jack and Malcolm are heading to the solicitors for a meeting. I hear you are The Agenda. Life here is unbearable since you left. I am frozen out and management are all blaming each other for you leaving. Jack is getting the brunt of it.

Paul: I have just been summoned to a meeting with Leonard, Jack, and Malcolm. Leonard spoke to me and said it is uncomfortable being stuck in the middle here and not being able to say I am the owner. In other words, who is to blame? He asked me to take ownership of this problem.

I will call you later.

Maria: Good luck. Sounds like you need it.

2 hours later the phone rings.

"Hey Maria. Well, I survived."

"So, tell me. What happened?"

"Jack opened by telling us you were leaving to go to work for the sports shop owners. They were furious and felt you were stolen away from them, and we had a part of it.

I decided to meet fire with fire. Pretty much what I said was, Jack, I had the pleasure of working with Maria for months and saw how she worked with the staff in London and the job she did. As I got to know her, she spent a huge amount of time complaining about being unappreciated at work. She was good at her job and when promotions came up, she was passed over again. She felt no woman ever made a partner and all she got were excuses and she wanted to move.

She booked holidays, the first this year, and the night before she went, she got emails looking for expense reports and other updates. Complaints when she got back that she did not submit paperwork while away and all senior people need to be contactable while away.

When she was asked to fix a problem created by the person promoted over her, she said she was too busy for the additional work, she was punished with low-level work to put her in her place. She told me she was leaving, and the last few months showed her, she had no way forward in DAF.

When she came back from holiday, she told me she was job hunting and looking at options but was limited by her contract.

I looked at her contract when she asked me to and gave her my opinion. She could not go to a competitor or an existing client or pretty much any accountancy practice within 100 miles for a year.

Jack and Malcolm were looking at each other and Leonard half in shock and half anger. They asked me why I advised you. I said why not. We are not your main legal practice as far as I know, and the executors just hired ye for the estate."

"For the love of God, Paul. You are taking the blame for advising me. "

"Oh, I was on a roll. I said I was working closely with the chain and advising them. I knew you were job hunting and maybe worth approaching. So, I approached you and offered you the job as operations manager to set up the new online shop and a hub. You would run operations.

You told me that DAF was not happy they did not get the accountancy contract. I said. Nobody did. The decision is to go in-house and centralise all account work, so, the only accountancy work will be external annual audit and some tax consultancy. Malcolm said I poached you. I told him no. I took the opportunity of a good person coming to the job market. That they drove you out and they know everything said by me was accurate.

Malcom responded. "We are retaining Leonard to injunct Maria. Sorry Malcolm, Maria already consulted us regarding her employment, so we are conflicted. We represent her and we represent the sports shops and their new owners.

1. We represent her new employers who have said they will underwrite the cost of any attempt to stop her working. The new job is not as an accountant, so I don't see how it breaches her contract.
2. Until the new offices are set up here and sales, admin and accountants, and employees she will be based in London so well outside the 100 miles. So even if she is found to be an accountant she is outside the radius. But please get advice and see if my advice is right. I am happy to let Leonard advise now when I leave. "What about the audit and tax work. Are we in the running for that Paul?"

"I stared back. Well, Maria will be running operations and day-to-day management. So, she will be left to select who she can work with or not. So, her support is what ye need there.

Honestly, I would not like to be on her wrong side. I do know 2 of your competitors have approached her and offered her a position when her restricted time is up.

So up to ye really. Stop her going in and risk her going to the competition with an axe to grind or let her go and she will never compete "

"I left them and said. Leonard and the company here had nothing to do with this. It was all the new owners who liked her style when London staff reported to them, and they saw her in action.

I know Leonard would find it easier if she was not employed with his clients. But outside of his control."

"One last question Paul. Why are we not being told who owns this company?"

"Because they don't want it out there and on need to know. Legal advisors, Maria, and whoever the tax advisors are the only ones who know. We are sworn to secrecy. Ye are left dealing with me and I am the point of contact with the shops."

"I left and let them to it."

"Paul. What will they do?"

"I don't know. But I am hoping Leonard will say get advice and I am probably right. I dangled the audit work, and they must be nice to you if they want to try for it. I was serious. Your call. You pick who you want in the end. Play them how you want."

"Ok. Hopefully this will end soon."

Paul says he must go and talk later.

I wonder what is coming next.

Nothing for me to do but wait.

Joan: Jack is back. I heard him and Malcolm argue. Looks like they are now blaming Jack for forcing you out.

Nothing much happens for the rest of the day. I don't wish for anything to happen for the rest of the day.

Joan calls me at 9:30 on Wednesday. "Maria. I have been asked to call you in for a meeting with Malcolm. Can you be here at 12?"

"Of course. How is the mood?"

"Not good."

Well, it would have been a surprise if the mood was good. I know how to deal with bad moods.

I arrive at the reception. I decide to wait and tell them I am there. After a few minutes, I am sent to a conference room.

As I walk into the conference room, I see Malcolm sitting there with one other manager.

He is polite and asks me to sit and offers me a coffee. I accept, wondering what is coming next.

"We met with Paul Bridges yesterday. I understand you have retained him in any employment issue."

"Yes. As I expected problems, I asked his advice, and my new employers offered his services."

"He told us how you felt working here, Unappreciated and short-changed and wanted out."

"Yes. I was leaving whatever happened and it came as a surprise to be offered the new job. I did not expect it. I was looking, though."

Malcolm: "If we moved you to another department here, would you be happier."

"Malcolm, honestly, after I gave notice and left there was a huge weight lifted and I know it was so right for me. Even partnership now would not change my mind."

Malcolm: "Ok. I expected that. If we were to leave you out of the contract now, what are our chances of the audit job with the companies."

"Honestly. We have a lot of setting up to do and effectively a start-up. If I have a choice, I will see who I and the new accounts department can work with. I will look at this office. But if it is Jack or Justin and those around them, I won't. I only have a few weeks to wait anyway, and I get to work."

Malcolm introduces Alan, who sits quietly next to him. He heads an audit team and hopes we can work together.

He handed me a letter, effectively telling me that my garden leave was at an end, and I am free to work for the sports shops. But my restrictions stand with respect to all other companies.

I thank Malcolm and I leave politely.

I leave and give Joan a smile as I pass.

Heading out I ring Paul.

"They caved. I can start work anytime you want me to."

"Great. Take a few days off. Relax. And how about you start on Monday?

Go out and buy a good laptop for yourself for work. Whatever you want, and we will get it set up with a new email address for you. Let's put you to work soon. Get my money's worth"

I call Mark and tell him the news.

I tell him that I want to go to London for the weekend. We should all go. I can use the company's apartment there that I usually stay in. Paul has told me to take it any time. A weekend away with him and the kids before I start the new job might be nice.

Mark surprisingly agrees very quickly. So, we plan. Take the kids out of school at lunchtime on Friday and get an early train down.

Get some shopping done and maybe do some sightseeing.

Paul said he will be in London on Thursdays and Fridays at the office so he will make sure that the apartment is empty of anything personal. This might be a nice weekend away.

I look at the ads that Paul has in for administration, accounts and marketing, and sales, thinking he is not wasting any time, I wonder who will reply.

Before the weekend I go laptop shopping. Well, he did say whatever I wanted. So, I got myself a new Microsoft Surface laptop. Lovely laptop. Long battery life and is very light and sleek.

We tell the children about the plans, and they are excited. Time off school and a weekend away. *This feels right. I needed some time with my kids. And I think, they also missed me, like I missed them.*

Even when they are around, even when I am at the house with them, I miss being there with them. Last few weeks, I have been preoccupied. I guess I have always been preoccupied.

We get to the train and take our seats to enjoy the views for our ride. Other than, a few exchanges, neither of us have a conversation. I guess we are all tired and need the quiet time. As soon as we reach our destination, I get a feeling. Oh, please let me not see Mr. 24a.

Thankfully no sign of him.

Chapter 9

We arrive in London and grab a cab to the apartment. Walking in, we look around, taking in the atmosphere.

"Maria, so, this is where it has all be happening when you are down here." I blush back a little and make a joke. "Oh yes, the account and the solicitor. Like a dictionary meeting an encyclopaedia." I change the subject. I sensed the subtle undertone in his voice. Not sure is it me being paranoid or what. I have been thinking, overthinking everything for a long time. Every facial expression, every possible double meaning in what is said.

The kids poke around, and I head up to the main bedroom. We open the wardrobe and drawers, and there is a change of clothes. Casual. "Oh, I forgot I left these old clothes here. Was always handy to have a change." The bed is fresh and clean with tidy bedding tightly tucked in all the corners. *'Always appreciate the neatly tucked-in bedding.'* The housekeeper here is very good.

The children find the spare room and sort themselves; the girls take the room and Liam says he is happy on the couch. Sometimes, I wonder if he will turn out to be a couch potato, he loves his couch. Sprawled out, all he is missing is a PlayStation remote control.

I tell Rebecca we will go to the Disney store tomorrow. For now, I tell them to drop their bags and head out. Watching the various personalities come through. From the couch potato that is Liam to the neat and organised girls. I watch and wait impatiently. Finally, they are ready to go. I walk with purpose and Mark remarks. "You seem to know your way around here." We walk around the corner and pass Adam's shop; Mark stops and glances in. "The other shop. Interesting."

I look back at him and then glance at the children. Liam spotted it, but the girls didn't. I can see Liam looking, while Mark is. "Mark" is saying with purpose, and he spots Laim watching him. As I walk on, I tell them, "Look up. That is where I work when I am in London."

"Mommy, can we see?" Rebecca squeaks.

"Maybe tomorrow if ye want to see when people aren't working." Honestly, it is more that I don't want to bump into anyone yet.

Paul told me he informed Nicola and Helen that I was joining the team full-time and would be between here and Manchester. He said that they were all surprised, but happy. I will face them next week and deal with that. Especially after they just gave me a going away party.

"Come on, Let's go to Leicester Square and ye can see M & M and Lego shops and we can get dinner. Wherever ye want." I finally shift their attention to their favourite things.

Rebecca runs out of steam, so Mark picks her up and gives her a piggyback ride to the square, up through Covent Garden and the shopping streets onto Leicester Square. Mark suggests the tube. "It is so far down and back up at the other end for a stop, it is not worth it. Anyway, let the kids enjoy window shopping and see where they want to go tomorrow. They can try the tube then when it is quieter." We walk on and look for somewhere for dinner. The city is bustling with activity and crowds everywhere. Sounds of horns as Friday afternoon traffic builds.

We enjoy an early dinner; the kids suggest the Italian, so we must agree to that. We are all hungry, it has been a busy day. We order, I just watch them enjoy the experience. It is a lovely evening. Mark is relaxed also and seems to be enjoying this and paying attention for a change. This feels like such a normal family on a weekend away. It is times like this that have me thinking about Paul and what am I doing.

'Am I a bad mother? Am I being deceitful to my kids? I shouldn't be hiding from my kids, they are kids, they should know their mother

completely. Or they too will have trust issues when they grow up. I should tell Paul ...'

"It's very delicious, Mom," Rebecca's squeal interrupts my thought. I shake it off and returned my attention back to the kids. "Anyone want dessert... ice cream?" I ask. Needless to say, they all look and go for Chocolate Fudge Sundaes. Markl just looks. "They will be sick; they had too much. "Oh, leave them enjoy the treat and they can leave them behind if they want."

I watch their eyes widen, as I sip my coffee, as the 3 tall Sundae glasses arrive, the cream overflowing on top. Poor Rebecca can hardly manage the glass, let alone the sundae. But she tries. I just smile. The others make it halfway before giving up.

After dinner, we wander around Leicester Square and the M & M and Lego stores for the kids. They have never been here by night and are amazed at the level of activity. As the night falls and the city lights up it looks even more mesmerizing to them. Before heading back to the apartment, we buy them their treats and take a taxi back, they are all tired.

Stepping out of the taxi the streets are so much quieter here. Far from the evening crowds. The children drag themselves up the stairs, complaining about the steps. They just go to bed and Liam settles down on the couch with the TV, soon falling asleep.

I head to bed with Mark, who seems very attentive, far more than I have seen in a long time. "Shame, the shop around the corner is closed, we might have picked up something for some fun."

"You alright, Mark? Anytime I have even tried to engage lately you have shown no interest and now toy shopping?"

"Well, I said I would try, you took me by surprise the other night trying to tie me up. I realised you were trying, so I should too. If that is what you want?"

What to say? "Well, something has got to give, our sex life is gone, and we aren't old yet. Anything to try and spice things up."

I have no idea where this has come from.

Mark is playful, so I engage. Who knows maybe we are turning a corner? Must be this apartment.

Mark continues to engage, and I can feel he is aroused for a change. He goes straight to undress me and himself and stretches me out on the bed. To see him like this, it has been so long. I can't remember the last time he acted like he wanted me, rather than just going through the motions. Feeling him against me he proceeds to make love to me. It's fun, feeling him aroused, passion like we used to, at least he is trying. For the first time in a long time.

The following morning, we wake. For a moment I am disorientated, I have ever only woken next to Paul here. Mark asks about breakfast, which soon brings me back to the moment. The children are already up and full of life asking about the day ahead. I ask them, even though I know the answer, "So breakfast. Will I get something and bring it back or would ye like to go out.?"

"Out! Out! Out!" I hear a chorus.

"Come on then, there are some nice restaurants in Covent Garden and then we will hit the shops."

We stroll up through the streets and everyone seems so happy. As we pass Adam's shop again, Mark whispers, "Might call in there later."

I have no idea what has got into him. How is he interested in me and why? I can't put a finger on the reason. What has changed, it can't be that I have suddenly become appealing to him. Or is there any motive behind this? With Mark, I am always rational, emotions rarely take the lead. In fact, never; emotions are never involved.

Enjoying a relaxed lazy breakfast, the calm Saturday morning atmosphere around us. We head to some of the Covent Garden stalls and shops. Wandering into the Apple store and eyeing up the latest technology and phones. Liam is playing with some of the gadgets there and we just say, all too expensive and head on. Liam seems disappointed, "Who knows Liam, Christmas is coming." I smile at him. I know he'll understand eventually. We have a lovely day; I just make it all about the children. After a morning shopping, we take a tube up to Buckingham Palace, and then Trafalgar Square, to take in a few of the sights.

Heading back to the apartment, everyone is getting tired, the legs walked off us. When we arrive in sharing dinner ideas, I see an envelope pushed under the door with my name on it, a note "There are 5 tickets to the Lion King at the box office for you. 8 PM show. Enjoy the weekend, ready for work on Monday."

I show it to Mark, he says "That is really nice of him, is he here in London?". "I don't think so, but I begin to wonder."

"Liam, can you watch the girls for a few minutes, I want to take Mom out for a short while. It looks like we are going to a live show tonight also. The Lion King. Something to look forward to."

"Where are we going?" I look quizzically. Then I guess to myself Can only be one place as he does not know anywhere around here.

"Come on, you will see."

We head out of the apartment and the next thing I know we are walking into Adam's shop. I panic, what if he says something? I don't want to shop here. Not with him. But I follow him inside, a part of me wants to give him a chance, but another part of me knows I have no choice.

As soon as we step inside the shop, I see Adam. He walks over to us. "Hi Maria, nice to see you. Are you collecting more paperwork? It is unusual to see you here."

"No, this is my husband, by the way, Mark."

"Nice to meet you, Paul told me ye were down. I dropped a note to the apartment, tickets for tonight's show. I hope it was ok, I know ye have the kids with ye. Paul asked me to organise them. I think he is in Scotland this weekend."

"Thanks, Adam, much appreciated."

"Now enjoy the poke around, I am sure we can organise decent discounts if ye want anything." He says with a reassuring smile, that my secret is safe.

I look at Mark, "Well you brought me in here, so let's see what you pick out.". So, I just follow him around.

I watch as he wanders around the shop first, taking it all in, as if getting his bearing, and then back to where he wants to go, he picks up some lingerie, a bit cheap looking, alas. Then a pair of cuffs. He held them up, "Well you wanted to try a tie, maybe these are better."

I do not really want them, as they are more of a Paul's thing. I could not say no and tried to look enthusiastic. We head to the cash register. Paying was very uncomfortable knowing what Adam knows. He adds them up on a piece of paper and then just gives us a discounted price.

"Have fun guys. We will miss Maria around here. I did not see much of her, but I know the girls in the office liked her."

He is so good, playing his part in the charade.

"Oh, didn't Paul tell you, I am joining the company? I don't think I will have anything to do with this shop, as not part of the sports shop group. But he may have me looking at your books occasionally." I laugh, "Better watch all those discounts and stock control write downs."

I blush at the mention of stock control. The guilt across my face, only Adam can see. Adam laughs and we head out, thankful that this uncomfortable experience is over.

"He seems nice enough, do you have much to do with him?"

"Not a lot, I met him a few times when we were trying to sort out what the client had. Adam and his wife were friends of Ralph, so we met with them, and they filled in some of the gaps. Ralph had an office behind the shop. You get into it from around the back."

"You seemed to like the shop?"

With a playful smile "It looked interesting. You like to try what we got?"

I don't have a lot to say, "Well, unless you got them for someone else, it would a shame to waste them."

I see a look on his face, but then he simply said, "I hope the kids go to sleep early."

I hope not. I am not sure what to make of him but why not.

We head back to the apartment and arrange for some food; we order from a nearby Chinese restaurant and the food turns out half decent. The children are excited about the show, especially Rebecca is elated by the idea of the Lion King. The others love the idea of going to a show, whatever it is.

We head down to the theatre in good time, collect the tickets and snacks for the children. Oh, Adam has got us very good seats. The children are excited as they sit down, watching the activity behind the curtain as they get ready. The show has such colour and life, Rebecca can't take her eyes off it, we had a good night. The kids enjoy popcorn and sweets and drinks as much as the show, I believe. Mark is unusually attentive. I begin to wonder but this is what I wanted all along. When we get back to the apartment, Rebecca is nearly asleep before we put her down. The others decide to go straight to bed, being up later than usual. We agree to head to Harrods in Knightsbridge in the morning before heading home.

When they all settle, I head to the bedroom. Mark has the lingerie laid out on the bed along with the cuffs. I look at them. I have mixed feelings, but I can't exactly knock them back now, especially after my behaviour trying to tie him up with a tie. I have started this. I have spent an age wanting him to try and here he is with his idea of sexy lingerie and bright pink cuffs. I never expected this, but then before Paul, I would never have really thought about it.

I open the outfit. It is a one-piece, one-size-fits-all all, and completely see-through.

While putting it on, I decide, I will let Mark, take control. So, I sit back on the bed and leave the cuffs.

"So, Mark, what now, you are the boss."

Mark undresses down to his black boxers. He looks interested. What is it, is there something in the air here?

He crawls up the bed with the cuffs, he puts them on my wrists. I let him take control, just to see where it is going. He starts to play with me, then figures out that he can't take off what I have on with the cuffs. Maybe I was not being too helpful. I am after getting used to Paul, who always has a plan when it comes to toys.

We play away and it is fun, all be it a bit awkward at times, Mark is trying to figure out how to enjoy me, and work around the lingerie with the cuffs. In the end, it just rips open. Either way, itis fun, and I can see how excited and aroused he is getting, as if my naked body is new to him. Ultimately his excitement takes over and I feel him push into me, as I pull against the cuffs., it may not have been Paul-standard fun. But then for me, I doubt anyone would be. Mark is trying and open to new things. Is this the start of something? Should I try harder to try and make it work? It was so much easier when Mark did not care. Maybe I am resisting his attempts because of Paul, with whom I am much more comfortable.

The following morning, we pack up and head down to Knightsbridge. "Maria, what about the laundry and tidy up?" I also watch him hold up the lingerie from last night. Not fit for much more than the bin now having been torn.

"Bin them, and don't worry, the cleaners come in once a week and change beds and clean up."

I do hope Paul is not around for the next few days. I really don't want him finding any evidence of last night here in the apartment.

"Ok" As we walk out, he just looks around, "The apartment is nice, basic, and maybe a little cold but nice."

"It does the job." If only he knew that it was the apartment downstairs, I use.

"Could I use it if ever I was working down here?"

"I don't know, I could ask. I presume if Paul is not here, he may not care." Strange question.

After a lovely morning in Harrods and lunch, we head home. Everyone had a great weekend. The train journey I have taken all so often now.

Sitting down, I think of work tomorrow. It dawns on me, where?

Taking out my phone, I text Paul.

Maria: Thanks for the apartment and the great show tickets. We had a great weekend. I know I am starting work tomorrow. It just dawned on me. Where am I to go to work?'

I type the message and send it to Paul.

Paul: LOL the manager who can't find her way to the office.

Maria: Well. Or do I need to go back to London?

Paul: Can't have that. Go to the new offices and we can talk there. I will meet you there at 9.

I am delighted about work, about meeting Paul and then I wonder, do I need to tell Paul about Mark's newfound passion for me … and toys?

Shaking off the idea, what am I thinking? He does not need to hear that.

Chapter 10

Monday morning, I head to work. Nervous, as I do not know, what to expect.

Paul is there before me when I walk in. That's a relief, I don't want to see all strange faces on my first day. Instead, there are no faces.

The place has desks and chairs and not a lot else.

He has my office ready, computer installed, a couple of wall hangings adding to the aesthetics, and some stationary in my desk drawers. It isn't too much, but it's enough.

"So, Maria, not the usual hustle and bustle you are used to. IT will be here this morning and they will be installing new servers and setting up your desktop computer and emails, so they should be working today or tomorrow until tied into London."

"Ok, but what am I to do? Well, your first job is to identify your staffing needs. What you need to set up an accountancy section. Hire a secretary who can man the phones and PA to you for when you are not here. There is a load of CVS on your desk to help you start. Basically, this is your show, set it up. Plan on how to take over the accounts for the shops from the existing accountants and absorb them as you see fit. You will be busy and remember we need to set up an online shop also. So, you need to hire someone for that and start there, for handling orders, etc., and keeping an eye on the stock."

"You have some shopping list there; I will be busy."

"For the online works, I want you to advertise the job, sales, and management role. Working from home is an option. But I want to show Matthew and encourage him to go for it. He needs a job, he is qualified, and it would be a way of introducing him to the business from the ground up, not knowing I own it. No favouritism, only hard work. and you are his boss. I will just say that I am doing the legal work etc. I will not be here much at all. We can still do Thursday and Friday in London, work and get our time."

"OK, that sounds like a plan. I get what you are saying about Matthew. A good idea too. Make him work and appreciate the business first."

"I am the ice maiden, no mercy shown. What are you looking for in a PA or Secretary?"

"Maria, whatever you want. Hire and employ as the boss. Who do you want and will work with? I am leaving it to you. If you want me to sit in on interviews, set for Thursday morning or late Friday as I am not in the day job those days and free to work here or London."

"Let's do London this week, introduce you back to the staff there, and have some fun ourselves."

"Shagging the staff on the first week. Shocking" I say with a smile. "Keep it up, Boss." And I give him a wink.

"So, what did you get up to over the weekend? Adam said you were in Scotland."

"Just looking around, really."

Paul tells me to get to work, he must go to the office, and we can talk later. I settle down for the morning and read through all the CVs and divide them into categories, for various roles, and whether I am interested or not. The office has a strange empty feeling, there are no staff, no ring phones, and no desk clutter as I looked around the office. The opposite of what I am used to. But that will change soon, I hope. IT work away to get everything set up over the 2 days. I see a few familiar names in the list of CVs and some more even too difficult to pronounce. I truly hope that I get along well with everyone here. A part of me wants to impress Paul and a part of me reels back to Mark's newfound passion. Backburning the thoughts of my twisted personal life, I focus on my tasks and soon it's 5 PM. I head home exhausted. From what I am not sure. Perhaps the tedium of little interaction with people dealing with the mundane of staff hunting.

Mark is home before me. "So how is the new job?"

"Well, will be a challenge. I must start from scratch and hire everyone needed including a secretary or assistant. I am the only one there for now. IT were there all day setting up and installing new servers and terminals on a few desks. I will be in London on Thursday and Friday."

"Who are you hiring? Why not poach Joan, ye have been together a long time. I am sure you can think of a few more?"

"She applied. Do you think I should consider her?"

"Of course, if she is looking to move. Why not, better the devil you know than don't."

I consider it overnight and drop Paul a message.

"Joan applied for a job. Am I tempting faith by asking her to be my assistant?"

"Maria, you are the boss. Hire who you need and want. If you want Joan, she is a good fit. Just call and offer her the job. Or invite her to lunch and discuss the job."

I take the night and think about it.

Heading to bed, Mark asks me about Joan again. "I just say I will talk to her tomorrow."

Mark strips down to his shorts and climbs into bed. I head for my usual t-shirt.

"No lingerie tonight?"

I look at him wondering where all this new interest has come from. "Frisky 2 nights in a row, are you on little blue friend and not telling me." I decide to play along, I get the lingerie I wore way back, which he did not even bat an eyelid at.

When I come out wearing it, "Mm new lingerie, what did you get that for?"

"You, a few months back, and I wore it one night in bed, you did not give it a second look."

Mark is not sure what to say. So, he just turns and kisses me. Just to distract from an awkward moment. I can see the level of his enthusiasm is feigning a little. But he plays away. It is some fun, but it feels as if he is trying hard, more than naturally enjoying.

I joke, "Wait until I use the rope cuffs on you." He freezes almost in shock.

"Not sure about that." I leave them and we just have the usual fun. Fairly unimaginative, but then this would have been perfect before I knew of more.

We eventually finish and head off to sleep. My lingerie a pile on the floor I grab my t-shirt.

The morning starts as usual. Rushing around, kids, breakfast etc.

I send Joan a text.

Maria: Hi Joan, I see you applied to the new company for a job. Would you like to meet me for lunch and discuss and see how interested you are in the role?

Joan: OK; How about just after 1 in the usual restaurant?

Maria: I will book a table.

I head into the office and am glad to see I have a computer working and a new email address.

The IT technician asks me for the laptop so they can set it up. It does not take long and when they give it back, they have set up a full Microsoft suite and Outlook for emails, and calendar events. I look at the menu and they say my new email address is set up and I can add a personal one if I want to.

There is a VPN link on the desktop for times when I travel so I can connect directly to the office system.

"Your new phone is also ready. "

"New phone?"

"Yes, weren't you told…… anyway."

He hands me a new iPhone; top of the line and the new number is on a card with it.

"Your work email address comes into this also. You can add other email addresses if you wish. Any contacts you create in your Outlook here will automatically update in your phone and vice versa. The same with your calendar. Security is set up for your fingerprint once you set it and the password also. I will bring you to settings and you can set your own. Your computer password is Lillyhook as was requested."

I just smile at Paul's little joke. Lilies hook

I drop Paul a text.

Maria: Why Mr Grey, phone laptop, very cliché LOL.

Paul: Well, every executive should have them. But seriously you will be travelling, and you need to stay connected, so this is not just a treat, it is very functional. It is a business phone if you want to use it for photos etc. I have put some in the album. You can delete it.

I open the photos and see the selfies we took on the Scotland trip. I smile. Lovely reminiscing some memories. I vividly remember where each photo was captured.

Maria: Thank you, BOSS.

Maria: Meant to ask. Last weekend. What were you up to? Scotland or wherever?

Paul: That is a breakfast chat for the train on Thursday.

Paul: Book 2 seats, please. As I can't book through here anymore.

Maria: yes, Boss

Lunchtime comes and I arrive to meet Joan. I get there before lunch and wait for her.

She walks in and spots me straight away.

"Hi Maria, how is the new job going?"

"All good, lots to do, effectively a start-up on the back of the existing shops. Sort of a jack of all trades. I am alone in the office for now, so need to recruit and set everything up here, and tie it into the London office also. We will centralise administration here and online sales. So effectively I am looking for a PA, reception and secretarial. We will build staff based on what the company needs. We are also setting up an accounts department to manage all the shops. So, within a short time, we will be a busy office."

"Where is the office?"

"It is a few minutes' walk. City centre over the Manchester shop. You are welcome to walk down there and see if you want."

"So, what are you thinking, are you looking for a move or just a curiosity application?"

"Honestly, I was not thinking of a move, but since you left, it is hell in there. I am frozen out as they think I know. I can't even get the gossip; everyone is afraid to be seen talking to me. So, what is on offer?"

"Well, I can offer you the job as my assistant or PA, like what you have been doing. But you also be answering phones for the office etc. Nothing to do with sales. Liaise with shops and suppliers etc. You are on a top salary scale where you are. I can match that and your existing package. We will review in 12 months when everything is set up and look at roles. To start as soon as possible."

"OK, let me think about it. We might walk back via the office for a look. I will let you know."

We enjoy the rest of lunch and talk about families, and office gossip. She asks about my kids and Mark, and what he thinks of my move. We continue the chat as we walk to the new offices for a look.

Walking into the office Joan looks over. It feels cold and sparse. I see her reaction. "Before long we will have a full accounts team here and staff. I need to decorate and may need help." I am trying to assure her that it will not just be us rattling around here. She doesn't seem too convinced, I believe.

She heads off and I stay. I set up interviews for accountants and put the online shop set up and management ads as Paul requested.

Maria: Here is a copy of the ad you were asking for. Good luck with Matthew.

Paul: thank you.

Thursday morning and I arrive at the train. Paul is waiting on the platform. "I hope you brought my tickets. Hard to find good help these days."

Walking down the platform together 24A is in front of us boarding the train. He turns and sees us together, chatting away. He just exchanges pleasantries and we all board. Smiling, as he passes our seats, "Looks like that is a lucky seat." We hear him mutter.

Sitting down, I take out a folder with some CVs. Looking to take advantage of the time on the journey and free up time for us later, I hope.

I start with, "Well Joan is coming over to work for us. She gave 2 weeks' notice yesterday, so we will see her in 2 weeks. I gave her the same package she is on; it may be a little high, but she would not come for less. The add-on was, she was not happy where she was. It gave her a chance at a new start. Her job title is PA. I can just imagine what will be said when they know where she is going. Now we need to get an accountant on board. We can build a department around them as we need to. I will leave that to you.

"I think you should be in that interview, as it will be a senior person, eventually anyway and you will have contact with them, they will be your financial controller. Junior people do not matter as much, but to entice someone into a new role and start-up we need to show an interested boss and owner and that everyone is professional. If they have any bigger questions about the group maybe you are better to answer them."

"Ok, set them up for next Thursday morning and Friday and we will skip London."

"Now tell me about last weekend, you have been coy."

"I headed to Scotland. I suggested to Matthew and Rachel we head to Scotland and spend a weekend and see Sarah. We headed up on Friday and stayed city centre Glasgow, on Friday night. It was nice to spend time with them, we don't do it often. I was telling them about Ralph's shops and what I had been doing when I was in Fort William. When they said, it sounded nice, I suggested we drive up Saturday to Fort William and stay there. Just to see that part of the country. Rachel headed to the room at one stage Friday, as she forgot her phone, and straight away Sarah pipes in grinning."

"So, who is Miss Lavender, Matthew was telling me you came home with a lovely new perfume. Mmmm. So, maybe not all in London. Come on Dad do tell?"

"They were laughing away at me, Matthew just grinned, saying they must talk about something and who knew old men had love lives."

"Miss Lavender am I; I suppose I have been called worse." I was laughing at him. "So, what did you say?"

"I just went red and said I was too old to be explaining myself to my kids. Thankfully Rachel came back and saved me. Sarah did not let go though."

"Don't worry, a long weekend, we will get it out of you, and by the way, good for you, have fun old man."

"I rang Caroline ahead and told her I might be in the shop with my kids. They don't know I own it. So, don't refer to it, please. They would know we met via work, just not that I own the shop. We chatted for a few minutes about the shop, and I asked about her family and life generally. It would be nice to get to know her a little, just with all the history."

"Interesting, bringing the kids up, why now?"

"I want to slowly introduce things and see what they think of them. I was more interested in seeing the cottage to be honest."

"We headed up Saturday after breakfast and it was a nice day, so plenty to see. We got there at 12, it was just under 2.5 hours. As we headed in, I said there was an old cottage Ralph had, I wanted to check it and see if it was ok as nobody goes there. When we got in, I told the kids to look around. It was sunny and nice, so a good day. When we got in Rachel commented first, 'This is old,' Sarah loved it. Telling me it was a gorgeous setting, a lovely place that could be gorgeous with some TLC. Matthew was laid back as usual. The inside was the same as it was when we were there, except a bit damper and colder. Colder inside than out. A coat of jus everywhere and an odd cloud of just rose as we disturbed things. The same old picture was there, and Sarah was curious who they were. Little did she know I told them the estate would probably have to sell it, going cheap as needs a lot of work. We headed into Fort William. I rang ahead and booked a hotel in town. We got lunch, in that small café we went to and called into the shop.

Caroline came straight over, she was great. "Hi Paul, unusual to see you here, I haven't seen you since the last shop managers meeting." I introduced my kids to her. She told them to look around if they wanted anything she was sure their dad would get the 20% staff discount, giving me a wink when they were not looking.

As they poked around, I asked Caroline to show me around. The shop looked great, so new and modern. Almost a complete transformation and nice new signage. She said since the outside was modernised and fresh, turnover has gone up.

Then she said that wall. Asked if she could take it down and move it.

I did not have the heart. I said, "No, the wall stays as is, but she could build a new one if she thought it would work."

She just looked at me. "What is with that wall, will anyone ever tell me, there is obviously a story or a reason I can't take it down? Ralph, I knew something stopping him, but you? Will I ever know?"

I just grinned at her and said, "No," and laughed. "But seriously I hardly recognised the shop."

She showed me the stock room and the old, outdated stock. We explored the area for the afternoon before heading to the hotel and getting dinner.

I asked the kids about the day, and they said it was a gorgeous area. Sarah was on about the cottage, saying it was gorgeous, so rustic. Could be a fabulous little house with some modernisation.

I asked them if it was going cheap and would it be nice as a holiday home, just an idea. Mountains, walking, relaxed, skiing in winter nearby, etc. Rachel was not bothered, but that was her age. Sarah loved the idea of a getaway and Matthew said it might be ok once there was internet."

"Oh, very clever idea, what were you going to do if they had no interest?"

"Well, if they had no interest, then I would know, and if interested maybe a project and fun. I will talk to Sarah and ask her to take the job of doing it up if she wants to and I will buy it. I think it would be good for her. I don't have the heart to sell it, as it is the only contact with my past that I have found, and I will apply the 10-year rule to it. In fairness, costs mean nothing really to keep it. The shop can continue maintaining it. Give Caroline keys to have them locally if there is a problem. I am sure she would not mind.

"Anyway, tell me about your week?"

We chat away over breakfast on the journey down. I don't know why but I am nervous going into the office, seeing everyone who, only a few weeks ago gave me a goodbye dinner.

Arriving in, we met Helen and Nicola. They greet us and I head to my office. There is a stack of posts. I start to sift through it. I can see it was all already checked by Helen. It still feels as if I am not needed here really and only stepping on their toes at this stage. We arranged a Thursday morning meeting as we did in the past. When they arrive, there is a slight edge. Paul senses it.

"OK, well ladies, looks like the team is back together. Helen and Nicola. London is as is. Maria will be setting up the central administration for accounts and stock control and the online shops. Other than co-ordinating information ye are just working together on mutual projects. The Online shop, when it comes to stock control and how best to address suppliers and buying. Maria won't be buying; she will just be dealing with credit and other terms with the suppliers. Please just continue working together as ye always did. Ye are part of the same management team."

They relaxed, I think they were just unsure as to whether I was now their boss, which I don't think they would appreciate. And I understand their hesitation. It would feel like a demotion and now having two bosses.

"Now, what about stock, if we are doing online sales, what is the idea regarding an online shop and stock control? Do we get a new warehouse down here and sell from here or set up the shop in Manchester? Really it does not matter where it is, once space, access to post and couriers. The IT side of it can be anywhere also."

Nicola comes in and adds, "IT has finished, and all shops are linked in to here and stock control is centralised. We are going to look at a 2-day stock take next week to enter them into the system, so the plan is to close all shops for Tuesday and Wednesday and do the stock take."

I tell them that the Manchester office is set up and tied into the servers here also, so we are all connected now.

Paul asks about the warehouse here and Nicola says, "Nothing's changed, it is at capacity, it is working away but has no capacity to grow and we cannot run online sales from it, as just no room."

We agree to source a new warehouse, Paul says, "Let's look at Manchester again, out near the airport as cheaper, and close for shipping and deliveries. I knew behind it, Paul had already made the decision, especially when Matthew was hopefully coming on board. He was making sure to include Nicola and Helen. We will leave London as is, it can supply the London shop and existing stock lines. Any new stock lines can go from the new warehouse. It can have an online sales shop also and we can put a person in shipping. They can supply products between shops also until online sales grow. If we need to work things around, we can do that when we have a new warehouse going. See what is most effective for distribution. Maria, time to go warehouse shopping please, can you organise that in Manchester?"

I agree. "I'll get to it."

"One last thing before ye go. The stock controls. 2 days next week. What about the old stock, is there much work in that? I saw a lot of it in the Fort William shop last week."

Helen looks at Paul and I can see her wondering. *What was he doing in Fort William?*

"If anything, a lot of work as lots of bits and pieces and end of lines. We need to try and sell them off."

"OK," Paul said, "We want local PR for the shops and let's call it a re-branding and re-open in a few weeks. So, tell each shop, to put all the old stock that is hard to sell and not moved in a long time to one side and don't bother including that in the control. Contact local homeless and children's charities and donate all the clothing to them. If there are local walking and climbing clubs donate any old equipment to them, making sure branded with the shop's name. Get the PR going and at the same time announce refurbished shops and reopening."

We all look at each other. "WOW a great idea, dumps the old stock, clears space in stock rooms and great PR with charities, and reminds local clubs we are here. Really what we would get in from the sales would be hard work and we would have to put bargain bins in the shops lowering the tone before we even start."

The meeting ends and we go about our day and back to the apartment. To be honest, that was a lot of planning in one day. I can see a lot of work ahead for me and set to do. This will keep me busy and there will be a lot of settling in to do between here and Manchester. Let's hope I don't thread on Helen and Nicola's toes too much. We need to work together.

As I start to unpack my bag and hang my clothes for the evening, I come across two ticket stubs in the side pocket of the bag. This was not my usual bag; I just grabbed the first one that was handy as I was late packing. Looking at the stubs, they are for a show in Amsterdam. Not sure of where they came from, I checked the dates and realised that they were the weekend that Mark was in Holland at a match. I also noticed that the time of the tickets coincided with the match, which would mean he was in Holland and never went to the game.

I must wonder who he was there with and what is going on. There are a lot of mixed messages from the last year, he was not paying me any attention to the renewed interest lately. I also began to wonder about his match weekends away and where he really was. I put the two tickets back in the side pocket and get sorted; Paul and I head out to dinner. This is beginning to annoy me, and I'm preoccupied to the point of Paul noticing.

I tell him what I found in the pocket of the bag and my suspicions. I leave out the fact that there is a renewed interest from Mark lately as I just don't want to discuss this with Paul. He does not need to know, and I do not need to be telling him.

After I finish my story, Paul does look at me and points out the obvious – however, annoyed I may be with Mark, I am doing the same thing. I realise it was stating the obvious and it was very hypocritical of me to challenge Mark at this point. Pauls sees me thinking, "If you are going to start this discussion, remember it is likely to have two sides and you may be explaining yourself also."

I tell Paul that I'm going to do nothing, but I do want to find out who it is. Paul asked me, do I have any suspicions. I do tell him there are times I have wondered about Ursula.

I just tell Paul that at this point, I will keep my eyes open and do a bit of digging, but I will say nothing, and can we just change the subject?

Paul tells me that he had a cup of coffee with Adam today and there is a club night coming up in two weeks' time, that they are heading to it, and wondered would we like to join them. We briefly discussed Wasteland in November. He did say that we should go to at least one more club before jumping in at the deep end there.

I know that next week we are staying in Manchester, so we can do interviews and could work that as an excuse to stay in London the following weekend for Friday night and we could go to the club that night.

I tell Paul that sounds like a good idea and without thinking, I tell them that I can always ask Ursula if she can do an overnight.

After dinner, we head our way back to the apartment, street busy as ever, and walk from the shoppers and theatre goers to the financial areas the crowd thins out and it gets quieter. Paul suggests that we drop into the shop and see if there is anything of interest for the next event or even for ourselves later. Heading in through the back office, less conspicuous, we wander around to look at the stock and see there are a few new pieces. I pick up something a little bit more revealing and tell Paul it might be fun. I decided I would wear that to the next event. Paul looks around and decides that he will wear the same outfit as he did last time, as really there are not too many more options.

It is only 10 PM when we arrive back to the apartment. We open a bottle of wine and Paul asks what I would like. Thinking, I'm not particularly sure but I would like to have some fun, I feel like a distraction. It is hard to shake the tickets. "Let's have some fun, feel like it has been too long."

Paul and I start to make out on the couch in the living area. It is a nice large coach with plenty of space. Paul starts to open and take off my clothes, starting with my pants. Almost feel like a couple of teenagers making out on the couch, struggling at a time for space and whose hand is under who. But before long he has stripped me down to my underwear. Not having shed any himself, telling me to hang on a minute, he heads to the bedroom and comes back with our rope cuffs. He puts them on my wrists, then walks me over to the wall, "Isn't it about time we used our hook?" Of anything we do these cuffs do ring special, our first toy and first adventure, so simple an item, but started a discussion. I suspect the affair may always have started at some stage, but the sight of Ralph's rope cuffs did send us down a road neither expected, nor almost prepared us for what was to come from Adam and the letter.

Attaching my hands in the ropes to the hook, I just stand, back against the wall in my underwear. Thankful I was wearing something nice, lace and elegant. Mind you I always do when we go out, knowing, hoping I end somewhere like this. It's nice to just stand there and let Paul do as he wants to me. Means I don't have to think, just enjoy, and let go. Sliding his hands into my panties I just feel his fingers massaging me until I am nice and wet. His breath is against my skin as he stands against me. Sliding his fingers into me, deep and hard using his other hand to grab my wrists, even though they are secure by the ropes. I can feel Paul's body pinning me to the wall. Paul pushes my panties down and off, having to remove his fingers for me for a moment to do so, all the time holding my wrists with his other hand. Stepping back, releasing me, he opens his own pants and pushes them off, stepping out of them. My eyes alight as I watch him strip, my anticipation building. Watching him spring free as his shorts come off. I am never tired of seeing him naked and watching him strip while already hard for me. Paul pushes me back against the wall, holding me, he works his body against me until finally, he slides himself into me. Always so good to feel him like this, inside me. I just want to feel him close and forget today.

Feeling Paul moving faster inside me, each thrust harder with the wall behind me, I just close my eyes and get lost in the feeling, lost in the building orgasm. His hands on me, just taking me, I eventually feel his release as he holds me tight, not forgetting me, knowing I am close, his fingers drop to work me, faster, and as I feel him slide out of me his finger slides in, holding the intensity that is until I finally let go with a loud moan, the orgasm releasing the days' frustrations from deep inside.

After a minute, he slides the rope off the hook and releases my hands. At that point, he unhooks my bra and slides it off, I am naked, finally. Pulling his own shirt off he says, "Come on, let's go to bed." We grab our clothes and just head to the bedroom, dropping them on a chair as we walk in and climb straight into bed, enjoying each other until we fall asleep, the hardness of the cuffs and replaces with the slow and soft as we are both already spent.

The following day we head into work as normal. Enjoying the more relaxed comfort of the casual Friday we start, following on with the plans started yesterday, I spend the morning with Helen and Nicola, sharing ideas as to how we can make this work. I decided the best thing is to all sit and work out who is doing what and responsible where and reassure them I am not here to change things and we will only change what we all agree needs to be reworked into the new structure.

As the day closes Paul calls me, our taxi has arrived. He has left us to ourselves for the day, intentionally I think so we could sort out a working relationship between us. Ultimately back to Manchester by train.

As I arrive in home that evening, I look at Mark and wonder about the tickets. It is hard for my mind not to see him with someone else, but who. I ask him about his last few days, and he tells me there was nothing new. He was working late last night, and Ursula stayed over to make life easier.

My mind thinks back to all the nights that Ursula stayed. How helpful she has been over the last number of months. Their cosy chats in the mornings. I wonder how many times she has had sex in my bed, has she ever, as the kids were in the house, how many times has she slept with Mark? I am convinced it is her, but I have no proof. I am losing my reason over this now.

I wonder to myself, even if I do get proof, what can I do, would I do anything? I am not exactly innocent in all of this, and I must keep reminding myself of this. *Has this been going on a lot longer than me and Paul? Is this why he lost interest? Why is he interested in me again now? What is going on here? All these questions and I come up with my own answers. If he was at this long before me, then I was right to start with Paul. Weak logic even if I do say so to myself. I never knew until the tickets. It never even crossed my mind.*

I ask Mark a few bits in passing about his weekends at the matches and has he any more planned. I remind him about that the trade show is in Holland in November and to mark that weekend as I am away.

"Do you know any good restaurants or things to go and see there, as you were there recently?" Let's see if I can catch him out.

He stops in his tracks and pauses, "Not a lot really, between the match and everything else I did not do much tourist stuff with the lads. Maybe nice to go back sometime."

I tell him I am around for the next two weeks as I need to interview staff but will be in London on Thursday and Friday week and back on Saturday at some stage. I tell him I might do more of that. Work on late Friday and come back Saturdays, to avoid going down every week. Sounds like a reasonable excuse. He does not answer or seem to care. Just "Fine let me know and I can sort it out if I need Ursula and I will talk to her. I will see if any games come up, so we don't clash." There it is. His dirty weekends away. I must remind myself, that is what I am organising.

Chapter 11

We arrive at the accountants' interviews on Thursday morning. I have narrowed it down to 3. Paul and I interview the first candidate, Oliver West He is 40 with plenty of experience. He wears a smart grey suit and matching tie. Well pressed and nothing out of place. He comes across as nervous. He is currently in-house with a department store and has been there for 10 years. His reason for applying is simply that he has no chance to advance there, and he wants a new challenge. He does a good interview and confirms he could start in a few weeks. As I watch him leave, he seems dower, but trying to put forward a more confident demeanour.

Paul excuses himself for a few minutes while we wait for the second candidate. A knock on the door comes and Joan lets Alex Jordon in. I nearly choke on my drink, when I see him as he walks over to the desk, he holds his hand out and as he looks at me, he stops dead. Not sure what to do. He obviously recognises me and knows I recognise him. Time stands still for both of us until Paul walks in and comes around the desk. Paul not giving any focus to the man standing before me. I look and watch Paul's face as he finally looks over and must take 2.

The look we share is the unspoken realisation, Alex is Mr. 24a from the train. Paul composes himself and asks him to take a seat. So, finally an introduction. Alex goes red and looks from one to the other of us. "I am sorry," he says.

"About what?" I ask.

"The train. I never knew ye worked together."

"Don't worry, if anything we should be sorry, we were entertaining ourselves at your expense. Take the mundane out of intercity travel and work." Having got that out of the way, it is nearly a relief going through the formality of the interview.

We interview him and he does an exceptional interview. I wish he hadn't done such a good interview. Easier to say no. He is currently working for a bank and operates between branches, which is why he goes up and down to London. He wants to leave as he finds the job isolating. He is more of an auditor and is seen as a threat when in a branch. He finds travelling tiring.

When he leaves. We just laugh out loud. "What are we going to do about him?" I say. Paul smiles, "Just as well you are the boss and decide."

"He is the best of the two so far, but maybe we messed too much with him. He did seem to want the job, not happy where he is. Almost makes our teasing worse. If there was nothing between us, then fine, but he may start putting 2 and 2 together and come up with 4 and it may be awkward. But it certainly reminds me that we are in a small world."

The third candidate comes in, Amanda Dobbs. Power dresser, dress, and zip down back, like the one I wore that first day in the apartment. Again around 40, experienced, and seems to know what she is doing. Another good interview. Paul tells me to choose as all three are good candidates on paper.

We offer the job to Oliver. I say that Oliver is used to a shop that ships and sells online, so his experience of the challenges may help. He also has extensive retail sector knowledge.

I spend the rest of the morning bringing Paul up to speed on what is happening. I tell him there are more interviews for the afternoon. They include a junior accounts person and of course Matthew. We have decided that Matthew will be in the new warehouse when it is set up and he is in stock control and online sales there until it builds up.

Matthew arrives for his interview at 2 PM. He is well dressed and outlines that he has graduated from college with a business degree. We spend time going through his CV. He seems nervous, trying to talk himself up.

I take on my ice-maiden serious persona. If anything, I may be trying too hard to be professional and avoid personal engagement.

I then explain that it is a start-up role and varied. The job would be based in a new warehouse. If he gets the job, stock for shops would come and go from there. He would monitor the stock level from there with shops and ship for online sale.

Effectively a shop within a warehouse. If the online sales grow, as we hope, the role may have scope to advance to a stock manager and assign a junior person to online shipping alone. He seems convinced by the scope. It was hard to appear neutral knowing he has the job. The starting salary is comparative with the role anywhere and 6 months' probation.

At the end, I ask him "How does the role sound and is it what you expected?"

He is articulate and says yes. He did not know there was a chance of advancement, which is good. He thought it was stock and online sales primarily and had no option to advance to stock manager for multiple shops. He is very interested as it has prospects.

I tell him, "We are completing the purchase of a new warehouse near the airport, and it should be ready in a few weeks."

He says, "It is fine, I do not need to give notice anywhere."

I tell him, "We'll get back to you in a few days." We shake hands and he leaves the interview room.

Once the interview ends, I call Paul.

"Matthew is gone. An impressive young man. Well-spoken and appears intelligent. His interest went up when he realised the job would lead to advancement. Anyway, I am sure he will get the job," I laugh. "I wonder what he will say about me when he tells you about the interview."

"I am sure, you'll make the right choice," Paul replies, I feel reassured.

"Now I have accounts and administrative assistants to interview. Work with Oliver and backup for Joan. We are taking in the accounts from the various shops and the accountants in a few weeks, so we will have a lot of work to get familiar with. The best approach is one at a time. We will monitor sales from the new systems and take over the accounts management from the local accounts offices one at a time and check each set as they arrive." I agree with him and wait for the interviewee to arrive.

I interview the assistants' applicants.

Abbey Hunt the first one, she was ok, 35. Had experience and seemed keen. But was very vague about the job she left 6 months ago and no new job since. There was something off. I don't like people who don't give clarity about their job experiences. Besides, I know there'll be better candidates applying for this vacancy.

Pamela Richards, 29, qualified about 2 years, she came across as conservative. Knew what she was doing when I put any questions to her. Dressed very professionally.

After 2 more applicants Pamela was the best.

I left it a day and called her and offered her the position. She was happy to accept it and she'll be able to start in a week. Finally, I am getting a full staff together. I can't wait for the day when the office will be buzzing, and we'll be as busy as any other firm.

I look at my schedule ahead with Joan. I tell her I will be in London next weekend until Saturday to make up for missing this week.

I ask her to book my tickets and give her my time. Usual seat, please. I book Paul's, later. I just did not want her to know that Paul was staying over too.

Joan asks if we can have the same Thursday arrangement, where she can work 8-4 rather than 9-5. So, she can get her shopping done. I tell her, "No, not for the next few weeks, until Pamela is settled in and able to handle the phones and the office. I don't want the office left unattended."

I could see she was about to say something, but she stopped. She was not used to me refusing her requests. Joan needed to understand that things were changing and that this was a new company with far fewer resources. As Joan and I continue chatting for a while, I asked her how life is going and is there any new man in her life. She goes a little red and then says, "Nobody special, just something casual when it suits." She is being vague, and I decided not to ask too many questions as Joan does not share unless she wants to. And I know, she'll share when it's time.

I head home for the weekend and things are quite normal. Mark is working away and getting ready to watch sports for his Saturday and I spent my time with the children. We head down to the Trafford Centre for lunch on Saturday and go shopping.

However, subconsciously, I am still stuck about Mark's whereabouts. I know I shouldn't be the one wondering if there is another woman whom I don't know about. I also have a man that he doesn't know about. But it's all too hard to shake it off, I can't, and I don't know why.

"Mommy, I am tired," my youngest informs me. "Let's go home, mommy."

"Alright, darling, let's go home." After a day of shopping, lunch, and roaming about the city with my kids, we call it a day and head home.

Will Mark be home? Mark can't have someone… stop, Maria, stop thinking about it. I remind myself, more like reprimanding myself for overthinking everything. *Let's just head home.*

Chapter 12

Paul and I take the usual train to work in London. This time we are hoping not to see 24A after we turned him down in his interview. At least we had the excuse of lack of retail experience to fall back on. Arriving at the office it is business as usual, and Nicola and Helen have everything running well. That's a relief.

In reality, there is little reason for me to be in London and there is nothing that I do here that I could not do from Manchester. Paul and I head out to dinner on Thursday night, and I do mention to him that I'm sure Nicola and Helen are wondering what I am doing in London when really there is nothing here for me to do that, I couldn't do from the Manchester office. They see me as a threat. This is their domain and I keep coming in.

"That is just something that we will have to work around, right now, we have very few options aside from London, to spend quality time together. While you're working away, as you normally would and not wasting time down here, then I don't think you'll raise too much attention, particularly not in the early stages of the new setup. Don't worry about it and it will work itself out, let's just enjoy the time we have."

We enjoyed dinner for the rest of the evening, before heading back to the apartment. I love these walks back, being able to link arms with Paul and just enjoy each other as if it's perfectly normal for us. The sense of normality I crave with him.

Friday is busy with new systems and testing and this is my excuse for being here, even though I know a better test would be if I was in Manchester and they were here. But we work away all-day evening comes on quickly, as we are swamped with work all day.   Online connections with shops and Manchester are being finalised, so we are fully integrated. The stock control system is tested before a reset to make sure sales in various shops are showing across the group.

Paul is working with warehousing, getting them ready to get the bulk of stock on the systems. He seems to be enjoying it. I ask him "Why spend a day with warehousing?"

"Simple really. I was curious, as I had not spent any real time there. I don't really know the business; it was a chance to see what happens from the ground up. Opening the door to the warehouse manager, so he knows there is a boss and owner who is interested. Settle them a bit. A lot of changes there when they see distribution, in part, moving to Manchester."

We pack up for the day and say goodbye to Helen and Nicola. Heading back to the apartment, I start to get excited.

"I am really excited about tonight. A little nervous but much more excited. At least I have an idea of what to expect."

"What time are Nicole and Adam arriving?"

"I hope they are here already. I asked them to join us for dinner and stay afterwards. Save them a long journey at the end of the night."

"Maybe more fun for you to get ready with Nicole." Laughing.

"No offence but you are probably right. I can see the glaze come over you when I mention hair and makeup. Ye have it so easy."

We arrived at the apartment at 5:30. I ordered dinner for delivery at 6, making for an easy meal. Take out Italian.

Walking in, I hear Nicole and Adam chatting. Little did I expect to be met with a sight like the one I was seeing. WOW, I see in the corner, a bondage cross all set up. I look at Paul. "What the hell!"

"Adam was getting one in for shop display so I asked him if he could put it here for a night to try. Maybe fun and also a chance to maybe try before going out. Or maybe when we get back."

"Don't get too excited. It is going down to the shop tomorrow. Housekeeping would get some shock walking into that. Or maybe she might enjoy." He laughs.

I walk over to the cross and Nicole greets me with a peck on the cheek. "Hi, Adam. You have been busy." Looking back at Paul. "WOW. Where to even start?"

It was tall, over 7 feet high is my guess. The centre was a square padded section. Maybe 16 inches square. Leather padded. The four sections were a dark timber. Maybe teak and each one was padded, and leather covered for half its length where arms or legs would be. From the top and bottom corners there was a chain hanging down. With thick leather cuffs on each one for ankles or wrists. I could see they clipped on or off to move along the chain.

It seemed hard, but elegant at the same time.

I run my hand over it. Lost in the whole essence of its presence, looking at it. Never ever, ever, ever did I see myself on a cross or anything like this. Now all I want is to try it out and be dressed for it and tied to it, experience it.

When I turn around, I see the other three watching me.

Adam laughs. "Looks like the work putting this together is being appreciated by someone anyway." I blush, saved by the bell. Takeout arrives. I hear the bell and head down to the front door.

As I go, I hear Paul. "Thanks, Adam. I know there was a bit of work getting this up here. Looks like Maria is a fan."

We enjoy a nice dinner. Chatting about the night ahead. Nicole and I discuss our outfits and compare them. Funny sitting and talking about latex and leather over an Italian,

Paul turns to Adam. "I see you got your hair done and makeup and what are you wearing, Adam? Do you need me to zip you up?"

We stop and look at him. "Smart ass!" I say, and he just laughs. "How about we get ready, I am sure we will find something to pass the time before we go out. Maybe learn more about using the cross. "

We all head off and get ready in our latex outfits for the night.

Arriving back to the living room, Nicole looks amazing, Adam not bad either. But the outfits make everyone look so different.

I look over at the cross and then at the others. Before I can say anything, I hear Nicole.

"How about we try the cross, some basic cuffs and whips and see if it feels as good as it looks. Maybe start with Maria, as she looks interested." She smiles over and laughs.

"We have been talking and will stay tonight, but we suggest when we get back maybe we will go to the apartment upstairs, give ye some privacy, and let ye explore whatever ye want with the new toy." She winks at me. I blush and know exactly what she means.

"That sounds like a plan Nicole, thank you."

"Come on," she says, and walking over to the cross she takes off the wrist cuffs.

Putting them on me, the boys watch us.

She then leads me to the cross saying nothing and faces me into it, lifts one wrist at a time, and secures me. This feels so surreal.

I hear her call Paul over, taking a whip in her hand, she gently whips me a few times and then gives it to Paul.

"There are loads of options here, face in or out, just wrist or ankles or both. We won't tell ye what is good, it all is really. Ye just need to find what ye enjoy and what works."

"It's like what ye may have tried with cuffs already." Adam pipes in "So that explains the drop-in shop stock." He laughs.

We all have a little laugh.

"This feels incredible," I say. "So much different to a wall or door." I think they know anyway, so what the hell. We are all heading to a fetish club dressed in latex. It is a bit late to be coy.

We enjoy some play and after a while, Nicole breaks the moment, "You can't have all the fun, my turn."

I think it is her way of showing by doing.

So, we swap places, Adam cuffs her and restrains her wrists and ankles.

I watch them as he uses the whip on her. Far more forceful and controlled than we were. Experience is obvious.

But alternates between whip and gently rubbing her, almost massaging her. Gentle, intimate touches, as he does. Though hard to use a whip, looks so intimate and caring at the same time. Sounds like a contradiction, I had to see it to realise it.

I spot his erection as he does. Well, it is hot to watch, and it has me wet also. Just as well that is not obvious.

Paul and I watch them, sharing glances with each other.

We watch them until they finish and as Nicole is released, they compose themselves and I watch her smile at Adam.

"Come on Adam, let's drop our bag upstairs before we go out, hate to cramp Maria and Paul's style having to interrupt them later." The cheeky grin over at us, all I could do was grin back.

She was right, with any luck we will just want each other by the time we get back.

The taxi arrives and we had long coats on over our outfits, off we went.

We arrive at the club and Adam leads the way, again obviously known to the doormen, we head straight in, paying our admission at the door.

"This is much smaller than the last club we went to." I said to Nicole, "This is more normal for London, that last one was the biggest of the year. Ye started at the top."

We look around, the subdued lighting and dark surroundings of the bar, there is a dance floor, and some playrooms. A DJ set up in the corner.

We had a drink, relaxed, and then agreed to split up and enjoy the club for a while. Easier to find each other here than last night.

Paul and I walked around the club, taking it all in. We went in and out of all the rooms and watched what was going on. One room was more interesting than the next.

We found one playroom, and there was a man in a cage, with a seat on top of it. There was a woman dressed head to toe in leather around it. We presume his partner. Moving on we saw crosses set up in a few places and being used.

We recognised the couple we saw at the rubber ball. They recognised us and said hello. "No cross tonight?" I said and she smiled "The night is young; we will get there. Would ye like a drink?"

I did not even look at Paul, "That would be nice."

I introduced myself and Paul and they introduced themselves as Geoff and Sarah.

We headed to the bar, they were a nice couple and we asked them how long they have been doing this. "5 or 6 years now, we sort of fell into this by accident."

"Must have been some fall." I laughed. "How do you fall in by accident?"

"We saw some of this in a movie and it just started a discussion and as we were both curious, we tried a little fun and games and realised it was a lot of fun and it grew from there. How about ye guys? How did ye end up here.?"

I said "Now that is a story, somewhat complicated but let's just say, we read about it and someone else's personal experiences and started to try a little and here we are. We were lucky enough to be introduced to a couple with a lot of experience who were good enough to give us a little help."

"Ah, that explains how you found yourself at the rubber ball. We did wonder. Well, here you are now."

We spend some time enjoying some friendly chat.

Geoff got up "We are going to find a playroom. Would ye like to join us?"

Paul looked at me and shrugged "Why not, can't hide forever." We all head off and follow them. We find a room and the cross is free. We head over and look at Geoff and Sarah. "Well Maria, how brave are you feeling?" She asks as she takes my hand and leads me to the cross. She starts to put on one cuff on my wrist, and I don't stop there. Then the other. My heart is pounding, this is nerve-racking and exciting.

I am standing tied to the cross and Sarah offers Paul a flogger. "Why not show us how it is done first, Sarah."

"You, ok?" She asks me and I nod yes. I feel her hand on my back as she asks. She strokes down gently as she removes it. With that, she stands back and a few seconds pass, heightening my anticipation.

I feel the tails strike me for the first time. My blood is pumping, my heart is pounding, and it lands again. I can hear the crack of it. But it feels so soft and before I know it, I say "harder" as my head looks down.

It lands again, and Sarah whispers, "You are enjoying this." She continues and I have completely lost any concept of where I am. Almost forgetting I am being watched by complete strangers. I don't care. It is liberating.

After a few minutes, I realise I have been hogging this. I had not noticed that Sarah had handed the whip over to Paul and it is him who is now using it.

I turn and look back, "Maybe time to let the pros use it. You want to untie me?"

Paul releases me and I need a few seconds to compose myself, and bring myself back to the reality of where I am.

Sarah takes up the position I was in. Geoff secures her like a pro and Sarah holds herself there as he does. We sit back and watch them. They are much more expressive than we were, watching them was so interesting. As if they are completely detached from us and anyone else around.

They are engrossed in each other. So, after a while, Paul says to Geoff, "We are going for a wander and drinks. Thank you, guys, hope to see ye later."

He smiles and says, "We hope so."

Heading back to the bar we bump into Adam and Nicole.

"We saw ye having fun," Adam says to Paul. "We saw ye met Geoff and Sarah, they are nice people, often come into the shop."

"Ye know them?" I ask.

"Yes. They would be in shock if they realised who owned the shop."

We enjoy the rest of the night and head back to the apartment about midnight.

We arrive back and Nicole and Adam go straight to the top floor. Nicole smiles, "You kids be good, if we hear any shouts, screams, or moans and groans, don't worry we won't come running, and the same goes for ye." She walks off laughing.

We both laugh, head in, and get sorted, I pour some wine and after a drink, we head for the cross, we play away for a short while, but we are both tired.

We move the fun to bed and the sex was intense. Paul whispers an image in my ear of me being tied and how he took me just like that. Being watched and admired by passers-by.

I came in no time at all. My mind was lost in the image of it.

The following morning, we slept in and got up at about 10, I texted Nicole.

Maria: Are ye around for breakfast or already up and gone?

Nicole: That would be good, how about 10 minutes, we'll call down.

Maria: Great, see you then.

When Nicole walks in she looks over at the cross. "Expected ye would have broken it at this stage." She laughs.

We head out for breakfast and enjoy a chat about last night and how much we are enjoying it.

Paul was quiet, I think tired. I joke to him, "This is all too much for the old man age catching up with you."

Smirking back. "Mm careful now. That cross is not gone back yet."

"Promises. Promises." I say.

Adam and Paul are chatting away, as Nicole and I are.

I hear Adam, asking, "What do you think of my idea for the shop? I don't think it would be too expensive to set up the way the shop is, so the risk is low, financially."

"What idea?" I ask.

"I will tell you later, easier than going into it now," Paul says. "Not a morning for business."

After breakfast, we head back and pack up. Adam tells us he will sort the cross on Monday.

Paul takes a few minutes and takes the cross apart. He said to make it easier for Adam. But I see he is curious also, about how to take it down and put it up.

We are only a few weeks away from the Holland trip. I can't wait. A weekend away with Paul. Being a normal couple so to speak.

Heading for the train. "What was Adam asking about the shop?"

"I will tell you on the train. Sounds interesting. But I need another opinion. Yours."

We head for the train and take up seats. The first class is quiet, and nobody is in earshot, thankfully.

We order coffee and sit back. "Go on. Curiosity is getting the better of me."

"Well, he wants to expand the shop. He said initially he wants to go into higher-end playroom equipment. The cross was one item, Cages, benches, etc. There is a lack of places where these can be seen or tried before purchase, bar expos, and otherwise special orders. A lot prefer to see privately rather than public events."

"He does not have space for that, does he want to move?"

"He mentioned the empty unit under the apartment,"

I say, "Not suitable. To be honest, I don't want to be over a sex shop if the kids are down or friends etc. Reduces value of the apartments."

He thinks for a while then says, "Ralph's office would be perfect. Dark wood sets the atmosphere and mood. Also private for people to look and if it works maybe they could use the private access via the side entrance for people who do not want to be seen coming in via the shop and mixing with others. Or rent it for use. Many options. That bondage room equipment is a huge price. The cross last night sells for over £1000 and many are way more expensive. What do you think?"

"I don't know. I really don't have much use for the office as most of the paperwork is now with you in Manchester and

I have a computer in the apartment. But is it right to use Ralph's office like that?"

"Interesting dilemma. Well, you don't need the office. You have the apartment and the main office here. Ralph was using it for his personal work. That's all back in Manchester now."

"Is it disrespectful."

"Probably what you are asking. For some maybe. But for Ralph. Maybe not. After all, the shop was set up to make fetish gear available here in London where the supply was limited. If anything, this may be expanding on his original goal. So, no, I don't think disrespecting. He also enjoyed the use of them himself. But the choice is yours?"

"I get what you are saying about not having a shop like this under the apartments and I agree."

"Ok, thanks."

"The fact that you would have a fully equipped room of toys and your own little playroom fitted, is just something we would have to cope with." I laugh, feeling thrilled at the idea.

"And tax deductible as shop stock as well. As an accountant my duty to say you are nearly obliged to set it up somewhere."

We both laugh out loud and get a look from a couple seated a few seats away. Thankfully, they can't hear the conversation.

I watch Paul take out his phone. He calls Adam. "Adam. Regarding the shop. My accountant here says almost criminal not to let you set up a playroom as it is tax deductible. But she has said she wants to break it in." I hear Adam laugh and so does Paul. I smile at him. "Remember it will be your ass I am breaking the room in with."

"I will take what is left in the office next week. But go in and measure it up. I would like to see a layout plan and remember; I want the room respectful to Ralph. As he and Lilly may have enjoyed a room like this. I am sure he would not object."

They hang up and I look over. "You don't hang about. Do you?"

"Not really. Less so in the last few months. Found I had to learn to make decisions I am responsible for, a bit faster."

"It suits you. You have changed. More confident and stronger. I like it. I really like it." he grinned a cheesy grin.

"Hang on, darling. Not now." He holds my hand and give it a squeeze.

For the rest of the journey, we chat about last night, the club, and that Amsterdam is coming soon. Only a few weeks away now.

It will be only me and Paul and the free streets of Amsterdam. I am thrilled with this trip. We have never had such a trip. A trip where we won't have to hide from anyone.

I start thinking about packing all the sexy outfits I have and of course, getting a few toys and lacy lingerie. It will be one heck of a getaway.

Chapter 13

For the next few weeks, we work away.

It is busy. The warehouse in Manchester is getting sorted and Matthew is working away.

He spends the first weeks or so in the main office before the new move to the warehouse. He is learning the stocking system, the stock we carry, and our specialised gear. Paul stays away when Matthew is in the office, as much as he can. It is interesting to watch him, seeing the other side of Paul's life, his son, and hear him talk about his family and sisters.

Paul arranges to send Matthew to the Fort William shop for training. So, he can learn about the more technical climbing stock. And also, he can deal with basic queries if they came in.

Knowing Caroline could keep his secret. He can trust the Manchester staff.

Paul stays away from the office for the greater part and when he is in, he is more as the owner's representative.

I speak with Joan and tell her that Paul does not want the staff to know just yet that he owns the shops. Staff in London know, but he does not want to highlight it.

Pamela is working well, though she is certainly not the conservative dresser who first turned up for the interview. I watch her coming in fitted clothing. Professional but certainly showing all her features and she wis very attractive. The looks she gets from delivery men when they call.

Over the weeks, the shops' accounts are being integrated one at a time. Oliver is working hard to make an impression and he was a good choice. He is taking Pamela under his wing and making sure she understands all that is happening. The two make quite a duo, curious to learn and teach.

We head out one evening after work when Pamela invited me for a drink. I was curious as to why. I agree, after all, it will be nice to get to know the staff I am working with.

"Maria, what is Paul's story? I know he is involved with the shops here. He seems nice. Is he single?"

I am taken aback. I feel a little threatened because I know she has all the potential to charm a guy. She has the looks, personality, and charm. No guy will say no to her. I trust Paul, but now that I know Pamela is eying Paul, my trust in her is weakening. *Thank goodness, Paul isn't here most of the time.* I thought.

"Isn't he a bit old for you?" I ask, trying to be a wise friend or colleague.

"I always preferred older men, and in fairness, he does seem really nice and relaxed when I see him around your office. I asked Joan and she did say that she thinks he is single, his wife passed away years ago. But suggested I ask you."

"Well, as far as I know, he is." It killed me to say it, but what else could I say? I couldn't have said yes, I know she would have pried about it, and my façade of 'not knowing Paul too personally' would give away.

"Good, thank you."

The conversation then moved on, but I stayed very distracted. I really did not like this. She was young and a stunning-looking woman, brimming in confidence and single. How could I compete with her? *I have competition. Do I need to keep an eye on her? And Paul?* Do I need to offer him more?

When I get home that evening there is no sign of Mark. I get a message that he is working late and will be a few hours. I am no sooner in the door than Ursula says she must go. My mind is all over the place. She has makeup on and is dressed for a night out. *Is she going to meet Mark?* I wonder.

I sort the kids, get their homework done and Mark arrives home at 9.

"Where were you? You usually don't work late without advance notice?"

"I had a meeting, it ran late. Why all the questions?"

I decide to let it go with Mark, but I log on later to the credit card. I see that there was dinner charged to the card this evening. That was no business meeting.

My suspicions are up and where was Ursula going?

I watch and the following morning as soon as she arrives Mark is straight over to her. *What is he saying? Am I right about them?* My mind is flustered, and I am frustrated after the conversation with Pamela.

We head off to work, going our separate ways as usual.

Joan is there ahead of me. We have our morning discussion about the day ahead and a coffee.

We work away until lunchtime and Paul arrives. He is no sooner in the door than Pamela is around him and starts chatting.

They chat for a few minutes and then he heads to my office.

As we discuss the warehouse and how stocking is going, Pamela arrives with a coffee for Paul.

"Hi Paul, said maybe you would like a coffee, as I was making one."

"Thanks, Pam, much appreciated."

"Ok Pam, maybe head to lunch and we can chat later." I interrupt.

Paul continues talking about the warehouse and when will it be stocked to the point we can move to online selling.

As he drinks his coffee "That was nice of Pam, I needed a coffee, been a long morning."

"You have an admirer," I say.

He laughs, "I am nearly old enough to be her father."

I say no more.

Paul leaves before Pam is back from lunch.

Joan arrives to tell me she has my train booked for Thursday.

"Now that Pamela is up to speed, can I leave early Thursday, when you are away."

"Ok, that is fine." I am just glad to hear that my train is booked.

The work is busy, and I am keeping an eye on Matthew. I know he does not have much experience.

In fairness, he is taking to the job. The warehouse is getting up and going and Matthew is working with the online sales. They are slow now, so he is helping with the warehouse work and main stock control. I like my team, they really are working hard to make an impression and committing to their jobs. Except for 'Pam,' who has her mind elsewhere.

The warehouse management is working away, supplying the northern shops. Paul is intentionally staying away from the warehouse, and I am keeping him informed.

When we head off to the train on Thursday, Paul is in good form. He spends a lot of time talking about Matthew and said he has been asking him about his new job, he seems to really like it and enjoys the work.

He tells me his boss is nice enough, but very serious as he laughs. I can only smile. He then moves to Sarah; he tells her that he bought the cottage and asks that she takes the job of renovating it. Gave her a budget, that would be tight but doable. £20,000

I was distracted and after a while he noticed. "What's up, Maria, you don't seem yourself?"

"It is Mark, I know I am in no position to judge, but I am sure he has something going on with Ursula. They always seem so cosy, chatting in the morning. She is staying over again tonight, as he will be late. I know there is something going on."

"What are you going to do?"

"I don't know, I have no real proof, all suspicion. Anyway, let's just move on from this."

We spend the day in London looking at stocking and supply chains. The trade shows are starting, and Paul makes sure the usual buyer heads to them and looks at all the stock options.

Nicola updates us on Holland.

"The Holland shop is coming together, and we hope to be able to open in the new year. A warehouse house has been found for temporary purposes and the shop premises and leases are being finalised."

Paul has requested that myself and Nicola head to Holland for a day or two and interview managers for the shop. "Set up interviews there and possible candidates. They then can take on the role of setting up the new shop and employ shop assistants. A requirement of the manager is fluent English speaking," as he does not want language barriers. He said, "I won't go, and you two are well able."

"I will check with home and Nicola, and we will work on a date. In the meantime, we will contact a recruitment agency for candidates. It may be the best option."

The centralisation of the IT is working well, with a few of the usual issues, but nothing major.

Nicola states that the London warehouse is working much better. Their level of stock and congestion is down as Manchester is running and they now have some capacity if we need it.

The day moves quickly as we are busy.

Thursday evening comes and Paul has arranged an early dinner as he wants to clear Ralph's office for Adam. We head down and the room now has a much colder feeling.

Nearly everything is gone, only Ralph's desk and chair are placed in the centre. Some minor personal effects and pictures including one of Lilly. We proceed to box all of them up and take them upstairs.

"I will ask Adam to have the desk and chair moved to the top floor apartment, or he can use it in his office and get rid of the old desk there. I don't want it thrown out."

We take our time and look around at what was a big part of Ralph's life. This is where he dealt with most of his non-shop activities, and we presume he spent two hours each day.

We look around and Paul then takes a sheet from his pocket. "This is an outline of what Adam wants to do here. We look at it and the different parts of the room where various pieces of equipment are to be set up. The cross, cage, bench, etc., a display for whips, floggers, and other implements. He wants to leave Ralph's leather armchair, for character."

"This 'looks like it could be fabulous, a little private club area, play space."

"Yes, he wants to look at it as a display for ordering, allow private side door access for discreet customers, and maybe in time either rent it by evening or so as a dungeon set up or for giving instruction or classes. He has many ideas, and I am letting him off. The display equipment is expensive, but the margin on selling is high also."

We finish up and head back to the apartment for what is left of the evening and open a bottle of wine. I know my form is distracted and I keep wondering what Mark is up to and with whom. We chat away for the evening, watch some TV, and look at the Amsterdam trip plans.

Friday passes like any other Friday at work and then we take the train for home.

Chapter 14

Back in Manchester I get home and see Ursula is still there, "Where is Mark?" I was a bit frosty.

"I don't know, he is not home yet, I told him I would stay on until you arrived. I need to go soon, as I have plans."

I call Mark. "Where are you? Working late again?"

"I am stuck at work; things are very busy here. I will be home around 10."

"On a Friday evening, that is unusual, you never work late on Friday."

"Look, I will be home at 10 or as close to it as I can," Mark says a little annoyed.

I go about my evening, and I can feel my annoyance. I hide it as best I can for the children.

I try to stay busy on the phone, pick up a book to read, but just reading the first page annoyed me further. *Shouldn't have picked up a romance novel at least.* I decide to join my children watching TV or trying to watch TV. But an argument breaks out between Liam and Natalie over which TV program to watch, and I just lose it with them. I am so angry they just both stop and look at me. They looked on in shock as I give out to them. My anger bubbling inside me at Mark. Ignoring the hypocrisy of it.

Their argument is no different from the one they have a few times every week, and not even an argument really in the scheme of things. I completely overreacted; it was my frustration taking over. I speak a little too much, without a thought to my words. I notice tears forming in Liam's eyes, and out of my guilt, I walk away. Later, I hear the TV buzzing and they both watch it in silence.

Mark arrives home and I try to stay calm. But he comes in and I can see he is annoyed.

"What was wrong with you earlier, I was working late?"

I snap back, "You never work late on a Friday, what is going on?"

"Look who is talking, all these weeks away in London, and some weekends. If anyone has the right to ask questions it is me. So, if you want to start asking me questions, be prepared to answer a few also."

He takes me by surprise, what to say? "Well, where were you, all I am saying is that this is unusual for you to be working Friday night and you working Thursday night also. As regards London, my time there is winding down, more time in Manchester now and you are the one heading away on your football weekends with the boys, Amsterdam, and God knows wherever else."

There is a silence as we stare each other down. The tension is palpable. Clearly neither of us are innocent, but who will break first? I know I am not too good at confrontation in my personal life, and this is a confrontation on a highly sensitive and personal topic.

"Well speaking of weekends away. I am away the weekend after the next match in London. I might as well make a weekend of it; I assume you have no problem as you are away in Amsterdam the weekend after at your trade show!" The suggestive undertone obvious in his voice.

Mark turns and walks away; it is less of a question and more of a statement.

The tension stays in the house all night, it could be cut with a knife. I was nearly dreading going to bed. I knew this was an argument that I started. I also know that I am not innocent at all.

I decide to try and defuse this, heading to bed. "Sorry Mark, it has been a long week and I, we have been so distant lately."

Mark looks back. "Well don't take that out on me, if you need to check up on me, call my office and check if we're working late tonight. If you want to play this game, we can both jump to conclusions." Clearly not wanting to back down.

We head to bed and no more is said. I am lying awake most of the night thinking.

This is consuming me, what if he is seeing someone else? Who? What would I do if I knew for sure?

That is the question, what would I do? If I left him what would Paul do? My head is all over the place. I know this will keep me consumed for a couple of more days. But if I challenge Paul more, he will question me, questions I can't answer. I can see he has suspicions.

The weekend arrives and there is still an edge, but I say no more. Sitting down Saturday night over dinner with the kids, I ask, "So, what is this match you going to? Is it a big one?"

I see I have taken him by surprise, but I act casually and supportive of him going. I need to cool this down and see where it goes before I lose control. "It is a premier league match, a few of us are going down."

"Where are ye staying?"

"I don't know, we must sort that out."

"Would you like me to ask if the company apartment is available for you? I doubt Paul would mind if it were available."

"Thanks, I will see if the others have anything booked."

I watch him move in his seat a little uncomfortable.

Looking back, "So what is your plan for Holland, will ye get any social time there? Where are ye staying?" Throwing it back at me, like a game of deflection.

"I think we are staying in the city centre; Paul and the buyers are arranging everything. I hope to get some time to look around. Can you suggest anywhere nice for dinner?" *Back at you, I think.*

He did not expect that coming.

"Nowhere in particular, when we are at matches, more fast and easy food. We not on expense accounts."

I remember his dinner receipt. Not exactly Pizza Hut. Dinner conversation moves on to the children. Neither of us I suspect wants to continue the game. What they are up to.

Natalie, I see is poking at Liam. "What is going on Liam?" Natalie whispers to him "Go on, tell them".

Liam blushes and then Natalie speaks up "Liam has a girlfriend. Woooooooo." And she giggles. Liam sits there with his eyes looking down, trying to find a place to hide himself.

Mark comes in, "Well done, Liam, what is her name?" Liam briefly looks up at his father and smiles, turning a bit more red.

Again, Natalie answers for him "Rachel." In a teasing voice through her giggles.

"Come on Natalie, leave him alone, remember your day will come when a boyfriend appears on the scene and do you want Liam getting you back for this?

Liam, I am happy for you and look forward to hearing about her and maybe meeting her sometime when you are ready." Trying to reduce his blushes.

"Mummmm," is all he can say.

I change the subject as I see Liam is uncomfortable. I know he will talk about it when he feels like it. *Will he, though? Do my children trust me enough to share their new experiences and discoveries with me?* I don't speak, and the rest of the dinner continues in silence.

Dinner ends and the kids run before they get clean-up duty, the only one who moves faster is Mark. I let it go as there is enough friction. I take my time to clear the table and wash up. My mind is full of distraction, to an extent I do not even know if I am washing everything properly. My mind raced from Mark to Paul and back. Every scenario being played in my mind. Will Mark leave me, will I leave Mark? What will Paul do if it all blows up?

Finally walking into the living room to the sound of television and silence. Not even a turned head to my arrival. I find a spare seat next to the kids. Mark and I clearly avoided eye contact.

Composing ourselves to return to the status quo.

The weekend moves on, and normality as it is continues. Domestic bliss. Mother, cleaner, housekeeper, and passionless marriage.

Work continues as usual. I at least have Amsterdam to look forward to. I continue to watch Mark. *What would Mark do if he found out about me? I know that would immediately end our marriage. But what will I do if I find out something about him? I won't even have a justified excuse, as I am doing wrong with our marriage, too. What will I do?* Staying at home, without work and Paul, I tend to create hypothetical scenarios and prepare myself for them in case they come true.

Thursday rolls around and I am not in London. I am not going down this weekend.

When I get home at 5:30, Mark is there already home from work. I think he works every Thursday evening. Is it just when I am away?

I make a plan in my head. I am going to let the next few weeks pass. I am not in London; Mark is away and so am I. I will then plan for London as usual and just not go. Say nothing and see where he goes on Thursdays. Am I losing it? Am I really going to follow him? Am I spying on him? Am I really that typical wife who suspects her husband?

I start to even question my own sanity at times.

The following morning, I meet with Paul. We spend most of the morning on general business. When we take a break, I tell Paul what I suspect, and I want to find out. He says very little, "What do you want me to do, if anything?" I look back "Nothing, I am just saying." I put my head down, go back to work, and say no more about this.

I can see the look on Paul's face. He seems cold, and distracted, finally, I ask "Are you ok, you seem distracted.".

"Maria it is fine, just let it go."

"But Paul. What have I done?"

"Nothing Maria. You just need to deal with you and Mark."

I continue, "But I know something is going on and I just want to find out. I need to know what he is doing."

I just hear a big sigh from Paul, "Just do whatever you need to do. It is not my business. Now I better be going." He gets up and goes.

I watch him leave. I feel alone and abandoned.

What if Paul leaves me? Mark and I aren't even on talking terms, and now Paul. For a moment, I want to bawl my eyes out, I know my suspicion will consume me if I don't find out the truth. And I know, Paul won't appreciate my quest for this truth.

I need Paul and the truth about Mark.

Chapter 15

AMSTERDAM

Walking off the plane, at Schiphol airport, my heart is racing. The cold in the air marks the beginning of November. Blue skies and the buzz of people.

I have come through dozens of airports. Why such excitement? Not that I need to ask. I have Paul next to me. We walk together like a couple. I am going to Wasteland tomorrow night, all so surreal. I have all the reasons in the world to be excited, a romantic weekend full of exciting adventures..

As we get through security, we find the baggage claim. Hope those bags are not security checked, I chuckle to Paul.

I have a gorgeous red latex dress that I picked out with Paul. I smile as we collect them from the conveyor. The dress is in Paul's bag. Would be fun to see him explain it.

It is not even from the shop. Buying from an online competitor. But my excuse, it was made to measure and of course like any prepared woman a backup outfit.

Adam and Nicole's flight landed 30 minutes earlier. So, we agreed to meet them in arrivals at a cafe.

Walking into the arrivals' hall, my phone pings.

Nicole: All-latex clad vixens to the Taxi exit, please. The light weights to the departure terminal.

Maria: Yes, mistress Nicole.

Oh, Nicole is already having fun. Love it, I smile.

The boys are more sedate. But I know Paul is excited and nervous at the same time. Paul has booked the hotel, but he did not tell me where. I know it will be a stunning hotel with luxurious rooms. I know his taste.

I wave as soon as I spot Nicole. I get to them first, just ahead of Paul. I get a big hug and a peck on the cheek from Nicole. "I am so excited and nervous," I tell her.

"So where are we going now?" Nicole asks.

Laughing back. "I was about to ask you. Paul booked it. I presumed you knew."

Adam piped in laughing "Don't look at me. I am just along for the ride and carry the bags."

Paul smiles, "Come on, ladies. Valuable shopping time being lost here."

It is 9 AM on Friday and Wasteland is tomorrow night. Heading out to the taxi rank, we wait for a taxi. Piling into the minibus cab. Paul tells the driver.

"Krasnapolski Dam Square, please. "

Nicole says. "Wow, great pick. I know that hotel. It is 5* right in the middle of the city on the square. Could not be a better location for a weekend." I have never been to Holland, so I look at everything going on.

We arrive and drop our bags. We check in but our rooms are not ready until after 1 PM. So, we head out and get breakfast on the square.

The weather is a bit cold here, but not too cold to be outside, the heaters under the canopy take the bite from the air. It's a bright day, the sun is out and no clouds to be seen. *It's going to be a good day,* I remind myself. The city is alive yet at a relaxed pace. There is none of the usual rushing we see in London or at home. It feels like we are on a holiday.

"So, boss, what is the plan?"

"Well. I have a meeting at 12 for about 2 hours. But they are coming to me. I booked a meeting room in the hotel. Otherwise, a day of shopping and seeing the sights with you after. Dinner is booked for tonight at 8:00. I am wide open to suggestions."

"How about ye ladies figure out if ye want to trail around all together or split?"

"Well, I would like to do some tourist things. Ann Frank museum and Flower market. Just relax and enjoy." Nicole suggests.

"Well as Paul is busy for a few hours. So how about we look around here a little? Do some shops in the high street and then ye can book Ann Frank for later and enjoy it together? And we meet for dinner."

"We have tomorrow as well. Expect to not hold out much hope for energy Sunday." She laughs.

That is agreed. Paul joins us and we just wander around by the canals and the palace, just looking at the sights. Christmas lights are up, I can feel the holiday excitement and bite in the air. We check a few shops selling souvenirs and decorative, I look for some for the apartment. But before I can decide on what to buy, Paul announces his departure. At 11:30, Paul heads off for his meeting.

"How about I meet you at 2 in the hotel, Maria? When I will be finished, I hope and rooms ready."

"Paul, what meeting? I don't know about it."

"Don't worry. Just work"

I head off with Nicole and Adam. They know their way around, obviously well-used for the city.

They suggest I book the museum for tomorrow. You will be tired later with an early start. Maybe a rest before going out tonight would be good.

For tonight, Paul has booked a restaurant called the Supper Club. Looks interesting. It has dinner on a bed, looks very high class and big, and with live entertainment. I googled it. Certainly not for the faint-hearted and not for bringing kids.

We hop on a tram and head out to one of the markets, the tram system looks so busy. Everywhere I go, they are passing all the time. Nearly run over by bikes at every turn. Honestly, I need eyes in the back of my head. The markets are just street stalls everywhere. We walk by every stall, stopping by a few of them and passing by most of them. A few stalls with handmade items grabbed my attention, but I noticed Adam and Nicole don't seem to have much interest. So, I drop the idea of checking the stall and move on with them. I don't want to be lost in this new city, on our first day.

Nothing unusual or extraordinary in the market, and we decide to sit by a small café, chat away our day and wait until 2 PM.

2 PM arrives and I am waiting in reception. It is a big open-plan reception, very modern. The varnish on the timberwork seems news, it seems to be just renovated. It is buzzing with activity. The hotel is huge. I reckon a city block on its own.

Paul arrives back and he has two very large holdall bags. "What were you doing? Shopping? For what?"

"I met a new supplier of Ski Wear for the shops. He brought me a selection of sample products I asked for, jackets, hats, adult, and children, etc. All the catalogues for the companies they are agents for also. They have an impressive range. He was keen to know we have 6 UK shops and opening soon in Rotterdam and online. I told him a preliminary meeting and I will send a buyer over at some point. Now, when you get home you have bags of samples and catalogues. Work done, so the rest of the weekend, I am all yours."

The concierge helps us with all our bags, and we head to our room. We unpack. I have black pants, heels, and a blouse for tonight. They said pants may be a good idea if we are getting on and off a bed for dinner. I hang my outfits for tomorrow as does Paul.

I am tired now and we are slowing down. We both stretch out on the bed and relax. I doze off for an hour and wake up refreshed.

"Come on," Paul says. "Let's wander out. So where to?" He asks me.

I tell him the Museum is booked for tomorrow. "So how about we look at the red-light district? I am curious."

Laughing, he says, "Well, when in Rome or Amsterdam as the case may be." We wrap up and look at a tourist map. It is only a few minutes' walk. We spend an hour wandering there.

In and out of the shops. A lot of them are just carrying more of the same. But they are fun to see.

We pass a sex museum, live shows, and a latex shop. Many girls in windows are selling their services. We look briefly at everything, wander in and out, and get our bearings.

We have little time, so we decide to explore the museum in the red light. Walking in, it just looks like a step back in history. It is entertaining, funny, and looks like a dark age of pain. It is fun just being able to hang onto Paul and look around. We enjoy the experience and each other.

As we head back out and down the canal, we turn back for the square. We walk past the shops and restaurants, trying to take in the newness of this city. Suddenly, I spot the restaurant matching Mark's receipt, I stop and look in. Paul asks me, "What do you see?"

"That was the restaurant I found a receipt for." I just hear a sigh from him. He says nothing, just waits for me. I look and think and eventually snap out of it. I can't let this become part of my trip, our trip. The last thing Paul needs to be listening to on a romantic breakaway, are my suspicions about my husband.

"Maria, let's get back, we can take the long way."

As we walk back up to the hotel, we pass an ice cream parlour and a few doors away a condomerie. A shop selling condoms from the fun to the useful, shape of buildings to whatever you can imagine. They had a window full of them. Fun to see. I say. "Can't see that in the Trafford centre anytime soon. Only in Amsterdam."

It is a fun city and we have hardly seen any yet. We arrive at the hotel and spot Nicole and Adam in the bar. We join them for a few minutes. Nicole has done some shopping. Looking at me, she says, "No shopping?"

"Not yet. There is tomorrow. We looked around."

Paul says, "Let's get sorted. See ye at 7:15 at reception. I have booked a taxi. I know it is not a long walk but, killer in heels I suspect. We can walk back if we want."

Nicole says, "Thanks. I will wear heels. Was in two minds. The cobbles are a killer in heels. But I love them when out."

We head up and get ready. We have plenty of time. We have a large room. Not a suite but spacious. Paul heads for a shower. The walls are glass frosted, can't really see but know he is there.

I decide to open the bathroom door and admire him. He is having a long shower. I am just enjoying seeing him there.

Paul sees me and calls me in. "Nope, I say. Not with this hair." It would be ruined before tonight. But definitely later, I would love to join him. My hair was done yesterday, and I am saving it for tonight.

Nicole booked a hairdresser for late tomorrow afternoon, so we look our best for Wasteland.

So easy for the boys. Shower and shave and off they go. I chuckle at the thought.

We get to the reception just before Nicole and Adam. When I see her getting off the lift, "Wow. Look at her. Sex on legs. She looks amazing. So tall and thin. And the heels, the outfit, and the makeup. She knows how to dress to impress."

I do think that she does make me look plain at times like this. I love what I am wearing, but she looks fabulous.

Paul whispers. "I know who I am admiring, and it isn't' Nicole." As he squeezes my hand. *And that is why I love him.* I smile broadly at him, wanting to kiss his whole face but I know I can't afford to right now.

"Come on." We head to the door and a taxi driver calls our name.

Walking into the club, it looks so unassuming from the outside. It is modern and comfortable inside. We get a drink in the bar and then our drinks will be brought to the table or bed, as the case may be. I see the club inside is all white. Lined walls with what looks like a huge, long bed. We must take our shoes off. I instantly go from towering over the boys to being shorter than them. It is a club rule. We are brought to the sections that are ours and a metal table/tray is in the centre. The sections are small but have just enough space for drinks really. We are asked about allergies.

Adam tells us they have been here before. "It is a mystery menu. Just enjoy. There is live music and a performer coming later." He says and looks around.

We sit back and I lay back into Paul's arms and Nicole does the same with Adam.

Looking around the club we see everyone is well dressed. Wine and drinks are flowing. We get up to the balcony in front of us to look at the entertainment and everyone.

Adam says, "Once dinner is over, at about 11, the club opens to a night club, but we can stay." We just enjoy the party atmosphere; the meal is good and lots of fun. We get the waitress to take a photo of the 4 of us sitting back in the bed, relaxed, happy, and having the time of our lives. Paul gives his phone for the photo; I know I can't have such photos on my phone.

We take some selfies of the two of us also. Some on the bed and more with the club behind us over the balcony. Nicole and Adam do the same.

The live show is a burlesque dancer and a singer followed. It was an amazing experience. Adam tells us there is a similar club in London with the same name.

We leave about 11. All tired from the day. There was a nightclub starting after and we could have stayed, but we have been up since 4 AM. Paul says, "It is late. I will just get a taxi." As we drive back, we notice Dam Square is still buzzing. More like 11 AM than 11 PM.

Paul says, "I am tired and let's just head up." Our rooms are all on the same floor.

When we get back, I ask Paul, "Who paid for dinner?"

"How are you working out the traditional who is paying argument? I hate those arguments."

"So, I spoke to Adam a few weeks back when I was booking, I said as a thank you for the help they have given us, this trip is a gift. No argument. I am paying for the hotel and dinner etc. And Adam and Nicole got us the Wasteland tickets. We agreed generally unless a reason, we will just split things. But this is from us to them. Anyway, it is a trade show. The company is booking the hotels and paying. One room in your name and one in mine. Can't have a suggestion, you are sleeping with the boss. So, it is all tax deductible. As an accountant, you should be proud of me. Yes, a deductible dirty weekend."

We are both tired. But we do have some fun as we head to bed. The feel of good hotel sheets always has something nice about them. I love curling up in bed with Paul. I could watch him sleep. I keep my head on his bare chest and close my eyes.

Morning comes and we go down for breakfast. I spotted what looked like a ballroom last night. It has a ceiling the full height of the hotel. I could imagine the dress balls that go on in there. A big glass dome ceiling and marble floors and pillar and just plush. I dreamt of Paul and me dancing in that ballroom, just like in those fairy tales. Breakfast is served and they call it the winter garden. It is a buffet down the middle like I never saw before and chefs in the middle of it making omelettes to order.

Looking around, everyone is so casual at breakfast, like any restaurant. But it is some spread. We enjoy a lazy breakfast and make our plans for the day.

We head over to the Ann Frank house for our booking at 11, line up in the fast-track line. Working our way through the museum, we read and listen to all the history that goes with it. A sombre story, interesting and grounding. A bit of serious on a fun weekend.

After spending the next few hours, we wander around the streets, and squares, drinking coffee and watching the world go by. I want to pause and enjoy this relaxed city. Is the city relaxed or is it just me, I can sense Paul is chilled out too. Maybe we all are away from our work, our usual hassles, and that's what keeps us relaxed. I remind Paul that we need to be back at the hotel for 4 as Nicole has a hairdresser's booking.

We just head for a light coffee and pastry, as we are already full, from breakfast. We sit across from each other, and I watch an elderly couple sitting next to us. We can see they still are so much in love and like to share the laughs with each other There is something about old couples that warms my heart. I look away, realizing they might not like my stares. We enjoy our coffee and pastry and watch the world go by, peacefully and at a much-relaxed pace.

We arrived back at the hotel at 3:45, time to drop a few bags and head to hairdressers. Some pampering, hair and nails, and ready for adventure. The hairdresser asked us about our weekend and if we hadanything nice planned. All we could say was maybe a club tonight.

We arranged to meet the boys at 6 for dinner. Paul has booked a restaurant around the corner for an early dinner before getting ready to head out.

I am so excited, who knew I was 43, more like 13 going to my first disco, than heading out to a huge fetish party? I had done some research but did not know what to expect. At least Adam and Nicole were there to keep us safe.

I could hardly eat; I was so giddy. But we enjoyed a nice meal. Nicole can see how giddy I am. "You seem excited about your night out. Just enjoy, take in the atmosphere. Fancy dress night club and theme. Plenty of time in the future to get more involved. We will be doing the same. We just enjoy the weekend away and the atmosphere."

We got back and changed. The taxi is ordered for 8:30 and we arrive at the event at 9:00.

I was wowed when we saw everyone, it looked amazing. The theme made it fun. Nicole made sure I was well sorted for it, dressed to the last, and prepared for it as much as I could be.

The entrance felt like crossing a barrier to an alternative universe. Paul insists we took a few selfies with the backdrop showing where we are. I think just a bit of reliving what Ralph and Lilly did. People around us were just laughing and chatting, their excitement filling the atmosphere, like a drug, with the sense of the excitement to come.

The outfits were something you would see in a movie; they were a wow factor.

We walk in and get our bearings. The place is huge. The atmosphere is fuelled by the music, the smell of leather and latex, and who knows what else. Moving through the ever-growing crowd the sense of adventure grows.

We reach one of the live shows. My jaw just dropped. There were women dancing inside a cage the size of a small room and putting on a show.

As we moved on, there were dancers on stage dressed in little enough to cover the essentials, in amazing outfits. They looked so daring, that words could hardly describe them.

We kept going, moving through crowds, now getting thick and jumping and dancing to the music, where each person was more elaborate than the next. Face makeup and masks like skeletons, hats, and headpieces. Yet the face behind is smiling and full of fun.

Acrobats suspended from the ceiling, twirling and putting on shows, in different costumes. We were definitely not at the circus.

The costumes were made of latex, chains, leather, feathers, and every other material known to man, cut and sculpted to the bodies underneath.

There were bondage and play scenes wherever the eye turned.

I shout to Paul over the music and crowd. "Let's get a drink"

We had already lost Nicole and Adam, but we were having so much fun we did not care.

The clubs in the UK look like teenage discos next to this. I had googled it and it was described as "The wildest party on earth." I presumed this was marketing hype, but now I get it. Everyone was having such fun.

Back at the bar, we just get a drink, watch the world go by and taking a breath. We chat about what we have seen. After a second drink, Paul takes my hand, "Come on, lots more to explore."

We headed in a different direction from which we came and found the shows got even more daring, the outfits more flamboyant and outrageous. I thought I looked amazing in my dress and now I see it was definitely on the timid end of the scale.

This was definitely an alternative universe and reality seemed a world away.

Three hours here and we have still not crossed paths with Nicole and Adam. Just as well we had set a meeting time and place. As the night went on the party got wilder. The crowds livened with the effects of alcohol and whatever else.

We circled a second time, the stage shows had changed and entertainment continued. The crowds included everything you could imagine in latex and leather, PVC, metal adornments, and makeup. Men as women, women as men, fantasy and fancy dress. Fire twirling entertainment and equipment like I had never seen. Even on Google.

We danced, we sang, we drank, and got drunk in the atmosphere. This was certainly not an experience I could ever have imagined, even after the London clubs.

We never tired, returning for drinks when the heat and atmosphere demanded before we knew it. It is 3 AM and the party is still going strong. Meeting our taxi and Adam and Nicole at the entrance, we head back to the city.

Dan Square is still full of activity. A city centre full of nightlife and revellers. But clear the messy end of the night.

Pulling up to the hotel, security checks for our identity and room number. Our hair and makeup certainly now look like the morning after. As Adam and Paul had to open jackets to get our wallets to prove we were guests, I could see him eye us up and down. Getting a clear view of what Adam and Paul were wearing. He eyed us up and down, we were still covered up. He was probably wondering what we had on underneath.

Ever polite and professional, he opens the doors and wishes us a good night. I am a little drunk and just laugh with Nicole if only he knew where we were.

Felt like a 20-something, sneaking in after a long night, hoping my parents do not see the condition I was in.

We sleep in the Sunday morning and crawl down for breakfast just before the last orders.

Certainly, the worst for wear after last night. We are not too energetic after breakfast, but we pack up and are ready to go home later. Paul says that one of the holdalls is for me to take. "That is full of the kid's gear, sizes should suit yours. Show you have samples, and they score." I look at him, he obviously planned it. "Always a step ahead."

We head out for some fresh air. Thankful for a late checkout, there is a fresh cold feel to the air. The square is quiet in comparison to 3 am. A few people are walking around, probably heading to work as department stores are getting ready to open. We then see the decorating of the giant tree in the square. There is sound of warnings from lifts and vans as they work around the empty square in front of the palace.

We pass the day at the nearby restaurant chatting. Not much energy for anything else. "How are your kids doing, have you told them anything about the shops yet?"

"The kids are good; Sarah is really enjoying the restoration project of the cottage. I was up there last week, and she is working hard, the cottage is coming along well, she got an IKEA kitchen, to cut costs and put it in with her boyfriend and a local carpenter. The budget is very tight, and I am surprised she is stretching it, but let's see how far she gets. We will go up over Christmas and take a fresh look. Rachel is being Rachel, a spoilt teenager, but she is fine. Matthew, you know, is loving this job and seems to have found his niche. He is getting a good handle on distribution and online sales."

"Yes, he is, I am keeping an eye on him and is keeping regular contact. He has the sales running smoothly and is taking a real interest in distribution and how it is all working."

"I am hoping it will make life easier when I tell them. I know it will be a shock."

Adam and Nicole Walk in, and we end the conversation. It is time to head to the airport. Our flights are close in time, so we share a taxi out. It was a lovely weekend and such fun. The event was amazing, But the weekend was relaxing, shopping, being together, and spending time is what made it memorable.

I am a bit sad going home, as I know it will be a long time before we can do this again. Heading back to reality and life, and mine is a bit more messed up currently. My mind drifts on the plane home. Back to the walk and investigating the restaurant, Mark went to. I wonder again who with.

Paul sees I am glazed over; my mind is somewhere else. "What's on your mind?" Before I think, I answer honestly, "Thinking of that restaurant. Who was here with Mark?"

I hear a sigh. Realising what I said, I immediately regret it. I can see Paul regretted asking. "Think about something good from the weekend. Not just what Mark did." There was an edge to his voice. Too nice to say more, but I can just imagine what he was thinking. He says no more and leans back in his seat.

Getting off the flight, the weather is cold and damp. We head to the terminal and reclaim our baggage. We head out to the taxi tank. Paul opens the door to a taxi and lets me in as the driver puts my bags in. Closing the door, I look at him, and say, "You not coming?"

"You need to check on Mark and get home." He gives me a quick peck on my cheek, far from the weekend's passion. I sense a little annoyance, I suppose, hard to blame him. I am away for a weekend and party, and coming back I mention Mark is on my mind.

When I arrive home, I take a deep breath. Getting out of the taxi and put on a mother face. Mark greets me with, "Looks like someone cleared out the shops," when he saw a packed holdall.

The taxi driver throws me a glance as he has seen me leave Paul and get a little kiss there. The kids come running up before I say anything, "What did you get us?" I open the holdall and say, "Help yourselves."

They pull everything out in seconds. Mark watches, "You went mad on all that gear, must have cost a fortune. Very expensive brands."

"Don't worry, cost nothing, these are all samples from the trade show and possible suppliers. I just took samples that matched the kids' sizes. Paul has more of the same that we will use to decide on orders." The kids love it.

I am distracted but try to focus on the kids and being home. Heading to bed, I feel deflated as to how Paul and I parted. I know it is my fault. Why did I say that? He went all out for me this weekend and covered every angle from hotels to kids' clothes to parties, and I mentioned my suspicions about Mark.

What a way to spoil someone's good mood! I am tired from the trip, but my mind keeps reprimanding me for saying such a thing to him. *I could have said anything, that I was sad that this weekend was over, or we wouldn't get to spend time like this. But no, I go on and mention Mark. I am such an idiot. I need to apologize to him.*

Chapter 16

Christmas is just around the corner, a week away and work is busy, the shops are going well and the new shop in Holland is due to open in the new year, everything is coming together there. All seems to be going according to plan and I seem to be well-adjusted with my new role and new responsibilities. I went for a 1-day visit to Holland to check on the progress, I couldn't be happier about how smoothly things are moving. A new norm is developing for me at work as if it was always my normality.

Certainly, I am working hard in this job, hours are long and challenging, but that is what I wanted. It gives me more time with Paul, and less time to bother about Mark and his whereabouts. Well, that's what I thought. I spend the morning going through all the paperwork and budgets for the shops and the Euro Brexit project as we now call it.

Pamela is coming and going with paperwork and always to Paul and I do see occasionally, yet intentionally, she rubs against him, she is some flirt, but subtle at the same time. I watch her, the days she knows he is coming in, the clothes are more fitted, the blouse opened that extra button and lacy lingerie evident when she leans over him. Today it is black fitted trousers and white open neck shirt with a pendant dangling and almost giving a direction to her cleavage. Some days I really want to call her out, but my ethics and mannerism hold me from doing so.

I half smile to myself, poor Paul is clueless. He could have anyone; I think once they know him. Pamela is in hot pursuit, and truth be known, I think Joan would take her chances if she thought she had one. Paul does not even acknowledge Pamela's flirtations, let alone react. And I see how much that upsets Pamela. *Poor Pamela, barking up the wrong tree.* I could only chuckle at her attempts. They are all in vain, and this makes me a bit proud about his loyalty and our relationship. But nervous as to the temptation if he ever wakes up to it.

When we take a break and start chatting about non-work matter, I tell Paul about my suspicions about Mark and what my plan is. I recount all my thoughts. He is always solid and lets me just vent. He usually says little, just supports me and is always there. *Do I want him to help me out with it?* That's a question I couldn't answer for sure for myself.

This time I watch Paul sit back. He looks at the me seriously, neither speaking a word nor reacting to what I say. Until finally he does. An ominous feeling comes over me. "I have always stayed out of your marriage, but you are getting obsessed here. If you find he is seeing someone. What are you going to do? It does seem that you have very strong feelings for Mark, and I must ask the question. If this is affecting you as much as it seems and considering what we have been doing, am I standing between you and him, and in making your marriage work? I told you I would never do that, irrespective of my feelings."

I am completely taken aback. *Do I make him feel insignificant? What is Paul thinking now? Am I coming across irrationally?* "What do you mean?" I ask.

"Well Maria, whatever happened you are entitled to be upset if you find Mark is playing away. But you are getting obsessed here and you have been playing offside with me for a long time now. So, you are not exactly innocent in this. The only reason I can think is you have strong feelings for Mark, enough to care rather than turning a blind eye knowing you are doing the same. Maybe you have shelved your feelings. You have always said you would not let us impact your home life, but one way or the other it has. So, think about it, and if you still feel this strongly, maybe you need to try with Mark again."

There is silence, I am too surprised to say a word. I watch him, hoping he would say something less severe, but he continues.

"I saw your reaction when you saw the Amsterdam restaurant, and coming home on the plane he was on your mind. Not the gorgeous weekend we just had." He rests his case. I knew my words on that flight were a mistake, now they are coming back to haunt me.

"But Paul, what are you saying?" I know what he is saying, I just don't want him to say it again.

"I am telling you; you have some serious thinking to do about what you want or not and what you see happening. Do you want a monogamous marriage? Do you want to continue with me? Do you want to stay obsessed and angry that Mark is doing exactly what you have been doing? Simple questions, you now must decide."

I see the solicitor coming out in him. Like he is laying things out for a stranger.
"Your options are simple. We finish and you give Mark another chance. We continue and you let Mark do whatever he is doing and say nothing. You stay obsessed with Mark and apply a double standard and see where that leaves everyone. Or we finish and you tear Mark a new one. Or whatever other option you come up with."

I feel like I am being hit by a wrecking ball. I did not see this coming. I am frozen and stuck at the mere mention of ending the relationship with Paul, and somewhat about letting Mark have an affair.

We are only a few weeks back from an amazing weekend away in Amsterdam. *Has this been brewing or what I wonder?*

"But Paul, you know it would be possi…"

"Your options are there, choosing an option is always possible," Paul interjects, before I can finish saying. I understand he is frustrated, perhaps with our relationship. Or just me.

"Paul, how long have you felt this way?" I become serious.

"Look, you know how I feel about you, but I don't want to be the cause of ending a marriage that could otherwise work and the way you are obsessed with who he may or may not be seeing, it is clear you still care a lot and have feelings. I am not asking you to choose, I am asking you to think about what you want and how you can get or keep it. Now Christmas is here, and it is time for kids and family, enjoy it with yours and take the time. I still have mine to deal with and juggle that they don't know about my newfound life and all the changes. That will be fun."

I nod my head wondering, how does it all come so easy for him, and I feel like my precious world is shattering around me. He stands up, says goodbye, and heads off. I can't even gather myself to look up to him, I hear his footsteps fade away. A part of me believes, he is fading away from my life. With Pamela bounding over to him like a lovesick teenager, as he walks out, my earlier dismissive attitude to her now forms a knot in my stomach. The competition.

I am left thinking what just happened.

I know Paul is right. I know what he is suggesting makes completes sense. And I know now or later, I will have to make the choice. I don't even know what I will do if I discover about Mark's affair. I don't either know how long I can have an affair with Paul. I don't even know how I will react if my family finds out about my affair. How will my kids feel? They will be left with severe trust issues. It will impact them the most. Paul is right, I need to think straight. He loves me, perhaps, that's why he doesn't want me to be stuck like this.

We have a lot of work to do, and I must focus on things more important than spying on Mark.

I pick my phone and see a few emails from Paul, all work related as if nothing happened. He seems to be able to compartmentalise work and personal, which is good. I suppose he must. I begin to think, maybe the advances of Pamela and who knows who else have not gone unnoticed by him. *Is there someone else?* My mind races all over the place.

Am I competing with someone else for Paul?

I realise thinking back that I have been so caught up with Mark and everything going on I really have not been paying attention to him and all that's going on. The last year has seen a lot of changes for me, work, personal and life in general. Paul had his life turned upside also. I have a complicated love-life, and work. Suddenly, he becomes a huge employer and company owner and has the responsibility of all that and his family, he needs to manage them on his own. He never really shares his worries, makes me think he has been keeping a distance of sorts and if I am being honest, I never really ask much about them. I, of all people, know the changes that have taken place.

I head home and Mark is there before me. I can only look at him, now I have a double distraction. With my behaviour, have I pushed Paul away and lost Mark to whoever? Mark doesn't acknowledge my presence. I hear my children welcoming me home, they are all excited about Christmas coming.

****

I see Mark smiling and laughing with the kids, enjoying as he asks them again what Santa is bringing. He looks over at me and smiles as if nothing is wrong. "And what does mum want from Santa?"

All eyes turn to me. What to say, I simply smile and say, "Oh a surprise, I hope I have been good enough to deserve one?"

"And dad, what is on your wish list this Christmas?" I look at him.

Laughing, he says, "That is easy, united to top the league."

Liam laughs, "Some miracles are even beyond Santa."

Everyone seems to be in good form. I must shake it off and try to get in the mood for them.

I resolve, for Christmas, and try to put all suspicions aside and see what Mark is like and is anything still there or not. Maybe that will help me see clearly.

When everyone is gone to bed. I sit down alone and look at my phone. A few unread emails and messages, and a couple of requests on my socials. I decide to explain myself to Paul.

Maria: Paul, you took me by surprise today, you have always been so supportive and never expressed an opinion or judged, so today was surprising. I completely accept what you said and how bad I was for you to have said it today. You are right, I need to get my act together. I need to get my head around everything. I am sorry I have not been paying attention to you and all you have going on. I will try and get myself sorted and come to grips with Mark and everything else.

Please forgive me xxxx

Paul: I know, you need to come to grips with what we are and have been doing and the same with Mark, if he is, decide what you want and accept it whatever it is. Double standards won't work. That is the real cake and eat it.

Take Christmas with your family and Mark. I will do the same. It has been a hectic year and I need to take time and evaluate how I am going to tell the kids and when.

XX Nite Nite.

Well, that was formal, that is it, I think. Sitting back on the chair, I wonder, is that it? Are we over? Have I blown it? What do I want from Mark? Is Paul right, do I still have strong feelings? I feel myself tearing up, but I resist sobbing. I need to be rational about all this, not emotional. But all I feel are emotions.

I decide to head to bed. I change into my t-shirt and climb into bed. Looking at Mark asleep next to me, I ask myself, what do I feel? Want? What does he want?

I lay awake most of the night thinking and wondering.

Is Paul right, should I be trying at home, and see if I can make it work or not?

Over the next few days, I put on a brave face, pretending that I am all fine when I am cracking underneath. Between work and home, I just keep going like routine. The kids are excited about Christmas, and I try to keep the Christmas spirit alive at home with shopping, decorations, Christmas dinner preps and presents for my kids. I am torn up inside and can't let it be seen.

Paul is emailing and communicating about work and limited to basic-only chat. I know he, too, is struggling emotionally, and trying to be brave about it.

The 23rd arrives and we are finishing up. Paul arranged for an end-of-the-year conference call with all the managers and me.

I open the call at 9 AM as Paul asked for an early pre-shop opening call.

When all are logged in and on camera, Paul immediately takes over.

"Morning all, this was supposed to be a review meeting, but I am going to make it a short and sweet one.

Thank you all for the year ye have put down. I know I have made a lot of changes and ye have worked with all involved to help transform your individual shops and work as a group. I appreciate ye were all faced with uncertainty after Ralph.

I committed a bonus for making this work and I can confirm that everyone will get a bonus as promised and that is being transferred into your accounts today and all tax is paid. You will get an email showing your gross and net figures, so you see exactly what is paid.

Thank you all for your support and the transition work. Next year is a new year. I know you have a busy Christmas period ahead with last-minute shopping and sales in the new year. Have a great Christmas and New Year. We shall arrange a New Year's meeting for the end of January to look at the year ahead. Another overnight in London or Manchester, with partners if you wish.

Now if nothing urgent, I will let ye back to it."

There were Christmas wishes all around and the meeting ended. Slowly, one by one, all started to exit the meeting. Some stayed a little longer, chatting with Paul, and discussing their plans with him, and some shared ideas with him. I stayed, watching all of them leave, until all were gone except me and Paul.

"Hi Paul, how are you, it feels like we haven't spoken all week."

"I am good, busy, will be glad of a break for Christmas and time with the kids, see what to do with them. I may even go up to Fort William for a few days in the new year. How are you?"

"Honestly, rough few days, a lot of thinking, and have to say you caught me unaware last week. But I know I have been consumed and neglected by you."

"Look you have a lot on your plate and Christmas is for the kids and family. Good chance for you to re-evaluate. Also, your bonus is going into your account. It is a one-off 20% of your salary. I hope you think it is enough. Whatever you do I want work to continue, you are good at this and what you do and a vital part of the company."

"20% is fine, thank you. I was not even thinking about it, more about us and everything else."
"I know, go away and have a good Christmas. Enjoy the kids and a break from work. Buy something nice with your bonus. A reward for you. Some pampering. I must go here. I promised I would take Rachel to town; shopping and she seems in a hurry. We will talk soon. I am always here; you know that if you need to talk. Now finish up there and enjoy Christmas." He hardly lets me get a word in. I can feel he does not want to talk about this.

Paul heads off and I sit and look at the screen. What now? I hear my email ping and open it. It is an email with my bonus details.

I read it and it is saying 30% not twenty and I see the figures. The two are 30%, not 20%.

I check my bank account and the amount there is as per the email.

I pick up my phone. I go to dial Paul and then decide to text.

Maria: Paul there was a mistake in the bonus. Accounts have sent me 30% not 20%. I will contact them and arrange a refund.

30 minutes pass and nothing. The phone pings.

Paul: No, 30% is right, I just mentioned 20% to see if you would complain or say it was not enough. Sorry, I was messing a bit with you, I wanted to surprise you. Go use the extra and get something nice. Not like I can get you a gift you can bring home. Buy something for you, knowing it was from me.

Maria: Thank you. It is way more than I expected. Enjoy your time with Rachel. Oh, to be a millionaire shopping at Christmas. 😊 If only Rachel knew, she would dent that wallet.

Paul: Just as well only you know so, isn't it?

I head off home and walking in I meet Mark and Ursula. "What are you doing home, Mark?"

"I could say the same to you. I finished early and came home to give Ursula the rest of the day off. And you?"

"Paul called it a day after the 9 AM meeting. Told me to finish up and go home and enjoy Christmas."

Looking over at Ursula I smile as best I can, wondering what they have been up to, "Thanks for all your help, Ursula. I know you have done a lot of late nights, enjoy Christmas and there are an extra week's wages as a thank you. I will transfer it today. Have a great Christmas."

I drop my stuff on the counter, go to freshen myself a little. But realise I can't watch Ursula with Mark anymore. I feel anger boiling in me, and I need some air before I lose my cool. I head out and two minutes later Mark follows.

"That was a bit generous, a week. We paid her for the extra hours."

"I know but it is Christmas and a long year. Without her, it would have been a strain. Anyway, it is done now, I thought you would be happy enough to give her a bonus."

"Done now, so I presume you will pay it."

The kids come bounding it, the school holiday start today. They are all excited. The excitement is contagious, and I just say, "Come on, let's go for lunch, I am feeling generous."

I glance over at Mark, and he asks, "Am I invited?"

"Of course." I know for kid's sake; I need to keep Mark with me.

We head off to the Trafford center.

First stop is lunch and then we hit the shops. I say no to very little. In fairness, demands were not too expensive.

Mark is enjoying the time with the kids and just going with the flow. I take the girls and we split up for a while. I got a new shirt and small bits for Mark for Christmas. But I decide to splash out a little on him. If I am going to try, I might as well. I go and get him a new camera; he may enjoy it for his new job. He seems to be spending more time onsite.

It was a lovely day and the kids run to their rooms with their shopping as soon as we got home. Mark comes into the kitchen to me.

"You were very generous today. How come? I know it is Christmas. But still."

"I got my bonus, it was 30%, way more than I expected."

"That was very generous, who am I to complain? Now let's just try and enjoy Christmas, it has been a long year."

I don't want to talk about work or what Paul gave me. It will bring my mind back to him. *Should I give Mark and me a shot? Have I been too uptight with Mark? Am I trying to ruin my marriage? Have I been trying to do this all along?* My mind broils query after query, and each leaves me speechless.

I have this Christmas to sort my life. The thought of it bothers me. While everyone else celebrates, I, on the other hand, have some life-changing decisions to make.

Chapter 17

PAUL'S POV

Christmas eve comes and finally everyone is home. We really don't get much time together anymore.

Over dinner, everyone is focusing on Rachel as always.

She may be growing up, but she is still the baby for everyone, and everyone takes care of her. She has her shopping list of what she wants, and it's a pretty long list. Come 9 PM, she heads to her room and is lost in her phone again.

I ask Matthew and Sarah to join me for a drink.

"So how are ye, been a busy year. Sarah, how is the cottage? Who knows Matthew may want a weekend away, I see things getting serious with his new girlfriend?" I smirk over at Sarah as Matthew goes red.

Sarah laughs and says, "Oh the love nest is ready, a few more small furnishings and good to go. "

I can see she is so proud of herself. She pulls out her phone and shows us photographs of the house.

It really looks great.

"So, how far over budget did you go?"

"Not at all, the budget is gone and a few things to get, but the cottage is done and on budget." There is a huge smile on her face, she feels proud of herself.

"Wow Sarah, that is amazing, I was expecting an extra few thousand, and budgeted on the same. You must have worked hard to do that. How about we all head up for a few days, enjoy it and maybe finish it together."

"Yes, I have stayed a few times, rough enough at the time, but nearly ready now. Fit to be used, maybe a few more home comforts are needed if the budget can be topped up. It is a gorgeous old house, a great escape, I can only imagine how old it must have been and who was there before."

Matthew comes in on the conversation, "I will be busy in the new year, the online sales at work are way above what we expected, and I expect an online Christmas rush. So, I don't think I will get time off and I want to make sure no problems. This is a good job and I want to keep it."

Sarah jokes, "Oh, Mr. Responsible, whoever saw you growing up. Worried about work. What are you looking for, a promotion to packing boy? You will be running it before you know it." She says laughing.

"Now, Sarah, be nice, from what I hear Matthew has really found a purpose there. The business took off and is far busier than expected and Matthew really rose to the challenge."

"Ok, my bad, I know he is working hard, just not used to seeing it. And what about you, Mr. Lavender, how was your project for the year? Up and down to London, surely you do not need to disappear from work every Thursday and Friday. Do tell. Who is she?"

Matthew jumps in, glad to move the focus off him. "Go on, who is she, we see how different you are. Happier, more confident, man about town, even new clothes. Have you picked up a younger model?" They both laugh at the remark.

I blush and hesitate.

"Oh, Dad, there must be a story. Go on, it's Christmas. When else do we all get together?"

"Ah, it is a long and complicated story. Not for tonight," I try to dodge the question, I have too much occupying my head to begin with.

Sarah looks on, "Complicated, now I am curious, does she make you happy?"

"It is complicated, not what you think. I will tell ye some time."

Rachel walks in, to our surprise. Neither of us thinks she will leave her phone alone tonight. It has become like an extension of her arm. "Where is my drink? Am I missing out on a party here?"

"Now, Rachel, you know, you are too young for a drink. What have you been up to?"

I know I need to change the subject fast.

Getting up, I say, "Give me a minute, I know Santa is coming tomorrow, but how about a Christmas Eve surprise from the old man."

I head out and come back with 3 small, wrapped presents, all identical looking. "But dad you gave us our presents. But never let us turn down another."

I hand them all the boxes and watch them. Sitting back, Rachel rips straight in and the others join her. They are children again, ripping of the paper without care and with curious playful smiles on their faces.

"An iPhone, but these cost a fortune," Sarah says with surprise. "These are the newest models, are you losing it?"

I laugh and say, "You want me to take them back?"

Rachel shouts in excitement, "No chance, my friends will be so jealous. I suppose you topped them up with credit as well." A cheeky smile on her face.

"No. No credit, I set up a contract plan, so we are all on contract, no more top-ups. A family plan"

"Quick call a doctor, the old man has lost it. Did you win the lottery and forget to tell us?"

Rachel comes over and gives me a big hug, this excitement is worth anything.

I watch them mess with the phones and think how nice it is to get everyone together like this and relax. We really don't do this enough. I am lucky to have three good kids and I get to watch them growing up so fast.

Snapping out of it, I did not see Sarah going out and coming back. She hands me a present, "We can't leave you out tonight." She hands me a small box. The same size as the phone boxes as it happens.

"What is this? Surely not a phone?"

"This is yours. Since we are opening a present tonight, join us."

I see the 2 of them look at me as I open it. It is a key. "A key, for what?"

"Your new key to the cottage, we had to change the locks and front door, as the old one was rotten. Not exactly a new home. But yours anyway."

I am overcome with a sense of nostalgia, the meaning of the cottage, the family history for me, and the kid's truth be known. Even if we don't know much, it is a history for us all. Now it has Sarah all over it, her work.

"I love it, now we are all definitely going up to see all your work and finish the place as a family."

We enjoy the rest of the evening and have dinner and drinks. Christmas day passes and it is a lovely day. The family are so happy and relaxed. Sarah's boyfriend calls around for a while, she looks at me and smiles before finding a corner to talk to him. I know I am eternally grateful for her gift. I may not have said enough to thank her, but deep down I know I am so grateful. Her interest is quite reassuring.

I announce we are going to Scotland on the 27th. There are a few moans and groans, from the kids, Rachel mostly.

She says, "I have plans, there is a party."

"No excuses, we are all going, and all will be relieved."

As the kids head to bed, I sit back and think of Maria, I have intentionally given her a wide berth for the last few days. Seeing the kids and knowing how important they are to me makes me realize that they need to be the priority. If I'm going to break the news to them as to what has happened this will take a lot of transition.

I will have to give them time to get used to the idea of this and to be there for them. I know the shock that this was for me I can only imagine when I land this on them all at once. This will be as big a life-changing event for them as it was for me. Do I really need to be dealing with Maria-drama at the same time?

Chapter 18

PAUL'S POV

Heading out early on the 27th, Rachel complains it is too early. Sarah, I can see is excited that she gets to show us all her work. Matthew moans he wants to sleep. Clearing some morning frost from the windscreen, the crisp air helping to jolt me awake for the journey ahead.

I am apprehensive, I am going to tell the kids, earlier than I planned but the time seems right. After a quick breakfast stop, we head again, and everyone feels more awake and chattier. Coming around Matthew starts on me, "Ok Dad, the great reveal. Spill. 3 against 1 here. You are dragging us up here, might as well tell us a story as we go."

I take a deep breath, "Ok, story time. I don't know what ye remember about my mum and her family. But you know she lived in a small house and did not have any family other than me."

"Dad, are you losing it, what has that got to do with anything? You are telling us about your new love life and Miss Lavender."

"Sarah, I said all would be revealed. Soon, all will." I spot a small roadside café open as we drive through the lakes, and I decide to stop again. "Let's get another coffee here and I will tell ye a story."

I watch them look at each other, serious suddenly. Probably, they are worried now that something very serious is going to be revealed. We get a table in the back corner, and I start with the story.

"OK, this is a complicated story. Don't worry, nothing bad in it, but listen and let me tell ye and we can talk after. Your granny is part of this, and I just want you to bear that in mind.

Earlier this year, I was given an estate job, the one that had me up and down to London, but ye know about that. It was the chain of sport shops and ye have all been to the Manchester one and it was that estate we bought the cottage from.

Yes, I did meet someone while on that job, but that looks like it is over, so no more about that. That is not part of this story so leave it.

I was a good few months into the job. It was good, different and me and the accountants were nearing an end, the estate was ready for distribution. We were getting ready to make a presentation to the beneficiaries in a few days.

My boss called me in and gave me a letter. I am going to read some to ye, as it tells a lot. Much better than I could explain."

I pause and I can see 3 serious faces around the table. Almost in shock and some concerned. I rethink my decision to tell them all. *Perhaps, I should leave something out. No, I need to be clear with my kids.*

"OK, please don't interrupt, just listen until I have finished."

They all look nervous; Rachel and Sarah hold each other's hands. "It's all OK. Don't worry." They weakly smile at me, and I start reading.

*5th **March 2013***

Dear Paul,

In opening this, you are probably in shock and wondering what is going on. Who is this man and why me?

I was born in 1950 to a family where I was brought up as an only child.

I discovered in my late teens that I had a sister. She was 10 years older than me. At the time, she was born my parents could not cope financially and it was wartime, so they put her up for adoption. When I was born, they were much better able to cope and raised me as their only child. I was raised near Fort William in Scotland.

When I found out about my sister and quizzed my parents, they eventually told me that they were financially unable to cope, and they put her up for adoption. My parents were young, 20 at the time, and had nothing.

I always had a huge sense of guilt over being raised in a loving, secure environment and that my parents chose to keep me and not my sister.

When I could afford to, I went about trying to track her down. I did not know what I was going to do when I found her. But felt I needed to know she was at least ok.

It took many years of investigation and with adoption records sealed, it was hard. But I found her. I am sure by now you have guessed; it was your mother. I am your uncle, be it that you never knew I existed.

I contacted her on a few occasions. Each time she replied, she did not want to meet me or know me. She was raised without a family. So, did not want to be shown what could have been or should have been. I respected her decision, but it only heightened my guilt. I could see how bitter she was, and I was only a reminder of that.

I know your mother has recently passed away, so I am writing this to you. I have respected that she did not want me to have contact.

I followed your career as best I could which is why I chose your firm for my will and for this reason, I specifically directed the partner to assign you to the estate. By doing this, I wanted you to explore my life and learn about it from an unbiased perspective. I did not want you bringing emotional baggage to this but make your own mind up as to who I was and what I was and whether, when you got this letter, you wanted to learn more or not. Which is why you have not been told about this until now.

By now, you know my financial makeup. I presume it has remained healthy and strong and maybe even improved since I have written this in 2013.

But really my objective was for you to learn how I ran my business and the value I placed on the people around me. Though I kept all aspects of my businesses separate. I valued those who make it all work and relied on good managers and people in place. By now, you have seen that I hope. Nicola and Helen, I hope are still at head office. Though their job descriptions may be one thing, they are two people I have the utmost trust in. They have always run any major decision by me, but in reality, I have just approved what they proposed or suggested, particularly over the last 5 years when I lost some focus. They may not realise this, but I hope you will tell them and show them the trust and respect I have placed in them.

The trust I have put in them is shown, I hope in their loyalty to me, by respect for my privacy and slightly eccentric ways.

I have always held a guilt about what I have, feeling that I accomplished this because of a start I got in life from my parents who helped me open my first shop in Fort William. I felt that the money they had, came at the expense of my sister. It is for this reason, I am letting everything I have to you, subject to conditions. I am leaving you everything as you are my only family, but also because the foundation of my wealth is because of my parents' decision regarding your mother.

The picture you have of me maybe of a lonely, solitary man, who lived sparingly, privately, and right now that is how I am.

I will come to the conditions later. But my story is not finished. A lot of who I am was moulded from the decisions on my parents, ...

Sincerely,
Your Uncle,
Ralph Michaels

I sit back and watch them. I see a look of shock and sadness as they hear parts. I see a tear in Sarah's eye.

Matthew speaks first, "Are you serious? What does this mean?"

Sarah finally talks, and I see her wipe her eyes. "That is so sad, you had a family and never knew, and so did he… The cottage."

"The cottage belonged to your great grandparents and where Ralph was raised. It was left as part of the estate. So, I did not buy it, but it was easier to say that. Hope you understand. I know this is a shock, but I had to come to grips with this also."

"Shall I go on? Or do ye want time to think about this and we talk later?"

"Go on, tell us a bit more about Ralph and we can talk about the rest later."

"Ok, Ralph was killed in a crash early this year, his car went off the road on ice. He spent most of his time in London and occasionally visited Scotland. He never married or had kids and led a quiet life.

The cottage is as it was when ye saw it. I asked the photos to be kept as they are your relatives, great grandparents, and though may not be left out, might be nice to look back on sometime. I wanted to keep the cottage, as it was Ralph's, but also in a way part of our history, all be it we never knew. Ralph was obviously very clever with his businesses and how he dealt with them. Always respecting your granny's wishes. Making me learn about his business and people not knowing what was going on.

I am a little guilty of that, not that I thought of it, but I took his lead, in giving Sarah the job of the cottage and hopefully learn a bit about it. But also, Matthew, I wanted to see how you worked in the business and did you have any real interest."

"You mean, when you pushed me into the job interview, you are involved in that business other than a solicitor?"

"Yes, and Maria knows everything, she had too really. She was also told to cut you no slack, other than had to hire you. She says you are very impressive and interested and speaks highly of your interest.

Come on let's hit the road, and maybe ye will look at this trip a bit differently now. Take your time, I have booked a hotel for tonight anyway, so we can look at the cottage and see what's next. Gives us time to talk over dinner as well tonight."

The drive was quiet, Rachel was asking about her grandmother on and off. She did not really know her or remember her.

The others I could see were thinking and absorbing it, the magnitude of it. As we approached Fort William, we turned down to the cottage.

"Come on Sarah. Give us all the guided tour." The outside was freshly painted white.

As we enter the house, Sarah leads, and we all follow in quietly. As if remembering what we never knew.

"Come on, guys. Show some excitement here. This will be our holiday home. Something to be excited about. Don't be so quiet. I know today was a surprise. But it is all good. We will look at Sarah's work and then head to town. Make a list of what's needed to finish. Sarah, do you have a list?"

"Yes, Dad. But let's see."

When leaving, "Will we call to the shop in town? Caroline runs it. She has always worked there. Her mother, Lilly used to be the manager. She worked there since it opened until she died. Caroline knew Ralph. She is very friendly."

We all agreed and headed to town. Walking towards the shop, Rachel starts. "Does this mean we get everything free? Oh, new clothes."

I laugh at that thought. "No, ye will get staff discount, each shop is the responsibility of the manager so any stock you take free, it affects them and profit and losses."

Walking in, Caroline sees me and heads over. "Hi, Paul. You are far from home. Is this your family?"

I introduce them. "I have been telling them today about Ralph and the history here and he was my uncle, and I am the new owner of the shops. So, excuse them if they are a little in shock. They have been told no liberties here or anywhere else. Staff discount as far as it goes."

Smiling at them, Caroline says, "Well, someone got a shock today. Why don't ye look around, ask me anything? Do ye know anything about the shops?"

Matthew interjects, "A little. I have been working online sales in Manchester in the distribution centre. But this is all news to me, too. I had no idea."

"Well, look around, I will talk to your dad. Staff discount is 20% off list or 10% off sale price."

I say, "Poke around and I will be back. I will talk to Caroline."

We head to a quiet corner. "Well, they must be in shock, anything you need me to do?"

"I don't think so. Answer any questions if they ask. Whatever they want to know. No real secrets or surprises there. Are you or your husband free for dinner tomorrow evening? If they have questions. Would be nice for Sarah or Matthew to have a friendly face if they come up here."

"I am free, I will check on a sitter. I will let you know."

As we walk back, Rachel comes up with a purple puffed jacket. Caroline says, "Oh, new stock good choice."

She smiles up at me, "Dad. Please. 20% off to you."

Caroline and I laugh. "So, it begins. Ok, go on. I will sort it. Ask if the others want anything and we will sort them."

When she goes, Caroline continues, "Do you just want to take for them or an account?" Caroline asks. "Seems a bit daft you are paying."

"No, I will pay and let them see me. If I pay, then they have no excuse. If I don't, they may think it is ok to just take and not pay. If I am on my own, I might just charge, and you can bill as returns so as not to show up as shop lift or loss. I don't want to affect your bottom line."

"Fair enough, boss." She smiles, approving my stance.

Sarah and Matthew don't buy anything. More taking it all in.

Over dinner, we chat about it and make a plan to finish the cottage, and furniture and agree to look tomorrow in the sales. They have loads of Ralph questions, so I suggest dinner with Caroline as she is the only one who knew him well.

They all agree, we enjoy a nice family dinner, the children are giving out to me for not telling them everything before now, mixed with some serious questions, as to, will this make any difference to them. The early start is catching up on them and we take an early night.

The rest of the trip is spent exploring the area and doing the rest of the furniture shopping for the cottage. Sarah will come back in a couple weeks and finish the cottage before we stay there ourselves. Caroline and Sarah get on very well over dinner and have agreed to meet up for a chat the next time Sarah is in Fort William.

By the time New Year comes round, we're all back in Manchester, the children are beginning to get their heads around the revelations. I reassure them nothing is going to change, their work and school will continue as normal and we will be continuing to live where we are.

Matthew heads back to work as normal and tells me that he does not wish to tell anybody the news. He really likes the job and does not want to change the relationship he has with his co-workers and if they knew that he was the owner's son, then the behaviour was bound to change towards him.

Sarah has nothing to do with the company so there is very little upheaval from her perspective.

Rachel, as expected, is taking the more teenage approach and is just more interested in finding out if we are wealthy. That was really only to be expected.

Over the Christmas period, I am in contact with Maria a little, more responding to her than anything else. I tell her that the children know Matthew and how he wants to approach it.

Having the children know the main part of the story and a change in my work position feels like a major load has been lifted. I no longer need to be hiding that part of life and pretending to just be at work as usual.

The big question now is, what about Maria? What am I going to do with her? The space has given me an opportunity to think, and I know we must sit down and talk about where this is going or isn't going as it may be.

Her behaviour over the last month or two has been very obsessive to Mark. It is clear that he is having some form of an affair, the question appears to be with who.

She does need to decide what she wants and who she wants. If she is just fixated on Mark and who he may or may not be seeing, it is obvious that she has not moved on from him to the point that she can be committed to any other relationship.

Everything seemed to be fine until she had heightened suspicions about Mark, which highlights that she is running a double standard. Things were much less complicated when we were in London, we just had our time away to ourselves and our other life was left behind. But since Maria got suspicious and then became obsessive about Mark, her behavior has changed. I have tried to put it to one side, waiting to see if Maria can combat this and what am I supposed to do if she can't.

We always said that what we were doing should not impact our families. So much has changed since we started this. Maria's situation is complicated by what Mark is doing and now I have everything to deal with in my life. Maybe it is time to look at a clean start. Let Maria focus on her family and let me focus on mine. Remove any complication that we being together has created.

Perhaps pulling back will just give her space, us some space.

Chapter 19

MARIA

By the time February rolls around, everything is running smoothly in the office. The Holland shop is up and running and staffed. Out of all the chaos going on, that is one thing I feel proud of. I am elated to have been a part of this process, and now I can watch it all come to fruition.

Matthew has stayed where he is in online sales and his interest is obvious. If anything, knowing that he has a vested interest now is motivating him. Matthew and I have been getting along. We had a coffee in January, and he told me of his surprise about Paul's inheritance and asked me not to tell anyone at work. Everyone knows Matthew is Paul's son, but do not know Paul owns the shops. It keeps him less of an intimidating figure, I guess. Or he doesn't want his staff to fear him like they would have feared the owner.

I am still trying to get my head around Mark. I have been shelving my suspicions of Mark since Christmas and not sharing with Paul, I told him I came to grips with it and there isn't a lot I can do about it. After all, it was only a suspicion.

I could see things were different with Paul. We had a little fun once, but he was keeping a bit more distance. Being guarded. I could not bear to lose him. I wanted what we had. I wanted a weekend. I wanted another romantic getaway with him. I wanted really to escape my realities with him. But then again, we all do return to our realities. My reality is being straddled between my family and Paul; I can't lose either. I felt like I was losing Paul.

I continued to pursue Mark's whereabouts. He booked a weekend in Germany for a match. I checked. Yes, it was on, and speaking to Sandra, Gordon's wife, he was going too.

So, I checked with Nicole and found a weekend there was an event on. The Torture Garden. When I researched it, it was a monthly event in London. The biggest in the UK. I booked two tickets and resolved I was giving Paul a playful weekend to remember.

I went shopping for a new outfit and as usual, there were so many options. But I wanted to be different. I want everything about this weekend to be a surprise for Paul.

Nicole sent me a picture of what was Ralph's office now. Wow, a bondage playroom that could put any club playroom to shame. I was due in London alone and arranged to meet Nicole for dinner and asked her to show me the room. I told her I wanted to surprise Paul with an evening there.

Getting down, I headed to the office and worked away. It was the usual routine, to check any correspondence. I spoke with Helen and said we must find some form of method to scan and share posts and save the delays of waiting for me to come down. Otherwise, it was the usual day, reviewing paperwork and discussion options for the shops.

I arranged to meet Nicole after work for dinner and drinks.

She called to the apartment, dressed from work, formal black pants and blouse, and sensible shoes. I always smile when I see her like this, knowing her alter ego. On arrival. I simply started with, "Come on, let's look at the playroom first. At least then you can ask me anything over dinner. We have an hour to the booking, and it is only 5 minutes away."

I could imagine Paul and I enjoying ourselves in the playroom, and Nicole had built enough anticipation to fuel my imagination. Walking in the side door, I was stopped in my tracks. There was a smell of rich leather, the lighting was dim, and there was a pin-drop silence in there. Looking more closely around the room, I noticed it was all dark panelling, from the original office. On the far wall, I could see a cross – the one

Paul and I played on. There was a dark timber on the floor. I believe everything here needs to be felt and sensed, sight doesn't have much to do here.

Nicole pressed a few more light switches. There were glass-fronted wall cabinets lit up. In each, there were selections of toys such as floggers, cuffs, restraints, feathers, ball gags, butt plugs, and more.

There was a suspended type of bench off one of the walls. It looked adjustable. I went over to feel it. It was padded and I had no idea what purpose that could serve. I asked, "How does this work?"

Nicole smiled and said, "Oh, that is fun."

She grabbed the chains that suspended it. I watched as she lay back against it. "You take whatever position is comfortable. You just lay back and put it simply. Just get fucked there. You can tilt the back higher and use cuffs to lift legs or arms high on the chains and cuffed in."

I lay on it and lifted my legs to see what she meant. Glad I was wearing pants; I think to myself. I can't wait to experiment with all these implements. Excitement surged in me.

Getting up, I see a bench in the centre of the room. Looks a bit like a raised bench with a padded top. I see Nicole trail her fingers over it, almost teasing it.

There is what looks like a cage underneath it, as I size it up. "That is dual purpose. A cage for those that like that and on top a surface that you can play on. And space for 2 on it, if people want to play as a group, if you get what I mean. You can secure legs or arms at the corners to the bar's underneath."

It seems like a complicated implement to work on, but I know it must be so much more fun. I can see that as Nicole touches it with a smile on her face. I smile in return, as I listen to her.

There are rings of various parts on the wall, some high and some low. Again, Nicole interjects, "Rings for ropes, there are more in the ceiling."

There is a long leather couch on the other wall, dark like all the others, but Low back and buttoned.

I take one more walk around the room and try some of the cabinets. The ones with floggers and cuffs are all open. So, I can feel the various cuffs and floggers and spreader bars and other similar restraints.

I try the next one. "Locked," I say looking at Nicole.

"Yes. All the restraints etc and big toys as we call them are open. So, if the room is rented for use, they can use all of them. The others are more intimate personal toys that may be inserted, if you get me. These are personal, so not for sharing. If someone is viewing this as a shop extension they can see and if interested, we can get samples or maybe leave the cabinets open so they can be looked at but not used."

"That does make sense."

"Come on, there is one more thing." I watch as Nicole walks over and presses a panel which opens as a door.

Walking in, it is bright. A bathroom with a walk-in shower. There is a door from the other side also.

"Wow, I never saw this coming. Why?"

"Well, by day, it is a bathroom for staff. But if the room is rented for evening use, then people do work up a sweat and in fairness, the shower is useful on its own." She laughs out loud.

I shrug and smile. "Well, I can't argue with that. That is smart and thoughtful."

"There is something more." She walks over to the small desk and bends down, "There is a fridge under the small desk in the corner. It has water in it and a selection of glasses next to it. In case, someone brings drinks. Wine or whatever." She closes the fridge door and checks all the locks of the cabinets, I give the room another good roam around, trying to envision Paul and I in it.

"Come one let's get dinner. I am hungry." Nicole hits the switches off and we both headed out.

We went to our usual place, ordered our dinner, and once I had a few drinks, I ask, "So the new part of the shop. Wow.

Even the shower. Have you tried it?" As I look over, I see a little blush. "Oh, you have, you bad girl," I laugh.

Nicole chuckles a little and say, "Well, come on. Having that available. Got to try it out. Health and safety checks and all that. Make sure it can take the use and abuse."

"So, you? Are you going to try it?"

Looking over, I take a drink. "Yes. I want to give Paul a weekend to remember. I was going to surprise him with an evening in the playroom and then torture garden the night after. Honestly, things have been a bit flat. Things are a bit complicated at home for me. And Paul, I think, is stepping back to give me space. So, I want to try a nice weekend of fun."

Nicole says little, "I hope it works out, complicated is not easy."

"But complicated is all I have," I say glumly. I feel like I can cry in front of her. My mind is chaotic, and nothing seems to be going right. But then again, I blame myself, I should have made a choice by now.

We are served our dinners, which we finished a lot quieter than we started, a much more sombre mood from me, and Nicole I suspect not sure what to say. After that, we head our separate ways. I head back to the shop alone for a chance to examine it all more closely and look through the new playroom. I am just fixated on everything. Also, I need the time alone to enjoy the 'things' that could be envisioned and done here. All the options, they are tremendous.

I head through the main shop to see what else I might use. I decide to go different. I order the gorgeous corset I saw online and a couple of new lingerie sets. I don't want him to think that I just took from stock.

Heading back to the apartment, I head for a shower, get to bed early with a laptop, and back to the corsetry shop. They have an exceptional collection of corsets and lingerie; I'll remember this shop for the next time and save to my favourites.

I decide on my playroom outfit and come up with a plan for the evening.

I text Paul sitting up in bed, I can't afford to have him distanced from me.

Maria: hey Baby. The bed here is empty without you.

Paul: Hi how are you?

Maria: good. I Miss you.

Maria: I had dinner with Nicole. There is a club down here that is organized every month. Torture Garden. The next one is 2 weeks. Do you want to go?

Paul: sure, sounds like fun. Nice to try somewhere new. Tell Nicole they're welcome to stay after if they are going. Where is it.

Maria: I will. Good question. I will check the address. But city centre.

Paul: How are things otherwise? All ok down there. I need to get down for a day or two.

Maria: pic sent. (I send a selfie of myself sitting up in bed with low-cut chemise on).

Paul: Mm, someone looking sexy tonight.

Maria: yes, I am. A bit too much drunk and feeling horny. I slide a strap off my shoulder.

Maria: pic sent. (I send another selfie)

Maria: should I keep going? You want to play?

Paul: why not. You the giddy one. What would you like?

Maria: Send me a picture.

Paul: pic sent.

I gasp. It came instantly and I saw Paul there. Exposed chest. Hair and his smile. He looks so good. I miss him.

Paul: what now?

Maria: are you hard?

Paul: getting there.

I decide that the text is too slow.

I call Paul.

"Hey baby. Isn't this better. Now for a change let me tell you what to do."

"Ok."

"I am taking off my chemise. Slowly. Imagine me naked here."

I take a selfie. Kneeling naked in the bed. My nipples are hard. I am just imagining Paul in the playroom.

"Now, baby. Stretch out and take those shorts off."

I can hear him move around as he takes them off.

I send another selfie. This time on knees upright in bed and touching myself.

"Baby, I am imagining you naked and hard there as I lean over next to you. Taking your cock in my hand, I slowly rub it before I push my mouth down over it. My lips are tight, so it feels like you are pushing into me. I can see you react."

My phone pings and it is a picture of Paul naked and hard. Oh, I love seeing him aroused.

"Close your eyes and stroke yourself. Imagine me sucking. I want to hear you release."

I whisper down the phone "Just feel me against you. Going faster and harder. I want to taste you and keep going."

Finally, I hear the moan and release.

"Oh, baby now listen I am close. I need to cum."

I am soaking. I just go faster against myself, knowing exactly how I want to be touched until I finally let out a moan and release onto my fingers.

"Oh, I needed that. I wish you were doing this to me "

"Me too Maria. But soon. We will have that weekend. Now I am tired, how about we talk tomorrow."

"Nite Paul." And I blow him a kiss.

"Nite Maria, talk tomorrow."

Hanging up the phone, I put back on my chemise and head in under the quilt.

Thinking back on what just happened, it was fun. We did both orgasm, but it was missing something. The playfulness we used to have. The way the call ended, it just ended, a little cold.

I am resolved to make the next weekend a good one. I need to get him back, I must.

He has withdrawn from me. Who could blame him?

I think of all the things we could do in the playroom – all the toys, restraints, benches – I can just orgasm at the thought of Paul doing all of it to me.

He will be back. We'll be back. I know.
I head off to sleep.

Chapter 20

PAUL

The last month, since I have told the kids, has been interesting. Matthew has surprised me in one way, a good way.

He has really got stuck into work, he does not want to change job, but wants to make what he is doing work.

We all agreed not to tell anyone about all that has happened. Matthew does not want to tell anyone at work, as he feels they would change towards him, and he is getting on well and has made friends. Sarah is just continuing as normal and said it really does not affect her as she is not involved in the business, but she agreed that it shall remain a secret for now.

Rachel is Rachel, a bit spoilt trying to get her head around it. All she seems to see is that we might now have a lot of money. She asked me for a credit card, to which I said no. But had to smile to myself, have to love a trier. I gave her a small increase in her allowance, nothing out of the way. She will not go mad about it. I am elated that my kids are sorted and have navigated their way around this new discovery. Far easier than I did.

Work is another story; the shops are going well, and everyone seems happy and getting on with the job. Maria is working hard and in fairness she is doing a great job with the new management structure, and all the shops' accounts are now integrated fully, and the Holland shop is up and running and selling away. My business is better than ever, I feel a sense of relief. Happy that I am making this work,

She has spent a lot of the last few weeks working with Oliver West on the online sales division. Oliver has really settled in well; he seems to like the smaller office structure and more responsibility and autonomy. They work well together, maybe as they are both accountants, and they speak the same language.

They approach me with an agenda for a management meeting, they proposed an online plan and platform.

I opened the proposal to check costing they have put together. They have done their analysis.

The most cost-effective proposal is to move all UK distribution to the Manchester HUB, and the new warehouse as it has huge capacity. They suggested that London could be used for online sales if I wanted, but really it would be like supplying another shop for the sake of it.

The online sales would be run as a stocked shop in the warehouse in Manchester, so all the stock is there onsite. They would supply from the warehouse as needed It made a lot of sense. I hardly find anything objectionable in that proposal.

Holland then would be a small stock for now and holding for the Dutch shop and could be ramped up if international sales took off, so we are Brexit-ready. Before I leave the single market and must factor in border taxes, we can see how sales go and gauge the level of stock. They both tell me that if a Hard Brexit happens, we could have single market tariffs for goods coming in and out and customs checks. Oliver comments, "Could be a real shit show if no trade deal. But we are but small pawns and all we can do is prepare. We set up as an EU division out of Holland and the UK here."

The budget is mainly for getting a large online sales platform going and an additional person in Manchester to deal with online sales. "Online has really taken off and does not seem to be affecting the shop sales so far," Maria advises me.

Maria smiles over at me, "So, boss, what do you want to do?" Oliver looks at her, he does not need to say anything, his face asks the question. "BOSS?"

Maria checks herself, badly, "I mean, who do you need to run this by for a decision?" Checking herself almost makes it more obvious.

Sitting back, I say, "Well, there is one problem in this. The idea looks perfect, but you know, we promised all the key staff job security for 10 years so long as viable. The London warehouse, you want it closed? That would mean job losses. I agree it is the best option, but as the owners are honourable, they will stick to the conditions. Find another option, or more to the point find a way to keep London running cost-effectively and move primary distribution to Manchester. Online sales can all be from Manchester as that is where it is set up anyway."

Oliver asks, "The 10 years, what is that?" We had both forgotten that Oliver was not here for all last year's changes and probably did not know of the conditions and 10 years security. Maria explains it to him, "So, you see, we must allow for this. We could try and wind the warehouse down if people leave but I think the new owners won't break the conditions, even if we could find a loophole."

The meeting ends and Oliver and Maria get up to leave, "Maria, can you hang on a few minutes? We can look at the next agenda for London."

Oliver leaves and Maria turns "I am sorry, at times I forget the secret is such a secret."

"It is ok, I know I can't keep this much longer, people will have to know soon enough, or they will feel betrayed that I have been messing with them. But Matthew's position will change then as he will be a boss in the eyes of those around him at work."

"I understand Paul," I smile.

"Now, what is this club you have been talking about?"

I smile more warmly, "Oh Paul, we have not got out in a while for a club or play, since Amsterdam, really. I just said it has been a long 2 months and maybe some fun might help, so I asked Nicole, and she told me about Torture Garden, they are not going, so our training wheels are coming off. I said maybe a weekend of fun might be nice."

"And home? What about Mark?"

"He has some matches abroad coming up so, I said I was going to stay on in London and do some shopping and get a slow weekend. He did not seem to care much."

"Ok, well I look forward to a break away, trying to juggle work and company here is tiring and I need a time out."

As we are finishing talking, we hear a knock on the door and Pamela comes in with coffee for me. "Oh, I do need it."

She makes a point of leaning over the desk to put it down, I see Maria staring at her.

When I look, I see that Pamela has a button or 2 extra open in her blouse, making sure I get an eye full.

"Anything else you need Paul?" the glint in her eye and double meaning becoming more obvious.

"Thanks, Pamela, all good for now, I needed this."

Maria just stands there. Pamela leaves and I take a sip of coffee.

"Really, could she be any more obvious? If she was any more obvious, she would have served herself up, to, you on the table."

"Are you jealous? She is a kid, and I am way too old for her."

"Mm, well that is not, a not interested, just you are too old. I don't like it."

"Come on, Maria, I have never given any encouragement and what do you expect me to do? Tell her to cover up, I am not interested. She has never tried anything."

"Well, she is flirting her ass off." and the big mistake follows next. "And a nice ass it is."

Maria goes red, "Seriously, I say she is flirting, and I don't like it and you tell me she has a nice ass. You not turning her away or discouraging her is a hint that you are interested. And that is all she needs. She will keep serving you with an unbuttoned blouse, who knows how many buttons will be undone the next time."

She turns and storms out.

What was I thinking with that comment? But seriously that was some overreaction.

Maria really got cranky. Maybe the ice maiden is surfacing. Best put it down to a bad day.

Pamela walks back in, "You finished there, Paul?"

Clearing the cup, she makes a point of brushing off me. Ok, now I see it. She is flirting and making a point of leaning over and coming closer than needs be. But in fairness, that is not my fault. Maria was overreacting.

I decide to text Maria.

Paul: Maria, if you want to talk about what just happened let's talk, but in fairness, I did nothing wrong except maybe a playful comment meant as a joke. It is not my fault if Pamela is flirty.

2 minutes later, Maria walks into the meeting room. "I know I was off, sorry. But I hate seeing her flirt with you."

"I am not defending her, but as far as she knows, I am single and available. Look, people, thinking I am available is part of what needs to be for us to be together. I have no interest in Pamela whatsoever. But I am not taking grief over this."

"I am sorry, it is hard to see her making a play for you. It is so obvious."

"I don't know what has come over you, and why such a reaction, but you need to get a grip. I have never given you any cause for jealousy. Now, I need to go."

I head off and leave Maria standing there, I am more annoyed now than when she came back in. Realising that I am being blamed for Pamela and this is the same jealously she is expressing about Mark.

I go for a walk and end up at the hotel we have met for coffee and lunch so often. Sitting back, I think of what happened and over the last few months.

Has Maria changed or has this been her always? Did I just get a social version? She seems to want me, and Mark, and now jealous at someone flirting with me, I don't understand this. I come to reason with myself, our reason for being together. I resolve. I will give her a few weeks and see how it goes, if she is still on a jealousy run, it may be a good time for a full break.

I have enough going on with the shops and business and the kids.

Heading home, I am surprised to see Sarah, I had not expected this.

"Hi, Dad, how are you?"

"Good, surprised to see you, are you ok?"

"Yes, I am fine. Really, I have just been thinking. I spent some time in Scotland and working on the cottage. I have it all done, by the way. Thanks for the extra budget."

"I have also been in and out of the shop in Fort William and seeing things running, I have been thinking. When I looked there and absorbed that it is just one shop of 6 and not even one of the bigger ones. I know we are keeping this a secret, but really when this comes out or not, what will it mean for us."

"Where has this come from? You seemed to take it all in your stride."

"I have been thinking, I have been talking with Matthew, also. He is happy in the new job but does not know what will happen when this all comes out, at work. Will he be able to continue doing what he does?"

I look at her wondering, should I have told them, what if I didn't? But I did, so here we are.

"Ye have been thinking. What about Rachel? Has she been in on this also? I am glad you have come to me with this. We need to sort this out as a family."

"We have been talking, always have. She is fine, she just says we are rich and is not really phased. Just don't spoil her. "

"Matthew will be home soon, Rachel is out and won't be back until 10, something at school. How about we go out and get some dinner and chat, the 3 of us?" I look at her approvingly, I am happy that my kids have matured enough to tackle such conversations.

Matthew arrives in, "Hi Sarah. You are home. That's a surprise."

She gives him a sarcastic eye roll and continues, "So, I have been talking to dad, I told him I want to talk about what is going on, and that you are worried also. He suggested we go to dinner and have a chat."

"Great, I am starving,"

We head down to a nearby Thai restaurant and thankfully it is quiet.

"Well, who is going to start? Tell me what ye are thinking. I know this has been huge for everyone. Remember it was news to me also and took me ages to get my head around all of this."

"Ok, dad, well, I better start. The cottage was a great project and I loved it. But now there is so much history, it feels different. A life we never knew. Then going in and out of the shop, Caroline is so nice. But she often mentions, that she wonders what you have in mind for the shops, and you are expanding into Europe and online. It just gets me thinking you have a big business, and wealth, life could be so much different."

"I feel the same, I can see what is going on, the online sales. I see the turnover of just what I am doing, and I know this is just a small part of the business. I love the job, but I know when I am the owner's son, things will change, the usual banter, and complaining will all stop around me, and will they think I was a planted management spy. What will happen to me, what will I do?"

"Two big statements. Ok, let me ask a question. Where do ye want this to take ye and when do you think we should say I own this?"

"I don't know. Either way it is going to affect my working with others. But I suppose the longer you wait the worse it will be. I can try and give some of the story and say we were only recently told." Matthew then looks at Sarah.

"I don't have the work complication so really no difference to me. I am more interested in knowing what changes to our lives may be coming. The ones that affect us all."

"Both fair summaries. I was going to wait but I can see recently at work it is far more complicated trying to hide it than not. After all, all the shop owners know and those in London."

"Ok, I have a plan. How about I say we will let everyone know Friday of next week and between here and there tell who you want Matthew that you just found out and tell people as friends. Tell basic story details also, long lost uncle and all that. Also, Matthew needs to decide and see if he can stay where he is. I think you can, a new sector of the business and all new staff. So, they knew no different."

We agree on that, change the subject, and enjoy dinner. I am looking at how mature my 2 kids are, they are trying to deal with this and not just thinking we are wealthy or how can we spend it. I know they are going to make some huge and impactful decisions in their lives. Thinking about decisions, my mind travels back to Maria, that is one decision I need to make.

Heading to work the next day, I call Maria and Oliver to the meeting room. I am still annoyed with Maria after yesterday.

They walk in and sit down. "Oliver, Maria knows this, but I asked to keep it quiet for a while, but you need to know, and it will be public knowledge soon anyway. The owners of the company. It's me. I am not just legal here; I own the business. Maria will be running things as normal so no change there, but we can't hide this forever. Keep to yourself for another week as Matthew wants to tell some work friends before everyone. Explain why nobody was told and avoid him being labelled as a plant or spy."

"Thanks, Paul. I was wondering about Maria's boss's comment yesterday and attempt to cover it. Look, it makes no difference to me who owns it. My job is the same. But maybe easier that we know. Faster decisions if needed."

"Thanks, Oliver. Maria, can you hang on a minute?"

Oliver leaves and Maria stares at me, "You didn't give me a heads up."

"I only decided on the way in. But I have decided everyone can know next week. Honestly, I have enough to deal with besides yesterday's unnecessary jealousy outburst. So, it is easier if everyone knows. I will tell my boss today the secret is over and next week; I don't care who knows."

"Sorry, Paul. I just felt Pamela moving in on you and with what is happening with Mark, I lost it."

"Honestly. You need to get your head around Mark. Not nice he is cheating, but in fairness, you have been a bit hypocritical if I say so. If you feel that strongly about Mark cheating on you, you should not be cheating on him. Now, I must go to my day job."

I get up and head out.

My head is all over the shop with the changes and Maria's jealousy fits are not helping. She seems almost a different person back in Manchester than I have always seen in London. Like two separate worlds, we were in colliding in a chaotic and frenzied fashion.

I arrive at work and head straight to Leonard's office. He is inside when I walk in.

"Hi Paul, how are things? What can I do for you?"

"Leonard, I have been thinking and decided that trying to keep my identity as the owner of the shops a secret is causing more problems than it is solving, and I know it is awkward for you, also. So, I am not saying take an ad out, but no need to keep a secret, also."

"What brought this on, I agree, but what changed your mind to let it get out?"

"I told the children in the new year, and they have been dealing with it. Matthew works in the company, and he is afraid the longer we wait the worse it will be with his friends there. It is just too messy dodging around it in the office here also. So, no reason to delay now as the kids know and have had time to get used to the idea."

"Well, that solves one problem. I am sure interesting times are ahead for you. Well, keep me informed."

Heading back to my desk, there is almost a sense of relief. With this no longer a secret, there is no more watching what I am saying or explaining why I am on a 3-day week. That has required some explanation as to why I am working a second job effectively. I am glad Leonard is on board with us. One thing off my rather messy table. Time to deal with another thing, hopefully, they'll be easy to deal with like with Leonard.

Chapter 21

MARIA

Everything feels like it is going wrong. And I don't seem to be getting a grip on any of it. Why did I react to Pamela and her flirting the way I did and bring my frustration with Mark into the discussion? I can see Paul is getting fed up with it. Or fed up with me? After all, who wants to be with a person who just complains about things?

Things have changed now; we are not just seeing each other in London and day to day life is much closer to us. It was good when Paul and home were in different cities. Honestly, more like my life is much closer to us. It is just that my baggage is causing problems, and my frustration seems to get the better of me.

Mark and I are just ships passing in the night and neither of us is making any effort. The house is running fine, but life is strained and there is no real interaction, and the bedroom is non-existent and neither of us is trying. Mark and I have rarely been together anymore, we are two strangers living under the same roof. We are only there for our kids. And I sometimes feel guilty about it, that I don't share any sort of relationship with my kids' father.

And then there is Pamela. I cannot look at Pamela without seeing someone young, attractive that's after Paul. I am almost getting irrational in my thoughts. Losing myself in work is the only place that is working well.

The shops have really fallen into place and Oliver was a real find, he really knows the market and how to get online sales running effectively. Pamela, much as it pains me, is good at her job and working well.

Sitting at home at night, all I want is the old Paul back, to enjoy London as we used to and the escapism. Paul is the only one that helps me cope with the lack of engagement from Mark, whatever he is up to or who. I dearly miss those old days. I don't know what I would trade to have those days back. I hear my phone ping, hoping it is from Paul.

It's a text from Mark.

Mark: Maria, I got called away for work next week, Thursday night only. I know you are supposed to be in London. Can you change?

Maria: I am due in London, but if you are only away Thursday night I can stay at home and head down Friday morning. I can catch up on work on Saturday.

I wonder where he is going and why. He is rarely away for work and all his jobs are in Manchester now. I am just angry, he is messing with my weekend with Paul and London, and we get so few chances anymore, let alone a club.

I call Joan, "Joan, my plans have changed next week, I am going down Friday on the 9 am train, can you cancel the booking please and rebook me?"

"No problem, remember I am finishing early Thursday, as I had made plans as I do when you are away."

It is unlike Joan not to be nosey as to why my plans are changing.

I begin to wonder, Joan finishing early and Mark working late Thursday all started together, and now these mysterious plans. Mark and Joan have been in contact when booking my holidays etc and I wonder.

Surely not, Joan and Mark. Is that who he is seeing? I know she is a bit predatory when it comes to men, but would she go after Mark? I am about to text Paul my suspicions and stop myself. That is the last thing he needs, and I will appear unhinged. I put my phone down and start reconnecting all the dots.

It does make sense, I think back. She took a weekend away the same weekend Mark was in Holland and the restaurant receipt. She ever only changed her Thursdays when I was away, and they have met at the Christmas party and been in contact. I convince myself I have found Mark's lover – my only good friend at work.

Getting back to the office, composing myself, I walk in as happy as I can appear. "Hi Joan, thanks for changing the booking, are you going somewhere nice next week?"

She blushes, "Just a girl's night, it will be on Friday, just an old friend."

"Ok, can you get me Paul on the phone please?"

"Hi Paul, just to let you know I won't be in London until Friday next week, clash at home."

"That is fine, hope all is, ok?"

"All is fine, just a diary clash. How are you?"

"I am good, I have told Leonard the secret is no longer a secret. So maybe you might want to tell Joan if you wish."

"I suppose I better, she will be surprised and better she hears from me. Are you free for a coffee or lunch, away from the office? I want to stop the tension; I know it is my fault."

"Ok, how about 5 pm, I can come to the usual restaurant near the office there."

"Ok thanks, baby, see you later."

I hang up, Paul seems a bit more relaxed, hopefully, he has calmed down, I can see how annoyed he was. I remind myself not to mention my latest discovery about Mark to him. He is already annoyed; I can't afford to annoy him any further.

"Joan, can you come in a minute?"

"Sure," she smiles and walks into my office.

I say, "Sit down, I have some news for you."

"OK, what is it?"

"The owners of the shops, I can tell you who it is."

"Go on." She says.

"It is Paul, he owns the shops and everything really. He did not know when all this started and only found out when most of the work was done."

Watching her, she does not seem too surprised. "Oh, that explains things, I suppose, why didn't you tell me before?"

"I was told not to, he wanted to keep this private, and you know when we were back at the old job, would have been awkward for you anyway. You could plead ignorance about the owners when Jack pushed you."

"Does Jack know?"

"I don't think so, but Paul's boss has known long before even Paul did, and he too was sworn to secrecy. Nothing Jack can do now anyway. There is no further secret, and it doesn't change anything here. Except now Paul is the owner, not just an advisor. But nothing should change. OK, thanks, Joan. You can leave now. I need to get back to work, too." I see her face as I give such a direct instruction to leave. Unlike me.

Joan leaves and I note she has not had too many questions and did not even seem too surprised. Did she know? I wonder, but how, and then I remember, Mark knows, so maybe he told her.

I meet Paul at 5. He is on time as always. I watch him walk in and smiling over at me, he takes a seat.

"Well, did you tell Joan?"

"Yes, I did, and I am sure office gossip will work from there."

"Telling Leonard that there was no more secrecy was like a load off. I can stop pretending and just get on with things. Needless to say, I have not advertised that I am the owner of an adult shop." He laughs.

It is good to see him laugh and relax again. "I am sorry for the Pamela thing…"

He stops me. "Look, Maria, I have no idea what is going on with you at home, you seem obsessed with finding out who Mark is seeing if he is seeing anyone. But really, I don't need to be on the receiving end of that. We are far from innocent."

I look back, "You mean I am far from innocent."

"No, I mean we, I knew you were married, and I got involved, I know I should have said no and never tried. Ye were still together."

"Ok?"

"What are we doing Maria? I know we said it was what it was and just fun and escapism. But really what are we doing? This is affecting you and you obviously have a lot going on at home. So, Maria, what are we doing?"

I did not expect this conversation, I didn't prepare this. I could never prepare for this. I somehow know where this is headed. I don't want to be hit by a wrecking ball.

"Well, you know I love you and all the fun we have had and can have."

"Yes, Maria, but you are not free and the fun we have or had been like a different world or alternative life in London. Things are different back here. You don't seem to be able to manage Mark and could only cope when we had the double life in London. You came and went simply from both."

"I know, but I don't want to lose you."

"Ok, but what do you want? I am not asking you to leave Mark, I told you that would never happen, but in fairness, you are looking for your cake and eating it, too."

"I don't know what to say."

"I know, well how about this. I told you our personal life would never interfere with work. You have a lot to sort at home. You need to get your own home sorted and decide what you are doing. I am staying out of it. You need to sort that. Ignoring us, you need to decide what you want with Mark and your kids. As if I was not here. You know I would do the same if I were in your position."

"What are you saying, Paul?"

"I am saying we need to take a break, for a while anyway. All that is going on with us is messing with your head and home. You need to get yourself sorted."

"But Paul, I don't want to stop."

"I know, but honestly what Mark is doing is eating you up and you are ignoring that you are doing the same. You have 3 lovely kids, a home, a husband, and a life. You need to decide where that is going. We have turned into work meetings, odd dinners in London, and hotels occasionally. That was fine for me, as I knew what it was. You woke me from a 10-year sleep. But it is not enough for you, and I don't know what is."

He takes a pause, and an awkward silence imbues. He takes a sip of water, clears his throat, and for some reason I know, he is going to say something important now. Or hurtful, for me, for that matter.

"Don't get me wrong, I loved every minute of it. But it can't go on forever. I am the other man, and it is not fair to anyone. I did not care initially as I didn't have a life really and had no intention of meeting anyone. But my life has changed significantly, not that I am looking to meet anyone, but I have had to change and change for the kids."

"I know that I have been all over the shop. I had a lovely weekend booked in London next week. Enjoy a club and dress up and each other."

"Maria, I know if we go, we will have great fun, but if sex and a club and night in London is what we are and that is the fix, then what are we, just sex? I know we have been more, but that is not the issue. The thing is you are so conflicted and your reaction to Mark, just shows how wrong we are in what we are doing. Surely, you see that. What Mark is doing to you, you are doing to him."

"I don't think Mark knows anything."

"Come on, surely, he suspects something and maybe just not saying it. Maybe not suspect me. But who knows? Either way that is not the issue. All you talk about is you, never us, never anything that is not you. We can't have a good non-work-related chat and coffee and just enjoy each other, which you only seem to be able to do in London."

My heart sinks. Is this the end? I know he is right in what he is saying but I don't want to accept it. I don't want to end this. What will I be left with? A non-existent life with Mark.

"Paul don't do this. Let's go to London and enjoy. I had a great weekend planned. Remember all our fun?"

"Oh, I remember. Honestly, I could do with a weekend of fun and games, but I don't want to use you for sex and then take time out. That would not be nice or fair."

"Really, Paul. Please come. The new playroom is finished in the shop, and I booked it. It looks amazing. Think of the toys and play. Then Saturday night, a club. A fun-filled weekend."

I feel like I am begging him not to end it. I never begged anyone for anything. And here I am begging the apparent love of my life to keep me with him.

"There is nothing that would be more fun, I know that. But I also know that I would feel guilty if I played all weekend and then said time out. It would be harder to come back as I feel I disrespected you. We will still see each other at work and hopefully, things will sort out for you at home one way or the other. We can then see if there is a future there. But how you are now, can't continue for you. You need to make some life choices about you and Mark. Are ye finished or is there a future? Then you will know how to go forward. For me, I need to deal with my new reality too. My job. My kids and the shops. My entire reality has been turned on its head. I do sympathise with what you have going on. But I have a lot going on also and must keep the kids grounded and prepare for a future."

"Paul, you know I love you. I don't want us to end."

"I know Maria, but you obviously still care enough for Mark to be eaten up by his behaviour and we are nothing but playing cloak and dagger, for what? We both need time to get ourselves sorted. I don't want to hurt you, but we must deal with the reality of everything back here now, that our few nights, a week in London are no longer and everything else that changed."

I can barely hold myself together, it feels like I am losing everything and everyone. I know I have lost everything. My happiness, my love, and myself.

"I must go, Paul, I need to think, I understand what you are saying." I pick up the glass of water, trying hard not to show my trembling hands, I take a sip of water.

"I have things on, so I won't be in the office for the next few days at least, so you won't see me for a while." I have no clue when I'll recover from this. A few days might not be enough to heal me.

I stop and pause as Paul says, "OK" and then I leave.

I know there is no looking back from this. All I ever owned and loved is gone. In a moment, my entire life flashed before me, and all our memories danced in my head, mocking us, mocking our love.

Chapter 22

PAUL

I watch Maria walk out of the restaurant. A part of me wanted to take back everything I said, but a stronger part of me knew it had to be said. I feel bad for her, I know she loved me, and I believed we could have been together, if only our circumstances were different. But here we are, she is married with children, and I don't believe in breaking families, even if it means sacrificing my love.

Finally, everything is coming out in the open, the secret is no longer a secret, and it is just to deal with the perception of it to those around us. Things might feel easier now, I think.

I sit with a drink and think about Maria, are we over, I wonder to myself or is it just a time-out. Is that strong attraction going to return? Are we going to continue the way it was going? How long can I be hiding this from my kids?

I know the answers, but I need to find a stronger conviction to keep it this way – distanced from her and not hiding from my kids. Even though I know, I feel a void in my life, but things could not go on as they were. Maria was like an awakening to me, both socially and sexually.

Whatever about Ralph and his letter and life, I could never have explored it without Maria. I wonder if that is over. I will miss that adventure and for the first time in my life, I have enough money that I can do anything I want, without thinking twice.

Finishing my drink, I get up and leave. A real sadness hits me. After a long time, I feel alone. I never felt alone before Maria, but now I do.

I head home and on arriving I find my kids there. Almost a relief, distracts me.

"Hi all, what has everyone home again?"

"We just think that maybe we need to be around and deal with this news together. We had dinner, we expected you earlier. There is some in the kitchen, just to reheat."

"Thanks, Sarah, maybe later. So how are ye all feeling now that ye can talk about everything?" I appreciate their honesty with me, and the fact that we can talk about things so openly.

Rachel speaks first, "Honestly dad, I don't really know what this all means to me. What will change? Will we move house or what?"

Smiling at her, I say, "Excellent question. Nothing needs to change; we can stay living here and I don't see why we should move. Really what it means is that we have a bit more than we did before, and shops. But that means a lot of hard work ahead for me running those. But for you, nothing needs to change unless you want it to. We are not going anywhere." I smile reassuringly and receive the same in return from Rachel. "So, that's what Rachel had to ask. Sarah, what do you have in mind?"

"Sure. I am not asking what anything is worth, but what is there, what do you have now?" Sarah looks seriously as she asks me.

"Ok let's all sit down, and I try and give you an idea. Matthew has some idea of the size of the shops. But there is a chain of sports shops, 1 in London, Manchester and Fort William and around Scotland. 6 in total and 1 online. The head office was in London, but we are setting up a new centre in Manchester. There is an apartment in London and some property there. We are setting up a new shop in Holland and a warehouse to sell in Europe after Brexit. There is some money, but most of the value is tied up in the shops and businesses and we have had to modernise all of them. There was a big tax bill from inheriting all of this. There is the cottage as well, of course."

I look around the table. "Is the London apartment rented out or what?"

"No, Sarah, I use it when I am there, and if ye need to go to London it is there also. I think if anyone asks anything just say that I inherited an interest in sports shops and a big tax bill to go with it. For me the biggest decision I have is, do I leave my job as a solicitor and just go into the business or try and double job, honestly, it is getting a bit harder." I look around, Sarah and Rachel seem quiet, maybe I have answered their questions for now.

The next questions caught me by surprise. Matthew finally spoke.

"Miss Lavender. Have you met someone? Before you say anything, we have all spoken and we really hope you have. You deserve happiness and we now see you put your life on hold to raise us and that now that is nearly done. So, if you have, please don't be afraid to tell us. We think you should enjoy life more."

"Thanks, Matthew, but no, I was seeing someone for a while, but it is not going anywhere, it is over."

It hit me like a hammer, it is over. I ended it, it may come back, but I don't know. It's like the more I sit and think about it, the deeper it cuts, the more it shatters me.

"Let's all see how this works out. Let's just all agree to share concerns or worries or any problems from this. If ye go into any of the shops, just pay for what you get, don't use that we own it for free gear. Ye can get staff discounts, but in fairness, ye can get what ye need. For now, let's not make any drastic changes, but know we have some financial options if we need them."

"OK. What else is going on outside of all of this? How's all your lives been?"

"Dad, I have a party Saturday night. Can I go? It is at Fiona's house." I know there was always one of them asking for permission for some party or another. This time it is Rachel. And as much as I want to protect her, I can't cage her.

"Ok, but I will collect you at 11."

"11, it will only be starting, how about 1. Fiona's dad said he will drop me home."

"12 and that's it, I am sure Liam will have more to do than drive you home at 1."

She is excited, not been to too many parties. "Thanks, dad."

Sarah and Matthew seem to share some glances, I know there is more than just permission to the party. I laugh and say, "Why do I feel I have been played?"

Sarah laughs, "We are teaching her well."

Everyone then gets on with their night. I go to text Maria until I realise that I can't, she is no longer there for me, texting her would only open the door I just closed and give false hope.

I take a deep breath and decide on an early night. Just as I am going, Rachel bounces up a big smile, "I am really looking forward to the party, thank you. So, can Sarah take me shopping for some new clothes for it?"

"New clothes, why?"

"Ah dad, I haven't got anything new in a while, not like you can't spring for it." She smiled.

"Ok, you know you are spoilt, ask Sarah if she can take you Saturday morning and I will bring ye to town."

"Oh, she already agreed, all I need is your credit card."

I cannot but laugh, "I am not that generous, I will give Sarah some cash for Saturday and ye can work with it." She is a little disappointed, whatever plan they were hatching, I believe my credit card was a part of it. I can rarely stop myself from spoiling her.

Saturday morning, I head to town with Sarah and Rachel. We make a morning of it, and head for breakfast first. It is lovely seeing Rachel so excited about her party and shopping.

"Ok I give in, Sarah here is my card, you can spend up to £300 on a few new outfits for Rachel. Have fun and give me a call when ye are finished." I hand over my credit card to Sarah and their faces light up.

The girls head off and I just decide to go for a walk, nowhere in particular, to pass some time. Perhaps reflect on things and get a grip on myself. I don't want to feel like the loneliest man. I know Maria and I were never going to work in the long run. Also, it just wasn't right. *Or did I end it too soon? Maybe we could have worked out what to do. Maria must hate me now. Did I hurt her? I hurt her, I never meant to hurt her. I want things to be easier, and things weren't getting easier. I ruined her plan for the weekend away; she was so excited…*

Deep into introspection, my phone rings, it is Sarah. "Dad, come quick, there has been an accident, Rachel fell on an escalator and hit her head, she is unconscious, an ambulance was called."

"Where are you?" I stand up and run toward the street, not even sure where I am going.

"We are in the shopping centre, on the ground floor. Now."

I run as fast as I can, and I arrive just as the paramedics do.

Rachel is on the ground, unconscious and covered by a coat, and Sarah's, jacket is under her head. I watch the paramedics check her and as they do, I see the blood coming from the back of her head.

I panic, there is a lot of blood, and she is not moving. It's my Rachel, it's my baby. They work on her, and Sarah comes over to me.

"I don't know what happened. One minute we were talking and the next minute she seemed to fall backward and hit her head on the escalator step."

I look over, the escalator is stopped, and I see some blood on the front edge of one of the metal steps.

As they move her, the paramedics turn to us. "Are ye family?"

"Yes, I am her father, and this is her sister."

"One of ye can come with us in the ambulance."

I hand my keys to Sarah, "Go get the car and meet me at the hospital."

"Dad!" Her eyes bloodshot and tears stream down her face.

"Now, Sarah, go and I will call Matthew."

As we arrive at the hospital, there is still no movement from Rachel.

We are rushed through A&E, and I hear the paramedics call out several numbers that mean nothing to me, and tell the doctors she is not responsive, airways clear, and severe head trauma.

10 minutes later, I see Sarah rush in, and shortly followed by Matthew.

"What is happening?"

"I don't know they are working on her. I don't know any more than that. She wasn't moving when we were coming out."

We spend the day in the hospital and watch as they carry out test after test and send her for scans. It is not long before she is wired up to all sorts of monitors and they move her to ICU.

I just can't leave her. I send Sarah home that evening to get a bag for Rachel, whatever she might need. "Also pack some toiletries, a shaver and a change for me," I tell her as she heads out.

I sit outside the ICU waiting for the doctors to tell me something positive and all I can do is have flashbacks. It has been 10 years since I was last here, and I lost Stephanie then. I can't lose Rachel. I can't lose my baby.

I sit there with my head in my hands. I watch the medical staff coming and going from the various rooms and the sounds coming from all sorts of machines. The activity is a bit of a blur but all I can do is focus on the door leading to Rachel's room. I see Rachel's doctor approaching me with a serious look on her face. She sits down next to me and asks me, "Do you know exactly what happened?"

I tell her "As much as I know is that Rachel had been out shopping and they were coming down an escalator. I'm not sure how, but Rachel fell backward and hit her head on the step."

"Rachel's condition is critical; she fractured her skull off the edge of the step and there is some internal brain swelling. She hasn't regained consciousness at all, she is critical but stable and all we can do is monitor her condition and hope that the brain swelling will go down. I hope when the brain swelling reduces then she will regain consciousness and then we can assess if there was any more damage from there. I suggest you go home for the night, get some sleep, and come back in the morning, there is little chance of anything happening overnight but if anything does, we will call you."

"I will stay a little longer and see how she does."

"That is up to you, there is a cafeteria on the ground floor, and you will find some vending machines and coffee machines near the lifts. I would suggest you get some sleep as there is little else that will happen tonight."

As I watched the doctor head off, I see Sarah and Matthew coming down the hall to me with two bags. One, I presume is for Rachel and the other is for me.

"Dad, how is she? I am so sorry. I don't know what happened." Sarah sobs she is so upset.

"She is critical but stable. Sarah don't blame yourself. She fell somehow, it was not your fault. You just happened to be there. Now the doctor just left and said nothing is going to happen tonight and she will call us if needs be. She suggested we go home."

Matthew has been quiet. Just listening. "What is wrong with her? What will we do?"

"She is still unconscious. Whatever way she fell and hit her head on the escalator she suffered some kind of brain injury, and her brain is swollen. They hope that will reduce and she will come around."

Matthew stands back. Looking at Rachel through the glass. She is all wired up and monitors are all around her. She has an oxygen tube on. A nurse is checking her and making notes.

I watch her giving one last look at the monitors before walking out. I excuse and ask, "How is she?"

The nurse has a serious look on her face. "She is the same. There is no change. But early days. Be positive, she is young and strong. Would you like a cup of tea I know you have been here hours?"

"Thank you, nurse. We are ok. We will get some soon. You are busy, just take care of Rachel."

"Don't worry. There is a great team here and thankfully we are quiet at the moment, so plenty of attention for everyone here. Try and get some rest."

The three of us sit around, unusually quiet. I know Sarah is still blaming herself, Matthew is getting around the fact that we all are in the hospital when only last night we were at home – happy and chatty with each other. And for me, I want to wake my baby up and take my three kids home and never leave their sides. I look at Sarah and Matthew, stunned and quiet, I say "I am getting a coffee. What would ye like?"

"Nothing thanks." Both reply, I don't force them.

I take my bag and head to the bathroom. I need to freshen up.

Coming back, I bring 3 coffees and snacks from the vending machine.

"How is she?"

"Same," Matthew says glumly.

We drink the coffee in silence and then I see midnight is here. "Ye two go home. Get some sleep. Ye can come back in the morning."

"What about you?"

"I will stay. Someone should be here. But we can't all be here all the time."

"We are not going, dad."

"Go. I will call ye if anything happens."

Under protest, they head off. We three hug each other, holding each other tightly, knowing how uncertain and unpredictable this fragile life is. "That was a nice group hug," I try to be a little cheerful, they smile and head off.

"Call us as soon as something comes up," Sarah reinforces her request while walking away.

I find a 2nd chair. The place is not too busy. The waiting room is empty. I stretch out and begin to nod off. But with the slightest movement, I seem to jerk awake. I guess, I just can't sleep anywhere I like.

The same nurse calls in. "You are still here? You need rest."

"I am fine. I will wait. Oh. We brought a bag for Rachel. Not sure what she needs."

I hand her the bag. "I will put it in her room."

A few minutes later, she comes back with a tea and sandwich. "You need to eat, try and get some rest."

I take a walk down to Rachel's room. Looking in, I just watch her. The sound of the machines and wires everywhere. She just looks asleep. Not moving. How I wish she was just sleeping. This time, she needs to wake up. "Wake up, Rachel. My darling, wake up," I whisper like I used to when I woke her up in the morning.

A doctor walks in. When passing me, he says, "Hello. Don't worry. Just doing rounds making sure all is ok."

I watch the doctor check her. A small torch shining into Rachel's eyes with no reaction.

A few notes on the chart and he walks out. "How is she?"

"No deterioration. All is the same. She is stable. Try and rest, Mr. Bridges."

"Thank you, doctor." I stand looking at her through the glass, I feel helpless. How can I with all my strength, all this acquired wealth, help her at all? I feel so weak and small, I just wanted to hold my child and tell her everything will be okay, but I can't. I don't know if everything will be fine.

After a few more minutes of standing there. I head for her room door. "Sorry Mr. Bridges, you can't go in. Go get rest, I will watch her and let you know if anything happens."

I am sent packing back to the waiting room. She seems very serious but caring at the same time. I suppose that is her job, to care for the patient.

Eventually, daylight begins to break, and the place comes back to life.

I look at my watch. I must have slept a few hours.

I head to Rachel's room. It is empty.

I panic. Where is she? Where is her bed?

I rush to the nurse's station, and I don't recognise any of them. All the nurses change with a change of shift. It seems like the start of a nightmare.

"Where is Rachel? A young dark-haired nurse looks up?"

"I am sorry. Who are you?

"Paul Bridges. Her dad."

"Ah, Mr. Bridges. I did not know you were here. She is gone for a scan. She was first on the list this morning."

"Oh okay," I believe, I must have turned pale and after knowing where she is, colour returned to my face.

"Mr. Bridges, she is fine. There was no change. There are a few tests scheduled for today. So, she will be coming and going. Have you been here all night?"

"Yes. How long will she be?"

"She could be another hour."

With that my phone rings.

"How is she?" It is Sarah.

"No change. She is gone for some tests. I am told she will be back in an hour. I am going to change and get something to eat."

"We will be there in half an hour."

"I will be in the cafeteria or here."

The day passes. Drags. We see Rachel coming and going for test after test.

Finally, a doctor calls me. "Ok, Mr. Bridges. There is still brain swelling. The good news is that she is stable and not deteriorating. I would have hoped for her swelling to reduce by now. But these things can be slow sometimes. We are going to keep her asleep so the body can heal. When she comes around, we will know more."

"All the tests?"

"They show no other injuries. We wanted to make sure nothing else was going on. Now, I am going off duty. She is in good hands." I shake hands with the doctor, and we walk out of his room.

There is a hive of activity and staff changing over. I see the nurse from last night. Familiar faces give me some relief.

After an hour she comes down to us. "Hello again. Mr. Bridges. Have you gone home at all?"

"No. But I am fine."

"Mr Bridges. You won't do her any good if you fall over."

Sarah wades in. "We have been telling him. But he won't listen. Dad, please go home. We will stay."

"I know she is right. But I don't want to leave. I don't want to leave my Rachel like this."

Finally, I relent at 10. When I walk out of the hospital, I spot a Holiday Inn. I decide I will go there. So, at least I will be next door, not half an hour drive away in home.

Checking in, I order a family room so that we can all use it.

I head to the room. Finally, I take a shower, I felt dirty and stale.

As soon as I put my head down, I fall asleep.

I wake at 4 AM. I look at the watch and panic hits me. Rachel. I pick my phone and see no one called me. *Why did no one call me yet?*

I get up, dressed and rush back to hospital. Walking into Rachel's corridor, I head straight for her room. Looking in, I see her nurse checking her. As she walks out, she spots me at the door.

"Mr. Bridges. You are back. Not much rest."

"I got some. I took a room next door in the Holiday Inn."

"Mm. Come on, have a cup of tea."

"No, thank you. I am fine."

"Mm," I hear and see a disapproving look.

Five minutes later, she comes back with a tea for me. "Please, Mr Bridges."

"I am afraid to leave her."

"She is ok. Look, I am going on a short break. Have your tea with me. It is just in the kitchen there. Tell me about her."

I agree, as it is only down the corridor.

I follow her down. Then I realise, I don't even know her name. What am I like? As she tells me sit. I just do. She makes herself a tea and sits down. I look at her name tag. Staff Nurse Victoria Edwards.

"So, Mr. Bridges. Tell me about Rachel. You know, exhausted you are no good to her when she wakes up."

I almost feel like I am being a child who is being scolded. But I know she is doing her job, and I am doing my part as a father.

"I look down. She is my baby. A good kid really like any other teenager. Has her moments. But our baby. Only yesterday morning after we had breakfast, she went shopping for a party she was going to. Fell and here we are."

"Her mum?" She asks.

"There is only the 4 of us. Me and 3 kids. Their mum passed away over 10 years ago. Not far from this room. Cancer. I can't bear to lose Rachel here. She reminds me so much of her mother."

"I am sorry. Look, she is in good hands here. The doctors know what they are doing. Have faith, Mr. Bridges."

"I know. But seeing her like this breaks me. She is just a little girl, she should be out there exploring the world, and being herself. But she is tied up to monitors and…" I stop as I know I will bawl my eyes out if I speak any further.

"Paul. There is a long road ahead. One day at a time. You need to pace yourself. Now sorry, my break is over. I better get back. Sit here a few minutes if you like."

We both get up and I head back to the waiting room.

Matthew is asleep and Sarah is on her phone. She looks up as I walk in.

"Sarah. Wake Matthew and go get some sleep."

"Rachel is the same."

"I know I just spoke to the nurse. She filled me in."

"Nurse Ratchet." Sarah smiles a little. "She is just really serious."

"I know, but I suppose they have seriously ill patients and can't really say anything that can be taken up the wrong way. So, must be careful. Anyway. She is taking care of Rachel. I have taken a family room in the Holiday Inn while we are here. So, here's a key. Use that or go home."

She is exhausted. "Ok. Thanks, dad," we hug each other, knowing these hugs are all we have for each other. "I love you, dad."

"I know. Love you more."

We both are teary-eyed when we part, we wipe each other's eyes, and Sarah wakes Matthew up.

They head off and I get comfortable, as much as I can.

Taking out my phone I check my diary. Busy day ahead of meetings. I check the time, it is 6 am.

I send Leonard a text.

Paul: Leonard sorry about this. Rachel was in an accident over the weekend, and I have been here in hospital. My diary is full, and I know I will be here all week. My diary is busy today. I will text my secretary and tell him to talk to you. Rather than cancel I suggest distributing as this could go on for a little while anyway.

My phone rings and I am shocked. I did not expect a call. At this time, it can't be good.

 Answering, "Hello."

"Paul, it's Leonard. What happened are you ok?"

Relieved to hear his voice, I reply, "It's Rachel, she fell on an escalator in town Saturday morning. She hit her head."

"Is she ok?"

I don't know where it came from, but I just broke down. Speaking through the tears.

"I don't know, she is in a coma and her brain is swollen, critical but stable is what we are told. I can't lose her."

"I am so sorry, is there anything you need?"

"No, Sarah and Matthew were here so between us we are sorted. Can you sort work?"

"Paul, forget work, I will get your diary sorted and we will redistribute everything for the next few weeks, you can do what you want, but presume we have it covered. I will tell the others that you are only to be contacted if they must, we will sort everything, I know your diary is always accurate."

"Thank you, I am a real pain in the ass this last while, for one reason or another." I feel at my lowest. If I can't help my child as a father, what good am I?

"Hey, life has thrown you a lot of curve balls in the last year. We will work this out one way or the other."

"Thank you, Leonard, I will let you know when I will be back to work."

"Don't worry about work, we will take care of that, just take care of Rachel and let us know if there's anything you need."

At least that is sorted, I access my email account to set an out-of-office with a general message to contact Leonard with any queries.

Victoria sticks her head around the door, "I'm heading off duty now, she is the same, stable. I will be back this evening. I am on duty every night until Friday."

"Thank you for everything."

Monday passes with little change. Sarah, Matthew, and I set up a rota to make sure to get a break to go for a walk, something to eat or a rest. We make sure there is always at least one person here. I tell Matthew to contact somebody in the warehouse so they can fill in for him at work.

I do not contact the other office or Maria. Sitting down and waiting for news gives me plenty of opportunity to think. I realise even if I contacted Maria, other than covering me for work there is very little she could do. It's not like she could be here with us or provide any significant support without drawing attention to the relationship. I think breaking this off was the right decision.

Monday night comes and I decide to stay in the hospital until about 2:00, Matthew then comes to relieve me. Victoria, in fairness, has been very attentive to Rachel and she does keep checking in on me as well. The corridor seemed a little busier tonight and there is another family sharing the waiting room.

I arrive back at the hospital at about 9:00 AM, just in time to meet Rachel's doctor. Thankfully, this morning, she says that the news is good, Rachel's vitals are improving, and they will try later in the day to bring her around.

The day passes slowly, we wait to see when they will make an effort to wake Rachel. At about 3:00 pm the doctor calls me, Rachel has started to come around and the indications appear good. The swelling has gone down a little, and she was responsive to tests. She has gone back to sleep now.

"Why didn't you call me when she came around?"

"We were just trying to wake her and carry out some simple tests, it is a slow process, and I did not want you to see if it failed. Rest assured that all the indications are good."

"Thank you, doctor, thank you so much. Can I go in and see her?"

"I will arrange for you to go in but for no more than 15 minutes at a time. If you wish to talk to her, please do not try to wake her and just call the staff if she begins to come around."

At this point, I'm happy with anything. I finally get to go in and sit down with Rachel, at least hold her hand. She feels cold and appears somewhat lifeless. Despite the request of the doctor, I stay in Rachel's room.

"Rachel, it's dad. You're going to be all good, okay? Doctors are saying you're coming around. I know you will. You're such a fighter. I know my baby is stronger than everything." I pause for a while; I don't want to cry and waste my time. I haven't talked to my baby for so many days, I want to talk to her now. "Rachel, come around, my baby, and I promise you, nothing will ever hurt you again. Your dad will keep you safe, just like you used to hide under my arm when you were little. Just like that, I will keep you safe."

Matthew and Sarah came back and let me know that they are in the family room, so I swap over with them for a few minutes so they can at least sit with Rachel for a while. "Goodbye, Rachel. I will be here, baby. I am always here." I kiss her hand and head out.

Victoria arrives back on duty at 8:00 and calls to the room and simply says "I hear Rachel had a very good day and that all the indications are positive."

"Yes, she came around briefly, but unfortunately, I wasn't here, but the doctor is telling us that the news is good so far. Her swelling has reduced a little but still a long way to go, I understand."

"I see from the notes that you are really supposed to be in here for 15 or 20 minutes. Don't worry, so long as you don't interfere with anything I won't say anything if you don't. I know how worried you are. I am around all evening if you need anything, the corridor is quiet again and I only have a few patients."

"Thank you." I feel a great sense of relief knowing that Rachel is improving and thankfully all the indications from the doctors are positive, I do note they haven't given any assurances, but at least they're not being negative.

Sarah and Matthew come and go during the evening, and we swap places so that everybody has a good chance to sit with Rachel. About midnight, I head out and walking towards the lifts I pass the nurse's station. That regular walk I make to the vending machines. Victoria looks up as I pass, and probably for the first time I see a real smile from her. "You must be relieved from the day?"

"Yes, we're all a bit happier, a long way to go we know, but at least she is improving. I am heading to the vending machine; would you like a coffee or anything?"

"No, thank you, I'm just going on my break, perhaps you would like to join me for a coffee? I'm sure nothing is better than the coloured water that comes from those machines. We have our own coffee here. Instant but no worse than the vending machine."

"Thank you, that will be nice. The coffee here is terrible, but any port in the storm."

I follow Victoria to the kitchen area behind the nurse's station. Sitting at a small table, I watch her as she makes 2 cups of coffee and takes some pastries from the box in the corner. She offers me one which I gladly take. Anything fresh is a change from the hospital's stale sandwiches and prepacked food we have been living on.

"Thank you, Victoria this is very nice of you."

"It is no trouble."

"Tell me about you Victoria, how long have you been working here?"

"Too long, I have been working in this hospital for the last 15 years and a few more before that."

"Night shift must be hard, particularly on home life."

"It's not too bad, you get used to it. I tend to only do night shifts; this allows me to work a week on and a week off. There is nobody at home anymore, my two girls have grown up and have moved out. So, I am pretty much okay with whatever shift."

"That happens, my kids are still at home, Sarah's away at college as much as she is at home. but technically nobody's moved out yet. How old are your girls?"

"Amanda is 30, she's married in Liverpool and Pamela is 25 and she is living here in Manchester with her boyfriend. I'm lucky they come and go from me a lot and we try and make a point of catching up for a coffee at least once a week. We have always been very close since their dad was killed 10 years ago. Night shifts meant that I could be around a lot for them during the day and thankfully they were old enough to stay at home alone, being 15 and 20 at the time."

"Sorry to hear about your husband, can't have been easy bringing the children up on your own."

"I'm sure you know yourself; you just get on with it. Thank you for the chat, I better get back to my rounds."

It's always nice to talk to her, she seems like a genuine person.

Rachel continues to make steady improvements as the week goes on. On Friday afternoon I get a message from Maria.

Maria: I am in London, I had half hoped that you would come down for work this week, giving us a chance to talk. Are you avoiding me, I have not heard from you in over a week, and you have not contacted the office.

I take a deep breath and I wonder how Maria has not heard what has happened. I know I didn't contact the office, but I thought it might have filtered back from the warehouse.

Paul: I have been tied up all week, Rachel got injured last weekend and I have been in the hospital since Saturday.

Maria: What happened, why didn't you call me?

Before I can answer the phone rings.

"Paul, why didn't you call me? All I was thinking all week was just you had no more interest and did not want any more to do with me or even talk to me. What happened to Rachel?"

"Rachel fell and hit her head on Saturday, she was in a coma until the middle of the week and is still only coming and going from consciousness."

"Paul, I am so sorry to hear this, is there anything that I can do?"

"Not really, I've taken some time off work and Leonard is covering me there, I know you and the others have the shops in good hands."

"You know I don't just mean work, is there anything at all that I can do?"

"Honestly no, even if there was, it is not like I could have rung you on a Saturday night or Sunday and said I need you to come down to the hospital. It is not like you could explain that away."

There was silence at the other end of the phone, I think of what I've said and realise, do I sound possibly angry or just annoyed. Before she speaks, I excuse my tone.

"Don't worry I am not annoyed; I have always known what we were. I'm tired and I suppose I have not applied a filter. Look I must go here, I must check on Rachel."

"OK, please call me if there's anything that I can do."

We hang up and I sit back for a minute thinking about the conversation, short and all that it was. I know that I was the one who was abrupt.

I think back on the conversation, the first words that we had, when she did ring me other than the first few words asking what happened, she went straight into how things affected her.

Why had I not contacted her in the last week and had I finished with her? Maybe I am over analysing this, but I do feel that her only concern in all this is her. Perhaps I'm being too hard, I don't know. I guess I did the right thing. Every time I reflect on our relationship, I conclude the same. I made the right decision.

My phone pings and I see a message from Matthew who is sitting with Rachel now.

Matthew: She is waking.

I read the message and go running to her room. I watch her laying there in the bed as she is beginning to move and quickly, we press the call bell for a nurse to come. She sounds like she's in pain and in discomfort. But in many ways, I'm relieved to at least see that she is moving and trying to wake up.

The staff are coming, and we are asked to leave. Matthew gets up and goes.

They call the doctor. I protest leaving, "I want to stay."

"Please, Mr Bridges, leave us to our job. We will call you, shortly."

I leave, even though I don't want to. As I'm going out the door Rachel's doctor is coming in quickly against me. The door remains slightly open, and I stand where I can hear.

I stand outside and look through the glass and I can see the nurse checking her eyes with his torch and I hear.

"Rachel, can you hear me?" I see her trying to move her head.

"Rachel don't try to speak, if you can understand me just nod."

I see an attempt to nod. It kills me to see how much discomfort she is in, but a sense of relief comes over me, that at least she understands something – that she is responding.

They check her over and I see them injecting something into her drip.

The doctor comes out. Sarah has arrived and we stand there in anticipation.

"The good news is she is coming around, and it is extremely positive to see that she came around herself. I asked her one or two simple questions just to see if she would react or understand and thankfully, she did react. Her pupils responded well to light, far better than before. I would not expect her to be talking for a while, but she is showing some recognition and acknowledgment, it is extremely positive. We will send her for another scan shortly to check for the level of brain swelling. But I suspect it is reducing. We gave her a sedative so don't expect any more from her this evening. Why not get out of here for a while."

A huge sense of relief runs over us. We watch her for a few minutes as she sleeps. I can't help but smile. I feel like I am seeing her get a new life, I am getting a new life. I feel like running around and jumping in joy, my heart brims with happiness. Sarah breaks the silence.

"Come on, let's go to the restaurant in the hotel and get something to eat. Would be nice to all sit down away from here."

I hesitate but agree. How about we book a table for 7. I am going to run home for a few bits. I take the car and head home. I get a quick shower there, fresh clothes, and my laptop. It is only now I realised how detached I became from work. Bar checking email on my phone I was really paying no attention. In fairness, Leonard text every day to check on Rachel and told me to forget about work.

I pick up a few changes of clothes and head back to the hotel. Dinner at 7 is nice. Sarah and Matthew are tired. But for the first time in a week, seems more upbeat. We chat about Rachel and the staff. We all like her doctor. Sarah comments on how nice the staff are, even nurse Ratchet.

"Ah, she is ok, very serious but she has been very good to Rachel."

When dinner is over, I head back to the hospital. Getting back at 8:30 pm I meet Victoria, "Good to see ye finally got a breakout. I checked Rachel's chart. She is making good progress. She is just back."

"Back?"

"Yes, she had another scan."

"I did not expect that today. How was it?"

"I should not be telling you; this is for the doctor to explain. But the swelling is going down."

"Thank you so much, that is a real relief."

"Why don't you go in and sit with her, I won't say anything if you don't."

Sarah and Matthew arrive and check on her. "Go home guys. Things are all good here. Come back tomorrow."

"You sure, dad?"

"Yes, she is ok, and she had a scan a while ago, Victoria told me the swelling is going down. The doctor will tell us more tomorrow, but all looks stable."

"Thanks, dad, we will head back to the hotel."

"No, go home, your own beds for a change. We have weeks ahead of us and she is out of the woods for now." They both agree and head for home.

I sit in peace and as midnight arrives, Victoria comes in again. This is her third time since I got here. "I am going on my break; you like a coffee. You really are not taking care of yourself."

"Thank you, that would be nice."

Sitting down, I watch her make coffee and take out the pastries once again.

I thank her. "Enjoy it, I am off duty now for a week after tonight."

"Thank you for everything all week."

We sit down and chat, about her kids. She talks so proudly about them. For the first time in a week, I feel somewhat relaxed. Knowing Rachel is out of real danger.

She heads back after her usual 15-minute break, and I go back to take up position next to Rachel. I sit there and recall how she grew up so fast.

Chapter 23

MARIA

I finally get back from London, it felt like a long week. The journeys were lonely, and a reminder of what was and what I was losing. I was not in the mood for anything. I had such lovely plans made for the weekend that I was so looking forward to. Nicole sent me a message on Saturday.

Nicole: how did the night go? how did the playroom workout, how was everything working? Maria: We did not get there. Paul is giving us a bit of a break so I can try and sort out life at home. His daughter was in an accident, and she is in hospital in Manchester and very sick.

Arriving at the door on Sunday afternoon, I am met with the usual greeting. The children are all happy to see me and looking to be fed. Mark is on his chair watching the football and reacts as if I am not even there. Stranger is what he is to me.

We sit down after dinner, and I decide to challenge him.

"Mark, what is going on with us? We hardly see each other anymore and we just appear to be passing each other at the front door. Our social life is non-existent, and our sex life seems like a dim and distant memory. Are we turning into one of those couples who just coexist, and this is what our future holds? "

I can see Mark is very much taken by surprise and certainly did not expect this from me on a Sunday night.

He sits at the table and stares back at me. "You tell me, you are the one who is running around with your new job. Ever since you started working in London you have been different. So, don't try and put all of this on me."

I certainly did not expect this, he came right back at me and when I opened the conversation getting ready to challenge him, I find I'm the one answering questions. "I have just been busy, and you know all the crap I put up with at work, not to mention changing jobs."

"Come on, do you really have to be up and down to London that much, now you have an office in Manchester and working full-time, not to mention weekend work?" I am surprised how he has been observing all this time and staying silent all along.

"What are you suggesting, you are the one out every Thursday that I am away, and weekends on city breaks for matches. Oh, I found the Amsterdam restaurant receipt and for the same time the match was on. You left it in a suitcase."

"Well, what about your lingerie collection? Oh, I saw some nice black lingerie in your drawer that I have never seen you wear, not to mention new dresses, and then they were gone. So, don't play all innocent with me. So, who were you in London with this weekend?" He knows, all this time, he knew.

"Nobody, I was alone, working."

"What about your boss? You are sleeping with your boss, aren't you?" HE KNOWS! My mind starts panicking. Why did I even start this argument?

"Well, for your information Paul's daughter has been in hospital for over a week, she was critical. He was nowhere near London, and you were where on Thursday night? How is Joan?"

"Joan, what are you on about?"

"Ever since you started working late on Thursday, Joan has finished early, and only when I am away, and she was away for the night last Thursday night. I remember ye planned our holiday dates last year."

"Are you mad? Joan!"

"Well, if not Joan, who?"

"You are very quick to change the subject. So, who are you sleeping with and trying to tie me up a while back, that was a new departure even for you? You did not pick that up at an account seminar. So, lingerie, bondage, weekends away, apartment in London. My money is on your boss."

What to say, I am back to the wall here. He knew it all this time. I don't know how to recover from this. He is right, I can't say no without coming up with solid reasons. And I can't think of any, my mind is numb.

"Honestly, yes, I was seeing someone from my old job. Why the hell not? I wasn't getting any at home and I have needs. You weren't shagging me so someone might as well. So there. I was for a while but that ended. You have been driving me mad, I know you are seeing someone, new clothes, new look and no interest in me and away for weekends and late night every night I am away. You never did Thursday night meetings, bar once in a blue moon and suddenly every week. Come on."

I sit and watch him.

"Joan? Seriously, are you mad?"

"Well, you are not denying it, only Joan. So…"

Things begin to get heated; I am conscious the kids are in the house.

"Well, you tell me, and I will tell you."

He is good, he had turned this completely on me. He revealed my secret before I could even come close to putting the blame on him. Was he always this slick?

"So, we were both cheating, what has brought us to this."

"Honestly, I felt ignored. I tried to make it work. I tried for sex, but you just ignored me. All I heard was work, promotion, and annoyance at Jack. You ran the house like a business and whatever I did was wrong. I felt like an inconvenience."

"I tried."

"You tried? I saw you occasionally strut in some new lingerie, but that was long after you kept knocking me back. Walked around waiting for me to say or do whatever. How many times had you knocked me back and then expected me to just give you what you wanted? You never spoke to me about anything. So, in the end, I gave into temptation, and you know what, she made me happy. There I said it. I love you and the kids, but you did not want me and ran the kids like a scheduled timetable for everything.”

I just burst out crying. I can’t hold it in. I surprise myself and Mark. Everything comes out. Was it all my fault? I pushed Mark away and then Paul.

Mark does not know what to do. He can’t exactly comfort me and say it will be alright.

He sits there quietly. When I calm down, he says “Well what now?”

I sob, “I don’t know, what do you want?”

“Oh no, you opened this can of worms. You must have had a plan. What now? What do you want?”

“I don’t know, I want what we had and then some. But can we come back from this?”

“Look, tear me a new one, if you want and I will do the same to you. One of us is as bad as the other.”

I lose it. I just start ranting at him. “It’s your fault, you paid me no attention, you, and your bloody football. I was left with the kids, house, work, and everything else and you just got on with life. You were then seeing someone else all the time while I took care of the kids.”

“Get off your pedestal. Ursula saw more of our children than either of us.”

Mark really was not cutting me any slack. He was way calmer than me. Did he care that little? Or was he prepared for this?

“They don’t call you the ice maiden for nothing. But that used to be only at work and then you brought it home.”

Natalie walks in. “Mom, what is wrong? I hear crying.” She looks scared.

What to say, I try to cover it. “Oh, I am upset because my boss’s daughter is very sick in hospital. It is really upsetting. She is not much older than you.”

“Oh, mom, will she be, ok?”

“I don’t know, she is in a coma. It is ok, you can go back to the TV.”

Mark looks at me, "She will be ok; we can talk about this later. Maybe you need a walk for yourself. I will watch the kids. They don't need to see this "

I realise he is not asking me. He is telling me to go and cool off. Where to go? I head out and call Sandra. "Can you meet me; I need to talk?"

"Now?"

"Yes, I need someone to talk to."

"Ok, give me a few minutes, how about the hotel that is always dead on a Sunday evening,"

"Ok, I will be in the bar, quiet corner."

I head down and parking up, I head in. Find a quiet corner, poor lights as I am conscious my eyes are red. I ask the waitress as I pass to send over 2 glasses of wine.

Sandra walks in and looking around she spots me and heads over.

"Hi, what is wrong?"

The 2 glasses of wine arrive as she does.

"Oh Sandra, it is a mess. I don't know what to do. Mark is seeing someone, and I think for a good while. I thought it was Joan, my secretary. But I don't know."

"Are you sure?"

"He admitted it, but not who. We had a big argument and he told me go and cool off. He has used his football weekends I think as cover. Until I said it, it did not dawn on me that Gordon was on all those weekends."

I watch Sandra face go red. She is putting 2 and 2 together also, Gordon knows.

"It gets worse. I was seeing someone also."

Sandra looks at me. "That is not news, in fairness, I have suspected for ages, but said you seemed to be happier. Come on, you spent way too much time in London and new clothes. Honestly anyone paying attention to you would have guessed. You still seeing him?"

"No. it is over, I think, I don't know. I have been fixated with who Mark is seeing for months and he got tired of listening to it, so told me to take time and sort out what I wanted."

"Is he married?"

"No. So, he is free to see who he wants. Sandra, what will I do?" I hold her hands, hoping for an answer.

"Honestly, only you know that. If I am honest, I suspect Gordon is seeing someone, but I ignore it. Home is ok and otherwise; we get on fine. I am afraid if I challenge him, I will push him out and I don't want that. I just accept it."

We talk for an hour, unfortunately can't have another wine as driving.

"Sandra, can you ask Gordon who it is?"

She pauses, "Honestly no. I won't. If I ask him, he will know I know the weekends with Mark are a cover and it will blow up my marriage too and I can't risk that. So please don't tell Mark you came to me."

"What will I do?"

"Nobody can tell you that. You have only one question to answer. Do you want to make it work with Mark or not? If the answer is yes, you better talk to him and tell him, or he may just go. If you don't want to save it, well then you need a plan for yourself."

I think and I know she is right. The question is, what do I want.

I text Mark:

Maria: We need to talk, not argue. If you want, I can stay away tonight, and we can meet tomorrow. My case from London is still in the car.

Mark: Yes, I think that is a plan. I will tell the kids you went to see Paul's daughter at the hospital and staying in town.

Maria: Ok: I will find a hotel and let me know what suits you tomorrow. I am light at work and can suit myself.

Mark: Ok.

What do I want? I need to answer the question to myself before tomorrow.

Is Mark my future? Will I come around that he cheated on me? Can we restart all this? And most importantly, do I love him enough him to stay with him?

Chapter 24

PAUL

By Monday, Rachel starts improving. She is more alert. She knows us but can't seem to speak properly. Still, any improvement is a big deal for us. For days, I have watched my baby lie on that bed lifeless, a hospital gown covering her lifeless body, her head all wrapped in bandages, attached to all kinds of tubes and monitors. How much I have craved for any response from her in those days, only a father knows. The continuous beeping of machines is that reassures me she is still alive.

We have a meeting scheduled with the medical team at 4. It is a long wait as ever, as we watch them coming and going all say as if we were not here. They spend the day doing test. Finally, 4 pm comes and they arrange a sit down to update me.

I ask Matthew and Sarah, "The consultant has called a meeting for 4 today with me. I don't know what the news is. We can all see how she is. So, it could be good or bad. Do ye want to come or have me update ye after?"

Looking at each other, Sarah asks, "What do you want, dad?"

"Honestly, I am not going to hide any of this from ye, so up to ye."

They look at each other. "Ok, let's all face this together."

At 4 O' clock, we all sit down and wait for the consultant. She arrives in and sits down, placing several files on the desk. A serious, almost distracted look on her face.

Then as if a switch is thrown her face and look are present in the room with us. "How are ye all holding up? Ye have had a long week?"

"Yes, honestly, we are sick to death about what has happened and what is to come. Can you just be direct with us?"

"Ok Mr. Bridges, the good news is she is responding well to the point she knows when we are talking to her, and she understands us. There is still some swelling, and we hope that will reduce further. Her speech, or lack of it is a concern and we can't assess her gross motor until she is a bit stronger. There is a road to go here and though not out of the woods yet, she is going in the right direction. Prepare for what could be a long haul here. Rehabilitation for speech and movement. Now, her condition could greatly improve yet and I am hopeful. But I think it is best to be realistic. As this is a long haul, you need to look obviously at the effect on everyone who cares for her. Work and home, etc. I am sure ye all have lives that can't stay on hold for the long term and a plan needs to be put in place. We will see how the next week develops, and the picture will get clearer in time. Some make exceptional recoveries, and she is young and strong. Let's all hope for the best." She smiles a little and hands me the file to review, pamphlets on recovery treatments and long-term needs. She inquires if anything specific concerns us.

Rachel stays in ICU and is stable and certainly, the hospital has said that staying 24/7 is no longer practical or realistic. And suggested at least go home every night. She is in no immediate danger.

I have told Matthew he needs to go back to work, and Sarah needs to look at where she needs to be also. Matthew agrees to go back to work, and he can visit in the evening and Sarah can cover what she needs from home. So, she says she is staying around for a while and can call in every day allowing me time.

I decide that I am going to take this week with Rachel and see how she works out, knowing when I am back, I am back. The week is filled with tests, scans and thankfully Rachel is getting stronger by the day. She is attempting to speak and trying hard. By the time the weekend arrives she is in great discomfort but making good headway.

As I sit by her bedside Saturday evening, Victoria arrives in, "Do you ever go home?"

I look up and see her. It is almost like I have seen her for the first time. I think for the first week I was so engrossed in Rachel I saw nothing. She was so good to me, yet seems like a vivid memory. The same white uniform, something says she looks a little different, but I dismiss it.

"Occasionally. How are you? Did you enjoy your week off?"

"Ah yes, nice week, had a wedding yesterday, so hair, makeup and everything done. Always makes me feel better."

So that must be it, I think to myself,

"You look very nice. was it a close wedding?"

"Yes, my niece. My daughter was my plus one, what an exciting life I lead. Now, I better check on your little treasure here. I hear she is doing much better."

I watch her check on the chart and then check her vitals etc and note them down. I watch her move around the bed with authority and control, focused on what she is doing, and adjusting the machine, checking drips, etc.

Victoria is about 5'6, I reckon, mid 50 maybe 55 or 56, looks in good enough shape for her age, and medium build. Hair looks good now, but I remember a fair share of grey in it now that I think back. She is much friendlier this week than the last. Or is it that I am more present than lost in Rachel?

When she is finished with Rachel, she turns to me and says, "Ok, I must keep going, I am sure I will see you later. If you are around at 12, I will buy you a coffee. That vending machine must be rotting you inside out." She joked.

"Thanks, that will be nice."

I sit with Rachel, reading a book and talking to her. Making plans for her, a holiday to Disney Florida, for all the family. I tell her that we will stay in an international drive, head to the Disney Parks, over to Cape Canaveral. Part of me wonders how she would have reacted if she weren't tied to the tubes and monitors. She would be ecstatic, and probably jump around the house for an entire day. My Rachel loves holidays, and any outing we do as a family. She is such a vibrant child underneath everything. I was chatting away to her and do not hear the door opening. When I look up Victoria is standing in the doorway listening to me.

"It is 12, would you like that coffee?"

"Thanks, Victoria."

"Please call me Vicky, my friends do."

"Ok thanks, Vicky."

We head to the kitchenette, and she makes me the usual coffee, and a few pastries from her box. I am starting to become a fan of those pastries; they always taste so good. The week has been stale plastic vending machine food and cafeteria food.

"This coffee is not great either, instant but better than the machine."

"Are ye big coffee drinkers here?"

"Oh yes, in fairness a lot of the nurses here are, and they are a great bunch. ICU is not an easy posting."

"No, it is not, families in turmoil and patients fighting for life. Ye must be careful what ye say and always attentive."

"Yes, we must, if we say something that may give hope where there is none, or taken wrongly by the family, can lead to trouble."

"Ye have all been fabulous while we have been here. I could not say a bad word. You have been so nice to me, these coffees, and chats."

"Ye seem like a lovely family, and I can see you all are devoted to Rachel, so nice. Now back to work for me, skeleton crew at night, you know. Must let Samantha have her break, maybe you can finish your coffee with her."

"Thanks, Vicky." We both get up and leave.

I say, "Good night. Thanks for the coffee, I will head back to the hotel, get sleep. Thankfully Rachel is out of danger so there is no need to be at her side 24/7."

"Nite." She replies, and I head off.

The following morning, I decide it is time to check out of the hotel. We can commute in and out from now. Not too far a drive. Matthew texts me.

Matthew: I am heading in for 9, you take a breather for the morning, get some air, and walk. I will let you know how she is.

Paul: Thanks, Matthew, I think I will.

I head home and drop my clothes and bag. Take a long fresh shower, I feel so stale living from a bag. Changing into fresh clothes and I head to town. I need a walk and some normality. I also want to see where Rachel fell. I have no doubt it will tell me nothing, but I want to see. Maybe I just want to know if I could have been able to save her, my father-guilt is eating me, and I need to tell it if I would have been able to save my baby if I got there sooner. I know I am being stupid, but I need to see. It was an accident.

I sit back in the coffee shop and enjoy a large Latte, watching the escalator. Seeing everyone going up and down. It looks like any other escalator. I get up and head off. I pass a coffee emporium and spot the machines in the window, all shapes, and colours.

I think of all the coffee I drank in the last few weeks, the joke from Maria, "Charmer, buying staff off with a coffee machine." My universal cure, coffee.

I head in and look at the machines. After speaking with the salesperson, I settle on a Nespresso, there is a new machine out, allows for many different sizes of cups. I buy the machine with 4 large boxes of the selections of capsules. Enough coffee to keep them for ages.

The whole thing is very bulky, so I order a taxi, and write a note. "For all the care you have been giving to Rachel and her family. Enjoy. The Bridges Family."

I address the card to "The Nursing staff of ICU." I tell the taxi driver where to bring it.

He looks at me and says, "Coffee?"

"Yes, my daughter is in ICU for the last 2 weeks and will be there a while more. Coffee is terrible there, but the staff are lovely."

"I am sorry to hear that, lovely gesture. I will deliver it straight away." He estimates the costs and I give him extra, make sure to deliver to the nurse's station in ICU, please. As I watch the taxi pull off, I am pulled back to reality.

I wander down and pass the sports shop. I head in and wander around the shop, watching the customers shopping and staff serving, life going on as if nothing had happened, everyone oblivious to my worries. The manager spots me and immediately walks over. "Mr. Bridges, how are you? Do you need something?"

"Paul, please. No, I am just wandering around, passing time, and felt like watching the world go by here. Don't worry not checking on you. Everything is ok here."

"All good, turnover way up since the shop was rebranded and modernised."

"I let you back to it, don't mind me."

I head out into lunchtime rush of the well-dressed office staff on their breaks. Replacing the bustle of mothers doing their shopping and older couples out passing the morning, I grab a quick lunch and watch a family at the table in front of me. Never really thought I would want to spend time with my family as much as I do now, having taken all our time for granted. I finish my lunch and head to the hospital. Arriving at the room, Matthew and Sarah are sitting there. "How is she?"

"She is good, we got a few words from her. Weak, but she asked Sarah for water."

We all look relieved and look over at her as she sleeps — peaceful and lovely, like she usually looked. None of us speak a word, we can watch her all day.

"Go get lunch guys, I will stay for the rest of the afternoon."

"Ok, by the way, what did you do? The duty nurse came in with two cups of coffee for us a while ago, thanked us, and gave us coffee, nice coffee at that for a change."

"Oh, I bought them a coffee machine and capsules. They have been so good, and we will be here a while longer. Never hurts to be nice or say thank you."

They head off and I make myself comfortable. The staff nurse comes in to check on Rachel, and thanks me for the coffee machine. "We are delighted, thank you. We have put it in the staff kitchenette. You know where it is, help yourself anytime."

I pass the afternoon with a book and watching Rachel, she comes around a few times, recognises me, and heads back to sleep. The kids come back at 6 and I head for dinner. I tell them to head away soon, I will pop back later and check on her before going home.

I head back in around 9, really a late-night review on her. When I walk in Vicky is giving her a check over. "How is she?"

"She is good, speaking a few words, a great start. I hear you were shopping, that is so generous. You know a way to a nurse's heart." She also informs me that her vitals are better, and we can be hopeful for more improvement in the way she is going.

On Monday, we have a scheduled meeting with the consultant. She informs us that Rachel is progressing slowly but steadily and with speech coming back and some movement appearing in her legs we should be very positive.

"Let's see how this week goes, and we will move her to more of a rehab setting. She is stable and improving and getting stronger. Let's now start getting to work. Physio and rehab. It will be slow, small steps to start and she how she copes. We will move from CCU later in the week."

We are all positive. Lots of work ahead, but positive. I stay all evening with her as I am back to work tomorrow. When Vicky arrives, I tell her the news.

"That is great. No more late-night coffee and pastries. Seriously though great news."

"Well, a few more nights anyway, I may just have to stay late to sample the coffee."

"Maybe you will, pastry is not bad either, coffee has improved lately." Vicky and I joke, and I believe, we sort of bonded over coffee and pastries.

By the end of the week, Rachel is making headway. She is improving with her speech and movement. I am elated that she has been moved from the ICU. Past couple of weeks have been stressful to say the least, but I am looking forward to the next couple of weeks and continued improvements.

The neurologist has arranged a meeting with the rehab team. They outline a road ahead where she will spend some time in the hospital in the rehab centre, her progress will be monitored, and she will eventually go home once her rehab is complete. They will assess her and look at our home, asking is there a ground-floor bedroom for her and potentially a bathroom with space for her wheelchair and help if needed.

The last night in CCU I decide to stay late. Thinking about what is coming next, what if she does not get properly mobile again, what level of brain injury will there be and how long will it last? For the last couple of days, I was so happy to have my baby back. But now, I wonder how much of her will return, will she ever recover fully and get back on with her life like before? Vicky comes on duty, and she checks her over. "All good here, great that she is moving on to general wards and rehab. Bet you will be glad to get out of here."

"Yes, it has been a long road. Thank you so much for the care you have given her and for being so nice to me. Letting me intrude on your breaks."

"Well, tonight is the last one, if you are here at midnight."

Midnight arrives soon enough, we enjoy a coffee and pastry, and a good chat. I make sure not to talk about Rachel, but more about her children and what they are doing. She tells me her eldest has her first child now. She is now a granny and feeling old, with a small laugh, as soon as the chat gets going it is over, as she must return to duty.

As I pack to leave, she tells me to let her know how Rachel is doing and gives me her number. We exchange numbers and goodbyes, and I head off – staring at the ICU/CCU corridor, promising myself never to return here. But not all was in vain, in my bleakest time, I found good people here who cared for her. Watching them go about their duties, I see the same compassion and understanding being given to various families and patients in different degrees of turmoil. From the new arrivals to those who have been here longer than us. I see Vicky being to them as she was to me.

Chapter 25

MARIA

Mark: I have asked Ursula to work late, and I suggest we meet at 4. We can then talk for as long or short as we need to.

Maria: Where?

Mark: Bar in the Hilton, at least in public we might all be calm. It will be quiet at that time.

Maria: ok.

I get nothing done all day, I spend the time daydreaming and wondering what will happen. I don't even know what I really want. I don't know what I am going to say to Mark. I know he will be ready with his questions, and I won't have anything to say. I am blanking out on the most important decision of my life. All the confidence I once had, I feel stupid and naïve.

I feel I have lost Paul, but even if I haven't, do I want to break up my home, my family or do I try? I head out at lunchtime and go for a long walk. Not making it back to work. I think of everything. My old life with Mark and the fun we had and the life we lead. The awakening that is Paul and the adventures we went on, and the change that took place when we were all based back here in reality. Was he effectively a long holiday romance, worked when away in London then back to reality? Did I never enjoy anything with Mark, or did I let the fire between us die?

At 3:30 I am outside the hotel; I decide to go in and wait. I look around, taking in the atmosphere of the hotel. The waitstaff welcomes me, I simply inform them I am waiting for someone. And that someone is going to bombard me with questions very soon. I check my watch, 3.40, still no sign of

Mark. A part of me wishes that this meeting gets rescheduled. I decide to wait for another 10 minutes before texting him. Forgetting I am early. Much to my dismay, Mark lands at 3:45, he looks around, spots me, and heads straight for me. His strides tell that he came determined to deal with all this. this now.

However, as I watch him walk over, I know what to do, like a moment of inspiration inspired by the pending doom.

Mark sits down and says, "How are you? You, ok?"

I am surprised, I expected an argument straight out. "Honestly, I am a mess, I have been a while. You?"

"Maria, I feel we drifted apart a long time ago. As you got busier, you got more distant, ran the house like business, diary dictated, and everything seemed to be on your terms. I just waited for my weekly to do list. And I know you are aware of it. So, I need to know what you want to do Maria?"

"If we are to ever see where this all went wrong, we need help?"

"Well, what are you suggesting?"

"Will we try seeing somebody?"

"Maria, does that mean you want to fix this?" I hear the surprise in his voice.

"Well, let's see what comes out of this, we used to be happy with each other, but it feels so long ago. What do you want?"

"I will go, but if you are going to walk in and just blame me, there is no point. Honestly, you seemed to cut me out long ago except when you wanted me. Two-way street. I know I shut down and gave up. So, we both have to blame here. If you accept that, we will give this a try."

"I know. I understand that. We equally wronged each other, I am not going into who started first, wrong is wrong no matter whenever it is done. I am ready to give us a try. Yes. I never wanted to break my family."

"Okay, we will go. With equally shared blame and accepted wrongs."

We spend some time talking, and surprisingly it was calm enough. Probably more than we have in a long time. We agree to try counselling and that I will come back home tonight and continue as normal.

I head into work and business continues as usual. I am still glued to Joan; I feel there is something between her and Mark.

I must head to Holland, to help sort out paperwork for the new shop and warehouse. It is well up and running and selling away, the online needs more set up and more funding for stock. As soon as I tell Joan I am away for 2 days in Holland, she books leaving early again.

Is she still seeing Mark, I wonder? Or am I losing my mind?

We finally get our first counselling session just before I go. I am not sure where it will go.

All I heard was Mark outline how I just went cold. Stopped engaging except when I wanted and turned the house into a calendar-run business. I functioned based on a checklist for him and once done, nothing else mattered. Intimacy went out of the window unless I wanted. it

His weekly to-do list always came. The only thing he said was never on the list, was me.

He told her I was called the ice maiden at work, and though that never came home for years, it found its way in. All I was interested in was work and making partner.

I described him as much the same, tuned out from me, and only interested in work. Did what he had to do and that's all. Romance and intimacy were rare, non-existent, to be honest.

She stayed away from us cheating and except to acknowledge we both strayed and tried and focus on what brought us here rather than anything else. How to go forward not backwards.

It gives me a lot to think about when I am away. Not to mention wondering if Mark is meeting Joan. I think how much I miss Paul.

He has just been a guest appearing in the office the last few weeks. I know that is because of Rachel, but it feels like he is avoiding me. He is not talking to me about her, no more than in passing.

It has been a month since her accident, and I know she is in physio and rehab. Paul is spending a huge amount of time with her and juggling all the work he has. I can feel his distance and detachment. Whatever chance there was in fixing this, I think Rachel's accident put pay to that. He is fixated with her and that is understandable. I just wish he would talk to me.

Sitting in my hotel room in Rotterdam, at 8 pm, I know it is 7 at home. I call Joan, if for no other reason than to see where she is. I rarely call her out of hours. There is no answer. Straight to voicemail. I then call home. Going to ask where dad is.

Liam answers. "Hi Liam. Just checking how everything is."

"All great here mom, we are just back from dinner."

"Back from where?" I am surprised to hear that.

"Dad came home and took us for a pizza."

"I thought he was working late."

"Hi Maria, is everything ok there?"

I hear Marks, voice. "Oh, I thought you were working. I was just checking on the kids."

"Everything is fine. I finished early so came home and took them out. Make more time for them. Isn't that what you wanted? Me to make more of an effort."

"That is good to hear. Would you like anything back from Holland.?"

"Surprise me."

That was an unusual answer from Mark. Is he trying?

"Ok. I will."

"I will let you back to the kids there. Enjoy the evening." I decide to do some work and strike up the laptop. I have an email notification from Nicole.

To: Maria

Hi Maria

How are you? I have not heard from you in a while. Is Paul's daughter, ok?

I feel sad reading it, but I reply immediately.

I work away for the evening.

Checking my diary for tomorrow, I see Joan had set up a meeting with Jan, at the shop. He has new lines in and wants to show me.

I drop him an email and ask him to bring some samples in adult medium and large. I might get some new men's samples that fit Mark, the surprise, I think. Is that all I want to surprise him with? A raincoat. Should I be trying something more playful?

Life is returning to the mundane. I miss Paul. The excitement. The passion he awoke in me. Is that what the future holds?

****

When I arrive back home, Mark is there with the kids. They are all sorted, and a dinner was made for me.

I give the kids some sweets from Schiphol airport and a down RAB jacket to Mark. "Well, you said surprise you. A new line, not in the shops yet."

"Thanks, great for the site visits when it gets cold. This was expensive. "

Is Mark really trying, what about whoever he is seeing? Now I am confused. I never expected that. Honestly, I nearly half hoped he would not want to. I could then blame him.

Over the coming weeks, I just focus on work.

I make a point of sending Paul regular texts asking for Rachel, inviting him to lunch and finally, he accepts.

I book a restaurant for a Friday, one of our usual. I am nervous, this is the first time in nearly 2 months that we have had some non-work time together. I hope we can have a conversation like we had before. I cannot hope for all the other things we did, but a conversation was a bare minimum.

I arrive early and see Paul arrive after me. I watch him walk across the floor. Well dressed, pants and shirt open at the neck. He looks as good as ever but a bit tired.

Sitting down, I get a smile from him. I return the smile.

"Hi Maria, been a while since we had one of our lunches. How have you been?"

He has disarmed me, he seems like himself, not sure what I expected.

"Yes, it has. How are you? We have not had any time to really talk when you are in the office."

"I am ok. Been a long few months, in every front. Rachel is making slow but steady progress. But a long road ahead, I think. You never know what any day brings for any of us, do you?"

"How are you? Are you ok and are things at home settling for you?"

"Messy. But we won't even go there. Let's just say complicated and very up in the air."

"Sorry to hear that. Hopefully, it will work out in whatever way you want it to. I know after our last discussion about us a lot changed very fast. I am sorry if I hurt you."

"I feel like you are avoiding me. Though it did hurt I suppose you were right and then Rachel's accident, I sort of felt helpless. Nothing much I could do or have done even if we were together. Brought a lot home to me about us and you, really. What little I had to offer you."

"Look Maria, it is what it is now. You have a lot to sort out at home and obviously you still feel strongly about Mark because of how you reacted to him playing away also. What we had was amazing, it woke me up to life and adventure and fun again. But I had closed down that part of my life. I think you got a lot also from this and if we were both single, who knows? But you are not and have a world of your own to sort one way or the other and I am overly complicating that. Here is what I want. We are lucky that nobody, bar Adam and Nicole, knows about us. We work well together, and I don't want to lose a friendship and a great manager. I am still happy to be here for you even if you want to talk or complain about home. I don't want awkwardness. If we can manage this as friendship, it will be much more open in, and we won't be hiding around corners. Also, we both are well aware that we didn't want to break your family up. I didn't want to be the reason of breaking your marriage. So, even if we continued, there was no point."

I look back at him. I am upset but can't show him. I know he is right.

"I know, I never knew life could be so much fun again and so relaxed. I know we were in a bubble in London and that was eventually going to end. I love this job also; great challenge and I am in control. Honestly, I hate the idea of losing you, but I know I have been all over the place for the last few months. Can we just do our best to go forward with a friendship and be there for each other?"

"Sounds like a plan, I would like that."

"And I know, much as I hate it, but I know someone will snap you up. Just please not Pamela or someone at work."

"Look, I don't know if I will meet anyone. But if I do, it won't be someone at work, and certainly not Pamela. But forget that. Now, we just need to get back on track and communicate properly. Things with Rachel are going in the right direction. So, let's make today the first day of a way forward."

"Ok that would be good. Aside from everything else I do miss talking to you and would be nice to be able to sit down and chat."

He seems relieved, maybe that I did not try and get things started again.

"There is one more thing, that you need to know first. I am thinking of leaving my job, to be here more for the shops, but really because I need to be there for Rachel and help her. In the long term, it is hard to juggle everything. In fairness, the shops are too big a business to just be looking in from the outside. I need to be more available for them and for the staff to feel I am fully invested."

I am surprised by this; I don't know why. One way or the other it was bound to happen.

"What does that mean for me, my position?"

"Nothing, your role is the same and job is the same, it just means I am not confined to Thursday and Friday here. For now, though Rachel will be taking the time freed up. So please nothing has changed just takes pressure off me. Now let's just enjoy lunch." We enjoy lunch, and he tells me about Rachel and the rehab she is going through, and they don't know if she tripped or had some sort of a spell. He tells me about an idea he has got from a TV program.

He is thinking of maybe working in the shop here, for a few Saturdays, just working and talking to customers and seeing what is happening. Just more to learn the business ground up so to speak. He wondered what I thought.

"That sounds interesting, have you said it to the manager here?"

"No, not yet, just an idea. I don't want staff thinking I am watching them."

"Have a chat with him and see what he says. Better success if you have him realising what you are trying to accomplish. Could be interesting."

We chat a bit about Mark, and I tell him that we are going to try counselling. "See what went wrong and where. I was surprised, I presumed that he would take the chance to leave."

"I hope you get some resolution to this one way or the other."

Chapter 26

PAUL

The 2 months since Rachel's accident have been hell for all of us. She has spent most of the time in hospital and a rehab centre. The kids have been great, and Rachel is fighting a fight back. Quite honestly, I feel proud of my children; they came together when they needed each other the most and believed in each other. It is days like these when I miss my wife the most, I wish she could see this – the love, togetherness, and care her children have for each other. A part of me feels proud of myself, I know somewhere I did the right things, made the right decisions and choices, and have my children together. Oh, how much I love them.

My baby is recovering speedily, she is due to come home soon. She can't stay in her room as she can't climb stairs for now. I converted my study downstairs to a bedroom for her and a small extension gave her a bathroom. Never was I so happy to have had money to be able to do this. Sarah and Matthew brought some stuff to decorate the room and give Rachel a proper welcome back to her home. We all are ecstatic.

We all go and collect Rachel from the rehab centre. Sitting in on her review meeting she hears everything. Struggling to talk properly she gets to ask some questions.

"Will I get better? When will I be back to myself?"

Her consultant looks back at us and advises that there is a long road to getting well. "Rachel you've made a great recovery so far, you may not realise, but your speech is far better than it was, not to mention your mobility. With a bit more work you will become more mobile, and we can only wait and see how well the recovery goes, but it's all looking positive, and we will keep it under review. There is a lot of work ahead of you, young lady, but I know with the support of your family you will be given every chance."

"You're a fighter, Rachel. You'll be completely fine at the end of it. I know it. I just know it," Matthew says to Rachel, patting her shoulder and trying to keep her spirits up.

"Let's go home. We have a surprise for you," Sarah announces.

We're all happy to be driving home with Rachel and she seems relieved to be getting out of the hospital. We get a wheelchair for her at this point as we feel it will be easier to take her out and for her to be able to move around when she's strong enough. Sarah has done a fantastic job of relocating everything in Rachel's room downstairs so that when she goes into her new bedroom it feels like her own.

When we reach home, Sarah tells Rachel to close her eyes, which she obeys. "No peeking," Sarah teases Rachel. We roll her wheelchair to my newly renovated study.

"Open them now!" Sarah is eager to know Rachel's response. She couldn't say much, but we all could see the spark in her eyes. "This is your new room. We've got all your stuff here." The sisters hugged each other for a while, Matthew and I joined in later.

Days go by, Rachel starts learning things on her own and tries to adjust to her new life. We see her struggle with little things, and it is difficult to see Rachel so incapacitated. She has always been doing things on her own, so she finds it hard to get help from us. We agree to bring in some home help and a nurse. Thankfully, Julia is still working with us, and she agrees that she will provide a lot of support for Rachel and any extra hours that are required. As much as we can do now is help Rachel through her rehab and hopefully, she will recover fully.

With Rachel struggling, we make a point of trying to continue as normal as much as possible. Sarah and Matthew go about life as normal. I however make a decision. Going into the office I arrange a meeting with Leonard.

"Morning Paul, how is Rachel?"

"She is getting there, struggling at home but determined to get better. That is why I am here to be honest. I know I have been a pain, firstly going back to 3 days a week and then Rachel. I am more of a liability than an asset."

"What are you saying, do you need more leave and time off?"

"No, I think it is time I leave fully, we both know the shops and business are more than enough and though I was happy to split my time, really Rachel is going to be long-term care and I need to be there. I can't do a 3-way split."

"Paul, we don't want to lose you, you know that."

"I know Leonard, but honestly, I need to be fair to everyone here. You included. I am happy to work out my notice."

"Honestly, I am not surprised. Leaving Rachel to one side, you own a huge business, shops, and retail. I presumed eventually you would go to them and enjoy some of your good fortune."

"Don't worry, I will still retain this office for all external legal work, maybe help with some in-house legal."

"Why don't you take the next few days working and do a summary of the status of your work. We can hand off then as you suggest. The team here have been covering so it should be easy enough. In fairness, you have been here a long time, and we hate to lose you."

"I know, I appreciate that, but I think we both know this is the right thing to do."

"I do, we both do."

Walking out of Leonard's office, there is a sense of relief. I head back to my office and tell my secretary that I am leaving. "Honestly Paul, it is no surprise. Between your new business and Rachel, we wondered why you had not left. But we will miss you. We all appreciate your work and dedication, but we understand your situation. We all wish you well and hope Rachel makes a full recovery."

I drive back home content that people around me support me and understand me. I can't be thankful enough for all the people who lent their support to me at this difficult time.

Saturday comes and I head into the shop in town. I am looking forward to a day working there, a distraction. The manager appreciated the idea of me working there to see what goes on in the shops. The shop is busy by 11, being a Saturday. I see the young assistants working away and honestly putting me to shame with their knowledge and interaction with the customers.

Around 1, I am about to take a break for lunch when I see what looks like a familiar face. I have to take two and see, it is Victoria. I head over to her. "Afternoon Madam, can I help you?"

"Yes, I am looking for a set of waterproofs. . ." She stops mid-sentence, starts looking at me.

I laugh, "Hi Victoria, how are you?"

"Good, what are you doing here, I thought you were a solicitor." As she looks at me wearing a staff shirt.

"This is my daughter, Amanda, by the way." The young lady waves at me and smiles as if she knows me.

"Hi Amanda, nice to meet you. I am Paul, your mother was good to me when my daughter was in the hospital recently."

"How is Rachel?"

"She is good, thank you for asking. She is home, at least, but a long way to go."

"So, what are you doing here? Moonlighting?"

"It is a long story. But now, waterproofs. What are you looking for?"

"Me and the girls are taking a holiday in Scotland soon, and planning some hill walking, we walk a lot but usually woodlands and lakes. I said it is time I got a new set of waterproofs. But nothing too expensive. I know they can be expensive."

I spot Amanda out the side of my eye with a small smile, watching us chat away. She has been smiling ever since we met.

I walk them over to the ladies' section. "So, does anything catch your interest here?"

"Honestly, it has been years since I bought walking waterproofs. Amanda, are you looking, also?"

"No, I am fine, thanks. We are just on a day's shopping. Only mom today."

I take one of the nicest jackets off the rack. "Try this on." As Victoria goes for the tag, I say don't worry about that. I am sure I can get you a staff discount. Let's find what is nice first."

Amanda looks, she sees it is RAB jacket, one of the more expensive in the shop. Before she looks too closely, I help her try it on. It is a lovely purple jacket, and it seems to fit perfectly. "It is comfortable, can you move freely in it?"

Victoria looks in the mirror. "It is lovely. How much is it?"

"Do you need the leggings also?"

"Yes, but a cheaper pair are fine, I don't intend to be in the rain too much."

I pick up the matching pair. "Medium, I presume?"

"Yes, but they do not need to match."

As she takes off the jacket. I just chat. "So, Amanda, your mum was telling me about you and your sister. She was very good to me when I was in the hospital late at night."

"Amanda, Paul here got us the new coffee machine I told you about."

"That was nice of you. Mom was really happy with that coffee machine. And the other staff members, too, of course."

"Your mum was amazing. The care she gave Rachel, let alone the time she gave me and genuine concern. Nice to have someone to talk to, even if only for a few minutes. Especially in such difficult times. It is rare these days to find people who genuinely care. You and your sister are lucky to have her as a mother."

"Yes, we are lucky. I am glad my mother could be of help to you and your family. I hope your daughter feels better, soon."

I look at the clock, "Ok let's get these sorted. I am due on lunch now anyway." The manager comes over to me. "Paul, aren't you supposed to be on lunch?"

"Yes, just finishing with this customer, this is Victoria she was taking care of Rachel in hospital."

"Nice to meet you. Do you want me to ring these up?"

"One minute, how much are they, I don't want to go too expensive?"

I look at Amanda then Richard. "Can you apply my maximum discount and credits to these?"

"Full?"

"Yes, she was exceptional in caring for Rachel and me."

"Ok," and he walks off.

"Paul, how much are they? Honestly, I don't want to spend too much."

"Is there anything else you need?"

"No, thank you."

"Ok, give me a minute."

We watch the manager head to the desk and when returning he hands her the bag. "How much are they?"

"It is taken care of."

"What do you mean?"

"Take it up with Paul. I am staying out of it. See you in an hour Paul." The manager leaves us, Amanda and Victoria look at me confused.

Victoria inquires, "Paul? What?"

"Don't worry about it, it is the least I could do for you. You paid in pastry."

She walks over to the rack and looks at the tag on the jacket. £350. "This is mad, you can't get this for me. Working here you can hardly afford this."

"Please take it. I do a little more than work here."

Amanda pipes in. "Mom, I really don't think Paul is just a sales assistant here, but look I have a job to do, the least you can do is buy the man lunch. How about I let ye to it and see ye back here in an hour."

Amanda walks off before Victoria can say anything.

"Paul, I can't take these. How much with the discount?"

"Victoria, forget it please, how about you get me lunch as suggested and we call it quits."

We head out and into the nearby café.

We sit and chat about everything and anything. It is lovely to hear about Victoria, her family, and plans for her holidays. I tell her about Rachel and her siblings, and how everything else is. I am yet to tell her about my owning the shop. But we talk in general, and it's refreshing to connect with her.

Before we knew it an hour and a half passed as we finished the 2nd coffee. The bill arrives and as I reach for it, Victoria grabs it. "Lunch is mine. And I still need to pay for these waterproofs."

She pays and I don't argue. As we get back to the shop, Amanda is poking around inside. As we walk in, she spots us and comes over. "Long lunch?"

"Paul, sorry you are late for work. Will you get into trouble?"

Amanda just laughs, "Mom, I think he is safe enough." Looking at her she continues, "Richard came over to me and offered to help when I arrived back. I asked to pay for the clothes, and he told me, Paul works with the shop, so he could not take anything. Paul covered it."

I just shrug at them.

"Now, ladies, enjoy your afternoon and please say hello anytime. It was a lovely lunch, maybe we can do it again sometime."

"Paul, thank you, there was no need, even the coffee machine was too much. Can you let me know how Rachel is getting on?"

"Gladly, Victoria, if you ever want to check up on her or me, please call, I would be happy to buy you lunch next time and fill you in. Enjoy Scotland." And I hand her a card with my mobile number on it.

I can see Amanda smirking, to the side. When they begin to move away, I hear her say. "Mum, I think he likes you."

"Don't be daft. He was just being nice." She looks back and I see a slight blush on her face.

"Mon, why not ask him for dinner, to thank him for the jacket?"

They then move out of earshot.

About 10 minutes later, Amanda comes back into the shop and heads straight for me. "Hi Amanda, did ye forget something?"

"No, Paul, I am sorry, I nearly feel awkward, but if I am not mistaken ye seemed to get along. Can I ask you to come for dinner? To thank you for the jacket."

"Amanda, what can I say? Did Vicky send you or are you playing matchmaker?"

With that, I see Victoria follow in. "Paul, I am so sorry. Amanda is just sticking her nose in where it does not belong. I am sorry; you have been so kind and now being put on the spot. Come on Amanda, before you embarrass me and Paul any further."

"Vicky, don't worry, sometimes us oldies need a push. You asked about Rachel, if you would like to come and see her someday, it would be nice for her to meet a nurse who took such good care of her. We can have a coffee and chat. The children can stay at home." I laugh.

She blushes, "Thank you, here is mom's number, maybe you can text her and let her know when a good time is. She is off for the next week." Amanda says.

I laugh, "Someone isn't letting this go, are they? I will drop you a text later and suggest an afternoon. I will see when Rachel is not in treatment."

"Thanks, Paul. Now, come on Amanda."

"I am so happy for you," I hear Amanda say as she gives her mother a side hug.

I watch them leave. Smiling, I am not sure if that was funny or embarrassing. Maybe funny for me and embarrassing to Vicky. I would kill the kids if they did that to me.

I wait until Sunday and text.

Paul: I hope this is your number Victoria and Amanda have not given me some random person's number. Because then it would be really embarrassing.

Paul: Rachel is in therapy on Tuesday Thursday and Friday. If you would like a coffee and say hello to her, you are more than welcome.

I wait for her response, which came after a few minutes.

Victoria: Thank you, Paul, yes, she gave the right number.

Victoria: It would be lovely, but I don't want to impose and you to feel pressurised into this by Amanda. I am free any day this week.

Paul: No pressure, honestly, after all, I did not have to send the message. Come around tomorrow and have some lunch with us.

Victoria: Ok and I will bring some dessert. Is there anything Rachel likes and is almost embarrassed to ask, but the address?

Paul: I am sending you a map pin by text and honestly no need to bring anything. Kids and friends are afraid I am going hungry and always have a house full of food. See you at about 12:30 tomorrow.

I don't say anything to the kids that Vicky is coming around. I get up a little early to make food arrangements and check if anything needs to be done. I don't want anything taking up my time once Vicky comes tomorrow. She arrives bang on 12:30. I answer the door and am greeted by a smiling face.

"Hi Paul, at least I found the place. This is a lovely house." Smiling as she walks in.

"Thank you, yes, we have been here forever really, the last 20 years."

I take her jacket and hang it on the nearby hook.

Other than Saturday, this was the first time I had seen her out of the hospital. She was wearing a nice pair of fitted jeans and open neck fitted blouse. She is in good shape for her age.

"I have lunch, Rachel is a bit tired today, so I expect she will go for a sleep after."

We walk into the kitchen, and I have the table ready.

"I hope you don't mind, I am not a great cook, so it is just quiche, salads, and some dessert."

With that, she hands me a cake box. "I could not come empty-handed; I hope you like chocolate."

The door opens and Rachel works her way in. She is on 2 crutches and struggles but is determined to do it herself.

"Hello." She says, still working on her speech. She smiles as she sees the chocolate cake.

"Hello, Rachel. You don't remember me I am sure, but I was one of your nurses for the first few weeks."

"Rachel, this is Vicky, she was the ICU nurse I told you about, she was nice to you and took great care of you and us. I bumped into her on Saturday, and she asked about you. So, I asked her to call around and say hello."

I watch Vicky as she moves to one side and at the same time turns a chair to the side. So, Rachel could sit without help.

We enjoy a nice lunch, Vicky asks Rachel about how she feels, and Rachel is curious about how she was in the hospital. They both talked a little, and I watch them connect with a smile. But before desert Rachel gets tired. "Nice to meet you. I need to go lay down."

Rachel gets herself up with a struggle and makes her way.

"How is she, Paul?" The nurse reappears in Vicky. I can feel my face drop.

"She is ok, been a long haul. Closest description I have is some form of a stroke. But she is determined and hates when we try and help her. It kills me not to at times. But rehab have told me if she can do something, let her. Pushing is the only way forward. Just don't risk her injuring herself again. A fine line. Anyway. Really nice of you to come and see her."

"It is rough on her. It is rough on all of ye. How are the rest of your kids coping?"

"They are fine. Great kids. Always just been the 4 of us really. Sarah has a boyfriend. Matthew is seeing someone also. The two of them have been a great help and support through all of this. Really, I am lucky. They are great kids."

With that the door opens, and Julie walks in with bags of shopping. "Sorry, Paul. I did not know you had company. How is Rachel, today?"

"She is good. She had lunch and is gone for a rest."

"Ok. I am here for the afternoon if you want to get out for a while."

I introduce Victoria as one of Rachel's nurses who came to see her.

"Sorry. I did not know she had a home visit in the calendar."

"No, Vicky was her ICU nurse. I bumped into her, and she was asking about Rachel so called around to see her."

"Ah. Ok. Nice to meet you. As you're here, any cure for this one?"

We both look at her.

"He is either here with Rachel or working. He needs to take care of himself too."

" Ok, I let ye too to it. It's lovely out Paul. Try and get some air."

"Excuse me. Where is the bathroom?"

I tell her and when she leaves, "She seems nice. Lovely of her to call around."

"Yes. She was so good to Rachel in the hospital and me. Always made sure I was ok when overnight in the hospital. She did night shifts."

"Paul. I think she may have an interest in you as well."

Vicky walks back in.

"Any chance you take him out for some air? Give me a chance to get this shopping away and give him a break. I see you have not had coffee yet. There is a lovely French bakery and coffee shop by the park."

I look at Vicky and she smiles. "I have no plans for the day if you would like to stroll down."

I am not left with much choice. But happy to go. I wasn't aware that Julie was rather professional at setting people up. But I have nothing to complain about.

We grab our jackets and head out. We head down toward the park chatting. "She worries about you."

"I would have been lost without her. She was like a mother to Rachel and a much older sister to Sarah. She was a godsend after Stephanie."

"How long has it been?"

"Over 10 years."

"And you never remarried?"

. "No. Never really got out there. Between work and the kids, life settled into a routine. Going out meant planning and babysitting or asking Sarah or Matthew to sit. And honestly, I did not want them seeing me with anyone other than their mother and so I never tried."

"Never? I am surprised."

"Ah, there was one person for a while. When I was working in London last year. But really was complicated and going nowhere so I ended it. What about you?" I am eager to know her status, and my biggest worry has been if she is with someone.

"Similar really. When my husband was killed 10 years ago, it was me and the girls and things were tight. So, I worked mostly nights, I was around by day and pay was better, so it helped them through college. The girls are brilliant and make sure one is around anytime I am off on Saturdays and get me to town and pop around when they can."

"You never met anyone? Not really no. The girls put me on a dating site a few years ago. I lasted 3 days. Then some other site, I can't remember. All I got was idiots looking to sleep with me. I am too old for that. One-night stands were never my thing. I do get out. I am part of a walking club and love to head off to the lakes and woodlands when free. So, I get plenty of time now. No real ties with the girls gone. Haven't met anyone yet, not that Amanda isn't always trying."

I see a blush and smile. "In fairness, she nearly forced me on you last Saturday. Sorry about that."

"It is ok. Sarah encourages me also, and I am glad Amanda did. Nice to get out and chat with someone I can relate to."

"So, how do you manage working in the shop and Rachel? Must be tiring. I thought you were a solicitor."

"Mixing me up with your other men, are you?" I tease her and see an embarrassed smile on her face.

"Stop. no. Sorry, my mistake."

"It is ok. I am messing with you. Yes, I am a solicitor. But taking a break to care for Rachel. Shops were a big client project. I had to help run them when he died."

"So, the shop? You are working there to keep it all going. Sorry, I am being nosey. But I am a little curious."

"It is ok. I can see the confusion. Long and complicated story, not for today. "

We arrive at the pastry shop. "What would you like?"

"Surprise me."

I look at her. "Ok. Grab a bench in the park there and I will surprise you."

I return a few minutes later with a cappuccino and pear and almond tart for her. Americano for myself.

As I hand them to her. She looks in the bag. "Mm, looks nice. Good choice."

"So, thanks for coming around today. Thank Amanda for me." We both laugh.

"Oh, she is already checking to see if I survived. She is a great daughter."

"I know. Glad she forced you to come today."

We chat away and I quiz her about her walking club and what brought her there. She tells me she loves to travel anywhere and the outdoors. But with work and things being tight, she never managed too much. The walking club gave her a chance.

I ask a bit about her husband. He was killed in a car crash. It was his fault. Working too hard and falling asleep at the wheel. They enjoyed life as much as they could and said they had their own life outside of kids. Always making time for each other. I could see a look of sadness and a slight blush as she remembered. I take the opportunity to quickly change the subject and try and lighten the mood a little. "It is good that ye kept a personal life for yourselves, can often be forgotten when the kids come along. Other than walking now, what do you do for pastime?”

“Not an awful lot really, I meet the girls and go for coffee or lunch, catch up with friends occasionally. It sounds a little bit like yourself so after my husband passed away my focus really went on to the children and work. Used them as an excuse to hide from the world.”

“We are a sad old pair, really, aren't we?” I laugh.

I smile to myself and Vicky notices it. “What is so funny?”

“I can blame the kids for this one, but in the first few nights in the hospital Sarah had you nicknamed Nurse Ratchet.”

“Mm, dare I even ask?”

“I think it was probably the early nights when we were in the hospital when Rachel was critical, you had a difficult job to do, and everything seemed so serious.”

“Yes, those early days can often be difficult, and we must be supportive of the family, when somebody is critical, we must be very careful not to give false hope or appear to be making light of a situation. It often makes things easier to keep a distance.”

“I have to say that you were always very kind to me, I really appreciated the late-night coffees. I can’t tell how much I hated that vending machine coffee.”

“You seem so nice and devoted to Rachel, I know how hard it is to sit by somebody’s bedside getting little response. We see all sorts coming in and out, and many of the families are angry and make life difficult for us when we can't give them straight answers.”

“I understand. Thank you, again for everything, really, Vicky.”

The afternoon slips away as we chat about everything from life to kids to work. Looking at my watch, I say to Vicky, “I better get back.”

We start to walk back towards home and as we walk up to the front door Sarah arrives. “Thank you for a lovely afternoon, Paul, I will head away and let you to your family”.

Before she goes Sarah comes over, I had not told her that Vicky was calling this afternoon, as she walks over to us, Vicky says, "Hi Sarah, it is nice to see you out of the hospital setting, and good to see that Rachel is coming along."

Sarah looks on, a little confused. "Sorry Sarah, maybe you don't remember me, I am nurse ratchet from the hospital."

I cannot help myself but laugh and Sarah goes bright red. I see a cheeky smile on Vicky's face as she heads away.

"Dad, seriously why did you tell her I called her nurse ratchet? What is she doing here anyway?"

"She came into the shop in town last Saturday with her daughter and she was asking me how Rachel was. I said if she ever wanted to call around and see her, she was welcome to, and it went from there. She called around at lunchtime by arrangement and when Julie arrived in for the afternoon, she pretty much kicked me out to go for a walk."

"Mm, picking up nurses in the hospital now, are you?" Sarah laughs.

We head in and Julie has Rachel up and is working on dinner. Rachel asks. "Why did the nurse come today?" She was suspicious. She often worries we are doing things and not telling her.

I tell her about the shop on Saturday, the coffee and that is how she was here. Sarah is listening. "Coffee. Saturday? You kept that quiet. What's going on, dad?"

I can see her antenna going up. Julie then joins the chorus. "She seemed very nice. Even brought a cake."

I say nothing. Best approach. Sarah looks at me, and I know she will get me talking soon enough, that's how she is.

Later in the evening, my phone pings, it's Vicky.

Vicky: Thanks for a lovely afternoon. It was unexpected.

Paul: unexpected. You dread it that much.

Vicky: no. Just I did not expect to be there so long and seemed to fly by.

Paul: oh, I know. Just toying with you.

Sarah was giving out, sort of, about the nurse Ratchet comment. You knew exactly what you were doing.

Vicky: was a bit of fun. Before I ran.

Paul: it is fine. Even Rachel quizzed me when I got in.

Vicky: Amanda did the same. Was on the phone before I got home.

Vicky: I know this might be forward. But the company was nice today. Would you like to come to dinner with me at home some evening?

I was surprised by the invite. What to say.

Paul: thank you, Vicky. That would be nice. I enjoyed today, also. Been a while since I got a break from everything.

Vicky. How about Thursday evening? If you are free.

I take a little time. I text Julie and see if she is free. I just say I have a meeting at work.

Paul: that would be nice. Sorry just had to sort Julie for Rachel first. What time? And now I must ask for the address?

Vicky. 7:00. And I will send you the address.

The pin arrives.

I sit around for the evening with Rachel and a movie. Wondering what this dinner invite was. Was it just a thank you dinner or the start of a friendship? Or something more?

Do I want something more than a friendship? I do enjoy being around her. And we do open up to each other easily. Will my kids be okay with it? Am I okay with it? Will Vicky be okay with it? Only one way to find out. After all, she is a lovely person.

<h1 style="text-align:center">Chapter 27</h1>

Work thankfully has been going ok. Paul is coming and going from the office. We grab a coffee sometimes and catch up on our lives. I comment that he is more relaxed.

"Yes. Giving up work was the right call. Means I am not being pulled in too many directions. In fairness, you are doing a great job, I am not needed really but to sign off. And I can give Rachel all the time she needs."

"I am happy for you. I am happy we can talk. Just so you know, I was in London last week, in your apartment, and I packed up my things and moved most to the top apartment. Our fancy dress I have in a case and put in the top floor attic. So, if you are down again soon or the kids want to use it, there is nothing to question."

"Not really sure what to say."

"Nothing to say. It was great fun, and I would not take back a minute of it. But we both know we are moving on. I did not want to make my outfits a problem for you. Now you just need to hide your own. I hope you get to use them again sometime. Onward and upwards."

2 months into therapy and much to my surprise we are getting somewhere. I can hope for something about my marriage. Perhaps one of the most interesting suggestions was what the therapist called media-free dating.

It was suggested we get 1 or 1 each ready-to-go mobile. A call and text only phone. When we are out, our smartphones phones left behind and the kids and sitters have the new numbers. So, no matter what, we have no incoming calls and cannot hide in our phones.

It worked. The distractions and temptations were gone, and it forced us to talk. Initially, I kept going for my phone and noticed more than Mark. It then became a joke. But a good one. I am surprised that Mark and I can share a joke and laugh about it without getting offended. In fairness, I am surprised that our marriage lasted so far without either of us attempting to save it up until now.

I could see I was as much to blame for this mess in the marriage as Mark was. If not more so. I got so fixated on my work that my family suffered. At least with this new job, I am well paid, like it, and have a good balance.

Mark finally opened up a bit. We both agreed to try and go forward. Coming to an agreement with him was something I never expected. Little intimacy existed. We tried occasionally but it was forced and hard to relax.

****

We entered the session and as sitting down she asked how we were and was everything ok. No speed bumps. The counsellor then addressed the intimacy question. When we said none, she said "Intimacy. I heard a lot about how both of ye wanted it. But not on the other's terms, so ye deprived yourself to punish the other. So, your thoughts?"

We looked at each other and neither said anything. "Ok. Do ye want to be intimate again or not?"

"Well, yes. I miss it, but it just seemed to end." Mark agreed.

"Ok. When ye were, were ye very active? How was it?"

Mark comes in first. "It was great. We really enjoyed ourselves. Lots of fun and adventurous."

"Ok, well, the thing is, fading is very common and normal, and kids take over. So, it becomes harder. Then you need to make time. Did ye try?"

"Yes, we did. But time and work and life became so hectic by the time we got to bed we were both exhausted."

Mark followed, "Sounds normal but does not mean I did not want or miss it."

We discuss it for a while and the counsellor leaves us with homework as she usually does.

"Before the next session, I want ye to either make time or to agree time away from the kids, home, and try and do something ye may have done years ago. No distraction."

Heading away, we talked about it. We were both nervous, but we agreed to try a night locally and go from there.

I asked Mark to book a hotel and I would sort Ursula.

We booked a city centre hotel in Manchester. It was not too far from home, but distance was not the idea. I was half excited and half nervous. It's unusual trying something with Mark. But I guess, I need to accept the awkwardness to overcome it. I must put all my efforts in. After all, Mark wants to reignite this relationship, too.

As the Friday night approached, I became more nervous. In an effort to try, I looked at some nice lingerie. The sexiest I had; all I could do was think about when I wore them for Paul. So, I went shopping to the Trafford Centre lingerie shops once again. I looked around a little and picked out a nice set. It's strange to think of wearing this in front of Mark unless I am drunk. Again, I backburner the thought of being awkward with Mark. We have been intimate with each other before and we can be now.

Mark lets me know that a room and dinner are booked. We arrive home from work, and I already have an overnight bag packed. Mark is home first and plans with Ursula. "Our private mobiles if you need us," I hear him say.

I am in the bedroom and just leaving and Mark takes out his phone and turns it off leaving it on its charger. He looks at me, "No phones." I am left with little choice.

Dinner is booked for 8 and we arrive to check in at 7. Changing for dinner, I have a dress and lingerie. It is black, a strappy set with gold-coloured detail and clasps. I am conscious that Mark is watching me change. It is not like he has not seen me take on and take off clothes before, thousands of times. But this time, awkwardness is palpable.

"What are you looking at, Mark?"

"You, I am looking at you, the lingerie and you and it feels like I am seeing you for the first time in a long time like this. The lingerie looks gorgeous on you. I am wondering why we stopped."

"Stopped what?"

"Stopped this, having fun, where did it go wrong?"

I take a minute, looking at him. "Well, we are here now, let's see what we can do to fix this if you still want to." As I finish dressing, I think about what he said. I know he is right, might have been nicer to hear I was gorgeous in the lingerie, but that is me finding fault. I hope that was what he meant.

We head down for dinner, and it is a quiet start to it. Mark seems to be deep in thought. I stare at him, clear my throat, drop my spoon, nothing, he seems too deep in his thought. I finally break the silence, "Spit it out, you are miles away."

He looks at me, "I am just thinking back. Remember a while back, you had a little too much to drink."

Where is he going with this I wonder, looking back at him. "Which time?"

"We were out, and you had a bit too much to drink, when we came back you were very playful. You tried to tie me up."

Oh shit, I think, is he going to ask where I learned that? I am not ready to tell who or where.

"Yes, I remember," is all I can say.

"Is that something that interests you sober? Or was it just the drink?"

I sigh deeply, "Honestly, I am not sure where that came from that night, but it seemed fun and harmless and playful. I was just trying to enjoy myself, so I suppose it was so long since we had fun, what was the harm in anything? And you? Does it float your boat?"

"At the time, you took me by surprise, I have looked back on the night a lot more recently and it could be fun, Maria. At this stage, I think I would try anything if it would help and hopefully, we could learn to enjoy each other again. I don't just mean in the bedroom."

I can see he is serious about this. He is really trying. He wants to reignite the lost fire in our marriage. I do wonder about his other woman, but maybe she is gone and the one thing I have learned is that I can't judge. I am every bit as offside. And I hope he is not judging me for it.

"Ok, Mark, and just so we know where we are with that. Do you want to tie me up or be tied?" If I learned anything from Ralph and Paul and the last year, no space for guessing, and more fun when everyone is on the same page.

He looks back and the first real smile of the evening from him. "Oh, there is a question, well either worth a try and who knows. And you?"

"The same." How did we get to this, from a serious dinner to talking about who is tying up who? I am glad we are talking about it.

"So, what else is on your wish list? We have not spoken like this in years, if ever really."

I watch and wait for his reply.

"Let's just say. To have fun and be open to new things."

"Good answer." I laugh, I know the options are endless. The rest of the meal passes chatting for a change.

Heading back to the room, we are both in a good mood, laughing, talking, and not being frustrated with each other. But I was nervous, there was no reason, but could we reconnect physically as much as we spoke?

Looking at Mark, "What would you like?"

"Let's go one step at a time, let's just enjoy each other and we have time to explore. Hey, your boss has a shop full of toys in London, maybe if we graduate to a weekend we could go there."

"One step at a time, and maybe we can." That would take some explaining to Adam and Nicole.

Mark did exactly as he said, taking his time undressing and exploring me. Compliments my lingerie more than once, takes in my fragrance, and compliments that, kiss my neck and face

— I can feel myself relaxing with every touch. It is a start, and I know once we are relaxed physically, we'll take it up from there.

We enjoyed the night, heading home we both agreed to make time and try for now to get one night away a month and all going well a weekend occasionally.

The weekend was busy. Running and racing after kids and shopping etc. Mark was far more helpful than usual. He still needed direction, but I appreciate he is trying.

Monday comes fast, and I head to work. Paul is there before me. "Hello, stranger, unusual to see you here on a Monday let alone this early. Is there something up?"

"No, I just said I would come in and review the accounts. See where there is money and not. Now that I am gone from the day job, I better take a wage from somewhere. Can you look and see what company it is best to take from? There are also rents which may be the place, after all, Ralph built those up and lived off them at the same time. Anyway. Also, we need to employ Sarah in one of the businesses. So how was your weekend.?"

I wonder why he needs to take a salary, there was a few million in available funds he inherited outside of the shops. Anyway, not my place to question.

"It was a good one, for a change. Almost embarrassed to say, but Mark and I are giving it a go. Counselling is working." I feel embarrassed to share it with Paul.

"Why embarrassed, I am happy for you, I said from day 1 your family first, and if you can save it, then do."

"When we were talking over the weekend, Mark suggested London and mentioned Adam's shop. That would be embarrassing."

"Relax, I will talk to Adam and Nicole. I will tell them what is going on and you and Mark are trying. So, when they see or bump into ye they will know and play along. Don't worry, leave it to me. If ye are in London, the top apartment will always be there for you and ye."

"Thanks, boss, how is Rachel?"

"She is ok, getting better slowly."

We both move on from the apartments and Mark's discussion. Paul is being good about this. He is handling this far better than I am, maybe it is Rachel, or he can just detach. I am still fixated on the time Paul, and I had together, and I need to put that aside now. It's gone, never to return and now I must focus on my marriage and Mark. I need to make it work. I can't spend the rest of my life finding another man to be intimate with when I have Mark. And I know I can't lose him; I don't want to.

I try to focus on Mark and making things work.

Maria: We need to look at a family holiday, if for nothing else the kids. Let's agree and look at options.

Mark: OK, look at your dates. It is unusual for you to take holidays let alone want to.

Maria: New job and able to manage my time more easily. So, let's look and make a plan.

Getting home we begin to look at the options. Mark suggests the same villa holiday as last year. I look at him and say, "Your golf holiday is it." He goes a little red.

"Ok I know I was offside; I spent too much time golfing and left you with the kids."

"What do you want.?"

"I want a family holiday. Fine if you want a game of golf or even 2 in 2 weeks. But then I get the same time to go and do whatever I want to. Be it a day on the beach with a book, or shopping, or whatever. The kids need to see us together, our problems affect them also."
"How about we ask the kids what they want, or will we just tell them the same place as last year?" Mark suggests we call the kids and ask them if the same place as last year will work or if they want to go somewhere new.

The kids all say last year was good fun when they did things out there. It was a bit of a shot across the bow, they want the holiday, but not just sitting around doing nothing.

We book for the same first 2 weeks in August again. It will be hot, but I know it will be great.

We have another counselling session. We leave the house together and head in.

After the usual pleasantries and I assume the counsellor checking the temperature so to speak, we get into it. She brings up the intimacy topic once again.

We both recount the night away and how we opened up a bit and agreed it needs work. Mark surprisingly continued and said we both missed the adventurous side of play and effort. I was hoping he was not going to go into a whole, who is tying who up discussion. But thankfully no, he just kept it concise.

The counsellor responds, "It's great, the important thing is consistency. Don't let it be a one-night wonder. Make a plan and follow it in principle. Anyway, where ye are going to make time for each other?

I mentioned we were booking a family holiday. This led to a new discussion.

"How did the last one go and when was it?"

This time I started, "The holiday was ok for the kids, but I was having a hard time at work at that time and was thinking of leaving my job."

"How was the holiday for you?"

"Not great, I was left with the kids more often than not. Mark was golfing a lot and we really had to look for time."

"Was Mark golfing agreed beforehand?"

"No, I only saw the clubs when we were going."

"I felt like a childminder and barely managed a few walks to myself."

"Mark?"

He goes red. "I suppose I was golfing a bit too much, but it was my holiday too, and felt I needed a break."

"What about Maria, did she get much of a break?"

"I thought she was happy with the kids, but I know I was probably avoiding too much time together. But we have agreed this year. I get two rounds of golf; 1 a week and she gets 2 days also to do what she wants. Something for everyone."

"Ok but what about ye?" We both looked at her.

"I am hearing how each of ye get time alone to do what ye enjoy, what I am not hearing is ye getting any time alone together. Are there kids' clubs or anything like that? What ye need to work on is ye time, not me time. Both are important."

The session was good and when we left, we talked and agreed, maybe we could bring Ursula, even for a week. The villa will take it.

When we get home, we talk to Ursula, and she agrees to come for the second week. We tell the kids, and they are all happy. I feel a pang of pain as they cheer and say Ursula is great fun. That means I am not. *How absent I have been from my kids' lives?*

I mark mine and Paul's diary with the holiday dates. I send him an email also flagging the 2 weeks I am away and where I will be in Portugal.

I just got a call from him.

"Maria, hi."

"Are my holidays a problem?"

"No not at all, I hope you have a good holiday and better than last year. So, enjoy that. I meant to say I was in London and had a drink with Adam and Nicole. I told them that you were giving things a go with Mark again and we had agreed to let things lie between us, we were both ok with it all, and no issues between us. I hope they can make time for ye also. I told them ye may be in London from time to time and using the apartment and maybe even going into the shop. Obviously, Mark does not know about us, so just play it that they know you from work etc, and whatever ye do is a matter for ye and not my business."

"Thanks, Paul."

He then jokes, "Try not to break the cross in the playroom in Ralph's old office."

"Not funny Paul. You know I would not go there."

"Why? You enjoyed it; we both did. In all fairness, if you learned to enjoy it and it works, don't let what we learned stop you from enjoying it again. I am not exactly asking to be kept informed, all I am saying is if it makes you happy then why not?

Honestly, we must be able to accept that each other will have love and sex lives if we are going to work together. We can't dodge each other's private life if we are to try friendship."

"Have you met someone?" I ask.

"No, but what everything has taught me is that I need to be open to meeting someone. Life is too valuable to let pass it by. So, I am open to it."

It is hard to hear that he has or will move on from me, but again, we are finished, and I am trying again so I must accept it. Even though I know I still love him, I just blew it. We didn't plan our relationship through, we just went day by day. Neither of us thought of our future, we were so lost in the fun we had together.

"Before you go. The trade show for Berlin, the last weekend in May. Are you going or just the buyer? It is only 3 weeks away and need to book tickets for you if you are going."

"Not this time. I don't want to be far away. The buyers know more than we do anyway."

"Ok, I will ask for a full report when they come back. You have enough on your plate without worrying about trade shows. Maybe next year when Rachel is back on her feet you might go and enjoy a trade show and city break."

Chapter 28

PAUL

I arrive at Victoria's house; it has been long since I felt eager to visit someone. Maria is in my past, and somehow, I always knew it would come to end. But still, I haven't been this eager; I feel like a teenager visiting his crush's house, hoping to not be disappointed or rejected at the end of it all.

'Here we go,' I say to myself, suppressing every raging hope all the while hoping against all the odds.

I snap out of my thoughts and look around the neighbourhood. It looks like a quiet area, a mid-terrace house, flowers outside the door. Walking up to the door my nervousness soars; I appreciate this nervousness. It has been so long since I felt this way, and I am surprised I feel this way. I stand in front of a fresh dark green door with brass door knocker, very traditional. I run my hand in my hair to get rid of any frizz in my hair and knock. Within a few seconds, Victoria opens the door.

She greets me with a big smile and welcomes me in. I feel a little awkward, not even sure how to greet her. Is it a peck on the cheek, hello, or nothing or what? The moment passes and I do nothing. *Should have gone for the side hug. Get hold of your nervousness.* I try to calm my nerves; *I am never this nervous. And I need to stop smiling like an idiot.* My mind, heart, and nerves are all over the place.

I admire her, dressed in a summer dress – a floral summer dress that perfectly complements her silhouette. *Is she dressed up for a dinner at home or is this normal?* I think to myself, impressed by her choice of the dress. I really know little about her. For all the times I have seen her, only twice was it not in uniform.

As I look around the hall, I see photographs following the stairway up. I look quickly at them as I hand Victoria a bottle of wine. I notice Victoria, 2 girls and some with a man. Many seem to be a good few years old, so I guess the photos are hers and her husband and the girls.

"Thank you for the wine. Come inside, make yourself comfortable. Would you like a drink?"

"Thank you, water please." I reply as I continue to look around.

"Water? You don't want a glass of wine?"

"I do. But later with dinner, I am driving so must behave."

"Very sensible, keep your wits about you for a fast getaway." I chuckle, as we rarely share a joke with each other.

"I love all your photographs. Really like how they are arranged. And the photography is exceptional. Are you into photography?"

"Used to take a lot more. Loved seeing photos of my family, and places I visited. They are all sorts and have memories for me. A bit of a sentimentalist."

I look at one photo, a gorgeous Lakeland setting. "Where is that?"

"That is Windermere, that last family holiday we all went on. Come on dinner is ready, you can talk to me in the kitchen as I get it sorted. I hope you like nutloaf. I think Nutloaf, isn't that vegetarian, only had once and like eating cardboard."

Walking into the kitchen, there is a lovely smell, "I was joking, how do you like your steak." She laughs, "I am sure you were thinking, Nutloaf, what the hell? Anyway, nothing too adventurous here, kept it simple as I did not know what you liked, and steak is always a safe bet."

"I thought you knew I was vegetarian, so I was impressed with the nutloaf. Must never have come up in the hospital."

I kept a straight face, "I am sure the veg will be just fine."

"Oh, I am sorry, let me see what I can rustle up." My turn to laugh, "Steak is perfect, you are not the only one who can have a laugh."

"Oh, thank God. I nearly dropped."

I watch her move around the kitchen and she produces a starter of stuffed mushroom and salad. Sitting, we start talking, or more to the point I start asking questions. I realized I have been more curious about her.

"Tell me about your photos, they look lovely. Such a homely feeling when I came in. You must be a proud mother."

"I love photos, always did, they are full of memories. I am sure I told you I loved to travel, not that I have done too much. But albums full of everything and anything. Memories of the kids and Richard."

"What travel have you done? Been anywhere interesting?" I ask as I keep munching the appetizers.

"We often went up to Scotland, we loved the mountains and the outdoors, I haven't gone back much in the last 10 years. The trip next week, I got waterproofs for, with Amanda and Pamela is to do some walking around Ben Nevis and Glencoe. I had always wanted to do Ben Nevis with Richard, but we never got there. So, the girls are bringing me up. Have you done it?"

"Ben Nevis, no. I am just getting to know the area in the last year. It is a lovely place and area. Are ye walking yourselves or guided?"

"We are staying in the Nevis hostel, and we think Ben Nevis is ok on our own as a trail. But we will do one guided somewhere just to see the area."

"Why don't you call into the shop I was working in, up there? They do guided walk, if you want, just tell them you know me, and I suggested you try them. I am sure they would have something. Ask for the staff discount, tell them use mine. We have credits for walks and gear."

"Oh, that would be great." I notice she is hesitant, considering the discount I got for her last time.

"Where else have you gone?" I finally stop my hand from getting into the delicious appetizers.

"We were in Holland once about 12 years ago, an anniversary present to ourselves, some South of England caravanning. What about you, you like travel?"

"Family holidays again, we did not do much in the last year or so before my wife died and then after, a few sun holidays with the kids, nothing too exciting. We were in Fort William in December for a few days. Work had me in London a lot in the last year and Holland a few times. But normally not too far. Would love to try to Ben Nevis. And the places in its vicinity."

"How is work now? You under pressure there with Rachel?"

"I am giving the office a break for a while, the shop client now, I was working as solicitor, in the same office the last nearly 20 years. They were great, but really Rachel needs me at home, so I found working a strain, so I am reducing my workload. They told me come back when ready, so a sort of extended leave if you get me. I am in a managerial type of role with the sports shops now. Was working on floor that day to get a feel for the business."

"That must have been hard, are ye coping, not easy when not working. Are you in the shops part time or what?"

"Shops are a long story; I was only there for a few days. And I must say, your girl, Amanda is a character. A very interesting character."

She laughs out loud, "You have no idea. She has pushed me to get out more, enjoy life like I used to. The two girls are great kids. What about yours, they know where you are tonight with Nurse Ratchet."

She gets back at me, I blush, "Honestly, I did not tell them, I got in a sitter for Rachel. If they knew I was here, I would get quizzed before and after. Sarah is at me too, as she says, get a life. Matthew says the same, but he is more relaxed. Does Amanda know you are having a strange man to dinner? What would she say? I think she'll be ecstatic."

"I didn't tell her. She was at me to call you after Monday, but I said no, you are busy with Rachel, and you were just being polite to me. Not to mention I am a much older woman. And yes, she will be over the moon if she finds out you are here tonight."

We talk about a little more about our kids, realizing and appreciating how much of a blessing they have been. As we talk on, Victoria serves up the main course, and a glass of wine for me. We talk away about travel, our hobbies, and our lives so to speak.

"Paul, you have been 20 questions tonight, you were being a bit evasive and changing the subject. Would you prefer not to be here? Is something on your mind? Don't worry, I understand."

"Vicky don't be daft, if I didn't want to be here, I wouldn't be. This is a nice evening." *And I really like being here with you,* I didn't say all that I wanted to say.

"Then sorry, but why the avoidance about you personally. Are you seeing someone? Really, I don't want to be a nuisance. You are a younger successful, attractive professional man, with everything going. I am just happy with talking to someone, not work related for a change."

"Vicky, you are reading way too much here. OK, me in a nutshell. I am 49, widower 11 years now. 3 kids, Rachel 17 recovering from a serious injury, Sarah 21 doing this and that, went to college, Matthew 23 did a business degree and is now working in online sales and shipping out at the airport. I am a solicitor, only child, brought up by my mother. Never had much and worked my way up. My mother died over 12 years ago also. My wife died 11 years ago of cancer. I stayed mid-level in my company as could not raise the kids and work partner hours. I have been in the same firm for 20 years or so. I cut back recently to take care of Rachel and get a home life balance back. I am single, I had a few single dates several years back and never went beyond 1 evening. Convinced me too much like hard work and never really tried. I did meet someone over a year ago in London, she worked for another company. We saw each other for a while. But I ended it, she never met the kids, so no complication there. It was good while lasted, woke me so to speak and showed me I am not too old to enjoy some life yet. We live a simple enough life, comfortable but not extravagant by any means. There are a few other things that I just don't want to talk about. But they do not involve another woman, or man or anything like that. Just old family stuff. Not for now if you don't mind. Some old family issues came back to haunt in the last year and complicated our lives a little. That's all."

She watches me as I conclude my part, "Wow, that is a mouth full. I am sorry I pushed. I just felt you were dodging personal for some reason and maybe did not want to be here or just being polite and I did not want to be nuisance. I had no idea about all this."

"As regards you, don't sell yourself short Vicky, you are a kind, caring, attractive lady, who brought up nice kids and sentimental side and great loyalty. Showed compassion to a distraught family member of a patient, far beyond what you needed to."

"Well, that's part of my job. And thank you for all the compliments. Really appreciate that," she says, and I notice she felt a bit shy receiving the compliments.

"Don't mention it. You deserve all that and more. Now, with that Vicky, I must unfortunately call it a night. I told the sitter I would be home by 10:30. It was a lovely evening." *I really want to stay a little longer. Maybe the entire night. Maybe never leave.* Oh, how much I wanted to say everything I felt.

"I understand." Her smile fades and reappears. "It was lovely to have you here. I hope we are, okay?"

"Of course, we are more than okay. Don't worry. Thank you again, for hosting me. You are a stellar cook, I must say."

"You're being quite generous there, now." She chuckles at the remark, and we walk to the door. She bids me good night. With that, I lean in and give her a peck on the cheek, just catching the corner of her lips, saying. "I hope we can do this again soon."

She slightly nods her head and says, "Of course. See you soon."

I get in my car, turning around to see her standing at the door with her beaming smile. She closes the door only when I drive away.

All the way home, I keep wishing I could have stayed there for a while longer. I know for sure that I will be getting a sitter later than 10.30 next time. As I arrive home, I let Julie go. "Nice evening Paul?"

"You know, one meeting like the next."

"Yes, I am sure, they all have the same shade of lipstick. Night Paul."

She heads off smiling and a laugh and I look into the hall mirror. Some of Vicky's lipstick was on my lip and the side of my mouth. I just blush, wiping the lipstick off. *Oh, Julie enjoyed that. So much for under the radar.* I am just glad it wasn't Sarah.

Before checking on Rachel, I sit down and check my phone and see a message.

Victoria: Thank you for a lovely evening. I am sorry I pushed you on being evasive, it is none of my business. We hardly know each other; I had no right. Anyway, really enjoyed myself, thank you for the happy ending.

Paul: Happy ending, indeed. When I got home Julie asked about my meeting. I told her like any other meeting. She smirked and asked do they all have the same shade of lipstick. Looks like you left your mark. Sorry for the kiss and run, by the way.

Victoria: So, which are you sorry for, the kiss or the run?

Paul: The run.

I enjoy the humour I share with Vicky. I wait for a reply, but nothing comes instantly. I decide to go check on Rachel. Her room seems silent, I assume she must be asleep however, as I slowly open the door, I find her chatting online to her friends on her phone.

I knock on the door to introduce my presence. "How was your evening, Rachel?"

"Good, can I have some friends over tomorrow night?"

"Of course, darling!"

I watch her slowly, but with a smile, she says to her friends: "He said yes, 7, and take out when ye get here."

I look back at her. "Take out, what have I agreed to?" I smile and close the door.

I don't care she tricked me. I am just so happy she is having friends around and wants them. She has not invited anyone around since the accident. A few called to see her. But sounds like she is after a girl's night, like the old Rachel.

I stick my head back in. She looks up nervously. "If you want any of them to stay over it is fine, they can stay."

She smiles with excitement, "If any of ye want to stay over it is ok."

As I hear the youthful laughter coming from the room and plans being made, I feel genuinely happy for my little girl returning to life and being herself. Honestly, I can't want anything more than Rachel being her teenager self. My phone pings:

Victoria: Well, if you want to try again, don't run.

Paul: How about dinner after your holiday? You pick the restaurant.

Victoria: Sounds lovely. Friday next week. You tell me where.

Victoria: Don't be a stranger. X and I will check out those walking tours you mentioned. Nite

Paul: I will pick you up at 7 next Friday.

I let it at that, and I can't wait for our next meeting. I hope it's a different shade of red the next time. I blush at my own remark. *Slow down, Paul, slow down.* I try to convince myself, against all the excitement I feel right now.

I call Sarah, "Sarah, Rachel is having a group of girls around tomorrow night. Some may be staying over. Any chance you can be here? I will be hiding out in my bedroom as don't want to spoil the night. The big sister might be ok to keep an eye on them and not embarrass her. Take away and food required. All on my credit card."

"You ok with this, really?"

"If she is having friends, I take it as a start back to herself."

"Ok, let it to me."

The slumber party night arrives and brings in the teenagers' roars and chatter in the house. As much as some of it may seem annoying, I am happier about my baby being happy and comfortable around people. And I am glad Rachel found friends who accept her in all conditions. Twice, Sarah came to my room, looking disoriented. She didn't say anything, but I know her sisterly duty took a toll on her.

"I am not doing this again." With that, she returned to her sisterly duty.

The slumber party night passes off, and it looks like a tornado hit the house, but Rachel was so happy and sounded like great fun. I stayed hidden for the evening. I trust my children and I know they wouldn't do anything to upset me.

On Saturday, I call the shop in Fort William. Just to let them know a Victoria and her daughter may contact them to book a walk. Get them onto a group with spaces and don't charge. Say I asked for them to be given the employee tag along with rate, of free when spaces to employees, as a favour. They are just to know I occasionally do some work for the shops and not that I own them.

Finally, life is beginning to regain structure. Rachel is improving and coming back out of herself. Sarah and Matthew are getting on with their own things and I am just working when needs be and involved with the shops and business. Then along comes Victoria, and I feel like a teenager with a huge crush on her. God!

Not that I have anyone to talk to about this. She is older, but good company and very grounded. Attractive. A year ago, sex was hardly on my radar but now if I go into a relationship, I want it all. Not just companionship. But what does she want? She is out of practise too, so to speak. I decide I am interested to explore and find out if we are on the same page. I can't just keep feeling like this, we are grownups now, and clear communication is the only way through. But I am not yet ready to let her know my full story.

I book dinner for Friday. Kept it simple, Italian, and not too far from her house. The place looks nice and has some good reviews. I decide to wear something casual, as much excited I was, I could have worn a tuxedo. I go to pick her up and reach her home 10 minutes before 7. I walk to the front door to call and seeing me, she comes out. Quite gladly, she was ready much before I arrived. I assume, she too is too excited to see me. She is wearing her summer dress again and looking lovely in it. Summer dresses suit her – a lot. Closing the door behind her, I am greeted with a lovely warm smile. I turn and walk back to the car with her, and she briefly catches my arm. I had thought of a peck on the cheek to greet her. But maybe not in public with her neighbours seeing. I would like to keep 'us' private.

"How was your holiday?" *I hope no one told her about the owner of the shops.* This has been a worry whenever she visits my shops.

"It was a lovely few days. I got to go up Ben Nevis and we called to the walking shop. Thank you for ringing ahead. The manager said you called, and the company policy is if last minute spare spaces on a walking group, staff can tag along, and you asked for us to get staff rates. You do too much. Amanda quizzed her about you."

"What did she say?" If anyone, it will be Amanda who will dig out the whole truth about anyone and anything.

"Just that she only met you last year and your company did the legal work for the shops when the owner died, and you had to act for the estate and manage until recently. Otherwise, she did not know much. You have 3 kids Late teens to early 20's. Amanda was a bit disappointed. Got little information."

"Well, not much to say."

I sat and listened to Victoria recount her holiday and beautiful scenery on the walks. Describing the hostel and how nice it was. She had some lovely photos on her phone, and she showed me. Her and the girls, all smiling in the selfies and there were also some scenic views that she captured. She described every scenery, and I can see how much she already misses that place.

"You enjoy being in the nature a lot, don't you? I asked her while she converses about her trip.

"I do. A lot. I'm sorry if I am boring you with all this nature's beauty talk. We can talk about anything else you want to," she replies.

"I absolutely adore you when you talk about things you like doing. You just glow different, and your eyes lit up when you talk about those things. And I enjoy the conversation even more. I can listen to you talk about your trips for hours, don't worry about boring me at all." I know she wanted to talk about the trip a little more.

As the evening drew to a close, I brought Victoria home. She came across as so bubbly, vibrant, and full of life and fun after her holiday. She recounted with a laugh how on the day coming home she detoured into the woodland's parks. Walking around a gorgeous forest lake they stopped for a packed lunch. Nobody was around and she just stripped off and went for a quick swim. "The girls were surprised at me, and I don't know why I felt like it."

"WHOAA! Was that out of character?"

"Yes and no, now yes. They would never have seen that. But years ago, would not have been too unusual. Once secluded, I enjoyed it. I was surprised I still had it in me. But only because nobody was around. Good to shock Amanda," she laughed. "Would you like to come in for a coffee?"

I hesitate.

"Don't worry I don't usually bite. Usually." She smiles with a glint.

"Ok, why not, as you don't bite."

Heading in, I walk behind her. Watching her walk with purpose she opens the door and kicks off her shoes. She is someone who isn't afraid to be herself, someone who is comfortable with her truth and stays true to herself.

"Tea or coffee?"

"Coffee please, milk no sugar.".

She makes me coffee and tea for herself. "Head into the living room and I will be a minute."

I head in and take a seat on the couch. Looking at the photos again, I just see a smile and playful sense of adventure on most of her photos, all be it they look from a while back.

Coming back, she sits down next to me, rather than on the chair opposite. Curling her legs up on the couch under her, so she is comfortable and looking at me. "So, Paul, you are a bit of a mystery. Those we met in the shops seemed to know little about you, except you were a lawyer who worked on the shops for the deceased owner and until the new owners came along, you ran them. You are all questions and not a lot of answers. Yet you seem a lovely man who adores his children and obviously kind, even calling the Fort William shop in case we called in. Can I ask this? It is obvious you are being evasive about something, and we all have our histories, but is there something stopping you from meeting someone new? I am sorry to be direct, but I am curious and want to know what page we are on, if any?"

If anything, I truly like people who are direct, and ask what they want to ask without playing around.

"Yes, I have a history and I am being cautious, it has been a hell of a year for me and the kids. Really, I can't talk about it. Only it does not affect me meeting anyone else and I am free. There is no skeleton in the closet or bunny boilers waiting for me. Unless you are one." I laugh.

"Ok. That's a good enough answer."

"Any more questions? After all, you said I do all the asking."

She smirks, "Ok, why peck and run last week?"

I blush. She really is direct. "I was avoiding being shot down. If you had no interest, I would hear no more from you and easily pass as polite and friendly. I missed your lipstick mark on me though."

As I talk, Victoria moves on the couch, one leg out in front of her, and she rocks her foot. I try to answer further, but I do feel her foot rubs off my shin, gently, passively.

She smiles at me. "Go on. Your sitter said what?"

"She commented ….."

I see Victoria smiles and now I know her foot rubbing me is no mistake. I, however, continue, "That lipstick same for every meeting. Laughed and left. I know her for years and she's like a mother to Rachel and the kids. ...... What are you doing?" I ask as she sips her tea.

"Nothing. Go on." I see the foot bounce up and down and rub off my shin.

"Are you playing footsie?"

"No. I haven't touched your foot." She laughs. "You know what I mean." I watch her put her tea down. "You know." I then watch her raise a finger and put it over my lips to silence me. She then leans in and softly kisses me on the lips. Gently, softly and I kiss her back. She then pulls away.

"Sorry I am a bit out of practise. I needed the wine at dinner to be able to do that, been a long time since I have kissed a man. I hope that was ok. I have been thinking of your peck last week and how soft your lips felt on the edge of mine."

"More than ok, and as I said other than one person last year, I have not really dated in 10 years."

"If I am too old, or not your type, please say. I can take it." I lean back in and kiss her again, a little deeper and harder.

Smiling at her, I say, "So, how close to pension are you granny?" As I laugh. She blushed. "I am 54. I know a lot older." I see her a bit embarrassed. So, I lean in and kiss her again. This time, neither of us want to let go. She tenderly puts her hand on my neck, gently pulling me in.

"I am happy to try if you are, let's just see where it goes, I too have been thinking about the peck and you, I wondered if you were just being nice and friendly. Now, with that unfortunately, I need to go, Julie is babysitting, and I said I would be home half an hour ago. But I am glad I came in."

"So am I, very happy." She walks me to the door. As she reaches to open it, "Vicky, one more thing." She turns to look at me, I rub my hand over her cheek, lean in and kiss her, softly and then deeper, as she leans back against the door. Never too hard, our lips and tongue gently caress each other's. When we finish, I whisper, "I just wanted one more kiss and to taste you before I left."

"That was breath taking, I have not been kissed like that since I don't know when. You can do that anytime."

"Now, I better go before ….."

"I know. Next time, try not to be on the clock."

I arrive home, and Julie is there. Sitting at the kitchen table with a coffee, reading a book. Looking up, I know when she is suppressing her smirk. "How was your evening? Was it the same meeting?" She smiles and laughs. I smile back and laugh. "Actually, it was. But please I don't want the kids to know anything, That I why I have not asked them to sit. It is very early."

"I hope someone nice, really you deserve it. You are too nice to be alone. Anyone we know? If you don't mind me asking."

"It is the nurse you met, Vicky."

"Ah, I wondered, was it. But please, kids don't need to know. Maybe if it goes somewhere."

"Paul, your secret is safe, you are a grown man and deserve your own life, and I don't tell you the kids' secrets, lol sometimes I feel like the confessional here."

"The kids have secrets from me?"

Julie laughs out loud. "How about the next night you have a meeting, if you want, I can stay over. Just let me know."

"Thank you, Julie. I don't know what to say."

"Just let me know and I will be here if needs be."

With this, she packs up her book and clears away the coffee. "I am heading away, have a good weekend."

I check on Rachel, she is sleeping. Going back to the kitchen, I sit with a coffee and pick up my phone.

Victoria: xxx thank you for tonight, Paul. Sorry if I was forward, it took a bottle of wine for the Dutch courage. I am way out of practise. I regret none of it though. That kiss. XX I am sitting here and can feel you on me.

Paul: Thank you. I know what you mean. I just could not leave without kissing you again. Watching you at home. You are so comfortable in your own skin. Seem so confident. Full of life. Gorgeous to see. You are a surprise.

Victoria: I hope Julie is ok with you being late. Sorry if the sitter is annoyed.

Paul: She was fine, had her fun, asked me was it the same meeting. She enjoyed it.

Victoria: And

Paul: I said it was and was a surprise. But I don't want the kids to know just yet I am seeing someone.

Victoria: So, you are seeing me now, are you?

Paul: Well, I hope we are starting to.

Victoria: Joking, let's hope this is the start of something new. But be warned, you have set a high bar with that kiss. Hope you can stay later next night.

Paul: Julie offered. Said she would do an overnight if I wanted to have a later evening.

Victoria: Good. Don't think I am a sure thing, but let's see where a night goes, if anywhere. Now this old lady needs her bed. Nite xxx

Paul: Oh, you're one gorgeous old lady. Haha. Nite Nite, Vicky. xxxx

Chapter 29

MARIA

The second week of our holidays rolls around, and Ursula arrives. Mark goes to the airport to collect her as I head to the beach with the kids.

The first week flew by. Mark took his afternoon for golf, and I spent a quiet afternoon on the beach with a book and a resort waiter keeping my drinks topped up. Absolute bliss.

As the kids mess around in the sand and water, I have a chance to sit back and watch them. These last three months have seen the kids so much happier, not to mention me. Calm seems to have been restored and Mark and I are sticking to the rules we have set.

With that Mark and Ursula arrive, "That was quick Mark."

"The flight was early, and we just dropped her bags, quickly changed and came straight down."

"Well, I hope she did not fly in that outfit. Not exactly much of that bikini there." "I know." Mark smiles and laughs. Rebecca runs up and hugs her screaming "Ursula!" Liam looks on with a smile also. "Looks like the bikini not lost on Liam either." Mark says.

"Stop. He is still my baby."

12 months ago, I know I was thinking Mark was shagging her. In fairness, looking at her, hard to blame him. I smile, nearly tempted myself, I think. Young fit attractive. But now I can see the joke he is having, and we can laugh about it. Though I do wonder who it was. Joan's Thursday afternoons early departure have continued. So, I don't worry about her now.

As a beach ball from Natalie lands on me, I snap out of my thoughts. "Heyyy!" I laugh and throw the ball back. Ursula is playing away with them like a big kid. "How about tomorrow we get kids sorted and head down to a different beach ourselves?"

I look at Mark as he suggests. He continues, "Well, we have cover and that is why she is here."

"Ok." I haven't seen this part of Mark in a long time. I am pleasantly surprised to see this, Mark.

The next morning the kids are sorted, and Ursula has the lay of the land. Mark tells me to get my things and let's go. He obviously has an idea of where we are going.

We head to a beach a few miles away, heading for a walk along it we round a corner and meet a sign. "Nudist beach. No children allowed". I stop in my tracks. Looking at him with my eyes wide open. He just smiles. "Well, you wanted an adventure. If we are not going to try here, we never will."

I must think and then what the hell. This is mild next to some of what I have done over the last year. We strip off and head on down. It is quiet, but a lot busier than expected and many people are our age and older. We enjoy the day and liberation. Before we leave, we head back to dunes area as it seemed to be popular. We see this is a hot spot of voyeurism and exhibitionism. We walk and watch some of what is going on and admire one couple.

They see us watching. They are our age and quite attractive. I can see Mark reacting to them.

Heading back to the beach, we are both turned on. But nobody bats an eye lid, after all, everybody here looks the same – naked, turned on, and liberated. A few minutes later, the couple we admire pass by. They stop and say hello, introducing themselves as Max and Lara and ask did we enjoy the show. We are embarrassed. They laugh. "Don't worry nobody cares here and all strangers." They are English also and we chat a little. Before leaving they invite us for a drink, they are in the next resort to ours. I get Lara's number and we decided to go.

We enjoy a lovely sociable drink that evening with them and chatted and agreed to meet next day at the beach. We all enjoyed each other's company and as they went back to the dunes for themselves, we also decided to try. Being brave in strange lands. It was exciting being seen and watched and we know Max and Lara watched us also.

That evening we met for dinner, and it was a lovely night. An adventure ending up back in a hot tub in their villa. There was some adventure and just meeting another couple like that.

We had coffee and I even went shopping with Lara on my second last day. It was nice to get some girly time. We agreed to stay in touch back home. They are London based and I said we occasionally get there.

As the holiday came to an end, we had our last dinner in a five-star restaurant. Upon asking the children if they had fun, they all said they loved it this year much more fun than last year. "We did way more stuff this year." Liam added.

We both knew why. Because we were a family this year not a couple avoiding each other.

"Oh, this year was way more fun," Mark remarked and winked at me. I smiled, knowing he was teasing me.

Getting back to Manchester, we had a session booked a few days later. We both recounted how well the holiday went. Making time worked and agreeing our own time also helped. We agree to try and keep that going back here.

She asks for any standout memories together. I blushed and so did Mark. Our minds going to the same place, I think.

She laughs, before we reply. "I take the 2 blushes as promising. What happened in Portugal stayed in Portugal. Aside from the blushing moment. How was it all as a family holiday?"

I answer, "It was good. The kids said much better than last year. We got some time to enjoy ourselves and away from everyone and got a few nights out together also." Mark agrees and adds, "Reminds us of what it should be, rather than what last year was."

"Now, going forward. Ye are on a good track. I am suggesting we schedule a follow up for a few months but no need for regular sessions, unless ye want one. Ye seem to be looking forward, not back and that's how ye need to go." We both agree and head off back to reality.

"So, what are we going to do with Lara and Max?" I ask.

"How about next weekend we get away we head to London and invite them to dinner and if they come, they come and if not, they don't. Can we still use the apartment?"

"So long as I am working with the shops the apartment is there. So, I will see when I am down next."

I get back to work and find Paul in my office. "How was the holiday?"

"Great thanks. Very relaxing for a change. Was all ok here. I heard nothing. "

"All was fine, I came in every day and told everyone you were not to be contacted on anything unless no other option and directed. You are entitled to a holiday and break away. Anyway, all was fine. Everything ok with Mark?"

"Yes, all is good thank you. Looks like we are back on track. I do miss us sometimes, but I know this is for the best. Sorry, I had to say it."

"Maria, I know. Last year was more like a novel or someone else's life but this is better for you and your family and good to see you are happy. You seem so much more relaxed."

"I know, what about you? Any love in your life or are you only looking after Rachel?" I see a change in his face.

"Actually, yes. I wasn't sure how to say to you. I did meet someone a few months back. It is going ok, being true to me, she does not know about the shops and all that. Just that I am taking time to mind Rachel."

"Really? Who?"

"She was one of Rachel's nurses. Was very good to me when she was in ICU. We then bumped into each other by chance a few months after and had a coffee and chat and went from there."

"Ah. You dirty old man. A young nurse."

"Actually, she is older. Widowed and a few grown up children. Anyway, things are moving along there, so I am about to come clean about the shops. Ralph and all that."

I feel a pang of jealousy. But I am happy now. I am happy with Mark, a year back, I couldn't say a single good thing about my marriage with Mark. But now, I am gladly happy with him. So, Paul has the right to be happy, and should be.

"I am happy for you. If we are to move on as friends with a secret past. We must be able to share as friends do and I may bump into ye also. Especially if we use London."

"On London, I am hoping to go down for a weekend soon with Mark. Can I use the apartment?"

"Maria, the apartment is empty really all the time. You use the top floor anytime you want. If I am down, I will use the middle one and so will my kids. So, top is for you and anyone from here who needs accommodation. If I am ever using it, I will let you know. Or set up a booking calendar here if you want."

"Calendar might be a good idea. So, is there anything else on the agenda?"

"No, everything is fine, I will head to London in the next week or two and see how everything is going there. I have not been down in months, and I don't want them thinking I have lost interest."

Thursday comes and Joan has arranged for her usual 4 PM departure. My nose is getting the better of me, so I decide to follow her. She heads back to her car and picks up a bag. I hold back. Where is she going? She heads down to a hotel down the street, and I see her check in. *She is meeting someone.*

I sit and wait to see who arrives in. Ordering a coffee, I find a quiet corner with a view of the reception and lift. My jaw drops. Who walks in, but Jack?

Surely not, surely, she is not seeing Jack. She never seemed to like him. I sit and wait, and I see him heading to the bar. Maybe it is just a coincidence. Five minutes later, Joan walks in and heads straight to him. Leaning in for a peck on the cheek, she sits down next to him, and I watch as she rests a hand on his leg.

My head is fried, I can't get my head around this. Jack of all people. Was she feeding him information in the early part of this? Then I think no, Jack never saw me leaving was coming, mind you I told Joan little. Well, at least now I know it was not Mark. I must wait until they leave, if I move now there is a good chance, they will see me. They enjoy a drink and then head to the elevator.

It sends a shiver to think of them doing whatever up there. No wonder she is keeping it quiet, it is Jack.

Heading back to work, I can only smile that I know. I think of telling Mark, but then I can't really as I accused him of sleeping with her and if I say to Paul, he will think my OCD is back about this.

Mark and I are back on track, getting back to what we once had. I have destroyed one relationship, and I won't risk this anymore. I don't want to lose my family.

Chapter 30

Friday night arrives and Sarah walks into the kitchen and sees Vicky sitting at the table. "Hi Vicky, you kids going out again tonight?"

"Yes Sarah, heading to a movie. What are you up to?"

"Nothing, where is dad?"

"He is not back yet."

"How long ye been seeing each other now?"

"Maybe 3 months, I hope ye are ok with it."

"Vicky, we are happy to see him happy. He was alone for so long taking care of us. Hope he still knows how to date. You know what I mean."

Vicky laughs, "Oh, I think us oldies can figure it out."

I was standing outside the kitchen door listening to the exchange, glad that my family is getting along with Vicky. I walk in and notice the two ladies sitting opposite to each other. "What are ye girls chatting about?"

"Nothing dad, mmmm 3 months. Do I need to have the talk with you kids?" She laughs and the two ladies share playful smirk at each other.

Rachel walks in. She is now moving much more freely and uses one crutch, and hopefully none soon. Her speech is also much improved, she slurs a little but with time, I believe, our old Rachel will be back.

Schools started 4 weeks back, at the start of September and hopefully she will be able to go back and do her final year again. I suggested a private school, but she wanted to go back to her own. It is nearby, and she has all her friends there.

"Come on, Vicky, movie starts soon." I extend my arm for Vicky to hold.

"You kids behave now; I don't want to be a big sister again anytime soon." Sarah folds her arms and raises her eyebrow, as if being our mother.

Rachel laughs. We cannot but smile and Vicky pipes in, "Ah Paul, better start being careful."

She grabs my arm, and we head out. No smart comments follow. But I know my two daughters are glad that I am going on a date, that I have someone to share my life with.

"Oh, that was bad." I laugh. "If you can't beat them, shock them."

Vicky really turned out to be playful with wicked sense of humour. It took a while to let the kids know we were seeing each other, but they were great, and Vicky was so nice they all got on like a house on fire. We head to the movies quite a while before the movie starts. We sit at a nearby café and chat a little before heading to order our popcorn for the movie. The movie theatre wasn't too full, so we have the chance to be more relaxed. It was a romantic comedy movie, during which we held our hands and shared hearty laughter's.

"I don't know why the theatre wasn't full. It was a good movie," Vicky chimes praises of the movie as we head, hand in hand, like teenagers, ignoring the fact that it is either that or pensioners.

Saturday morning comes, I arrive in about 11. "You dirty stop out dad."

Then Sarah goes serious on me. "Sit down, I need to ask you something." I sit.

"What's up?" I know she is being serious, but this was kind of new to me.

"Have you told her yet about who you are or more to point that you own the shops?"

"Not yet, I was waiting to see if it was going anywhere."

"In all fairness, the longer you wait now the worse it is, ye are like a pair of teenagers together. Tell her." Sarah insists. *It felt like I was getting a telling off.*

"I know, it is probably time." But I need to be very thoughtful before revealing this to her, as for now, I have been playing that I don't own any of the shops. I don't want to come off as a liar to her.

I go about my day and drop Vicky a text.

Paul: Hey babe, I hope you are having a good day.

Vicky: Good day, lunch with Amanda. She is asking for you.

Paul: Good, can you check your roster for the next few weeks. I am wondering would you like a weekend away. I was thinking London.

Vicky: I am working next Friday for a week. You need me to book a day off?

Paul: Well, if you could make a weekend of it would be great if we could go down Friday morning.

Vicky: Ok I will book Thursday night off for holidays. Let me know where we are staying. You know my rule. Go Dutch. Prefer to pay my way.

Paul: OK, I will book for Friday and Saturday night.

Vicky: Good. What are ye doing tomorrow?

Paul: Nothing, I think.

Vicky: Amanda and Pamela are coming for lunch. I was wondering if you would like to come with Sarah and Rachel.

Vicky: If it is not too soon just saying it.

Paul: I will talk to Sarah and let you know.

I sit back and think. What will I do? Is it too soon? If our families are meeting each other . . . but should I tell her my truth first?

Paul: Sarah and Rachel have plans, how about if we are going to introduce them, we book lunch somewhere or some evening and at least you are not rushing around cooking.

Vicky: Well, that makes sense. But if you are free tomorrow. You join us.

Paul: ok. Nice to meet Amanda properly. Only been fleeting hellos usually.

My head is pacing wildly, recollecting all the wrong things I have told her about me, I can't come off as a liar. No woman ever liked a liar. She will leave me if I come off as a liar. I need to be strategic about it. Or I can just be honest, plain honest that why I told her I didn't own anything. Honesty might hurt, but it will save me from a dozen excuses, strategies and perhaps lies.

My head keeps being stuck at telling my truth, that I forgot about getting the something for lunch. I head out a little early to lunch and buy the customary bottle of wine.

Ringing at the door, I wait. Vicky answers, "What are you doing, you forget your key?"

"I thought maybe best not to be too free with a key when your girls are inside."

"It's fine with the girls. Come on in." Vicky says and hugs me before we head inside.

The girls are inside working away in the kitchen. "Hi Paul, nice to see you."

"Hi Amanda, ye cooking up a storm."

"I hear you talking about whisking mom on a dirty weekend in London."

"Ah yes, all sorted."

"Good, where have you booked for us?" Pamela is much quieter than Amanda but comes in on this. "Ye guys getting on well, anything nice booked?"

"We are staying fairly central, dinner Friday and see what Saturday brings." The lunch is set, and the aroma tells how delicious the food must be. It teased my appetite instantly. Amanda and Pamela take turns in telling me about their lives, how their mother brought them up, and how much she meant to them. It's obvious that these two young ladies were brought up with love and attention that any child could ask for, and Vicky did it all by herself. I also felt they were marking my cards not to hurt her. Or maybe I was reading too much in knowing I might be about to.

"Your mother must be proud of you two. And I am sure she is. It's such a pleasure to get to know you two, and of course your mother."

"It's a pleasure meeting you, too, Paul," Pamela says, "We're glad our mother found someone who makes her happy finally."

We finish our dinner and I have to appreciate their efforts, "Amanda, Pamela, Vicky, the food was delicious. Unbelievably delicious. Thank you for cooking all this. You can't beat home cooked meals. I could get used to them."

The three of them laugh, and Amanda says, "You're always welcome. Just let us know when so that we can say all our magic spells on the food."

We all chuckle and while the girls are cleaning up, Vicky and I take our coffee to the sitting room. "Where have you booked, hope it is not too expensive."

"It is ok, I got a good deal. I will give you the bill when we are leaving. Fair enough."

"Ok, now … what is the plan? I have not gone to London in years. I can't even remember when."

"Ok. what would you like? I am easy I have been down a lot, just not this year."

"We know you are easy, but nice to just look around. Harrods would be nice, not to shop, just maybe get a coffee and see how the other half lives. Would they leave an unemployed solicitor and nurse in?" She laughs, "Seriously, are you sure you can afford this? I know you are not working much and been an expensive year."

"It is ok, I had a lot saved from 10 years of no social life and no mortgage from Stephanie's mortgage cover. So, I am ok."

I hate lying like this, or at best misleading. Sarah is right, she needs to know and the trip to London it is when I have decided to come completely clean. Show her Ralph's letter if needs be. I am nervous, this could make or break us.

Come mid-afternoon, I tell them, "I must head off. Sarah is going back to her apartment soon and Matthew is at his girlfriend's. Thanks for a lovely lunch girl.".

"Bye Paul, enjoy London and take care of mom for us," Pamela says.

Amanda finished, "If ye can't be good, have fun, we know at your age no need to be careful." Vicky throws her a look, "Amanda, behave."

I laugh. "She has a point. Bye, all. Hope to see you soon."

I work away for the next week, mostly from home. Monitoring what is going on in Maria's absence. All is quiet and she had everything set up running smoothly. I take time to review all the shops' financials and see how everything is going. Rotterdam is probably the most surprising. It is breaking even and on the verge of profit. Online sales are going very well in the UK. Matthew did say they were busy and should have known we are doing well.

European online sales are slow, but we have not pushed it. Maybe time to take a run at that, everything is going well.

Maria comes back from holiday, and I arrange to see her. See how she is and maybe talk about the EU and sales and the upcoming Brexit.

When we get to chat, it takes a turn, she tells me things are going well at home and asks about my love life. I tell her about Vicky, I can see a change in her face. She composes fast and then chats on. I decide not to go into a long work discussion. I keep things to the point, discussing what needs to be discussed, I don't want things to be awkward between us again.

When I get back to my office, I send an email. To Nicola, Helen, Maria, and Oliver.

Afternoon all.

I have had a chance in the last weeks to analyse the online sales and review the EU hub.

Firstly, ye have done great job, everything is going well, and I know I have not been in the game much this year. But normality is returning so, I am too.

The shops here are running themselves to a large degree and centralisation all went well. What I want to look at now is Europe. Do we need a separate EU website? And what else do we need to look at for more EU selling?

The infra structure is there, we have the capacity in the Manchester hub and some in London. So why not see what we can do with it?

Oliver, you have online experience, take a look and see what is there.

I would like to arrange an evening to suit everyone. Here in Manchester for all of us. Helen and Nicola might book rooms and stay.

I want to use it to discuss a way forward within the EU, let Nicola and Helen meet everyone here and see the Manchester hub at the airport. More of make sure everyone knows everyone and feels involved.

As always, I am open to all suggestions and directions.

Don't worry, Helen and Nicola, I am not landing more work on ye, I just want your knowledge and opinion and see what involvement ye might like.

We can look at any other business when ye are up. Plan on 2 days. Liaise with each other and what works, I will fall in with your plans.

Regards,
Paul.

<h1 style="text-align:center">Chapter 31</h1>

Friday comes and I pick Victoria up in time to make the 9 AM train. I am quiet, a nervous wreck really.

"Hello beautiful, ready four your trip?" I try not to show my nervousness.

"Oh, yes. So ready." She sounds excited, and I am terrified of ruining her excitement.

"Come on Paul, if we are cutting it tight, we will get bad seats or maybe not even end up sitting together on a busy train."

"Don't worry, we will be fine."

"You ok, seen very off the last week. You are quiet today. If this is too much, just say we can slow it down."

"Too much?" I want to just let her know my truth and be with her. I don't want to lie or make excuses, but I also don't want to lose her. *I can't lose her, no.*

"Yes, if a weekend away and how close we are getting is getting too serious, just say. I am happy but I do not want to force you. We are both grown up. We can just go home if you prefer."

"No, this is not too much at all, if anything it's perfect."

"Then what?"

"Come on, let's get the train. We are cutting it fine." I try not to keep it too uptight and deflect for now.

We head to the platform. 2 minutes to 9.

"We are going to scrape on, and it looks packed."

Getting onto the train just before leaving we walk down the carriages. It is full. But I lead the way. We reach the first-class carriage and go in.

"Paul, this is first class. We do not have tickets." Vicky tries to pull me out of there.

"We do, come on." And I lead her to our seats. Sitting down, facing each other.

"Paul, why book first class, for getting here on time we would have had no problem."

"I have a reason; I want to talk to you. here is a bit more private and you don't have anywhere to go, just a few uninterrupted hours to talk."

"You are worrying me. What is this about?"

The waiter comes around with the menu, "You want breakfast?"

"I have lost my appetite; I want to know what is going on," she says without even looking at the waiter.

Looking up, I hand back the menu. "Coffee for two and scones for two please."

"OK, Vicky, firstly this is not anything bad. Nothing for you to worry about. Please trust me, it is nothing to worry about," I hold her hands, hoping to reassure her. "You know how important you are to me, and because of that, I am telling you what I am going to tell you now. You remember, when we started seeing each other you asked what I was hiding, and I reassured you it was not bad, but was complicated."

"Ok, I remember. You did not want to talk about it and reassured me no bunny boilers coming for me and not to worry. But you are still scaring me a bit. This is very cloak and dagger. So, tell me now. All in one go."

"Ok, listen and let me tell you this story, it sounds incredible. But we have a long journey and I promise I will answer anything you ask after, no restrictions, ok?"

She nods her head, and I continue, "Now. you know most of my history, only child, my mother and brought up with little. I married and had the kids and Stephanie died 11 years ago. I have always been a mid-level solicitor in my practise. Last year, I was given a job, along with an accountancy firm. A client died, Ralph Michaels. He owned a chain of sports shops. He died in a road traffic accident. We were asked by the executors, my boss, to analyse all his holdings and shops and personal assets and help run his business until the new owners took over. An accountant and I got the job. I was up and down in London trying to run things and get everything sorted."

"Ok, but that is work, nothing new there. Get to the punchline, please."

"Ok, we finished the analysis and presented it to the executors. After that meeting, my boss called me back and handed me a letter. Maybe if you'll read the letter, well part of it, might help the rest of this."

I hand Vicky the first part of the letter. Our coffee arrives at the same time. She looks at me and opens it. "Are ye sure you want me to read this?"

"Positive." I take a sip of coffee, without realizing it is scalding hot. Spilling a little as I scald myself and not focusing on what I am doing, but Vicky facial expressions, which are serious.

I watch her intently as she reads the letter and notice the changes in her facial expression as she works her way down through it. See her occasionally life her gaze to me for a moment. When she is finished, she looks at me. Lost for words. I wait for her reaction, afraid of what is coming next.

"Paul, what the hell. What does this mean? What is in the rest of the letter? What was the other influence in his life?"

"The rest is another story. Let's deal with this first."

"Ok, but if you are coming clean, come completely clean. So, tell me. In simple terms, what does it mean?"

"Put simply, I was his only relative and he left me everything. He gave me a choice. Take everything or nothing. I was left with a position of making a choice. My kids knew nothing. It put me in a complete spin, wrestling with what to do. Knowing my mother wanted nothing to do with him and so on. Ultimately, I elected to follow his will and so I inherited everything. It was very complicated and brought huge responsibility. I did not tell the children. This was the summer of last year. I needed to see how to handle this and ultimately, I told them over Christmas. We went up to Fort William for a few days and I told them and showed them this part of the letter. As you can guess they had oceans of questions. They were getting used to this and then Rachel's accident."

"I still don't get this Paul, why not tell me? You inherited a sports shop. You could have just told me." The bit of disappointment in her voice shakes me to my core. Outwardly, I look calm but inwardly, I am terrified.

"Victoria, I always had a simple enough life, family, job, and the usual routine. We were comfortable but that was about it. Nothing wild financially. Never knew wealth and this was going to change things."

"Change things how? Surely the shop is not that big."

"It was a chain of 6 shops, property, investments, and money. This guy was seriously wealthy. He never spent anything. The reason I did not say was that wealth was not me. I had it now, but I did not want to be judged by it, it was not who I am."

"Do you think I would have judged you by that? You should know me better." She is taken aback by the remark, and for the first time, picks up her coffee and sips it.

"I am banking on that now. But you answer this, when you met me, if you knew I owned a chain of outdoor shops and was a millionaire, would you have asked me to dinner or agreed to go out with me?"

She pauses and I see her mind working.

"I don't know, but I get what you are saying."

"It explains how you could give up work and everything else. But for all you have, you seem normal."

I laugh. "Normal?"

"You know what I mean, and the kids are so level. They don't have any of the trappings, cars, expensive clothes. So, you are very wealthy."

"I told the kids no major changes. They have been great. Matthew is working in a warehouse and sales."

"Why not in one of the shops?"

"He is, the warehouse, online and distribution are part of the business."

"Ok, the rest of the letter. What is in it? I want to know it all."

"Ah, that is very personal about Ralph and his life."

"Ok, is it criminal or illegal?"

"No, but very personal details."

"Well, hit me with everything now. No exceptions. Give me the letter. I want to get this over with and if I don't know I will only be wondering. I don't want secrets."

I look at her and taking the rest of the letter from my pocket I hand it to her.

As she reads it, it feels like an eternity. Though I know it is only minutes. This time the changes in her facial expressions are dramatic.

"Wow, Paul, that is one hell of a story. Where to even start."

"Let's deal with this in two halves, the first part of the letter first, please."

"Ok, more in a nutshell, you are wealthy, lots of property money and the shops and you didn't tell me because you did not want me to judge you on that, but see you for who you are. Which I do."

"Exactly, you get it.", "Sort of, but I need to think on this, why wait until now? But those question for me to consider for a while. I will come back to them.".

"Now part two, bloody hell Paul. That is so romantic and so sad. Did he ever get over her?"

"No, he became reclusive."

"The adult shop, is it still there?"

"Yes, it is."

We spend the rest of the journey talking and nerves continue, and she has not given me any conclusions yet, only questions.

With that the train pulls into the station.

Getting off, we walk down the platform. "Well, what are you thinking of me now, do you want me to go home or are we ok?"

"This is all huge Paul; I get why you told me like this. No getting away. Let's talk about this, I want to learn more. But be warned. Don't let anything important out if I ask. So why London to tell me?"

"Well, I said, if here, we would have all the time needed, Undisturbed to talk and you could see some of it, maybe making it real."

I hail a taxi to the apartment.

During the ride, she asks me more about how my kids reacted to it, and where else are my shops. Pulling up outside, "Where is this?"

"I have an apartment here. Not been down all year. But this is one of Ralph's buildings and where he lived while here."

We walk in and I study Vicky as she scans the place. "This is all new?"

"Everything was let go a bit, so I renovated this last year as I was going to be here a lot and even if rented it, it needed an upgrade."

"It is very nice."

We drop our bags. Vicky takes a short tour of the apartment. "Would you like to go for a walk?"

"Air would be good."

We head out. Coming out of the front door, I see Vicky eyeing a bookshop on the ground floor. She says nothing and walks on. Rounding the corner, she stops outside the adult store. "Is this it?"

"Yes. Effectively it is Adam's. Run by him. Though Ralph financed it, he never took an active role in running it. Adam runs it away as he always has. The group London offices are up there." I point to them, and we walk on. "Other than the warehouse, the building with the apartments, and this building here, I don't own any other property."

"Must be hard, only own offices, apartments, and shop units here." She smiles. Trying to make light. But I see it is still a struggle for her. But she is trying, maybe hope for me yet. "Yeah, it is," I joke along.

We walk up to Covent Garden and find a restaurant and I suggest lunch. "You must be hungry." We sit and chat and she questions me away on Ralph and the shops and how it felt.

"So, the second part of the letter. Wow. He had some adventure. The Lilly story is such fun I guess and then sad in many ways. I am curious about the box and everything, but the big questions now for me is did you talk to Adam and look…" I visibly take a breath and pause looking at her. "Just be honest, we all have history, and it is all before me. I am curious really. No judgement."

"Ok. Well, I did say ask whatever and I will be honest. Only way forward. Yes, I spoke with Adam. And looked. Experienced some of Ralph's world."

"How was it?"

"It was very surprising, lots of fun and a real adventure. Alternate world of escapism. Different to what you expected." I answer concisely and honestly, I feel light, like taking the burden off myself. But nervous as to the next obvious question.

"Now the hard question. Did you explore with someone?"

I go red but I know I must be honest with her. "Well, I told you I was seeing someone last year and I ended it last year. But yes, I did explore with her for what little we got to explore it. Scratched the surface only."

"It is ok. I am not judging; I know you saw someone last year and we all had loves before. I just wanted to know. I was just curious."

"Now, Victoria, can I ask you something? And before you answer remember this. I told you about this because I don't want secrets between us. I hope this will go somewhere further than is and I showed you the letter because you are, I hope, my significant other. Is all this too much for you? I don't want to lose you, but I didn't want this secret any longer."

"I would have preferred if you had not kept from me, the shops and all that. But I get it. The letter, I can see why you showed it to me. It was not always you. As regards part two, I don't know what you want. Are you asking me to explore this alternative world and fetish scene and whatever? I do not know."

"Victoria. No, I am not asking anything of you, save to continue seeing me. You asked to see part two. I don't know if the fetish scene interests you or repulses you. But I know it is not a need for me. It is fun, if fun for both. An adventure."

"So, you don't want to explore it with me?" I see her raise an eyebrow.

"No, I ….." I am embarrassed again.

"So, you don't?"

An air of anxiety enters my voice. "I…"

"I am sorry, Paul. I can see your anxiety. I get it. I get the letter. I get why you explored it. When I was younger, I was always playful and adventurous. Though never tried fetish or the like. Who knows? Could be a lot of fun. Corsets were my thing, but only had one nice one. Too expensive. But let me take all this in."

I look at her. "And as for you, Paul. This is all a shock to be honest. But how I feel for you has not changed, though I may have more questions. Just remember despite your wealth, I am still an independent woman."

I lean in next to her. Gently touch her face and softly peck her on the lips. "You have no idea how relieved I am. I was so worried the last two weeks waiting to tell you. Afraid you might leave me."

"Very sensitive for a fetish man. Or is it dominant? So, if I misbehave, will I be punished?" She says with a serious look. But then laughs. "Sorry could not keep a straight face. Hey, looks like you may have a few tricks to show me. Always the quiet ones. Let us just enjoy the weekend. Show me the empire."

I sigh and agree. I was never so relieved. However, I got on with Maria. This had a different feel. I always knew with Maria it was what was and never really had a future. Vicky is different. She is different. Single and we could enjoy each other's company openly. We have a sense of relaxed normality; we aren't escaping from our boring family life. in fact, if anything, we are bringing our families together. And that's the best part about this relationship, about us.

We spend the next hours just browsing Covent gardens and we pass the London shop. "Can I go in Paul?" She cannot contain her curiosities.

"Of course, whatever you want."

We walk in and within a few minutes, the manager appeared. "Mr. Bridges, surprised to see you here. Is there anything I can do for you? Do you need something?"

"No thank you, just browsing, down for the weekend. I see you are busy; I won't keep you from it."

"Mr. Bridges, I have never heard you spoken to in that way. This is so much. I can just imagine the shock of one, let alone six of these and God knows what else. Have you changed anything since last year?"

"The shop just got a facelift, but we set up a Manchester office, warehouses and distribution and warehousing, and a shop in Rotterdam also. The shops needed to catch up with the times, Ralph sort of stopped and stagnated since Lilly died."

"This really is a side you kept to yourself."

As I look at her, I say, "I am glad I don't have too anymore. Would be nice to share what I am doing with someone. The kids are too young, and I don't want them getting notions. Do you want anything here?"

"Paul, no, this is yours, if I want something I will buy it. I have told you that, I am independent."

She browses a little more and we exit the shop. Wandering back to the apartment, we pass the offices, "Do you need to go in?"

"No, but if you want to go you can. Honestly, I want to be an open book."

"Maybe when empty. You don't need to be explaining me now."

We walk on, she looks at the coffee shop and travel agents. "These yours too?"

"No, I own the building, they rent the units from me." As we arrive outside the adult shop. "This is mine, but run by

Adam, as if it was his own. The same as he did for Ralph. But I told you that already. Sorry nervous and repeating myself".

I eye her wearily as she looks in the window. "I have never gone into a shop like this, bar once, with my husband when we were in Amsterdam. Very sheepishly."

"Well, if you want to go in at any stage we can. Even to ease a curiosity, I have keys in the apartment, if you want to go in when closed, and there is a back entrance through what was Ralph's office, so you can go in quietly."

"Was his office? What is it now?"

"Adam has changed it into a high-end showroom for larger fetish equipment and toys, for sale or rent the room. I have not actually seen it. I have not been in here since last year. Look, this weekend is yours, I am so relieved to have told you, but I know this is a shock. So, ask what you want, see what you want, and relax. Honestly, London is here to come back to whenever we want."

"Thanks, Paul, this has been overwhelming. Dinner tonight, can we just stay in, and talk? I would like to hear the full Ralph story and how you found out and your adventure."

We spend the evening with a bottle of wine, Chinese takeout and me recounting the story. We look briefly into Ralph's chest. "This looks like an alternate life like nothing I have ever seen or imagined. Tell me about what it was like?"

I recount the conversations with Adam and Nicole, the first club, what was seen, and the people we met. We head to bed to enjoy each other. I have a huge sense of relief and Vicky has moved to a sense of curiosity and playfulness. I am just enjoying her enthusiasm.

As I kiss her softly heading to bed, Vicky gets playful. "Paul, make love to me, like you are behind the curtain you mentioned, show me a little of this."

I am taken aback; I didn't expect this.

"Please, Paul."

I stretch her out on the bed and straddle her. "Tell me to stop anytime." I lean in and start to kiss her. Then sitting up, I take my shirt off. I start to kiss and touch her. With one hand

I pin her wrists over her head. I slowly push her cami-set shorts off. So soft, so silky. I tease her all over, with my free hand.

"What would you do here?" She asks.

"Well, I would probably tie your hands over your head. So, you can't use them. But….."

"Then do it, please, I want to experience what you did."

I stare down at her. I get up, walk to my wardrobe, and take out a tie. As I walk back, I finish undressing in front of her. She whispers, smiling up at me. "I love the sight and feel of your body against mine."

Straddling her again, I gently tie her wrists together and over her head to the bed.

I then explore every inch of her body with two hands. Kissing her, touching her, penetrating her with my fingers as I have done so often before.

I keep my touch gentle. Watching her react against me. I watch her hands strain against the tie as she pulls down. The intensity on her face as I slowly work her, reacting to her face and expressions of pleasure. Her eyes closed, the quiver on her lips and gasps of breath as her pleasure mounts.

Sliding my fingers out I move and parting her legs, watch her face as she looks at me, my eyes on hers as push into her, so open for me and slowly make love to her. We both watch each other as I do. My hands roam under her top and over her chest, gently teasing her erect nipples, and up her arms to the tie. Watching her reaction as tries to move her hands. Moving faster I feel my release coming, going fast, and pushing her back to the headboard. Finally releasing into her. Enjoying the feeling as out bodies and facial expression relaxing on motionless moments that followed.

When we are done, I untie her hands.

"Paul, that was gorgeous. You were so soft. I loved it."

I lay back and she takes off the top of her cami and lays naked against me. Her head on my chest as she falls asleep in my arms. Little more said of what just happened,

It is Saturday, I wake up first, put on my shirt and trousers, not bothering to find my shorts, I decide to head down to the

Deli and pick up fresh coffee and pastry. Bringing them back, Vicky is awake, and I bring her coffee and pastry in bed. Climbing into bed with her, we have breakfast. The sun is shining in from the lovely summer morning.

"You ok baby?"

"I am fine, last night was such fun. Can I ask, what else did you use?"

I just laugh, good morning to you too. So, the questions continue.

"You are curious. Well, a blindfold, or tie standing up, really anything can be fun."

"This does sound interesting, maybe you can teach me a little and see if we enjoy it. I like it so far."

"You are all surprises."

"Well, I told you. I was adventurous when younger. I just forgot how much," and she laughs.

"Now, it is too nice a morning to waste. Let's get up. Or should I say, get the rest of you up? I need a shower, come join me, and let's start the day as we mean to go on. Together."

I smile back at her. "Yes, madame. Whatever you instruct." Laughing, "Well we know you can be bossy. Sure, you have not played these games before?"

"Come on, get your ass into the shower, that way too nice a shower not to enjoy together." We enjoy a long shower before heading out into the sunshine.

We just enjoy the rest of the weekend. Walking, chatting and lunch in Harrods.

"How the other half lives." Then looking at me, "You are the other half, hell more like the other 1%." I blush as I never see myself that way.

"Please don't think of me like that, I am the man you have known since we met. I just happen to have some wealth, but other than that, I am what you know."

By the time we get back to Manchester on Sunday I have answered all the questions, I think. Except the one I assume she wants to ask but has not. Who was the woman last year? Well, if she does not ask, I won't say for now anyway.

We arrive back to my home and Victoria comes in. Sarah is there with Rachel. I excuse myself, and coming back, I hear Sarah and Vicky. "Your dad told me about the last year. Must have been a shock."

"Yes, it really was, took a while and honestly, I am still trying to get my head around the full extent of it. "

"Can I ask you something? How has Paul coped?"

"Hard to know. He did not change that we saw. Same old dad. Certainly, he does not show his newfound wealth. We never guessed anything. He dealt with it alone until he told us at Christmas. But I am glad he told you, he needs someone."

"Did he not tell anyone?"

"I think only those at work knew. We have no extended family and honestly, he has revolved life around us since mum. You are the first person he has dated that we met."

"Really?"

"Yes, I don't think he saw anyone seriously before now. There were a few dates here and there but nobody we ever heard of. You must be important to him."

I know that Sarah is talking me up to Vicky and making her feel special which she is. With that, I walk back to the kitchen.

"All good here?" They both smile.

"Oh yes, all good." I hear from Vicky.

"Now time for me to head home, thanks for the chat, Sarah. Paul, can I grab a lift?"

As we drive and get close to her home, she asks. "Paul, pull over." I look at her. "Now please."

I do so, wondering if something was bothering her. The next thing I know, she leans over, puts her arm around my neck and pulls me into a deep kiss. When she finally releases me, she says, "Thank you, thank you for letting me in this weekend. I know you have history and whatever that is, it is. I have thought long and hard and if you will have me, I want to be part of your future. I have not felt like this for anyone in the last ten years and if you want to bring me behind the curtain, I am happy to go with you. The demo was amazing."

I kiss her back, "Thank you. As regards the curtain, just remember the journey is the fun. The act is just the destination. Let's see where the journey brings us and what acts lay at the end. As regard who knows what, Adam and Nicole obviously know I have looked, but Sarah and kids and anyone I know really has no idea and never will. That part of my life is mine, and now yours if you want to look."

"I know. Your secret is safe. Now, if you want that dinner with all the kids, let's arrange it. It is time they all met. Let's go home. You wore me out with everything this weekend."

With that, I drop her home. Amanda is there to greet her. I kiss her goodbye as she walks to her front door with a smile. Going in, I just hear, "Someone looks happy. How was the weekend?"

The next few weeks were good, I felt my apprehension lift. We enjoyed each other and dinners and coffee. We arranged dinner for the kids. I book a nearby restaurant. It was a little bit nerve wracking getting them all together. Wondering how they would react to each other. This was a big step for me. I knew this was not something I would ever have to broach with Maria.

When the evening finally comes, I arrive first with the kids. We are no sooner sitting down, and Vicky arrives in with her girls. Thankfully, before we have a chance to do anything, they all introduce themselves to each other. Amanda, being Amanda, takes control and just makes a joke about the two teenagers being all coy that Saturday in the shop.

It doesn't take much for Sarah to start. It's amazing what you can pull with coffee and a pastry. Sarah and Vicky's girls all seem to get on extremely well. Though there is a little bit of an age gap, Sarah is old for her age.

Thankfully, they all had common ground to make fun of us. Vicky did throw a few nurse ratchet jokes back and her own girls for forcing them into meeting.

Dinner went off as well as anybody could expect or hope. I could see them exchange numbers with the girls as they left.

They were all talking as we headed home and simply said that Vicky's girls are genuinely nice.

We plan another trip to London.

Chapter 32

MARIA

Hearing about Paul dating someone hits me, but all I can do is remember, that I had my chance, and I blew it. I will remember the time we shared and perhaps will cherish those memories for a long time, but I can't be stuck at him. Now, I need to focus on what I have and try to save that. I have my marriage, my children, and my job, and I need to be there to fulfil each responsibility. I can't cheat on any of it now, not anymore.

Returning from holidays after a couple of weeks, I exchanged a few messages with Lara. We have decided to get a weekend away to London and have arranged to meet them for dinner. This will be interesting to see what they are like away from a holiday setting.

We book our weekend and Lara said they will book someplace interesting for dinner. They live a little bit out of the city, so I do offer them a place to stay in the apartment. Mark said that he does not mind and I've no doubt Paul could not care if we had anybody staying with us.

I'm looking forward to the weekend and getting some shopping therapy, it somehow always works for me. Getting a couple of new things that I have my eyes on gives me a different kind of pleasure – it makes me feel special. After my shopping therapy, we take the Friday afternoon train down. Dinner with the other two is booked for Saturday night so we have Friday to ourselves and all-day Saturday. I arranged to meet Lara in Oxford St. At 2:00 PM for some shopping and Mark and Max are going to find some place to watch a game for the afternoon.

This will be a good weekend away, Mark and I smile more often at each other, show affection more often, and we want to be with each other. And these weekends away from home contribute a lot to this. *Everything seems perfect.* Or so I thought.

The last thing I expect on a Saturday morning is to bump into Paul and Victoria. I had never met her, and he had not even told me her name. Mark and I are heading out for breakfast, and we meet them as they step out of their apartment. This is an incredibly awkward feeling. A sea of emotion comes over me, but all I can do is put on a good front.

Mark is in good form and looking forward to his day, and I don't want to ruin his mood. He says hello to Paul and asks them where they are heading. Paul says they are just going out for some breakfast and a walk. The ground could have opened up and swallowed me when Mark asks them to join us. What can I say?

I don't want to have this breakfast anymore.

I can see the look on Paul's face, too. But before anybody can say anything Victoria accepts the offer. We head out for breakfast and go up to the coffee shop on the corner. Probably not the first choice for any of us but, it was the easiest. Victoria introduces herself to me with a lovely warm welcoming smile. I can see she is a lovely, happy, and friendly person and just seems so relaxed.

Over breakfast, Victoria mostly speaks to me. She asks me how long I have known Paul and how long I have worked with the company. We have some general conversations about her plans for the weekend and we tell them we are heading out to dinner with friends that night. Victoria says they have little plans just to enjoy the day and they will pick something up later. I remember how often I have done with Paul.

Once we finish our coffee, I make a move and tell Mark we better get some shopping done. As we head out, I hear Mark tell Paul that he's going to watch a game for the afternoon and asks him to join them. Thankfully, Paul declines and says that he is not much for sport.

The other two stay behind and Mark wishes them a good day before we head out. I was never so relieved to be heading away from Paul. But this is how life has to be, and they look happy, and Victoria just seems lovely. I am glad that Paul found someone, though there is still a pang of jealousy. I wish them a happy life together. It would have been different if I had met Paul alone with Victoria, with Mark beside me, I wasn't too fazed upon seeing Paul with someone else.

Mark commented as we walked out that this is the first time he noticed Paul being relaxed.

"How long have they been together? Mark asks me.

I simply say, "I don't know. But they look happy together."

Mark nods his head, and we continue our walk to our next destination.

We spend the morning strolling through Covent gardens. We pick up a few things for the children. I know I will be going clothes shopping in the afternoon with Lara; my shopping therapy will surely make me forget about our awkward encounter with Paul and Victoria.

We head back to the apartment and drop off the few things we picked up for during the morning. As we pass Adams' shop, Mark suggests we call in.

"Let's explore this. A little exploration never hurt anyone." I can sense Mark is teasing me, as if something is on his mind. I agree to go in, inwardly hoping he really picks something 'exciting' from there, as hope not to bump into Paul and Victoria in there, Awkward enough meeting Adam.

We go in and take a look around and find that the shop is busy. Adam comes over to us as soon as he is free. We get a moment alone as Mark is looking on the shelves. Very quickly I ask Adam, "Is the playroom being used tonight?" His face immediately turns red. "There is no need to answer, thank you."

I have been wondering if it is a fun sort of evening with Max and Lara, I might just show it to them as something that is part of the shop. Not to use it, but just to show them.

"Maria, there is nobody in there now if you want to go in and take a look around, perhaps this is somewhere you want to show Mark."

Before I can answer, "Show me what?"

I have little choice now but to bring Mark into the playroom. "It is just a new addition to the shop here, a place where they have some big and specialized equipment, would you like to see it."

"Equipment?"

"Why don't you two go and take a look?" And Adam hands me a key.

Heading into the room, I turn on the light. Even with the lights on, there is a dark sultry feeling. The dark wood paneling of the floor and walls and the imposing cross standing in a corner give the room a dark ambiance. As we look over, I get a memory flash of that night when I used it. Snapped out of my flashback, hearing Mark, "Holy shit, whoever knew places like this existed other than in films. Do people actually use this room?"

"All of the equipment and displays are for sale to order. These smaller toys and extras can all be bought in the shop. I know Adam had a plan to hire out the room if people wanted it for private use, but I am not sure if that has actually happened."

We take our time looking around the room and they can see Mark trailing his fingers over the equipment, from the cross to the cage. Looking at him, I wonder was this how I looked like the first time I walked around here. A part of me is glad that Mark is more intrigued than disgusted at all this. I can only imagine if he, someday, wants to use it. Oh, I will be so happy to experience this with him. We sure have been more understanding with each other now, like he says, a little exploration never hurt anyone. I want him to cage me, chain me, tie me, and make love to me in this room. Or a room similar to this. Get back what we once had.

"OK, I'm done, Maria," Mark announces the end of his exploration, snapping me out of my thoughts – thoughts of us in this room.

We head out and hand the keys back to Adam, after all that we do not pick up anything. I think Mark was so overwhelmed by the room; he forgot what we were looking for.

We drop our bags back to the apartment and head up to meet the other two. Spotting us first, Lara walks over and simply jokes, "Hardly recognized you with your clothes on." Her humor is a breath of fresh air for the afternoon and we just shop. Mark takes Max back to the apartment and he drops their bags and changes for tonight. They head out and find a pub to watch a game for the afternoon.

We had all arranged to meet back at the apartment at 6:00 and Max and Lara told us they had a booking for eight and joked they hoped we had not lost our sense of adventure. Much as I tried, I could not get her to tell me where we were going.

Arriving at the apartment, Lara asks me, "Where did you find this place? Is this an Airbnb?"

"It was a company perk and I use this apartment when I work in London as our head office was around the corner. It belongs to Paul, my boss. He has the apartment downstairs, and the rest of the staff get to use this when we want to."

"Impressive. You work in a good company," she approves, and we begin to get ready for our dinner.

There was a taxi booked for 7:30. When we sit in the taxi, Lara gives the taxi driver an address and I do know from the address that it is in the warehouse district. I wonder what sort of a restaurant is out there. The extremely quiet and dark area and certainly not a place I would like to find myself alone on a dark night.

As we pull up, I see the name of it over the door. "The Supper Club." I do not think there is a club like this in London, not that I looked for it. I wondered if it is the same as the Amsterdam club, but I certainly cannot let on that I know anything about it.

Walking in, the layout is somewhat different, but inside the club, it is very much the same. The walls are lined with one big long bed with the eating tray in the middle, reminds me of the club in Amsterdam. There is live entertainment different from that in Amsterdam but at the same time very much in keeping with the theme. Mark asks Max if they had been here before, and he said they had come once or twice but this is more fun when you go with people.

"We don't think many of our friends would appreciate this, but said maybe ye would."

We had a very enjoyable evening with the drinks flowing and the mystery meals. By the time we left the club, it was nearly midnight and even the taxi ride back to the apartment met heavy traffic around Leicester Square. The square and the theatre district seemed almost busier at night than it was by day. Getting back to the apartment, we are all quite happy after having maybe a little too much to drink.

The taxi drops us at the corner outside of Adam's shop, and Mark proceeds to tell Max and Lara about the room he saw earlier today. They both seem quite interested to hear about it and Mark asks me if I had the keys.

"No, only Adam has keys that I am aware of, and I don't know if it is booked for the night. Maybe another time."

We head up to the apartment and sit around chatting a bit longer, opening some drinks and talking about the holiday. Heading to bed, Mark comments on how much he enjoyed the evening.

"Wasn't it a pity the room was locked?"

I look at him and say, "And Mark, what were you going to do in there if Max and Lara wanted to use the equipment and playroom?"

"I don't know, I hadn't even thought that far ahead. But I presume they would appreciate it or at the very least not be shocked by it." I presume some of this loss of inhibition is the drink talking and an interesting night out.

We head to bed and have to admit that it was a lovely evening, and it was really just a reminder of Paul threw me.

The following morning, I am up first and head out to pick up some fresh baking for breakfast. By the time I come back, I can hear the guest shower going, and from the sounds coming from it appeared to be a shower for two. Walking into the kitchen, Mark is already there making coffee.

"Looks like somebody is having fun this morning." He jokes nodding towards the bathroom.

After breakfast, Max and Lara pack up and head for the tube station and home. They look to meet up again sometime and suggested that they might come to Manchester, or we could all meet somewhere else. Lara is very full of fun and as she pecks both of us on the cheek she whispers to me. "Maybe next time find those keys and show us that very interesting room." I feel her hand on waist as she says it. And with that and glint in her eye, off she goes. I decide not to share that just now with Mark, but certainly I wonder about her now.

We have a lazier morning before we pack and head for the train back to Manchester. Other than being thrown from meeting Paul and Victoria, it was a very good weekend.

I stayed away from my work emails all weekend. I take a very quick look at my inbox and there is one e-mail marked urgent. I see this is from the Fort William shop. Subject line is "Personal time." I think to myself that I have never seen an urgent e-mail coming in from Caroline and normally she is well able to manage staffing and time off in her shop. I wonder what is going on. I hope nothing too bothering.

<h1 style="text-align:center;">Chapter 33</h1>

Vicky has been full of fun since the children have met. That is a big hurdle out of the way for both of us, we are just enjoying each other.

Vicki has loads of questions about the shops, Ralph and about me looking behind the curtain. We became more playful and adventurous in the bedroom as we are finding our way. I find this way more relaxed than when I did with Maria, and I'm not sure if it is because I have more experience, or because we don't have to hide when we meet. The whole relationship is so much more relaxed.

We headed down to London on the Friday morning train as I wanted to call into the office for a few hours and catch up with what was going on there. The video conference works extremely well but there is still nothing like face-to-face to connect with the staff. It is also good for them to see an employer who turns up as opposed to who just rings in.

Vicki took the afternoon to just explore the area more and felt brave enough to call into Adam's shop on her own. Adam recognized her and went over for a chat to see if she wanted anything. I showed her Adam's letter and said that Adam and Nicole knew everything. Vicki in her usual direct friendly manner dropped into the conversation with Adam that Paul had told her everything about the shop, looking behind the curtain, and she also had seen the letters.

They chatted for a few minutes and then Adam dropped me a quick text when he was dealing with another customer.

Adam: Paul, I was just talking to Vicky when I bumped into her. She told me that you told her everything and she had seen the letters. Before I put my foot in it is there anything she doesn't know.

Paul: The only thing she doesn't know is that it was Maria last year. She does know there was somebody but has never asked who. She does know we explored and that you were a significant help.

Adam: Thanks

I arrange to meet Vicky at 3:00 when I am finished with work. Arranging to meet her in the coffee shop, I decide now was as good a time as any. We have a quick coffee and I tell her that I want to show her something. She's relaxed and does not inquire too much only simply asks, "What?"

I tell her follow me and we head out the door. Heading out I lead her into the office, the first person we bump into is Helen. "Paul, did you forget something?" Helen asks as I had only left 10 minutes earlier.

"No, this is Victoria. I said I would show her the offices. She had never managed to make it in here with me before."

Rather than explaining anything to Helen, as I always suspected she might have known there was something going on with myself and Maria, I simply put an arm around Vicky's waist. This simple gesture told its own story and Helen then proceeded to introduce herself. "Paul has kept you quiet," she smiles.

Vicky politely replies, "That is Paul, he always does like a bit of mystery and keeps everybody somewhat in the dark."

Helen just laughs, "You can say that again, when he was first our boss here, we always felt he was three steps ahead of us. Now we know it was more like five steps. Would you like to meet some of the others?"

Without waiting for an answer, she introduces her to some of the other staff around before I interrupt. "I'm just going to give Vicki a brief tour and I'm sure you will meet her again in the not-too-distant future."

I take Vicki around and show her Ralph's office. Head on and look around the rest of the building. Heading back out,

Vicki asks me, "Why did you bring me in when everybody was there?"

"Simple, I wanted you to meet everybody, and I wanted them to know we were together."

"Oh. No more keeping us a secret, huh?'

"Oh no. I want to tell the entire world that we are together. That I am so lucky to have you with me."

"Aren't you cheesy? A big old marshmallow behind it all." Vicki and I laugh a little and continue our tour.

Once we had said our hellos to almost everyone in the office, we called it a day and headed back to the apartment. Passing Adam's shop, Vicky playfully asks me, "Are there any fun surprises in store for the weekend?"

"Whatever you want, And I know you have been curious. So, if you want, we can meet Adam and Nicole on Sunday evening for dinner. They're going out tomorrow night, so we're not free. But said they would happily meet us for dinner on Sunday if we wanted."

"When did you arrange that?"

"I called into the shop here for a couple of minutes when we arrived, just for a quick update on how things were going. I know you have been curious, so I asked Adam and Nicole if they were free for dinner over the weekend. I did not tell them that you know everything and said if nothing else it would be nice for you to meet the people I know down here."

Vicki smiles, "I have a confession. I was in the shop earlier and I was talking to Adam, I told him you told me everything. So, he knows I know."

I can't but smile, "I better warn him that you may have questions on Sunday." We both laugh.

"So, it could be an interesting weekend. Did you see anything else in the shop?"

"I did not end up looking really, more talking to Adam and half looking. Maybe you can show me more at some stage."

I smile, "Is that a question or an instruction?"

"Take it as a strong suggestion."

"Come on, let's get an early dinner and we can come back later if you wish for a look around."

"I went shopping, I would like to eat in, restaurants all the time are not really me. I will just make something simple if that is ok?"

"Of course, we will be out Sunday evening by the looks of it now anyway. I better book somewhere."

I watch Vicki making herself at home, working around the kitchen. I watch and laugh, I haven't watched and enjoyed watching a woman work in the kitchen other than Stephanie. Looking over, "What is so funny."

"I just realized. That is probably the first time the cooker was used."

"Really Paul, never! You are a disaster. Just as well you don't come down too often. Living on take out. You better learn somethings to cook. Simple recipes."

"Teach me, madame." I bow down, showing her the respect.

We enjoy dinner and wine. Deciding not to go too far. After the first glass is finished, we just relax with TV playing in the background.

"So, you want to show me more?"

"More, ah yes, your suggestion. Come on then."

I head to the desk and get a set of keys. As I look at them, I stare over at Vicki, "How much more do you want to see?"

"Give me your best shot Bridges, we are here now," she says with a giddy glint in her eye.

"OK, let's go."

Vicky leads on down the stairs. Heading out the front door and down the street. I call her back. "This way," as I begin to unlock the door to Ralph's old office. Heading in, I turn on the lights. Vicky comes in after me. The look on her face tells a hundred tales of surprise and shock. "Never seen you lost for words."

"Doubt if I ever have been like this."

I watch her eyes scan the room and then she begins to walk around, looking at everything. Interestingly, the cabinets are the first things she passes and stops to look at. "I see," she stops while looking at some extreme toys. "Have you used these?"

"No, that stuff looks extreme, I looked behind the curtain, not rushed in. These are all the shops and cater for all taste. They are locked in so just for display and not for use by the public. I have keys if you want to look closer at any."

I watch her walk on and she looks at the bigger things. The cross, running her hands over it. "Now Paul, this looks interesting. This looks like something you described."

"Yes, it is." I watch her leaning against it. Then she moves on to examine the whips, paddles, and canes. "These look hard."

"Yes, I have not tried them, only thing I ever tried was this." and I held up a flogger. "It looks hard, but in reality, it doesn't feel that hard."

As she does, I use it on my hand. She hears the sound, and says, "That sounds painful."

"You hardly feel it. I will show you," and I take her hands. Using it on her once, she looks up. "That feels soft, but it looks." Before she can say anymore… "I told you; pain is not my thing. This is only for fun. This is a huge sample of everything from the shop and extreme play."

We poke around the room and head into the shop then. As soon as we enter there, the mood is almost lighter. "This looks nearly timid compared to there." She picks up a whip and some other toys. Then goes to put them back. "I have to ask, what are you doing?"

"I forget the shop is closed, maybe we can call in tomorrow and get them."

I can only laugh aloud. "Vicky, I own this shop. Take whatever you want. Just tell Adam on Sunday that you did some quality control. He will enjoy the joke" She blushes, and I walk over and pick up what she put back.

"Come on, you need another wine."

"You better believe I do."

For the rest of the night, we just relax, curled on the couch, Vicky looks like she is taking it in. Out of curiosity, I ask, "Are you ok? Was it too much?"

She curls into me more. "Just the size of what you have and that part of you is becoming so real. This is another world. You have a big business and lots of staff. See the office and all those working there today in administration brings the size home to me. The shop and your experience in other things."

She wraps her arms tightly around me, "Now let's just watch the movie." We decided on a rom-com, shared a few laughs and kisses, and headed to bed eventually.

The following morning, Vicky gets up before me and comes back to bed with tea for us both. Sitting up enjoying it, like any couple having a lazy Saturday. We decide to head out for breakfast. Before we get up, I have to ask, "Vicky, you ok?"

"Yes, perfect. Just yesterday and then last evening. I am getting my head around what you have and the other stuff."

"Don't mind the other stuff. I barely looked, other than some basic toys and seeing what a club was like, I have not used any of the extreme toys. It is just fun."

"I know and we will have fun, trust me. Now, let's get some breakfast. It looks like a lovely morning." I love the mischievous undertones of thoughts untold.

We finish our tea and get ready to enjoy our day ahead. Vicky dresses up in her sundress, and I must say, I never thought sundresses could suit someone this much.

"You look really beautiful."

"Thanks, handsome." She gives a peck on my cheek, and we head out.

Little do we know that we will be meeting people first thing in the morning. We walk straight into Maria and Mark, coming down the stairs. I am taken aback. I had no idea they were down. I could see so did Maria. She never met Vicky. So, I can only guess what she is thinking.

We exchange pleasantries and Mark asks us to join them for breakfast. Before I can make an excuse, Vicky accepts.

Pulling the door out, she smiles at me. "I get to meet more of your staff and friends this weekend."

We walk to the corner café and order pastry and coffee. Vicky is chatting to Maria, I can only imagine how Maria is feeling. I hear some of the questions, how long with the company and know me, etc. Will she put two and two together and realise Maria is who I explored with. Breakfast ends and Maria quickly gets up to leave. She keeps up a good front all the way.

They are no sooner out the door. "Well, well, you are full of surprises this weekend. So that was last year's complication." She knew it, I should have guessed.

I watch to see her reaction. I know my face just answered it for her. "Married!!" she says. "Yes, it sort of came from nowhere on me and when started she told me her marriage was in trouble and was just going to be something casual and not interfere with her home."

I stop and watch. There is silence. "And?" is all she says. "And we enjoyed some good times. She was there when I was getting my head around all of this, she knew what was there. It was her job to figure that out. But then when this job ended, in many ways, so did we. We went back to reality in Manchester, and I could see she was conflicted. So, I ended it, told her work on Mark. Try and fix things. I never expected much."

"Was it good between ye?"

"When down here yes, I suppose it was. But always just here really. An alternative life away from reality. I realized it could never be more. I ended it. We work well together and when in Manchester, was always just work."

"Ok, more to get my head around. But look it is past. A bit awkward I must say. But I can only guess how this was awkward for her. One more question. The room we were in last night. Did ye?"

I look, hoping my expression won't answer the question, "I was never even in it with her as a playroom, only when it was Ralph's office, and no, we never used the room." I am so thankful that we didn't.

She gets up and simply looks, "Come on, let's get some air." I pay the bill, and we walk on. Nervously, I follow her lead. What is next? I feel some relief as she links my arm as we walk. Leaning up, "Don't worry, she is your ex. I have to get used to that. Everyone has a history. Easier if she was not working for you. But looks like she is back with her own life now also. Past is past. I will say no more about her. But may have a question or two."

I visibly relax. "Thank you."

"Well, I knew there was someone out there. I presumed was connected to your work here from what said. I just never asked. Now, let's enjoy the weekend."

We do, we just walk, browse the shops, and have a relaxed day. *No more surprises, I hope.* She stays away from Maria as a topic and sticks to everything else but continues to ask more about the business here and the shops.

Sunday evening was interesting, we had dinner with Nicole and Adam. This must be strange for them. Like Groundhog Day, Vicky had questions.

After the first glass of wine was drank, the conversation lightened. Nicole, being Nicole, opened the real conversation. "So, Vicky, I hear Paul has filled you in and I hear you have questions?"

A little smirk crosses Vicky's face. "Where to start. Paul showed me the back room yesterday. Is that what it is all about or what? Even as a nurse I haven't seen devices like some of those," She says laughing and lightening the mood.

Nicole jokes back. "As a GP I never seen them either. But can be fun to use," with a wink. "But no, they are not what it is all about. The toys and big equipment are a personal taste. A lot just like dress up, roll play and small bits. The clothes are a big part of it,"

I clear my throat. "Ladies, you like to order dinner." Almost dismissively, Vicky replies. "That would be nice, looks like we will be here a while." Nicole just laughs, "Well Paul, it looks like you will have your hands full here. Good for you, Vicky. He needs a firm hand."

Vicky takes a quick look at the menu, and I think almost orders the first thing that she sees, before going back to the conversation.

"So, Adam, I hear you have been giving Paul here some guidance. Is he trainable?"

I nearly spit my drink, and Adam does not know where to look. We all just laugh. Nicole answers, "They all are Vicky; you just need to find out how."

Adam breaks his silence,"Hard to argue with that."

As dinner goes on, the conversation moves away from playrooms and clubs to life as a whole.

As the coffee arrives, Vicky lands the last and unexpected questions. Sheepishly almost.

"So, you seem to know as much as anyone about everything Paul has dealt with. Is he ok? It does sound like a lot to absorb."

"He is fine, was a hell of a year for him. I can only imagine what all the revelations brought. But he seems fine."

"I am still here you know," I say to remind them.

Vicky smiles warmly at me. "I know you are." As she squeezes my leg under the table.

Heading to leave and pay the bill. I split the bill with Adam, no questions, just the rule we adopted to avoid awkwardness.

As we are paying, I watch Nicole and Vicky with phones, looks like exchanging numbers.

Heading out the door my hand grazes across Vicky's back. "You ok?"

"Oh yes, very enlightening. Not to mention the chat we had when you went to the restroom." The cheeky glint left me with more questions than answers.

"Adam and Nicole were at a club the night before, did you ask?"

"Of course, a few more bits quickly without your delicate ears."

Climbing into the taxi there was a sudden and awkward feeling about what was to come. What was she going to ask me later about me and Maria at a club.

Besides that, Vicky and Nicole hit it right off. Maybe that both are about same age, or both in the medical area. They seemed to get on so well.

Heading back, and Vicky seems so much more relaxed. "They are lovely, Nicole is so relaxed."

"You seem surprised."

"I suppose I did not know what to expect. But she surprised me. I like her."

Chapter 34

VICKY

The weeks since first meeting Nicole and Adam have been interesting, having quizzed and pushed Paul's boundaries.

It was fun knowing his past and discovering my desires. I have gone from decades of virtual celibacy to taking control of a man and filling my every desire and whim in the bedroom.

Taking the initiative, finally, I decided to call Nicole. We exchanged messages a spoke a few times.

The text message a few days after that first dinner was so comforting. Telling me how relaxed Paul has been the last while and confident in himself, settling into a new life. How he has spoken warmly about me, and they can see he is so happy. Suggesting if I need any help, or just a chat to call her.

I took the opportunity and called her; I ask her about the Paul. Starting light, I just ask about how it really was when he found out. Was there anything I needed to know?

Nicole is fairly open, and we touch on the clubs and Maria. Though I sense her unease around her,

Finally, I plucked up the courage.

"I have to ask about what you know about Paul and the exploring he has done? He has told me that he tried some restraint, some dress up and a whip. I don't want to press him, but I do want to know, is there anything I should avoid, or that he enjoys. I want to try but am a bit lost."

"Well, that is a big question. Not sure what I can say. Well, Adam and I are open enough and he would have seen us enjoy some bits at the clubs. Paul was more private; I probably know as much as you do really. I know he tried and seemed to enjoy what he told you. I think he enjoyed both being in charge and not, if you get me."

"OK"

"Look, if you need to learn more about toys and the bigger things, see, if you can get down here for a night and maybe we can visit the shop and back room and I can show you the basics. Maybe look at some outfits for you and what you may like."

"Ok, thank you, I will think about it."

I left it at that and back to my reality, doing some research online, but that confused me more than enlightened me.

****

Saturday rituals continue. Lunch with my girls,sitting down and catching up. I feel different. As the week goes on, I have as much news to share about my life as the girls.

The feeling of finally getting a life is liberating. It has taken years off me. Talking about dinners out, movies, places we visit, makes me feel more like I am talking to friends and not my daughters.

The girls talk me into occasional shopping trips, dressing me up, and reminding me that I now have a life worth dressing for,

We never did venture into a local lingerie shop, as we looked in one window, I just heard the comment. "Too much information, mum." Looking around, I see a smile.

If only they knew. I think to myself.

Shopping, I still can't bring myself to the labels boutiques. High street shopping good enough for me. I simply say, "I can't afford it." Reality is, I could afford some, but it did not feel like me.

Stopping for a coffee break, I sit as the girls go and order and wait to collect it.

My mind, when calm simply went to him. Thinking about the first time I saw him. The caring father, worried about his daughter. Never leaving her side. The image of him tired, unshaven, worried. Having to be kicked out of the ward just to get him to sleep.

Remembering his dedication to his kids. Sharing coffee and pastry, the simple to break from the vending machines. All the time he could afford whatever he wanted. But it was just not him.

Embarrassed by his wealth, all be it getting used to it. It did not seem to change him. Not that I knew him before. But he just seemed like such a decent person. That coffee machine certainly won him a few admirers on the ward,

And here we are now. Who knew behind the quiet professional family man, lay a fun sexually adventurous playful man, who had an alter personality that brought a whole new dimension, to not only him but me? A year earlier, I felt like a nun, now I am contemplating crosses of a whole other type. Lingerie and fetish dress-up. Smirking, as I think. *Easier to see myself in costume than a pair of stockings and suspenders.* How am I even thinking this?

Snapped from my daydream by the girls' return with a comment. "Do we even want to ask what that daydream smirk is about?"

"What … nothing."

"Oh, mum, we are only teasing, good for you."

I blush, I would have had fun at the girls' expense when they were younger, but harder to take it. They are getting their own back.

As the day ended, we all headed home. I headed to my bedroom and started to unpack. For every new item of clothes, I get, I decide that an older piece must go to a charity shop. Finding it hard to justify so much. So, I pack them up.

Having a night to myself, I grab a book I have half-finished and curl up on the couch for a read. Paul, having told me he wants a weekend with the kids, as he wants them to know he is still there and not off every weekend with me.

My mind wanders to what Paul wants, what I want, and how to try. I dropped Nicole a text.

Vicky: Hope all is good, Nicole. I wonder can I take you up on the offer to see what everything is and see what maybe I can explore?

I head back to my book and silence. No reply.

Finally heading to bed tired, I wonder had she changed her mind.

3 am and I hear my phone alert.

Nicole: Hi Vic… sorry late reply, we were just at a club. Great night, maybe you can come next time. Sorry a little dunk here. Yes lets explore .. talk tomorrow.

I smile to myself. *Never seen a typo from her before. She must be drunk.*

I headed back to sleep.

11 am, another message.

Nicole: Vicky, I am sorry, I hardly remember sending that last message. We were out for the night and a little drunk. Anyway. Yes, it would be great if you could come down. Stay a night and we can go in when the shop closes. I won't tell Paul you are coming. Stay with us, we have a guest room.

Vicky: Thanks, Nicole. Maybe someday Paul will be away with work, and I am free, thank you for the offer. Yes, it would be nice to stay,

I am nervous and excited but determined.

Vicky: Hey Paul, how is the weekend playing daddy going? Are you having fun? I am looking at my work roster for the coming weeks. Have you any travel plans I need to work around? I know you mentioned some trade shows and Holland.

Little does he know I just want to plan a trip down to London. Can't even tell the girls as I have no reason to and never have over the years,

Paul: Kids, great, took advantage of me and dragged me shopping, or more my credit card. I love seeing Rachel taking an interest again. Though she does tire quickly still.

Paul: Not much travel. Tomorrow week I am in Rotterdam for 2 days, looking at the shop and distribution for post-Brexit. Nothing then for a while.

Looking, this is short notice. I emailed work and booked 2 days off. Thankfully, I have a load of holidays due to me.

Texting Nicole and asked if Monday night is possible, as it is the only night Paul is away. She quickly agrees, suggesting we meet at the shop at 6 and go from there,

****

Arriving in London at 2 pm I have all I need in a small shoulder bag. I head to Oxford Street and work my way down. Window shopping and wandering.

Arriving at the shop around 5:30 I take a few minutes and just look up at the offices, seeing staff leaving for the night. Still trying to get my head around this reality.

I take up the station in the coffee shop and text Nicole where I am. Within a few minutes, she arrives in. Greeting me with a peck on the cheek, "You didn't go straight to the shop?"

"Sorry not sure what to do."

"I have the keys, Adam is gone home, he said he would leave us to it and said to remind you all shopping is quality control. No argument. Oh, and he said cameras are malfunctioning for a night." She smirks.

"Come on, if you are ready. We can get something to eat after and head home."

I feel so giddy heading down. Like a kid going to a toy shop. Walking in, Nicole turns on the lights and locks up. Heading to the back she unlocks the door to the display room, as they call it.

Beckoning me back. "Let's start here. Might be easier. Walking in she turns on a bank of switches and the subtle light illuminates the dark woods and the glass cabinets lighting an array of toys and what I can only describe as weapons from the Middle Ages.

Leading me to the cross she just told me to feel it. "This is obviously a cross, feel the restraints and cuffs there." As I do she takes one off the shelf and puts it on me. Tightening the cuffs, "See it is lovely soft padded leather." I am surprised at how comfortable it feels, even when tight.

"The cross is the upper end of this restraint. These can be used on a bed or even a door or wall. Whatever works."

We walk in and see swings and harnesses and a bench with a cage. Looking at her. "Ah, this is a spanking bench. But more painful if you want it and a cage underneath. If any help, I don't think I saw Paul show much interest in anything with much pain."

Opening a cabinet, she pulls out a flogger. The look on my face says it all. "Nicole, that looks…. All those strands on it."

She laughs, "Don't knock it till you try it. Hold your hand out, go on, it won't hurt."

As I see the whip come down, I brace myself. Memories of being slapped at school fill my head. Much to my surprise I hardly felt it. I look at her.

"See, it is all in the minds. The sounds of the whip and image half of it. Now you can go much harder and feel it. But that is the choice. A good flogger I very soft. The cheap ones will cut you to shreds."

With that, we head out of the shop. I stroll around and see some of the toys. Nicole picks up a box and shows me. Over the door restraint. "You would use the cuffs with these and any door. You don't need a cross for effect. Next to it was under the mattress restraint. I then see there is a whole section of restraint and cuffs and bars.

As the exploration continues, we come to clothes. Nicole picks up some leather outfits and holds them up to me. Look in the mirror. As I do, she picks a few more Latex and PVC from the racks.

"They look tiny and dull." I joke, pointing to the latex. "Ah, these latex ones stretch and hug your figure. Cold to put on but then nice. Once shined up, look amazing."

Pointing to a mannequin, dressed in one of those outfits she is holding, I did not even recognize it with the shine coming off it. "You want to try it on?"

It is a black and red latex dress with a little shoulder detail. It did not look like me, but I said it would be good to see what this felt like and what the attraction was.

"Ok, well I am here now, so why not."

Nicole hangs back up the one that was in her hand and moves to the display dress. I watch her remove it, "Best try this one, at least you will what it looks like all shined up."

Using the cover of the racks for little privacy I quickly undress and start to try it on. Nicole intentionally busies herself so as not to be intrusive. "Best take off the bra. These dresses show the lines of everything underneath."

"My goodness, this is freezing." As I put it on.

Nicole smiles, "Yes, but give it a minute, it will be fine."

I do as suggested, when nearly into it I ask Nicole to help with the last of the zip.

Looking at myself in the mirror I look so different. I don't really like the dress I have on but I do like the feel of it. "It feels surprisingly comfortable?" *Is this really me? I look like someone else. At least, I am in good shape.*

Moving to take it off and get my clothes back on, Nicole focuses on the shelves once again. I put the dress back on display.

"You are not going to take it?"

"Thank you, but not right now!"

When we finish in the shop and lock up, we head back toward the tube station. Looking for a restaurant, of which are plenty for a quick dinner. I could not believe we had spent 90 minutes in the shop. It was like an overload.

As we sit down, and order Nicole asks me if I have more questions. I think. "No, I think that is it."

"Well, if you have more just let me know, or if you need to go shopping again. One last piece o of advice and we will change the subject. Just try what you want and talk to Paul, he is lovely he is new to this also. Now tell me about your girls."

We talked over dinner for the next hour, and I told her a bit about me. My girls and what they are doing and the years since my husband died. Finally, getting to Nicole's house,

Adam was in there watching a movie. Looking over, he says, "Hi, how was the evening, no shopping bags?"

"Lovely, thank you. Nice to meet you again, Adam."

Nicole showed me my room and I dropped my bag and coat. Coming down stairs, I just admire the decor. Very modern and well furnished, it looks like a 4 bedroomed house. Plenty of space.

We enjoy a drink and chat; Adam does not even mention the shop and we just talk about Paul really and last year for him. He assures me that Paul seems so happy and relaxed and the Paul before the inheritance and the Paul after have not changed. The money has not changed him.

Heading to bed, Nicole shows me the kitchen and tells me they will be gone early tomorrow. Just pull out the front door when leaving and let her know I am gone, she can turn the alarm on from her phone.

Lying in bed I think of what next. Making a plan, I finally drifted to sleep.

The following morning, I headed back into the city and did some of my own shopping, not feeling right going to Adams's shop. I called Paul to see how he is getting on and what time he will be back in Manchester.

When he asks about me, I just pass it off. "I am shopping and relaxing."   No lie really. I suggest to Paul that maybe we will have a family dinner this weekend. Get the kids together again. No reason, just a dinner. He knows how important family is to me and just agrees. "Great idea. I will check are all of mine are around"

I arrange the dinner and cook at Paul's, he has more space than me.

Chapter 35

Arriving back to mine after dinner, Paul walks in behind me. He is laughing and enjoyed the night.

The kids had sent him to take me home and said as I cooked, they would clean up. Heading out the door, all I heard was, "See you tomorrow, dad."

As soon as my door closed, I feel Paul's hands on my waist. Pulling me back as I start my walk away, He leans down and I feel his lips on my neck, his grip tightening around my waist.

I try to turn but can't. His lips on my neck and his tongue teases me. I turn my head so our lips can find each other. I can feel his erection against me. *I love this man; how does he do this to me?* Is all I can think.

Kissing each other deeper, his grip finally relaxes so I can turn. I am so horny right now, I just want him. I move to open his shirt right there in the hallway, as his hands move to my bum, pulling me into him.

Opening his shirt, I kiss his gorgeous chest. Ripping one of his buttons in my enthusiasm. He releases his grip so the shirt can come off him.

I don't stop there and as my lips explore his chest, my fingers open his pants. The further I go the hornier I get. I just look up at him I finally win the battle with his pants button. "Fuck me. NOW."

The passion evident in my tone and my eyes. Pushing his pants and shorts off in one go, he kicks his shoes of and the pants off.

Naked before me, I kiss him and wrap my hands around his erection. "MMM, I want this now," I moan.

With that, he turns me around and faces me to the wall. I was never so thankful to be wearing a dress. I press my hands to the wall and push myself out to him. I feel him pull my dress up and moving my panties to one side he pushes into me with ease, My desire obvious from my wetness.

Grabbing my hips, I just feel him moving so hard and so fast that neither of us are able to last too long.

The sounds of skin on skin. His fingers pressing into my hips and the moans from both of us, until that final release into me.

Panting, we just hold there, and Paul just leans in against me. Between breaths, "What has gotten into you?"

My face flushed I just smiled "There is a long night there yet. You are not getting away with a quickie." *I had my own plans for tonight, I just could not wait.*

As he slides out, I feel him trickle down my thighs.

As he steps back, his clothes strewn around the floor, I let my dress drop back over me. "Excuse me, I must clean up the mess you made. Don't go anywhere."

By the time I returned, Paul was in the kitchen pouring 2 glasses of wine, dressed in his pants and shorts. He smiles over at me.

"Mmmm, someone is in a playful mood. Gorgeous."

I just smile back, "Let's hope you can keep up."

Taking our drinks through, we just sit on the couch, me taking my new favourite position, curled into Paul and his arm wrapped around me, Paul's feet up on the footstool in front of us.

"This is a gorgeous evening, so nice to see all the kids getting along and chatting as they did, and then my welcome home."

We relax and chat away about the weekend so far and then I ask. "I have been wondering, these clubs you went to before. What were they like, what did you do?"

I feel Paul shifted a little uncomfortably in his seat. "Don't worry, I am curious, you had a life before me and I would like to know more, I know who you went with and well, that is what it is. So please, what was it like."

Taking a moment and tightening his grip on me, as if to assure me everything was ok, "Well, the clubs were a bit of a scary idea to go to first, exciting as well. But then the best description was a bit of fancy-dress night club for adults. The outfits were amazing. A bit surreal really. Bar and dance area and then the play areas."

"Play areas? Did you go there, what did you do?"

"Well, of course, looked. There was a lot going on there, lots of equipment from crosses to cages to benches and people flogging, caning and even some discreetly having sex, through there were rules against that, they were dressed but managed."

"Sex! Could you see them?"

"Well, they were in discreet corners, but you knew exactly what's happening. Not floor shows so to speak."

"Did you do anything there, play?"

"Tried a cross a little once, when it was quiet, but really no, more watching, dressing up and enjoying the atmosphere and the night out. Adam and Nicole used to use the equipment."

"Did you see them, was it awkward?"

"Yes, I often saw them, and they knew I could see and watched a little. But they did not care, honestly, looked amazing. Knowing them in their day jobs, as it were and then seeing them like this, really showed that these were ordinary people enjoying an extraordinary side of life. Made it feel much more acceptable. Why all the questions?".

"Just curious, and the dress up, did you like it?"

"It was fun, made you feel like someone else really, and added to the excitement and almost danger of it. It was fun, but for the ladies the options are endless, seeing all the outfits in the club was just incredible."

"In private?"

I feel him shift again uncomfortably, "Its ok, I know what I am asking. Was it fun there, the dress up, playing?"

"OK, well, you asked, yes it was fun, so different and I knew it could be. Really it was all about fun and trust."

"Ok, last question… maybe. What did you like to try, equipment and toy etc.?"

"Well, really was not in the scene too long before it all ended. But the cuffs and restraints and cross were really as far as it ever went. I never got to use the new room in the shop, never went that far."

"Would you like to use it, if you could?"

"Hey, wasn't that the last question?"

"Woman prerogative, well?" As I smile up at him.

"OK, well who knows, might be fun, but only with you and only if you wanted to for you to try."

I curl in and simply say, "You are staying tonight, aren't you?"

As my finger roam inside his short, having opened a few buttons as he answered me. I could see he was getting a little aroused again. Maybe from remembering the clubs or play.

I think for a second, I hope it is not the idea of Maria. Until I hear his answer. "Of course. You can't kick me out after that welcome home."

Home, now there is a nice ring to it. I smile.

"Come on, take me to bed." As I get up and move. Walking upstairs, passing his shoes and socks on the hall floor as we do.

"Go on, get your ass to bed there. I need the bathroom."

A few minutes later, I emerge and take a deep breath. Looking in the half-opened door, I see Paul under the sheet and naked chest, sitting up waiting for me.

I walk in, watching his expression. "Vicky…." I smile, he is nearly speechless.

"Well, I was worried from earlier you may have ever exerted in the hall, so I said better charge to give you a physical."

I was wearing the nicest, sexiest nurse's outfit I could find in the lingerie shops. The short nurses dress, zip don't the front to show off the twins and sexy stocking underneath, though they were not the best fit."

As I walked over, I saw a huge smile on his face filled with desire. As I touch him, and my hand roams down over the sheet, I whisper in his ear, "Oh, I see your blood pressure is up."

As I rub him over the sheet, outlining the shape of him draped in white. His hands begin too slowly roam over me. Down the back of my very skimpy outfit as I leaned in. Passing off the material and finding it in area of exposed skin just above the stockings.

"Now, Mr. Bridges, I am here to give you a physical, and I give his roaming had a little slap." I could not help but smile and laugh, as did he.

"Sorry, Nurse Vicky…" He laughs through a smile.

I move him down on the bed and stretch him out. Making sure that as I move him, he finds my breast rubbing off him, and in his face.

My hand roamed down his body, over his chest and stomach. Pushing the sheet down to expose him, just above his erection.

"Now, Mr. Bridges, where does it hurt?"

"Everywhere," he softly whispers, as I see him twitch, standing very erect.

Leaning in from next to the bed, I just begin got kiss down his chest and stomach. My hands roaming over and under the sheet gently stroking him, and eyes looking up at him with a smile, a kiss, my hand tightening around him as my lips get closer.

I hear him take in a gasp of air as I do.

My other hand now roamed over the hair on his chest, which feels so warm. That hair on his chest feels so masculine, always love it against my skin.

Breaking the kiss just above his hip.

"Mr. Bridges, everything seems to be fine, do I need to keep going?"

Gasping, "Yesss," is all he can say, as my hand tightens around him again, covered by the sheet slowly stroking him.

My lips move down and pushing the sheet off as I do. "Oh, there is something here I better check for you." As my lips wrap around his tip and slide down his shaft, my fingers wrap around the base. The feel of the sheet is just below me.

The moans and sign increase from him, though faint. "Does that hurt Mr. Bridges?" I quickly say as my lips release him and back into position then, not giving him time to answer.

Seeing him react like this, I can feel I am soaking wet. As I taste him, I know I want hm again.

I release him and move, "Sorry, but …"

I quickly move and climb onto the bed. Pushing the sheet away I positioned it on top of him. His hands reach my bum under the dress. Finding my thong, he pushes it to one side and I push down on him.

I lean in and whisper, "Sorry but this had me so horny I had to have you."

His hands grab my bum and lift me up and down on him and I just fuck him hard and fast. Sitting up so he can see me and I can see him.

I open the front of the dress so he can see all of me.

I reach around and take his hands in mine and pull them over his head. Pin them to the pillows and I just ride him.

My naked breasts now against his chest. My mind lost in what we were doing, imagining everything, until I closed my eyes and the release I desperately needed came.

I was so wet I hardly knew whether it was him, or me or what. Taking a minute to enjoy the afterglow I then rolled off him. Panting from exertion, hot from the outfit and the sex, I just reached over for his hand.

"You ok?"

Laughing back, "Now I do think I need a nurse, you nearly gave me a heart attack."

We curl up and enjoy each other.

I move, only to take off the costume. As I do, Paul watches asking.

"Nurse's costume?"

"Well, I was in a nurse's uniform when we met, and went looking for something to try I saw this and said maybe fun. See if you like it. See if I like it."

Laughing out loud, "It certainly wasn't that costume you wore. Even I would not have been that distracted." We both laugh.

After a while we both agree we need a shower. Spent from sex we enjoy a refreshing and cleansing shower before climbing back into bed.

Paul is in his shorts only and I am wearing one of his T-shirts I do love to wear now.

A little more awake, I tell him about my trip to London and meeting Nicole.

I reassure him that everything is ok, and I just wanted to figure some of this out myself.

I tell him that she showed me the room and explained the equipment and the shop. "Don't worry, she did not help me select the costume out, I got that somewhere else. But she showed me so much more. I did not take anything."

"And did you like it, did you like tonight?" he asks.

"I was curious about it all and tonight, well I had no idea where it would go. Even walking in here, and would I just look silly. But it was such fun. I never tried this before. It was real fun, I think I want to explore more… if you will show me."

"Of course, it could be a lot of fun."

After that, we slowly drift off to sleep. Tomorrow being Sunday we were in no hurry to get up.

****

After breakfast, we dress, thankfully Paul keeps spare change of clothes here now, so he feels fresher. We head down the park, strolling hand in hand and enjoying the fresh air. Stopping to watch the activities and just chatting about everything and anything.

We bumped into his old boss Leonard and shared a coffee with him. I watched them catch up and office gossip and some of Paul's old work that he asked about

As we walked away. Paul draped an arm over my shoulder and kissed my forehead. "This is what it is all about."

343

"What do you mean?"

"Out for walk when we want, catch a coffee with friends and not cloak and dagger."

I realised that was new to him. Maria was all cloak and dagger, no public and no friends, no family. This is what he wants.

It gave me a warm feeling and security that Maria cannot compete with me on that and he has well left that behind.

It was 5 before Paul left to head home after a lovely day.

Chapter 36

PAUL

I cannot but smile at Vicky in that nurses costume. So playful, who saw that coming.

Meeting Leonard really brought home to me the normality that we have. I never had, nor could I have that with Maria. *I deserve this.* Thinking to myself.

Life finally seemed to be settling down, the kids are settled and get their heads around all the changes. Vicky has been made feel so welcome by them and me by her family that it surprised me.

My phone rings, breaking me away from my daydreams. "Hello"

"Paul, I think we have a problem in Rotterdam, the manager is talking of leaving. He is complaining about stock issues."

"What are the problems, why isn't he getting stock?"

"Some of the suppliers are slow to deliver because it is too small a shop."

"Well, get onto them and sort it out. Remind them that this maybe the only one in Europe for now, but we are chain for them and growing."

"Anything else I should do?"

"Maria, come back to me if you can't sort it. This is your job."

I know I am a bit sharp with her, but I feel I have to remind her of her job at times. From someone who wanted autonomy, she has been pushing more back to me lately.

Thinking about it I decide to deal with this. Calling her up I ask her to a working lunch and we arrange for 1 pm.

I arrive early and order a coffee and wait. I know this won't be one of our usual lunches. I have to be her boss.

I see her walk in and head straight for me. Sitting down she is relaxed. Thinking this will be one of our usual lunches, a chat, and a catch-up.

"So, Paul, how are you?"

"I am fine, but Maria I want to talk about you. I wasn't going to say anything, I know you have a lot going on with Mark, but your mind does not seem to be on the job. I let it slide until this morning. Really, you should have just sorted that and just updated me. That is your job. It has been happening a while. I don't want any problems and if you need help for a while, by all means I will. But I need to know, do I need to take more day to day management?"

I watch her face change. Going red. I watch for the reaction.

"Paul, I. . .I am sorry. Home has been difficult, trying to put things back together. Have I been that bad?"

"No, we all have bad times, but there has been slippage, I will help, but you need to know it is seen. Let me know what you need. Now let's order, I have another meeting at 2 pm"

"What's 2?"

"Nothing to worry about, it is not the shops, now let's order." I decide it is time to stop sharing everything with Maria. We need more distinct boundaries.

We have lunch, a bit strained, but that is to be expected. But, at least I had an exit strategy for 1:45.

As I leave I just tell Maria, "Take a few days off and see you on Monday. I will sort the distributors in Holland. Let me know what else is urgent."

I leave before she can answer.

I arrive at my dentist office at 2. Oh, the joys, polish and clean.

****

Over the following weeks, I see a change in Maria, she is back to being Maria, focused on work and determined to make it work.

In the month since the conversation, Maria has been head down and hardly bothers me with anything. I have been watching what she is doing just to make sure, I am not being bothered for the right reasons. Rotterdam was sorted and it was no harm, I took it over. It was a harsh discussion with the distributor there and there UK arm, as to our level of purchases and if they can't or won't supply us I will take it to the manufacturers directly.

The extra effort by Maria meant I had more time to myself. So, I ask Vicky to see if she could take a week for a working holiday.

I arranged to do a short notice visit to all the shops and bring Vicky with me. So, I told her to pack a bag and we are spending a day or two in each location, other than Manchester.

Sending an all managers an email and accounts and Maria here, deciding it was better if all saw that they were all being visited and also to show my interest after a rocky year.

Good Morning All,

Thank you for all the work that has gone into you shops in that last while. Over the next two week, I will visit each shop for a day. Everyone's shop will be getting the same visit. I would like to take the morning to look at any issues each individual shop is having, see what support you need to go forward and listen to any ideas you have. The agenda will be primarily yours, so please let me know.

We have made great strides in the last years or more, the efforts have been seen in turnover figures. Let's see what else we can do and look at what may be localized market. We may be a chain, but I want your local market to feel personalised service and meeting all of their needs.

If ye have any ideas or agenda please email me in advance, so I have time to consider in advance of meeting.

Regards

Paul Bridges

After I send the email I arrange to meet Maria and the admin team.

"Good Morning,

You all saw the email I sent the managers. Can we arrange an admin and accounts meeting here for tomorrow afternoon? Bring any issues you may be having with individual shops to me, or challenges they are having. Also their management accounts, so we can see their margin. Let me see if there is consistency in shops.

Any ideas ye may have for the next shop. Either here or EU or both.
Regards
Paul

Maria walked into my office a few minutes later. "Are we expanding?"

"Of course, the business stood still long enough. But I want to keep the ship steady in the shops we have."

I see her look and she heard my tone. It is business. So, I said I better lighten it. "You like a lunch today. Just a chat, see how life is, so to speak."

She takes a moment to gauge the invite. "OK, 1 pm usual place."

I nod in agreement and we get back to work.

Sitting down over lunch, we get a quiet corner. Exchanging the usual small talk on how the kids are, I ask the question.

"So how are things at home? How is Mark?"

"A struggle, to be honest, we are trying and maybe a bit better. But nothing like us."

"Maria, we were, well, we were what we were, more like a holiday thing, away from the reality of home. It would have been hard for us to be any more than we were and as life moved on I wanted more than that for me. I don't regret us for a minute, you and Ralph woke me up to a whole new world."

"I know." In a low somber tone.

"Now you need to get on with your life and me with mine. Let's be friends and let that work as it has."

"Ok, and Victoria, what does she know?" with a look in her eye I have trouble reading.

"Everything and I do mean everything. She is ok with it."

"The clubs and type of play …." With a shocked look.

"Pretty much. I had to come clean with her and the kids really like her."

I could see the last comment stung a little.

"Ok."

I then quickly moved on and asked her about holiday plans. Where they heading anywhere and I just avoid any more of the conversation. There was enough said. I just wanted to shut it down.

We lightened the tone of the chat and finally wandered back to work.

****

Monday morning, collecting Vicky for the first shop visit. We take the day to drive and enjoy the route over to Perth. Stopping for lunch and chatting. A real road trip to enjoy. The drive is long, as we decide to start the furthest north and work back down to London.

Vicky comments on everywhere we pass. Chatting, smiling, laughing, and commenting on the talk show conversation on the radio as we go.

It is interesting to just listen to her and the energy she has talking on random subjects as they arise. I cannot but smile at times, just listening to her.

"I meant to ask. So why bring me on this road trip? Not that I am complaining. I get to see the country."

"I wanted the time with you, the company, and maybe let you see what is there also. Don't worry, you can go exploring as I go to work."

"Mmmm, so will you be gone all day?"

"Well, for a good bit, maybe we can meet at lunchtime and see how the days are going. You can call in and see the shops also. I hope you won't be too bored."

We arrive to our hotel in time for dinner. Checking in, the room is booked in my name and the receptionist referring to Vicky and Mrs. Bridges did hit a slight cord for us both. Of what I lost and the idea of what I might have found in Vicky and I wonder does Vicky think, who she is not, Mrs. Bridges.

We shake it off, without a word, and head up. Dinner was nice and we look at the local tourist pamphlets for ideas for Vicky to pass the morning.

****

The morning in the shop was uneventful. Reviewing paperwork and just looking around.

I stroll out to the floor at 12:45. I stop Vicky wandering around. I walk over to her I see a bag in her hand. It is one of the shops. I know what happened. I am a bit annoyed.

"You were shopping."

"Yes, I needed a light rain jacket, nothing much."

"Did you tell them you were with me?"

"Of course not. Why would I, I can pay my own way. Don't you give me that look?"

"Vicky, you can't go buying things in the shops when you are with me. That is silly. We can just get you whatever you want. Please don't do that again."

With that, the manager walks over. I introduce him to Vicky, and tell him that I won't be back after lunch. Everything is just fine and he does not need me in his way.

I see a little mischievous grin on Vicky face as we walk out. I presume knowing she bought without my help in the shop. *She is so independent, how will she ever let me help?*

We drive down to Edinburgh for tomorrow's shop. Checking into a hotel just down the street from the shop, and looked out onto the park and castle.

We get time for an evening walk and some air. We looked around. Vicky was telling on the drive that she had never been to Edinburgh before. We make a plan to visit the castle tomorrow, together.

I ask Vicky to head into the shop for a look around early in the morning and she agrees.

As we head in, I walk over the checkouts. The manager is there and I introduced Vicky. "Now can you tell the staff, if she looks for anything, just put it down to me. Don't let her pay."

I give her a smile and she know what I am doing. Smiling back. "It is ok, I bought what I needed yesterday. Hate to have to call to Cotswolds instead."

The day and the week pass like a mini holiday. The shops were all going well and it was really more like a PR tour to show the managers reassuring them I am here and interested.

The time with Vicky just flew. She is full of fun. When we finally land into the London apartment. Dropping our bags at lunchtime, we head down to the coffee shop.

We stick our heads into Adam and let him know we are around. Before I can say a word, Adam starts chatting to Vicky as if old friends. I just watch and wonder where this came from. How do they know each other so well?

Heading out, I hear Vicky say, "Oh, by the way I texted Nicole earlier to see if she is around tomorrow for lunch or a coffee and if ye are free for dinner would be great. Bye, Adam."

Walking down the street, "How do you know Adam so well?"

"Ah, we chat the odd time when I call for Nicole. We talk regularly."

That was news, I knew they spoke but this surprised me.

By the time evening rolls around, we are tired of restaurant food, so Vicky makes a light dinner. Working away in the kitchen as if it was her own. This is so homely, relaxed.

Sitting down after dinner, a movie on I just feel her curled into me.

As the credit roll, Vicky heads to the bathroom, and few minutes later she comes back and standing in front of me she holds up a pair of rope cuffs. Smiling at me. "I think it's time you showed me how these work, don't you?"

She throws the cuff at me and jokes, "Well master… teach me."

Not sure how to react, I just stand up and walk over to kiss her, and then deeper and break only to whisper. "You are full of surprises." As we kiss deeper I move her back to the wall. Back to the hook where it all begun.

Sliding the cuffs on her wrists, I raise them up and slide them onto the hook. Kissing her, my hands explore her over her clothes. Touching, caressing and I watch as see her reacts to my touch. Over the front of her dress, I lift it a little to touch her, expose her skin to me.

I watch her face as she feels my fingers tease her and feel how wet she is through her panties and then as I slide my fingers in. Listening to her breath catch, as she tries to lower her hands. As she does I move to kiss her neck and whisper. "Having fun?"

"Yes," she gasps.

I continue to tease her until she is close. Touching her, teasing her with only my finger and her inability to move.

Then moving I try and open her dress, my fingers leave her and she relaxes. Her arousal moves to laughter when she smiles. "You did not plan this through with these cuffs and this dress." Knowing I can't get it off her without uncuffing her.

We both just laugh and I release her hands. "Come on, these work in bed also." And we head to the bedroom.

****

By the following evening, we are heading to dinner with Nicole and Adam. Vicky is all dressed up and almost giddy about the night out. The more I see her the more playful she gets.

Walking in, Nicole and Vicky greet like old friends. I almost feel like the guest. The conversation flows all evening, and two conversation for a lot of it. I hear the girls talk about family and shopping and TV. Anything everything, we talk sport and some shop. Noting too exciting.

As the evening goes on, there was not even a mention of the dress-up or clubs or anything else, until Nicole introduces it over coffee.

"So, the next club night, are ye going to come along?"

I don't know what to sat. I just look at Adam, and he shrugs, "Don't look at me."

Vicky is the one who answers, "Once you break me in gently, why not."

I look at her, we had not even discussed this. She sees my look. Laughing, she says, "Don't worry, Paul, we will mind you." And the three start laughing. "We spoke about it today over coffee." Nicole enlightens us.

"Vicky…."

I just see a radiant smile back. And that is my answer.

"Ok, looks like I am out numbered."

As the night ends, we walk back to the apartment, arms wrapped around each other. We talk. Vicky explains her curiosity and chats with Nicole and how she is not sure, but she wants to try.

Then we talk about last night. The cheeky grin returns. "Oh that was fun, I am curious, very curious. Let's explore together."

We chat and decide as it is Thursday we will just stay until Sunday. Maybe do some afterhours shopping in the shop, exploring and see what we can find.

That is exactly what we do. We spend the weekend relaxing and enjoying. Exploring the shop and even ventured into the back room. Just look see and explore a little, but not a lot, Vicky tried the padded cuffs for size.

Vicky absolutely blew my mind with how adventurous and open she was, but knew where her lines were also.

Chapter 37

PAUL

Monday morning, I check my email while I am still in London. We are going back at lunchtime when I notice an email from Caroline with subject "Personal time." Also, it is marked urgent and sent to me and Maria. *An urgent email with personal time as a subject always has something alarming about it.* I thought of opening it after lunch, but I knew Caroline must be expecting an immediate response. I click open the email. It reads:

Dear Paul and Maria,

I am sorry for the short notice; I need to take a few days off. My dad passed away today, and I need to organize things. I did not have time to organize the rosters fully, but the assistant manager should be fine to run things. I told him to roster extra staff for help.

Sorry again. I will check in on the shop every day and see if all is running fine.

Caroline

I see Maria replied last night.

Caroline,

I am sorry for your loss. Please let me know if there is anything we can do. If you need more time let us know and I will see if I can send up another manager to support you.

Let us know the details, please.

Take care.

Maria.

I pick up the phone and call Maria. "Maria, I just saw the emails. Send up some cover if needs be from the Glasgow shop. That is the closest shop. Now, I never heard Caroline mention her father. Always her mother." I see Vicky looking at me as I am on the phone. The look on her face asking me what went wrong. I whispered 'Caroline' to her to ease her worried look.

"Maria, leave this one to me, I know Caroline was important to Ralph so I will take care of things. You just get her a manager."

"Ok, I never remember a father either. Sort of presumed he was dead. All the times we met and even asked about her family he never came up. Always Lilly, but then I never asked."

"Neither did I. Ok, keep me informed."

I end the call and turn to Vicky. "Caroline, the manager in Fort William, her dad died, and she needs time off. She is Lilly's daughter and Ralph was always protective of her. From a distance."

"Just seeing you on the phone. Just straight to the point, no small talk even with Maria. Is that how ye are? Take control, give orders." Vicky seems surprised, almost not recognizing the 'boss' me.

"Pretty much, we can talk when we meet, and we get along fine. But yes, what you saw yesterday and that. That is about it. We get along fine and are able to put the past behind us, will always be there but it is in the past. At the end of the day, it works for me." I convince her, knowing she isn't bothered or too inquisitive about my past anymore. Whatever there was, I spilled all of it. there isn't anything left to tell.

"Ok, so what about Caroline, what are you going to do? Does she know about Ralph and her mother?" She asks the pertinent question.

"I will see what I can do to support her and not a lot more I can. She knows nothing, that I am aware of."

I pick up the phone and call Hellen. "Hellen, Caroline in Fort William, her father died. Did you hear?"

"No, what happened?" Helen has a surprised tone to her voice. Perhaps, Caroline didn't tell anyone about her father.

"I don't know yet, I just heard he died, Caroline emailed last night. She needs time off. Did you know much about her?"

"Not really other than meeting her at events. I know Ralph was good to her, but I just presumed because it was his first shop." Helen adds nothing much to the information that I know.

"Ok thanks, if you hear anything let me know. If ye want to go up, just take time and go, no pressure, your own choice. But take paid time and if you need a hotel just charge it to expenses. I will email the other managers."

"Give me 2 minutes Vicky." I see her watching me as if wanting to say something important. And I know she is waiting for us to leave for breakfast.

I send an email to all managers and senior staff.

"Good morning All,

I am sorry to say that Caroline, our Fort William manager, informed me that her father passed away yesterday, I would like ye to provide her with whatever support ye can across the shops. If anyone wants to attend the funeral, just arrange cover and please go, company time.

If any issues or suggestions to help, please email me directly.

Regards,

Paul Bridges."

When I am pressing send, I notice Vicky on my shoulder. "That is supportive. Good for staff to know the boss is there."

"Thanks, Vicky. I have to be there for them. They all have been a huge support." I see a smile crease on Vicky's face.

We pack up and head back to Manchester. I make what inquiries I can, discreetly, during the week. Nobody knows anything about him. That's strange.

I head up to the funeral the following week. I stay in the cottage. Sarah comes with me as she has gotten friendly with Caroline. I ask her to find out what she can, such as how close they were and any history. I cannot tell Sarah why I am interested and the connection with Lilly and Ralph beyond the shop.

As much as I get from Caroline when talking to her the night before the funeral, they were never very close. She was always with her mother really. She saw less and less of him after her mother died. For some reason, he really disliked Ralph and wanted her to work somewhere else. He would not tell her why but said he did not get along with many, drank a little too much and so was not nice to a lot of people. She has not seen him in a few years. No wonder no one knows about him.

I could see she did not want to talk about him much. I met some of Lilly's family. Caroline introduced me as her boss and Ralph's nephew. Lilly's mother was there, in her 80's, I guess. As soon as I was introduced, she went pale and said, "I did not know Ralph had a family."

"Neither did I until last year. I never knew him. Caroline is doing a great job here and I hear your Lilly was a great manager and well-liked."

I could nearly see her tearing up, not sure why, I knew it could not be good, so I decided to cut the conversation short. I decided to find Sarah and made an exit. I couldn't afford a scene at a funeral, and also with someone I hardly knew.

Definitely there is history there with Ralph. He seemed like a genuine guy to me and never did anything too objectionable.

When we make it to the graveyard, he is being buried with Lilly. I can see Ralph's grave from here. Reading the headstone, it hits me. There was only 1 day between Lilly's anniversary and Ralph's accident. Is that what he was doing here? Her anniversary, I wonder about the coincidence of those dates.

I spot DI Irwin and I wonder why she is here. I met her a few times in connection with Ralph's death. She is sure there is something off but would not tell me why. Typical DI behaviour. As we are walking away from the funeral, she approaches me.

"Mr. Bridges, surprised to see you here. Did you know the deceased?"

"No. but Caroline is one of my managers, and if we can't take care of our own then. . .Have you any more leads?"

"Not a lot, but you know, I still think something is off. Who knows I may be wrong."

We head on, and her words make me wonder. *The death of Caroline's father and his burial, and in fact no one knew about him. Detective is right, something is strange, if not wrong.*

"Dad, who is she?" Sarah's question interrupts my thoughts.

"She is a detective up here. She thinks something is off with Ralph's death. Just that he knew the roads so well, he would have known the conditions. She does not get into the accident details. There is more she says, she can't tell me."

We head back to town. I call into the shop. See if they need any help. I can stay a day or two and so can Sarah. We don't get up here often and nice to use the cottage. It is now like a home away from home and all comforts. Sarah threw the budget out the window in the end and said I can afford it. She enjoyed a budget-free finish and I agreed to it.

The shop was fine. We hung around a little bit. I had to visit the climbing wall. There was nothing much to do there, it was just Ralph's memory. I will insist it stays until it can't.

Chapter 38

MARIA

We attend the follow-up counselling session. I hope that this time we are better than before, in fact, I know. But somehow, I seek approval from our counsellor. Also, she can help us with a few ways to keep this alive. This togetherness that we get to cherish now.

We both drive out together. Walking in the counsellor looks at us with a smile and says, "Maria, Mark, nice to see ye arrive together. Can I assume things are going well?"

Mark starts. "Yes, we have our moments, but once we make an effort it is good."

She then looks at me and asks, "And how are things with you?"

"Same really, all is good, we had some good times and made a point of time away and getting out."

"Anything ye want to discuss or share? Is everything ok in the bedroom?"

There is that question. "Yes, all is fine. Better than it was at least. We are having fun again. We were trying more."

It was a short meeting and she told us no need to come back unless we what more support. Mark and I look at each other, relieved that we are on the right track with our relationship.

Over the next few months, I bump into Vicky occasionally, she attends with Paul at all company plus partner functions. No getting away from that message. But I convince myself, I have to be happy for him. He deserves it. And they look genuinely happy together.

We get up and down to London a bit, meet with Max and Lara when we are down. They are fun for a night out. I can see a sense of adventure and playfulness in them. Lara repeatedly asks about the playroom. Finally, I relent and how it to them, but I picked an evening I knew was rented out and we could only look around for a short while. That one visit was enough to see her interest. I can only imagine what they would be like there,

When she asked, I pointed clearly that we don't use the room, it is simply a curiosity. I never went there with Mark; I am drawing a line there unless Mark wants it. I live in hope and dread at the same time. Knowing I would always be comparing my experiences.

When I see the room I just wonder are Paul and Vicky there. Or does that playroom have memories of Paul and me only?

Paul is looking ahead. He is talking about opening another shop or maybe two next year. He has asked me to look at options. Maybe one more in the UK and see if another in Holland is a good idea. Paul is convinced that Brexit will be a trading nightmare for the UK. He says we will lose the EU market for everything. It will destroy our economy. The bigger problem might be in getting the stocks in and tariffs. He even suggests looking at a Belfast shop. I have to think he is losing it, but he is the boss.

I do my research and compile all my findings for Paul to review. *Can't wait for Christmas.*

Christmas finally arrives, and I am looking forward to the break. It has been a long year. I can't wait to have quality time with Mark, hopefully we will get to explore each other more. And of course, spend some more time with our kids. We really don't get enough time with our kids, and considering what impact Ursula had on my kids, I need to make a more regular place in their lives.. I want to be their mother and friend. Like every mother should be.

Quite unexpectedly, I get a call from Victoria. "Maria, how are you?" I have to wonder what she wants. She has never contacted me directly and I know she knows I am the ex. Paul told me, he said she was ok with it.

"Hi Victoria, is everything ok? Unusual for you to call."

"I know. But hey, everything is fine. We are arranging a surprise 50th for Paul in January. I wonder can you get me a contact list for work people who should be invited. I don't know who he likes to mix with and would be appropriate for a party like this. And of course, for you and Mark. I know he would like you there."

"I will make a list and send it to you."

"Thanks Maria. It's very kind of you."

"Oh really, it's no big deal. Have a good day."

With that we hang up the phone. She sends me a message after, and she gives me the dates and her email address.

I wonder who the 'we' is. I can only assume that it is Paul's kids. It is hard to get away from what I lost there, not that I ever had it. I have to focus on what I have. I have my kids with me, and they are a huge blessing in my life. And now with Mark, I feel wanted again.

I head out for Christmas Eve shopping with the kids. Stopping into a jewelry shop I bump into Jack. The sight of him still annoys me. Before I can turn and leave, he turns around and sees me. I can see he is as happy to see me as I am him.

"Jack, surprised to see you. Hope you are well, and all is good at work." I tried to be polite. Jack could not be.

"Maria. You are doing well I hear."

"You know Jack, it was the best move I ever made. Better pay and better hours and holidays. Life is far calmer." I try not to sound passive-aggressive.

"Well, I am glad you are happy, you left some mess behind you. Took us a year to try and fix it." He really wants to start an argument; he always wants an argument.

"Jack, my work was in perfect order. You and I both know that. Any mess left behind was all your own making, I had no big job going so it could not have been that difficult." I try not to lose my composure.

"You and your new boss, ye played me." His voice becomes stern.

I really wish I did not make the next comments, but anger was taking over. "We did not, I was shown where I was not wanted and never got that promotion. You care to tell me the reason why you kept that promotion from me?"

"Maria, we lost a lot of clients after you left."

"Good to know someone saw my value, even if not my boss." The pointless argument starts all over again.

"Maria, we saw that, offered you a raise, and the way ye played me so the shops were not clients, and I was blamed."

"Jack, well, not as much playing as you and my secretary. Is that for her or your wife?" Anger took over me, I could have been way ruder, but I know my limits.

"How dare you, Maria?"

"Oh, I dare, it is happy Thursday, after all. I saw ye in the hotel one Thursday evening." I spill his little dirty secret. He never was a man of character.

He goes red and quiet. Before more is said, I say, "Happy Christmas, I have shopping to do." And I head off.

Oh, I will pay for that. I am sure he will tell Joan and who knows how she will react. I will worry about it when it happens.

I review the end-of-year projections over Christmas. The shop managers had emailed in reports. The projections are as predicted at the end of Q3. All the shops have outperformed the previous years. They all put it down to face lift and branding. The shops look new, modern and enticing. Online ordering means they can each sell specialty products and just get them shipped.

Paul bonused me 20% this year, it was a good bonus but not like last year's 30%. Then again, last year's had integration projects.

I take what break I can, we are all tired from trying to Brexit-ready ourselves and make sure the supply chain is working.

Home is fine, we are all playing happy family. Never what it once was, but everyone is trying. And I need to try, too.

Maybe it is just in my head that I think everyone is trying and pretending. Perhaps, they all are happy now. You can't feign happiness, not for too long. And if everyone is happy up till now, they really feel contented with how our family behaves and acts now.

Whatever it is and however we achieved it, I can't let it go now.

Chapter 39

PAUL

The last quarter of the year I knew was a heavy one. We keep hearing to get Brexit ready. The queries keep coming to me from the shops, people are worried about their future, and rightly so. Will we be able to get stock in? What will change? Everything seems so uncertain. Tensions are high all round and I am feeling a little out of my dept as I am only new to the business in itself.

The reality is, that it is a mess. We can only try and prepare. At least, we are not exporting, any EU sales are going from Holland. The big question is, how will importing stock work?

I make a point of getting down to London once or twice a month now. We plan all visits to coincide when Vicky is on a week off. She travels with me. It is such a different feeling — perhaps a feeling of belonging that I haven't felt in so long.

Planning together, no cloak and dagger around who we meet or not and if we want a weekend, we take one. Vicky is settling right in and gets on great with the kids. She has a mischievous side, a playful woman, which means she tends to have a good sense of humor and gives as good as she gets from Sarah. They get on very well. The kids seem very settled with her and us.

Vicky is as stubborn as anything, always independent and looking to share all costs. It is as much as I can do to get her to agree that I pay for all travel. Telling her that it is all company-paid and deductible, and I am traveling for work.

I convinced her to come to Holland for a weekend and told her that I had to visit the Rotterdam shop and warehouse. Also, I wanted to make sure we are ready for any changes

January might bring. I don't think she was entirely convinced; it was not just an excuse for a dirty weekend away. I get her need for independence, but it gets tiring at times, as if she is not fully invested to being able to relax and ignore the money side.

We flew over Friday morning and took a train from Schiphol down to Rotterdam. I met the warehouse and shop managers there. Vicky looked around and went for a walk around the port area when I was working.

It was good to meet the managers in person and remind them I am more than a voice on a phone. The meeting went well, everyone working there seemed prepared for the big changes and were quite positive about it. Their optimism was refreshing. When I spoke to them about Brexit they seemed to care little. They said the only way it affected them was UK manufactured product, which was low enough. They said that was a UK problem. I had to think, they were right.

After the meeting, we returned to Amsterdam by six that evening; we were staying until Monday. On Friday evening we were tired and decided to take a short walk, soak in the surroundings, and grab dinner in the hotel restaurant.

Saturday is a lazy day, we leave our hotel and wander the streets, drinking coffee and taking the time to enjoy some museums. We stroll, talk, and look in the shops. Of course, we visit their 'red light shops.' There isn't much novelty going into them really, Adam's is so much better. However, some of the more specialized shops look interesting.

As we stroll into a shop specializing in fetish clothing Vicky looks and says, "Paul, do you miss clubs, I know you went before?" I did not see that coming. We had spoken about this at times but never got a chance to act on it.

"Vicky, honestly, yes, they were fun, but the fun was seeing what is possible and opening myself up again to new things and realizing life was yet to be lived. I know you are not too keen. I don't miss them, how could I, I have you. Anyway, you may not like the club, but you have certainly taken to Ralph's playroom. You dark horse you," I joke.

"Ok, well, maybe sometime, who knows. I am not saying no, just not yet. Now come on, let's get dinner, on me."

"On you! Here we go again. Can't you just let me take you away," I chuckle at her stubbornness.

"No, I pay my way. I am not a kept woman. Feels wrong. Take me somewhere for my birthday if you want. Now, dinner on me, anywhere. I have a nice dress for the evening."

I smile to myself, two can play this game. "OK! If I must, anything for a quiet life."

"You bet, good to see you give in easily for a change." Vicky teases me.

We head back and change, Vicky has a nice dress – as much as I want to take her out, I know she isn't going to change her mind.

"You look nice. And looking this gorgeous, you deserve to be taken out for dinner," I try to convince her. She raises her eyebrow looks at me sternly and I back off quietly without another word.

Heading out, I tell her I know exactly where I want to go. We head down a street lined with restaurants and shops. Steakhouses, Chinese and Thai, and so on.

I head across towards a Thai restaurant, Vicky heading towards the door, I divert, there is a small waffle, and fries stand next door. I walk up and order. These fries and toppings are known to be really nice. "I always wanted to try these, what do you want?"

"Really, Paul?"

I smile, "Well it is my choice, you said I could pick."

"I am all dressed up!"

"You look lovely dear, will go well with dinner." I smile as I see her scowl at me.

"I will give you this one, but you will pay for it." She can't hold back the laugh.

As we eat our fries, she smiles, "Have to admit, they are nice." We enjoy our fries in silence at the side of the street, watching the world and nightlife pass by. . .

We stroll on, she puts her head against my arm, and I wrap an arm around her. We finally find a bar and head for a drink. I just cherish this relaxed feeling, with her, I don't worry or think about things. Quite ironically, I smile to myself often, it feels right. Not trying to fit things in, enjoying what we do and always come back.

As the night rolls on, I have to admit, I could eat. Too stubborn to give her the satisfaction of telling her. I head for the rest room and on my return, I see that Vicky has ordered some light bites from the bar. Sitting down, I reach over for one, as there is more than enough for two. As I do, I get a little slap on the hand. "You had your dinner." As she takes a bite with a big smile. "I told you, you would pay for it."

I can only smile, "Heartless, but I suppose I deserve it." After a few minutes, she just pushes the plate to me. "Go on, can't have you hungry, you need your strength for later."

I resist, wanting her to insist more and I like teasing her. We finish up and my hunger growls are silenced.

By the time, we are back home. Monday night, I receive a message from Maria,

Maria: Wondering why were you in Rotterdam, was there a problem I do not know about?

Paul: No, I was just over for the weekend and took the chance to call and remind them who their owner was and let them know they were not forgotten.

Maria: OK, thanks

I know she knows now it was a weekend away, almost the same weekend as we were away a year earlier. But she has enough sense to say no more.

Life has a sense of normality, a purpose which I didn't have before. It is not just work. I have found a life. I am busy at work, and I see a future. I start laying a plan for two more shops. I see Northern Ireland. Maria thinks I am mad. But I suspect it may be a backdoor into Europe for stock. I am not sure how yet, but I feel like the North has almost dual citizenship, EU and UK.

Anyway, I need to be ready to move if we need to. Thankfully, property is plentiful there and the worst that can happen is that I buy into a Northern company and supply from there.

Never did I imagine 18 months ago this would be my life. Perhaps the biggest surprise is Matthew, he has really taken to this and is loving the responsibility.

I head into Christmas, and I am determined to enjoy it. Surrounded by family and now Vicky who is rapidly becoming part of the family.

Chapter 40

PAUL

As I walk out of the bathroom after a refreshing shower, Vicky walks in. She tells me she bumped into Nicole at Starbucks while picking up breakfast. Nicole joked that she hoped we did not break the playroom last night. We both laugh, and joke a little, and also kind of surprised that we enjoyed the playroom quite a lot. A new dimension for me/us.

Vicky looks at me, runs her hand through my hair, and says. "Ah, I missed the shower with the birthday boy. 29th of January, 50 years ago today you graced us. Who knew?"

"Thanks, Vicky," I kiss her lightly on the forehead.

She takes a small camera out of her bag. "This Christmas present of yours comes in handy," she says as she takes a photo of me.

"Not one for the living room wall I think as I stand there in a towel."

"So, Paul, what would you like to do today? Celebrate?"

"Enjoy breakfast and let the day pass away."

"That's one way to enjoy a birthday. But it definitely isn't a way to start your day with people acknowledging your steamy bedroom antics. I was so surprised to see Nicole here on a Saturday morning."

"I think she and Adam were at a club last night. Stayed upstairs."

"Let's hope you and your antics in the shop playroom did not wake them. Oh, is that a blush Vicky." I laugh.

"Leave me alone. Or I will tie you up again."

"Now that would be a way to pass my birthday," I say with a wink.

"Who knew 6 months ago this is where we would be today when you revealed all?

"I certainly didn't. Come on have breakfast and let's go for a walk. Our train is at 4."

As we walk, the birthday wishes and jokes come in from friends and family. We receive them all with grace and gratitude. I realize the number of people who remembered me today. Who knew so many cared enough to even remember it.

Arriving back in Manchester, we grab a cab back home. "I will be glad of a quiet evening with the kids. Sarah said she is cooking dinner for us all. Celebrate the half century she said."

"I know she invited me to dinner also."

"I hope she did. I hope you are staying over."

"My little joy toy looking for a birthday bang from his older woman." Vicky laughs out loud, and the taxi driver checks us out in the mirror. He tries to suppress his smile. We try to temper our playfulness for the rest of the journey.

We arrive at the house at 7:30 and Sarah's and Matthew's cars are there, and all seems quiet. As soon as I walk in, everyone shouts "SURPRISE!". I am completely taken aback; I had no idea. I stand in shock. Rachel comes over all excited.

"Happy birthday, Dad," She says as he hugs me tightly. I look around and the house is full. I am speechless. They all laugh, and clap and Sarah starts a happy birthday chorus. Oh, to have the ground swallow me up. I am not in a state to appear in front of so many people, a pair of old jeans and a plain sweater. Vicky is all smiles, she obviously knew.

"Ok, let's give the old man a few minutes to change and recover, don't want him keeling over with a heart attack."

"I need to change, too, Paul," Vicky announces, and we head upstairs, Vicky in front of me. I catch Maria watching us out of the side of my eye. She smiles, her eyes glued to us going up stairs to my bedroom, somewhere she has never been.

Getting to the bedroom, I close the door. "Were you in on this?"

"Of course, I was. I asked Sarah over Christmas, what do you get a man who wants for nothing? Between us, we came up with this idea. Why do you think I did not drag you into the shower this morning? I was sparing my hair. Now a quick change for you. You have a house full of guests. I will take a little longer."

Sarah has a fresh shirt and pants hanging ironed for me. So, I put them on dutifully. As I head down, Vicky says, "I will be a few minutes behind you. Everyone dressed up and there is a small Marquee with heaters out the back and food is set up there."

I pass Nicole on the stairs. "What are you doing here? You came?"

"Of course, we did. Thrilled when Vicky invited us. To be considered a part of your private life and not just taken out for occasions. Now Vicky texted me to come up a minute."

I work the room, or the room works me, I am not sure which. After a while, Maria and Mark come over. Maria leans in for a peck on my cheek like so many others. She whispers, "I am really happy for you. Vicky is lovely." As she smiles up at me. Mark then shakes hands. "Happy birthday, Paul." I see them arm in arm and looking happy together. I couldn't be happier for them.

It is good to see Maria finally got her life together and things with Mark are going well again. We make a point of lunch every week or two. She seems calm, relaxed, and back in control. However, she occasionally says how she looks back on our adventure.

Helen and Nicola came from London, and Leonard and his wife made it, too.

I receive the guests and also receive the lovely wishes; I look around and spot Vicky coming down the stairs. "Wow! What an entrance!" I inwardly compliment her. She is in heels with fitted black pants and a stunning black and red corset top. A simple gold pendant around her neck finishes up the look. All eyes were on her. She looked absolutely amazing. Nicole whispers, "Now you know what she needed help with? Bit hard to get into that corset on your own. Easier to get out of it."

Vicky got to know most of the guests over the previous six months. She and Nicole have become very good friends. Maybe the mix of medical background but also, no hiding in the background, and Nicole even came up for a weekend and stayed with Vicky in November. I could see Maria may have been slightly put out about that. But she would have found it hard to explain Nicole and Adam to Mark.

Vicky comes over to me and leans in to give me a little kiss. "Wow, Vicky. A new corset. You look amazing." I put my arm around her and hold her close to me.
As much as I want to stay like this for the rest of the night, I am drawn back into the crowd.

Vicky's daughters and their husbands were there also. Thankfully, all the kids get on so well. They are all just happy to see their parents happy. Of course, we, parents, are happier to see our kids happy and comfortable around each other.

The party was going great, Sarah had help with food and drink and she worked the room. There were two kinds of appetizers, a delicious chicken main course, and of course a stunning birthday cake. I was proud of her, for sure.

After everyone is fed, Sarah starts a speech. I hear the clink of glasses, I look at her and mouth, "NO." She laughs, knowing how awkward I will get.

I have to admire her. My baby commanding a room. They really do grow up so fast.

"Hi everyone. Thank you all for coming and keeping it a secret from Dad. Vicky asked us over Christmas, what do you get a man who wants nothing? We all agreed to get him what he didn't want. A big surprise party that puts him into the limelight. But really tonight is Dad's night. Surrounded by his friends from his old and new life, showing him that he has so many friends. Thank you to those who came up from London.

He put his life on hold for us three and reared us. Though at times, we may not have seen it. As we got older, we saw what he gave up for us. So now we're nearly done. He just gives us his credit card and we are gone. He can look forward to a life of his own. We are all thrilled he is so happy to have met

Victoria. We can thank Rachel for that. But she could have found an easier way in fairness, all so dramatic. But seriously it is great seeing 2020 come in and Dad so happy as he enters old age. To Dad or Paul or whatever else ye may call him." And she raises her glass.

The toast takes place and then calls for my speech. Reluctantly, I get up and begin, "Where to start? Thank you all for coming. I was in shock. I had no idea. I am lucky to have such friends as ye. And to be able to share this with ye.

Vicky and Sarah seem to adapt to keeping secrets from me. Not sure how this got by me. But it did. Here was Vicky today saying such a hard person to get a gift for, but they accomplished it, and got all my friends and family together. So, what do you get the man who wants nothing? Well, she got that answer this evening. When Sarah was asking the questions in her speech, that Vicky asked a few months ago. I answered it for her.

I told Vicky that the thing that I want is to marry her. Thankfully she said yes on the spot. So now, ye all know there is no backing out of that one. Vicky came into our lives nearly a year ago. Most of you know she was one of those who cared for Rachel. But what few know is during those long nights in the hospital, Vicky took pity. She often shared a coffee on her break, made sure I ate something other than from the vending machine and enquired about Rachel after she left her care. When we met outside of the hospital, it was relaxed and natural, and such a happy, genuine individual you will rarely come across. A bit stubborn at times, but maybe we will find a way to knock that out of her.

Now the real toast of the night. To the future Mrs Bridges and the next adventure."

Cheers go up and Sarah hugs me. "Dad, I am so happy for you." Rachel hugs Vicky and seeing them happy for us nearly makes me cry. What more could I ask for? Matthew congratulates us in his quieter way. He is no hugger.

The rest of the night passes with nothing but congratulation. Amanda comes over. "Hi, Amanda. Hope this is not too much of a shock to ye." She laughs. "Ye oldies don't hang about. I suppose not much time to. We are delighted for ye. I never remember her as happy as she has been this last year."

Maria raises her glass over at me and smiles. Though it maybe a little touch of sadness, I know it is genuine. I go over to Maria and Mark. "Mark, I hope we are not keeping Maria away from home too much. How are the kids?"

"Great thank you. No, it is good to have Maria home so much more. This new job suits her. Thank you."

"She is worth her weight to us. Now enjoy the evening and if you are down in London to see United lose any time, work away with the apartment, it is there for staff usage."

As the night winds down, Vicky approaches me and whispers, "Get me out of this. This may look gorgeous. But reacts badly to too much food and drink." I laugh a suppressed laugh; she really does seem in misery.

"Come to bed, Paul. We will worry about the clean-up tomorrow. I think the caterers will sort a lot."

Heading to bed. I look back down at my three children starting a clean-up. Laughing happily though tired.

"Kids." They look up. "Thank you for a fabulous evening."

"Well, Mrs Bridges. The lengths I must go to stop you arguing about going Dutch on everything. Just come to bed and get some sleep. We can plan a future tomorrow."

Smiling and tired, "Ok, Paul. But I am still not calling you master." She laughs.

"Oh, we both know who the boss is Vicky."

*****

374